ROBERT
URQUHART

ROBERT URQUHART

GABRIEI SETOUN

WILDSIDE PRESS

CONTENTS

O a bonny walk is the Sandy Loan
  When the round moon rises ayont the moss;
An' the loch's like a scythe frae the mawer's hone,
  Wi' the starnies' silver threads across.

Doun whaur the burnie wimples alang
  The siller saugh is a sicht to see;
An' I hear, as sweet as the linty's sang,
  Somebody whistlin' there for me.

The kye's i' the byre an' the horses sta'd;
  At the furrow-end the plough lies still;
For the starnies are out; an' lass an' lad
  Stravaig whaur love and fancy will.

He'll stroke the hair back frae my broo,
  An' keek faur ben into my e'en,
Syne lay a kiss upon my mou',
  An' whisper me his lass an' quean.

O bonny's the Sandy Loan at nicht
  When the moon hauds ower by our trystin' tree!
But bonnier than a' in a lass's sicht
  Is the lowe o' love in a leal lad's e'e.

CHAPTER FIRST

THE COCKBURN CLIQUE

To my memory dear as to thine
Those meetings we had every week,
When we went a-wooing the nine—
The nine of the Cockburn Clique.

"*Ballade of the Cockburn Clique.*"

THERE were very few people about. Eleven o'clock had struck, and the night was cold, with a thick drizzle that was neither mist nor rain. It hung about the street-lights, dimming them to a fungus yellow, and blotting them out entirely beyond the fourth lamp-post; it clung to the pavement mucky and greasy. At the corner of Cockburn Street and Market Street a crowd of young fellows stood talking, seven of them in all. They were well protected against cold and wet, and talk, for the time being, rendered them oblivious of damp or discomfort. The rattle of a cab now and again, the tinkle of a belated car and the patter of wearied hoofs now hurrying stablewards, the wheezy whistling of engines creeping cautiously about the station,—were the only sounds that sought to silence their talking; and it would have taken a good deal more than these to silence a member of the Cockburn Clique, especially Alexander Grant. At all their meetings Grant made himself heard, and to-night he had excelled himself, sticking tenaciously to one point,

9

and, now that the meeting was over, trying to open up the whole argument.

The meetings were not usually held in a hotel, but to-night there had been a dinner. It was the only special meeting the Clique had ever had, although it had been in existence now for more than a year. Its first anniversary might have been seized as a fit and proper occasion for a dinner and a toast-list, but the great day had come and gone uncelebrated. It may be that the members, individually, were modest men, certainly they did not think meanly of their club, for they had banded together in the enthusiasm of youth and founded the Clique for great things. Every Monday night at eight they met in the lodging of one or other of the members, Urquhart's by preference, and discussed Literature and Art. Five out of the seven working members affected poetry, and the whole of literature was their province; albeit the Elizabethan Period suffered most at their hands. The literary aspirant must tackle the Dramatists, and get into grips with Marlowe and Shakspeare right away, just as the schoolboy dreams of doing battle with giants and wizards. And both are healthy signs. Even Æschylus and Sophocles were at times requisitioned in the service of the Clique, but rarely, for only one had made a study of them, and those who liked to quote the Classics did so timidly, with an apologetic eye on Crombie.

It was only when art was under discussion that the other two had their innings, and then they talked of *their* giants, Rembrandt and Rubens, and of such wizards as Turner and Cox; patronising Pettie, preferring Orchardson, pitting school against school, and awarding the palm to the French. Peter Taylor did most of the talking, for he was an amateur, and held decided opinions, only appealing to Bernard Kaye for occasional confirmation. Kaye being a life-school student, was invaluable as an authority to whom Peter could turn for support; not that Peter needed it for himself, but it was gratifying to have the others note that one who exhibited regularly, and sometimes sold, was in entire accord with the theories he advocated. But Kaye was too fond of his pipe to be keen in discussion, and contented himself with a remark now and again to keep conversation to the subject in hand. Once the talk got back to the drama he was only a listener, and should Alexander Grant manœuvre it into philology he shrugged his shoulders and yawned. Only once had Grant roused him to interest in this subject, and that was when he first mentioned the name of Grimm, for Kaye delighted in fairy tales. But before he could get in a word the talk had shifted to law, and he subsided, confiding to his pipe some disparaging remarks about lawyers. He delighted to hear Duncan Gilchrist declaiming his poetry, there was such a flavour and gusto in the performance; he would have listened for hours while Gavin Crombie inveighed against society in general, and slipshod English in particular, but he could not understand a man who spelled Celtic with a K.

And the Clique existed for other things than discussion. Once a month the members essayed composition, airing their amateur efforts in a manuscript magazine, of which Gavin Crombie was editor. To this organ of the Cockburn Clique every member was expected to contribute, the editor's contribution being a critical review of the papers submitted, for his gift lay that way. And the criticisms were more frequently caustic than appreciative. Urquhart usually tried a short story or a character sketch; Duncan Gilchrist confined himself to poetry, and Taylor to art; while Kaye was responsible for the illustration. Robert Haldane, who was a journalist by profession, did little more than write out a table of contents, and stitch the papers together. Thereafter the magazine was ready for circulation.

But the meeting to-night had not been an ordinary meeting of the Clique. To begin with, it was held not on a Monday, but on a Friday night, and to Urquhart and Grant and Gilchrist, at least, Friday night was a time of rejoicing. The day of the week was written in their faces; one could hear it in their voices, it gave elasticity to their motions, and a springiness to their step. Their eyes, their gestures, their very bearing proclaimed the day. For they were teachers, and the work of the week was done. Every teacher lives for Friday night. It is the week's Eldorado, when there shall be rest. For two days there shall be no school; none of that strain and tension and worry that kill, slowly but surely, the finer parts of the being, and leave nothing for Death, when he comes, but a shattered physical system, which he contemptuously dispatches at a blow, considering himself defrauded of the higher pleasures of his profession.

And to Urquhart this was more indeed than an ordinary Friday night. On the morrow he would leave Edinburgh, for he had resigned his situation under the School Board, having been appointed to a small school in a country village. Hence the special meeting of the Clique on a Friday night and in a hotel. The occasion had been solemnised by a dinner, and his fellow-members had met to wish him success and bid him God-speed. Hence also Grant's unflagging loquacity; for it was incomprehensible to Sandy that a young man should leave the city to settle down in a country village. The whole night long had he been demonstrating to Urquhart the folly of such a step, and predicting for him a life of sheer vegetation. And now, since Urquhart would not have another chance of listening to his eloquence, he must needs recapitulate all that he had urged, before they parted. He placed himself under the street lamp, facing Urquhart, and emphasised his points with a walking stick.

"Look here, Urquhart," he was saying, "what was the use of working as you did for your B.A., just to drift away as soon as you had got it, and settle down in a desert—nothing more nor less than a desert? You'll have nobody to talk to but the minister and the doctor——"

"I don't think there is a doctor in Kinkelvinwood, Sandy."

"And they'll only tolerate you when they want a hand at whist," Grant proceeded; "and—upon my soul, Urquhart, they'd cut you dead after the first rubber—you play like a fool. Manse doors have rusty hinges, you'll find, when the dominie calls."

"Never mind, Urquhart," Gilchrist broke in with affected consolation, "Grant will write you now and again, and you've got a dictionary."

Urquhart yawned. He had deliberated and debated the whole question in his own mind, and now that the decision was made he did not regret it. There were influences at work which Grant could neither know nor understand. For all the years he had been in Edinburgh he had not yet become reconciled to its gigantic school-factories, and now he looked forward to teaching in a school where he could know and study every child, and where, he imagined, the personal element of the master might have free play. There was another reason that had had considerable weight with him, but it was known only to himself and to Crombie. He had dreams of becoming a writer, of severing his connection with teaching entirely, and launching into literature. In the quiet of the country he could devote his leisure to study, disciplining himself for the life he dreamed of. And it was of the country and country life that he meant to write. He had known it in boyhood, and been in touch with it always. Years of city life had intensified rather than dulled his delight in hill and dale and stream and sea, and the simple lives that were lived beside them. He would rather hear the songs of birds and the lowing of oxen than sit through an orchestral concert. Walking the streets of the town he dreamed of green fields and hawthorn hedges, and in a crowd he was lonely. The country was his home, he felt; he had been only sojourning in the city for a time, and now the term of his exile was at an end.

But what was the use of saying all this to Grant? Sandy would simply have sneered at it as a bit of sentimentality.

" And as for salary," Grant complacently proceeded —" salary's a historical word, Gilchrist; it carries you back to the days when wages were computed in salt; it's interesting to see old customs preserved in words. I 've often thought of an essay on the subject."

"Damn!" Kaye commented; "that's another historical word, Sandy, and a beauty."

"As for salary," Grant repeated, returning to the argument without answering Kaye; "you may have a little more than you have here as an assistant, but you know you should be in the running for the next first assistantship."

"Dear me, Sandy," Urquhart answered, with a touch of impatience, "can't you see that it is the very uncertainty of promotion under the Board that has helped me to a decision? I see men who are my seniors still working at the miserable pittance of an ordinary assistant, and others who are my juniors and inferiors occupying the places of better men. It's all a matter of influence, as you yourself know. A few years more of waiting, and I'd be as soured and disappointed as poor Macgilvray."

"Still it is your own fault," Grant told him bluntly, "if you let promotion go past you; you won't canvass."

Urquhart shrugged his shoulders. He hated the very sound of the word.

"How would you teach a lesson in grammar?" Gilchrist piped in a strident voice. "I don't agree with you. Anything more you'd like to say? *Good* morning!"

"I tell you what it is," Sandy summed up; "you're simply burying yourself, nothing more nor less than burying yourself."

"It's burying either the one way or the other, Sandy; and I choose the country. Better be happed with the eternal silence of the hills than drowned in the din of the streets."

"Rot!" Haldane muttered. "You're talking like a penny-a-liner."

Grant turned on Haldane, grinning. "I don't believe you know the derivation of 'rot,' Haldane."

"I don't," Haldane grunted, "and I don't want to. Derivation's rot."

"Most people will tell you that it is simply the same as the verb 'to rot,'" the philologist informed him; "but that is not my opinion. I believe it is shortened from 'rote,' a repetition of words without attending to their signification. It's only since philology——"

"Damn philology," Kaye ejaculated. "There's Sandy at it again. Who goes north? Ta-ta, Urquhart. Any good sketching, let me know. But the Academy has been off looms for a time; a water barrel's the correct thing just now."

"You try a whisky barrel for a change," Crombie advised, "with a study of that death's-head of a waiter we had. 'Ganymede the pall-bearer' would be a fetching title."

"Good-bye, old boy," Haldane shouted. "Any good copy I'll try to place for you."

And with a shower of good-byes and good wishes the company divided. Five went by the Waverley Bridge, and Urquhart and Crombie turned up Cockburn Street.

"Sandy's a terrible bore at times," Crombie confided. He himself was in a quiet mood to-night, and Grant had wearied him.

"He has never forgiven you that curt dismissal of his great effort on 'Words' in the first number. You called it a *Trenchant* summary of the subject, you remember. Sandy was on it last night again. He wouldn't have minded it a bit, he confided to me, if you had only spelled it with a small 't.'"

Crombie smiled. "That did Sandy a lot of good," he said. "He's all well enough in his own way, but his way is not yours; and now that you've picked your path keep straight ahead. I'm certain that novel you sent off to London will be accepted, and if it is, that will be a beginning for you. But don't idle your time away waiting. Keep on writing, and mind what I told you about Greek. If you would learn the secret of style, study Greek. Don't ask me how that can help you to write English. Read Greek, study it, love it, and you'll know for yourself. If your writing does not improve with that then you are hopeless. Above all things keep a diary, not of what you've done and said—Lord help you if you begin that—but of everything you see round about you, the daily phase of the lives you wish to chronicle; and if you can, do a bit of writing every day. I've no doubt we'll hear of you yet, my boy, but don't be in a hurry for all that."

Urquhart went along by his side listening and dreaming. They met nobody but a night policeman till they had crossed High Street. At the corner of the Tron Church, however, a figure staggered against them, and asked for a light. He appeared to be a man of about twenty-two or twenty-three, well dressed; but his hat, hanging to the back of his head, was bashed, and showed traces of mud, and he held between his fingers the stump of a cigar.

"Here, I say," Crombie objected, "you're never going to light that."

The fellow backed to a lamp-post. "N' light it? Can't smoke if n' lighted." He bleared on them with a beery smile, and then held out his hand to Urquhart. "Gla-to meet you, Mis'r Urk'rt. Tha's

B

your name, eh? Right? Eh? Knew it. We're joyin' ourselves."

"That is my name," Urquhart said; "but I don't know you."

"No! you're teassher, going to Kinkelvie. Eh? Right? We're 'joyin' ourselves. N' got tha' ligh' yet?"

Crombie handed him a box of matches, but after several ineffectual attempts to strike a light he again addressed Urquhart, appealing to him now with the cigar-stump in one hand, and now with the match-box in the other, "I'm 'stonished a' fel' like you going to Kinkelvie. I's dead 'n ough' be in's grave. 'S only one 'traction. Tha's Elsie. She's a knock out, you bet; she's—" He leered at a female figure taking the three of them in a glance as she passed, and laughed to himself. "Tha's not Elsie's style. She's all righ'. But the place's dead; too slow for Frank Downie—tha's me. You jus' tell any them you know Frank Downie, an' you're righ'. I'm tellin' you. Frank Downie—tha's me. You're R. Urk'rt an' I'm F. Downie. Tha's 'n 'ntr'duction. F. Downie!"

"Francis Downie!"

The name was uttered solemnly, and the young fellow, leaning against the lamp-post, started at the sound. His hands fell to his sides, dropping the cigar and matches, and he gazed in abject fear on the face of the man who had spoken his name.

"R-Ro-Rob!" he hiccoughed.

Urquhart and Crombie, turning, beheld the face of an old countryman. A pair of dark, fearless eyes gleamed under a thatch of eyebrow. There was more of sadness than of anger in their light   but they were eyes that would have looked on death without blinking, and dared the devil to do his worst. Every feature in the face was strong, nose and mouth, the broad shaven chin, and the full ears behind the grizzled side-whiskers. He wore the double-breasted sleeved vest of a country carter, adorned with large mother-of-pearl buttons; corduroy trousers belted at the knee, and thick-soled blucher boots tacketed for rough roads. A snouted cap came down to his eyes, and a black silk scarf was wound like a stock about his neck and knotted at the throat above a gray woollen shirt.

" Francis Downie ! " he repeated in the same passionless tone. " Is this how I find ye again, bringin' the gray hairs o' your father an' mother in sorrow to the grave ? "

Urquhart and Crombie looked on as men beholding a tragedy.

" Can this be his father ? " Crombie thought, and closed his eyes against the look in the old man's face. "God help him," he muttered.

The old man turned and regarded the two of them with a searching eye. " Amen to that, young man," he said, taking the prayer for the helpless figure by the lamp-post. " I see that you twa have neither airt nor pairt in this ; an' it 's weel for ye. What word can I tak' to a faither an' mither o' a son that I find waur nor the beasts that perish ? "

" They 're both — well — Rob ? " the young man asked, with something of penitence.

" Ay," Rob answered, " weel ! Would to God their son were as weel ! Man, man," he broke out almost tearfully, "after a' they 've done for ye ! How they 've toiled for you, an' slaved for you, it 's only the mornin' sun an' the midnicht stars can tell. After a' I 've done for ye mysel'! Frank! Frank!"

He turned on Crombie and Urquhart almost fiercely. "I'm an auld man," he growled at them. "Forget what ye 've seen; it 's wearin' late, and this is no' a sicht for a young man's e'en. Ou, I 'll see him safe to bed. I seek no man's help for a son o' Mich'el Downie. Guid nicht."

The two were turning away when the old man touched Crombie on the shoulder. "Excuse my harsh manners," he said; "I 'm a rough man at best, an' I 'm no' mysel' the nicht."

Crombie, always impulsive, seized the old fellow's hand in both of his own. "My own father's dead," he said, "but if I wanted one whom I could call father, I 'd come to you." Rob's lips tightened over his set teeth, he raised his cap slightly and left them.

They watched him almost carrying the helpless youth across the street, and heard his heavy step trudging on the pavement after he was lost to sight.

"That's the stuff the old Covenanters were made of," Crombie said.

The Tron clock boomed above them, and a dozen answers rumbled across the night. Urquhart was silent.

CHAPTER
SECOND

KINKELVINWOOD
CALLED KINKELVIE

IT had rained incessantly the whole day long, and the village with its thatch-roofed houses had a cheerless aspect. On a sharp frosty morning, when the ground rings to every footstep, and one can hear the very sunlight palpitating through the brittle air, thatch roofs have a look of cosiness and warmth, hanging over the houses like a thick winter happing fringed at the eaves. But in wet weather, soaked and swollen to saturation, they become black and sodden and smell of rot. Oozing from the straw, the rain came trickling down the walls, not dripping as it does from slated roofs, but crawling like some slimy exudation that made one shiver with a sense of dampness and distaste.

The street was a network of rivers rippling through ruts which only country carts could have made, widening here and there into lakes, and gurgling reluctantly into the burn at the foot of the Wabsters' Wynd. This wynd, with a burn making an open drain all its tortuous length, led with leisurely zig-zags, as old horses take a brae, to the foot of the hill, and the village tapering on either side of it, ended in a solitary cottage which the villagers called the Appex. But to-day the Appex was hardly visible. The hill beyond rose like a curtain of grey-green gauze, disappearing upwards in mist, while a scraggy fir-wood, shooting from a bend of the highway sheer up the eastern flank of the hill, wedged its way into cloudland.

On the south side of the village a flat expanse of fields, intersected with hedges, looked, through the rain, like diamonds and squares of green glass, black-edged and mournful. To the east the green darkened into a waste of deep purple-brown, bounded by a black paling. This was the peat-moss and a saw-edged strip of fir. Beyond the fields like a streak of lead lay the loch, and a line of distant hills drizzled along the horizon.

A heavy silence hung about the houses. Sound was deadened in the soaked air. There was a dull plash of rain in the puddles, lost now and again in the flip-flop of bauchled feet scurrying across the causeway, and, like a feeble sigh, the continuous buzz of rotting thatch. Under these thatch roofs too were hand-looms at work, but the doors were shut, and the precision of their rhythm was toned down to a mournful cadence.

In the sunny days of summer, when birds are singing outside, and the air ripples with the laughter of children; when the breeze laughing from beds of heather and banks of wild thyme, comes wandering in by the opened window, all the looms are lyrical. But after the flowers are dead; when the hill begins to hide in the mist, and the thatch to rot in the rain, then is their music elegiac.

Old Michael Downie, who had been seated at his loom from sunrise, had heard it singing to him the same refrain the lee-lang day—

"Wiry at daw',
Weary at fa',
Wearin' an' warrin' an' worn awa'."

It was dusk now, and he had to hold his pirns close to the little four-lozened window to tell their colour.

"Another twa shuttles," he murmured; "but I'll bid to be lowsin'."

He went to the door, and opening it a chink, peered outside. It was wet as ever. Donald Macvie stood at the door of the hotel on the other side of the street, and Michael, by way of remark, shook his head very slowly. It was a mild protest against the weather.

He closed the door again and began screwing up his web. Donald Macvie crossed the street and looked in, but Michael did not hear the click of the sneck.

"Ye're surely keen on 't 'e day, Mich'el?"

The old weaver straightened himself, holding his left arm across the small of his back.

"It's you, Donal? I didna hear the foot o' ye wi' 'e birrin' o' 'e ratch."

"Did ye say ye wouldna look ower 'e nicht?"

"Na; I was just remarkin' on the weather."

"Ou, ay? A grand day for 'e loch, man. There's a boat out, I see; it'll be frae 'e sluices. They'll be risin' fine, man. That's twa good days I've missed this week."

"An' twa good drookins forbye, Donal, though ye could get that an' no trail faur for it 'e day."

"Rob an' Watty 'll be drappin' in for certain. We're expectin' the master the nicht, ye ken. Mair nor likelys Ba'bingry——"

"Aiblins ! It 's a promisin' nicht for jauntin' . . . .
That 's Marg'et," he said, answering a knock through
the wall; "a way she found out hersel'. Sic a simple
thing would ne'er ha'e entered my head, but it saves
her frae comin' out. She has a sair fecht wi' thae
broun-keddies i' saft weather, an' it 's out an' out
sappy the nicht."

"It 's a tryin' thing the breath, Mich'el. I 'll be
stappin' than, an' ye can gie us a ca' after ye get your
drap tea. . . . . That 's Muiredge's by the trot."
They were at the door by this time, and both
stood listening to the sound of approaching wheels.
"She has a bit dink i' the aff hent hoof." A minute
afterwards a gig drew up at the hotel, and Donald
crossed over. The occupants were a lady and a
gentleman, both so muffled against the rain that
their faces were scarce visible.

"Anything for me, Donald?" the gentleman asked.

"I thought I kent your trot," Donald in his own
way answered. "She 's been pickin' up as she gaed :
her belly-band 's buried in clerts. Ay, there 's something 'at Rob broucht frae 'e town." He handed up
a parcel he had just received from his wife at the
door. "I kenna what it is, but it 's heavier than it
oucht to be for its size."

"Oh, it 'll be my books, Uncle," the young lady
said.

"Is that the Miss aside ye?" Mrs. Macvie called
from the door. "You men-folk 's a thouchtless band.
What a nicht for a genty body like her to be out in !"
She had been making her way round the gig while
she was talking, and now stood looking up half-
reproachfully, half-pitifully, on the young lady. "Ye
maun be fair soakin', Miss Elsie?"

But Miss Elsie—as she had been called—only laughed, a little ripple of laughter it was, and tossed her head. Closely buttoned up as she was, there was grace in the action. "If uncle had had his own way, Mrs. Macvie, I should have remained at home, but you see he had just to do as I told him. We women are all self-willed, aren't we, Donald?"

"I believe I've noticed that mysel'," Donald answered cautiously. "Now, I was dead set on 'e fishin' 'e day."

A peal of laughter cut short his complaint. "And Mrs. Macvie was dead set on your staying at home? Wasn't that it? Ah, Mrs. Macvie, we are all the same. But you did quite right in keeping him at home. The poor fellow might have caught a chill."

Donald, who stood stroking the pony's head, confided his thoughts to her ears. "She just laughs at me, Mysie, because she kens I'd do onything to pleasure her. But ye're a woman yoursel', lass, an' ken their ways. I've heard ye gie'in' a bit nicher, yoursel', when I was bringin' ye a feed."

"Ay," Muiredge agreed, "even Mysie takes tantrums at times, and insists on her own way. She answers to the touch of the whip, however, and yet she'll shy at its shadow."

"Look how she noses me the now," said Donald, with pride. "She's a rale frake when she's wantin' onything. Ha'e ye a bit o' cake, good-wife?"

"And she gets what she wants, I see. Elsie herself here could not have coaxed better, even for a drive on a rainy day."

"It's their way," Donald moralised; "an' we've just to tak' them as the Lord made them. . . . Here's your cake, Mysie; an' I'll uphaud Eesie as the best baker o' cakes i' the parish, though I say it mysel'."

"An' wha has a better richt?" the wife asked. "Ye can account for the feck o' them."

"Is that Michael at his door?" Elsie asked, and without waiting an answer calling his name. "Michael! Why don't you come and say 'Good evening'? Have you been standing there since we drove up, not thinking it worth while to say, 'How are you?' If I were a dignified young lady——"

"Which you're not," said her uncle.

"I should be deeply offended."

"Weel, Miss," old Michael came forward and explained, "I could hardly say 'Good e'en' on a sour nicht like this, that I'm no sair pleased at seein' ye out in. It would hae been wiser-like to bide at hame as Muiredge wanted ye."

Elsie drew herself up on the seat with a pretence of haughty indifference.

"But," Michael continued, "if I said na 'Good e'en' when ye drove up, I'll say it willin' enough gin you be drivin' awa'."

"Oh, Michael, Michael!" she burst out, shaking her head down at the old man, "you are incorrigible. If it had been a young man that had said anything so rude I should never have forgiven him."

"Ay, but the young men are gey an' thin sawn hereabout. We're a' auld folk an' bairns. How-somever, there's a young man comin' to 'e toun 'e nicht, an' bein' a man of eddication he'll read'lys be able to say the things ye like to hear, an' keep his thouchts to himsel'."

Elsie tossed her head. " I know the tribe, Michael, and you need not be afraid that *their* compliments will turn a giddy girl's head. They think so much of themselves that they can see nothing in others but faults. They're self-conceited, domineering, vulgar —bah ! "

Muiredge smiled to himself, listening to this outburst. He had heard it before. " Has the young gentleman arrived yet ? " he asked Donald.

" No," Donald answered, " but we're expectin' him the nicht. If he come by Inverorr he should draw up here about eight."

" Better give him an extra half-hour to-night, Donald ; the roads are heavy."

" Ay," Donald agreed, " an' thae trains is no' to be lippened on."

" Gentleman forsooth ! " Elsie spoke to herself, and thought that enough had been said. She changed the subject. " And how is Margaret, Michael ? "

" Weel, Miss, I may say she's no waur, but nothing to brag about. She's just aff an' on ; aye about her frail ordinar'."

" This is bad weather for her, isn't it ? "

" Bad for the young as weel as the auld, miss Excuse me sayin' it again."

" Have you had word from Frank lately ? "

" Ou ! " the old man answered in a constrained voice ; " a bit scart o' the pen now an' then, an' no' onless he be—— But it's no' for me to grum'le. Young folks hae their trokes as weel as the auld, an' the ways o' the toun are no' the ways o' Kinkelvie."

" I see," Elsie answered briefly, and then began fumbling about amongst the wraps.

"Here are some fine sweets I bought for Margaret," she said, handing out a little parcel. "They are very good for a cough."

"I thank ye, Miss; I thank ye, an' Marg'et 'll be awfu' pleased at bein' minded. A little thing like that pleasures an auld body, mair so be she onweel."

Elsie smiled to herself. She knew that the old man did not mean to depreciate the gift.

"Will ye manage hame without the lamps?" Donald asked. "It's wearin' darkwise."

"Easily," the farmer answered. "Mysie could go every step of the road blindfolded, and never once stumble. See, Donald, a touch of the whip does it. Good night."

"Guid nicht, guid nicht."

The carriage rolled away, and the three watched it disappearing along the road.

"She's a mettlesome ane, Mich'el; is she no'?" Donald asked.

Michael stood in his accustomed way, his left arm lying across the small of his back.

"She minds me o' a fuchsia," he said, "hingin' wi' sic a slender threed, an' laughin' an' dancin' the summer through. The good Lord keep her frae rouch hands."

"Man, but she has a spunk an' speerit o' her ain," Donald asserted.

"She'll settle down gin she get a man." Mrs. Macvie flung the words over her shoulder as she entered the hotel. "Marriage 'll tak' the spunk out o' her, if onything will."

Donald gave his head a side jerk towards the door. "D'ye hear her, Mich'el? Spunk, quo' she? Man, I've seen her let sixteen stane ken the road to the

door, if she thoucht he 'd haen enough. But it 's
Eesie's way. Ye 'll be ower than, Rob an' Watty an'
Ba' bingry ——? "

" Ay, Donald, ay ; I 'll be ower. I 'll awa' now.
Marg't 'll be wonderin'."

" If He 'd only blessed us wi' a dochter," were old
Michael's thoughts as he turned to his own door, " to
bide an' brichten the auld wa's! But we 're blind
an' dowtet cr'aturs, an' canna tell what would be for
our ain good. The Lord kens best, and He sent
a son."

CHAPTER THIRD · AN ACADEMICAL DISCUSSION

WHEN Michael dandered across to the inn he found several already assembled in the back-room. The lamp hanging from the ceiling was lit; but the chief light was from a fire of peats blazing between the white-washed jambs of an old-fashioned fireplace, wide enough for a score of ribs. The only furniture in the room was a long deal table and a couple of benches, white as a holy-stoned deck, and one chair. A few framed advertisements of whisky and ales looked down from the ochred walls, sadly out of place, although peat-reek had done its best to bring them into tone. Over the mantelpiece hung a picture which was the wonder of the neighbourhood. Looked at in front, it was a basket of flowers—a wonderful bouquet of all the seasons. Seen from the left side, it was a full-rigged ship sailing on a waveless sea; while from the right it appeared a peaceful homestead built by the margin of a lake. Such miraculous transformations Donald Macvie took care that all strangers should see and admire.

To-night, when Michael entered, he found the table pushed back against the wall, while the two benches opening out from the chair in the middle of the floor stretched to both sides of the fireplace. The land-lord himself sat on one side of the fire, and Balbingry opposite. Rob Buchan—better known to all the country-side as Carrier Rob—occupied the chair, and Watty Spence sat between him and Balbingry.

"Come in by," Donald cried; "inower to 'e body o' 'e kirk," indicating, with the stem of his pipe, a vacant place on his left.

Michael shook the rain from his cap, and, with his fingers, combed dry his gray whiskers. "No signs o' betterment," he announced; "the same steady pour."

"Pass ower a tumbler, Donald." Balbingry reached for a bottle on the table behind him as he spoke.

But Michael held up a hand in dissent. "I would rather no, Ba'bingry; I'm no carin' for 't 'e nicht."

"Hoots!" Balbingry objected, measuring out a glass. "It's no every nicht we meet to welcome an incomer. It has been a' the other way since I mind."

Michael took the glass under protest, and set it down on the bench at his side. "I like a neigh-bourly drap as weel as mony," he apologised; "but I haena so muckle to do wi' as I was wont."

"No a word," said Rob; "no a word mair. We a' ken whaur your money's gaun, an' we respect ye for 't."

"Ay," Balbingry corroborated, "it's me that kens what the college costs, for I keepit my brother at St. Andrew's; an' it's no little. Tak' your drap, an' keep your purse i' your pouch; the bottle's paid for."

From under his shaggy eyebrows Rob looked on the old weaver, and the expression on his stern face softened almost to pity.

"I saw Frank in Edinburgh, yesterday," he said, "an' the first thing he speired was about the auld folk."

"Ay, man, ay?" Michael asked eagerly. "An' was he weel; was Frank weel?"

"Ay, Mich'el, I left him weel."

"Of course, of course," Michael hastened to explain. "What was to ail him? But ye ken a father's way, Rob. It 'll be grand news to Marg'et; ay will 't."

"Mind an' tell her I left him weel, than, an' lookin' weel."

"I 'm hearin' that this ane we 're gettin' oursel' is college bred," Watty ventured. He spoke like one who had no interest in the matter at all, and gave the information for what it was worth. "Ye 'll be thinkin' yoursel' no sma' drink ower the head o 't, Ba'bingry?"

Balbingry crossed his legs, and self-complacently sipped his whisky.

"It was a unanimous appointment, no doubt; but Urquhart was my man frae the first."

"They tell me he 's a B.A.," said Rob.

"B.A.?" the landlord echoed. "What might that mean?"

"Bachelor of Arts," Balbingry explained. "My brother 's M.A. himsel, but that 's a bit higher."

"Ay, he 's married," said Donald; "but this young chap 'll be takin' a wife ana', as soon as he 's settled down."

"It 's no a question o' marriage at a'," Balbingry seriously explained. "He 'll be B.A., married or single."

Donald shook his head.

" I canna see that. Watty's a bachelor, an' you're a
bachelor yoursel'—no that I would cast ony reflection
—but ye canna say that o' Mich'el an' Rob an' me."

"But still anon, bachelor he is, an' bachelor he'll
be," Balbingry answered; "an' a waddin' winna
alter't. It just means that he's up in Latin an'
Greek."

"That's what Frank studied," Michael interrupted.
" He'll maybe ken Frank."

Rob helped himself to a pinch of snuff and handed
the mull to Michael.

" He micht an' he micht no, Mich'el ; the college is
a big place, ye ken."

"I'm doubtin' if he will," Balbingry admitted
reluctantly. " Ye see our man is a B.A. o' London."

This staggered Michael. He had thought London
a vast agglomeration of stores and shops, where
people bought and sold, and haggled, and cheated all
the days of their lives. It was to him a great maze
of miles and miles of streets, interminably winding,
thick with fog and swarming with rogues ; where
crowds surged and swayed daylight and dark, jost-
ling, maiming, robbing, killing every man his
neighbour, and all struggling for the Houses of
Parliament, at the centre of the maze. In such a
place education was out of the question.

" Is he no college-bred after a'?" he asked.

" Ou, he's college-bred richt enough."

Michael felt relieved.

" He'll be able to read Greek an' Latin then, like
his mother-tongue."

"Greek an' Latin!" Watty joined in the conversation, hurling out the words with a vehemence that
startled his friends. " Ye say the words as if they

C

were sacred, makin' to yoursel's gods o' godless
languages. An' what's your M.A.'s an' your B.A.'s
after a', but empty shibboleths, that no mair distinguish the learned frae the onlearned, than the
names their fathers ga'e them. Gold's stampet
because it is gold, no because it has come through
the meltin' pat."

The others looked at Watty, and, seeing he was in
earnest, let him go on. He was a strange man, and
read books they knew not the names of. Quiet,
almost taciturn indeed, yet at times he would burst
into eloquence, confounding with the very fulness
of his information.

"If a man can write M.A. ahent his name, an'
gabble in a tongue ye dinna understand, ye ca' him a
scholar; as if they'd been foundin' a college when
they begoud to build the tower o' Babel."

"But I dinna hud wi' ye there," Balbingry struck
in. "If nobody's to learn Greek an' Latin what's to
come o' the colleges?"

"I say no word again Greek an' Latin," Watty
answered. "I've wished I kent them mysel, for I've
read Pope's Homer, an' it's grand; but we've ballads
o' our ain, an' we should ken them afore we begin wi'
Homer an' Virgil."

Donald and Michael sipped their whisky and
listened. Watty had talked of Homer and Virgil
before now; but they knew nothing of either, and
took what he said on trust. Both Rob and
Balbingry, however, watched for an opportunity of
joining in.

"What about Shakspeare an' Milton?" Watty
asked.

"An' Burns?" Rob reminded him. "Dinna forget

Robbie, a namesake o' my ain.   But, of course, everybody kens Robbie."

"No, man ; everybody doesna ken *Robert Burns*; an' some that could gie ye screeds frae Horace, never read a line o' the ' Jolly Beggars' i' their lives."

Rob shook his head.   That was scarce credible. Even Michael and Donald appeared to have their doubts; while Balbingry sipped his whisky and smiled the smile of a sceptic.

"I was aince acquant wi' a college birkie," Watty began, and the others turned in their seats interested at once ; they liked a story.

"That would be when ye was at the Drums?" Donald surmised.

"No, Donal'. I was but a hafflin' at the time, a kind o' gardner an' orra-man, wi' a family out frae Milndour. That's no i' your rounds, Rob; an' I'm doubtin' if ony o' ye ken the name o' 't."

"Three mile i' the wast side o' Blairbogie," said Rob, with automatic gravity. "I've never been there mysel'. Ay?"

"That's so, Rob. Weel, there was a young chap cam' about the house—he's a minister now, but he was i' the Divinity Hall than—an' him an' me used to forgather about the gardens whiles. I was just at the age when ye read a' thing that comes i' your way, be it sacred or profane."

"But ye wouldna read profane books, Watty?" Michael looked quite distressed.

"No i' your sense o' the word, Mich'el ; but I fell foul o' onything i' the natur' o' print; an' mony a can'le-doup I've kent gutter an' gang out leavin' me to crawl into bed i' the dark."

"Ay?" said Donald. "I couldna thole that. I

bid to ha'e licht to lowse my laces. After that, I'm a' richt."

"When this chap came to ken I was a reader he used to lend me books, an' muckle I've regretted it since; no that they were bad books, for I learned a lot frae them. But books are no lent for nothing, an' I'd to wink at mair than sma' print i' thae days—but that's neither here nor there. What bothered me wi' him was the way he used to brag an' blaw about Sophocles, an' Aristophanes, an' Æschylus, an' other sic outlandish names."

"They're a' that," Donald concurred. "I wonder how their fathers an' mothers mou'banded them when they were bairns. Ase-kill-us, did ye say? He was a bad ane, that, I'll wager."

"I got tired o' aye hearin' about Agamemnon——"

"Aggie's mair Christian-like," Donald considered.

"An' the death o' Hector, an' sic-like; an' I speired if he kent Jamie Telfer. No, him; never heard tell o' him."

"He would belang thereawa?" Donald queried. "The name's no familiar hereabout."

But the others were better informed than Donald, and Watty continued:

> "But Willie was stricken ower the head,
>   An' through the knapscap the sword has gane;
> An' Harden grat for very rage
>   When Willie on the ground lay slain.
> But he's ta'en aff his gude steel-cap,
>   An' thrice he's waved it in the air—
> The Dinlay snaw was ne'er mair white,
>   Nor the lyart locks o' Harden's hair."

"It's a braw ane that," said Rob. "The pictur' o' auld Wat barin' his silver pow, an' vowin' ven-

geance afore the dead was cauld, man it aye tak's
me i' the thrapple here."

"But the young whelp saw nothing in 't," Watty
told him. "He thought I was giein' him some verse
frae the *News*. An' when I speired dumfoundered,
if he didna ken our auld ballads, he said he 'd aince
tried them, but they wouldna scan."

"Wouldna what?" asked Donald. "That was an
odd thing to say about them."

"He considered them vulgar," Watty continued.
"That was his word; an' you would ca' him educated
because he kent Greek an' Latin?"

"But he would ken Burns better?" Balbingry
supposed; for he himself was not on sure ground
with the ballads.

"No him," Watty grunted; "neither his Burns nor
his Bible. I mind o' him actually sayin' that that
verse Rob 's so fond o', a' anent poverty an' love, was
a translation frae a Greek poet."

"Eh?" said Rob. "Was he so bigoted as that?

> 'O Poortith cauld, an' restless love,
>   Ye wreck my peace atween 'e ;
> But, poortith, a' I could forgie,
>   And 'twerna for my Jeanie.'

That was gaun ower faur. Ye wouldna let him slip
canny wi' that?"

"I didna, Rob; for he angered me. 'Damn your
Greek,' says I. 'What need had Robbie o' trans-
latin'?' . . . 'Don't swear, Walter,' he says; 'don't
swear.'"

"That was very richt o' him, Watty," Michael
seriously observed; "mair so, as Frank has telled
me, the Testament bein' written in Greek."

"But that was a' he could say," Watty declared; "an' it was just by way o' turnin' me aff that he said it. I found out that he kent his Bible no better. An' that's your man o' education?" He rounded on Balbingry, holding out an open palm like one exposing a sham to the eyes of the company.

"Still, anon, he kent Greek an' Latin," Balbingry insisted, "an' that argues ony man a scholar."

"No a bit o't!" Watty flatly denied the assertion.

"But I say it does." Balbingry was angry at being contradicted so bluntly, and held the more tenaciously to the position he had taken up.

"What you say, or what I may say, canna alter the question. The man that kens Greek an' Latin an' no mair is no' educated. He's just like auld Bowbutts, that kens to a firlot a' his neighbours' craps, an' lettin' his ain farm look after itsel'."

The landlord looked from the one to the other with an expression of uneasiness on his honest face. He was unused to academical discussions, and feared the two were going to quarrel outright.

"It may be that you're both richt," he said. "There might be a way o' comin' to an understandin'. What do you say, Rob? Do you no' see a way out o't?"

"It minds me o' the story o' the twa knights," said Rob, who was always a peacemaker.

"Ay, let us hear a story, Rob," Michael advised; "a' things come richt in stories, i' the end."

"This happened lang syne," said Rob, "when knights were wont to gang ridin' the country lookin' for ony wenches that micht be chained up in high towers, an' settin' them free."

"I've heard about them," Balbingry said; "knight templars, they ca'd them."

"I've no' howf o' thae templars," Donald acknowledged, "makin' a great fracas about a drap drink."

"Well, a knight after ridin' about a' day cam' on an inn, an' bein' hungry he loupit down frae his naig an' stappit ben. It was a room the very marrow o' this; the lang deal table forenenst the fire, an' the same pictur' aboon the jambs."

"I dinna ken whaur the twin o' that pictur's to be found," Donald dubiously reflected.

"As it so happened there was another knight sittin' at the head o' the table regalin' himsel' wi' bread an' cheese, an' washin' it down wi' a tankard o' porter; so our friend staps down to the faur end an' orders in the same. There the twa sat than, munchin' an' drinkin', an' they couldna lift their heads frae the drink without starin' ane another stra'ght atween the e'en."

"An' that's rale uncomfortable," Michael remarked, "in a strange place. I was aince i' the same predicament in Edinburgh."

"Weel, our friend gets tired o' this, an' just by way o' breakin' the ice, he points to the pictur' ower the fire, an' says a kind o' creetically, 'Isna that farm weel painted, na?'

"The other looks up an' wi' a loud laugh he blaws the fro' o' the porter frae his mou'tache."

"That's richt," said Watty. "They aye laugh the fro' frae their beards i' the auld ballads."

"Weel, that's what he did," Rob continued. "'Farm,' says he. 'Are ye blind, man? It's a ship.'

"Our friend was a bit nettled at the nasty way he

said it, so he answered back as brave as ye like,
'Farm, I said, an' farm it is.'

"'Ship, I say, an' ship it is.'

"'I'm a liar then?'

"'That's just what I was thinkin'.'

"'Then you're another.'

"An' so it gaed aff an' on till they cam' to blows.
Up they sprang wi' drawn swords an' faced ane
another i' the middle o' the floor.

"'Farm,' cries our friend, pointin' wi' his sword.

"'Ship,' says the other, pointin' wi' *his* sword.

"An' then they both stood gapin' like a pair o'
fools. It was neither a ship nor a farm they saw, but
a basket o' flo'ers.

"'Friend,' says the ane, we're both wrang. This
house is bewitched an' we're safer out o' t.'

"'Your hand on 't,' says the second. 'I tak' back
my words.'

"So they loupet to their saddles an' galloped awa'
as fast as their naigs could carry them, sadder an'
wiser men, as the story ends."

"But they would pay their lawin' first?" Donald
asked.

"Knights were aye fed an' horsed free i' thae days,
Donald," was Rob's explanation, which Donald considered hard on landlords.

"I see your meanin'," Watty said. "Ba'bingry an'
me's both wrang?"

"Or both richt, Watty. The whole truth lies
atween ye."

Donald held up a hand for silence, and stood
with his ear to the door. "That's wheels," he said.
"D' ye hear?"

All listened intently. They heard the weary

dribbling of the rain, and the moan of the wind creeping across the bare fields; but Donald's practised ear heard more.

"She's puin' up Petmettle Brae," he said, making for the door.

He went outside; but the others sat still. Balbingry held up the bottle to the light, and set it down again, satisfied.

"That's her now," said Rob; "four wheels, I hear."

A few minutes afterwards the machine drew up, and presently, through the opened door, Balbingry and Watty saw a gentleman enter and stand talking with Donald at the bar.

Rob, who sat with his back to the door, did not trouble himself to turn round. His shaggy eyebrows hung low over his eyes, and his chin rested on the black silk scarf knotted at his throat. Evidently he was deep in thought.

Watty, in a whisper, communicated to him his impression of the stranger. "Five foot ten, or thereby," he said, measuring him up and down with his eye. "Saft felt; a hielan' cloak; his breeks turned up at the boddom—that bespeaks carefu'ness. It has been an open machine; his umbrella's dreepin'."

"Ssh!" Balbingry said. "He's comin' ben."

"A friend or twa to gie ye a welcome," Donald said, entering first.

"Good evening, gentlemen," said Urquhart. "This is an unexpected kindness, and doubly pleasant on such a night."

"This is Ba'bingry," Donald continued, "a member o' the Board. Ye'll ken him by name."

Urquhart saw a man a little over his own height,
but broader, and much more strongly built. A short
red beard and moustache covered a mouth large and
full-lipped. The eyes were of a light hazel brown,
and the forehead low and broad. His dress was that
of a working farmer—trousers of grey tweed, with
brown leather leggings buttoned to the knee; homespun jacket and vest, showing a grey woollen shirt.
He wore no necktie; but the linen collar on a week-
day was a badge of respectability. All the others
were content with the tie without a collar. He might
be a man of thirty or thirty-five; no more.

Urquhart felt his hand lost in this farmer's, gripped
as in a vice. He looked from the steady eyes to
the heavy mouth. A powerful ally as a friend, he
thought; an unscrupulous and vindictive foe.

"Muckersie's the name," the farmer explained,
answering a questioning look in Urquhart's eyes;
"but we a' gang by the name o' the farm here, an'
Ba'bingry's mine."

"Oh, yes," Urquhart answered. "I had your
letter to meet you here. You've secured rooms
for me?"

"Ay, until we see our way to build ye a school-
house. The Misses Birrell's to put ye up—twa fine
ladies, they are."

"An' this is Mich'el Downie," Donald continued.
"A'body kens auld Mich'el; an' Watty Spence——"

"Any relation to Sir Patrick of that ilk?"
Urquhart asked, with a smile.

Watty seized his hand, and shook it enthusiastically. Here was a young man after his own
heart.

"D'ye ken him?" he asked.

> "The king sits in Dunfermline town,
> Drinkin' the blude-red wine ;
> 'O where will I get a skeely skipper,
> To sail this new ship o' mine ?'

"D' ye ken him, sir ? D' ye ken Sir Patrick ?"

"He's an old acquaintance of mine," Urquhart answered, falling in with Watty's humour.

> "O up an' spak' an eldern knight,
> Sat at the king's right knee—
> 'Sir Patrick Spens is the best sailor
> That ever sailed the sea.'"

"He'll maybe ken Frank, too," said Michael, anxiously ; "my son, Francis Downie, sir, in Edinburgh, at the college——"

"Welcome to Kinkelvie," said Rob, breaking in abruptly, and compelling Urquhart's attention. "We a' ken ane another here; but Edinburgh's a big place, an' the face o' a friend 's no to be seen at ilka street corner."

Urquhart started at the sound of the voice ; and, turning, recognised the face of the old countryman he had seen the night before under the shadow of the Tron kirk.

"Rob Buchan," Donald whispered at Urquhart's ear. "He's a travelled man an' kens what he's speakin' about ; in Edinburgh ilka fortnight—a score o' times i' the year."

"Welcome to Kinkelvie," Rob repeated, with a look in his eyes warning Urquhart that they met as strangers.

"Mich'el's awfu' bound up in Frank," he explained, speaking a little less sternly, now that Urquhart understood on what footing they met. "He's an only bairn, an' the heart o' a father yearns ower him, fechtin' his way i' the world."

"It's Marg'et," Michael corrected with a plaintive smile; "ony body wi' word o' Frank has an easy road to Marg'et's heart."

"We met to drink your health," Balbingry announced, "an' wish ye success." He handed round the replenished tumblers. "Ye 'll be no waur o' a drap o' the hard stuff on a nicht like this."

"I 'm soaking through and through," Urquhart answered. "The sooner I get out of my clothes the better. Good health, gentlemen."

"Success to ye," they answered, "an' a lang acquaintance wi' Kinkelvie."

"A good wife to ye," Michael added; "an' that 's the best wish I ha'e for a young man."

"It 'll be a race atween him an' Ba'bingry here," Watty predicted; "an' we 'se a' ha'e a biddin' to both."

"Ye 're glib-mou'd on waddins, Watty," Mrs. Macvie's voice came from the door, "but your ain 's never no nearer."

"Would ye advise me, Eesie?"

"'Deed would I; an' it would be the best fa' that could fa' ye; though I would be wae for the wife's sake. Ay, ay," she said, turning to Urquhart, "ae bit glint o' love 's worth a' your book lear; an' I ken the pair o' e'en 'll gar your heart dirl—if so be ye 're no bespoke a'ready, to some shilpit, fusionless town-hizzie, I 've no doubt."

Urquhart smiled. He felt the wet clothes clinging to him, and was eager to be gone.

"I must say good-night, I fear, or I 'll be catching cold."

They all moved to the door where Michael edged
in alongside of him and again spoke of Frank.

"It was a kind o' a bit fancy cam' into my head at
the loom, that you an' him might ha'e forgathered,
but—good-night, sir, good-night."

"Did ye notice, Watty?" he asked, after Balbingry
and Urquhart had gone. "He wears just sic a
collar an' tie as Frank, that I thoucht maybe just
braw enough for ordinar' folk. It'll be the college
fashion, I'm thinkin'?"

"Ay, Mich'el, ay," Rob answered, meditating over
his mull, "that'll be it; no doubt, no doubt. Ay,
Mich'el!"

CHAPTER FOURTH

A SUNDAY MORNING SERVICE

AND far as the eye could see were undulating meadows and fields, narrowing into ribbons of light green, edged with the darker green of hawthorn hedges. Dreamy-eyed kine browsed under beech trees, and sheep showed like bulbs of white on the hill-side. The winds were still, and everywhere was peace. A brook gurgled unseen among rushes, and far away was heard the tinkle of a sheep bell; faint at first, but coming nearer and clearer until it sounded like the slow swing of a hammer on an anvil. Across the fields an organ pealed and swelled, and the air was filled with the softest music and the aroma of flowers.

Urquhart rubbed his eyes and listened. Soft as the whisper of children he heard the rustle of leaves pattering on the window, and in the distance, miles and miles away it seemed, the rhythmic tolling of a church bell. It was Sabbath morning. How still and peaceful life could be! Here was a place where the Sabbath was verily a day of rest.

The room, which had looked so quaint and cosy in the ruddy glow of a peat fire, and the guttering light of a single candle, as he had seen it the night before, was now suffused with the mellow sunlight of a November morning. Through the fawn-coloured window-blind it oozed, tinting everything in dim gold. The wall-paper; the two old prints above the fireplace; the china hen sitting unconcerned between a pair of purse-mouthed china dogs; the mahogany chest of drawers itself which they ornamented—all were sleeping in a golden haze. Everything appeared to have yellowed with a calm and peaceful age. This surely was a spot for rest and reflection.

He lay still for a while thinking. Now he understood the indefinable charm of the Misses Birrell. It was the sweetness of a pure and lovely life lived slowly, afar from the fret and fever of the city. Even yet the sun stands still, to the wayside gowans; for their eyes are on him the whole day long, and shadow is ever behind them unseen: night is oblivion and forgetfulness. So had Time stood still for the Misses Birrell, young in middle life, and ageing without the wrinkles and ravages of years. The snows of winter had whitened their heads, but its frosts had not chilled within them the heart of their youth. On meeting them last night he had felt like one carried away back to the days of chivalry and romance, when the whole world was young. Now he thought of them again as his eyes wandered round the room bathed in the morning light and mellowed with a century of suns.

The Misses Birrell represented the luxury and leisure of Kinkelvie. They occupied the best house in the town—a two-storeyed building, with attic windows. A little walled-in garden in front separated the house from the street, while a gate, opening on a graveled walk to the front door, gave it its claim to respectability and distinction. Moreover, it had a

slated roof, and held its head high above its neighbours. The two elderly ladies themselves upheld the
tradition of family greatness with lace caps and
alpaca aprons for indoor wear. When they walked
out in the afternoon they wore broad-brimmed hats
of black Leghorn straw, and the household apron
was laid aside. Their great, grey shawls and poke-
bonnets were only for the Sabbath day.

It was twenty years since their father's death, and
only the oldest of the old folk could remember his
coming to the village as assistant to Dr. Dewar.
The young student married Mary, the only daughter
of the old doctor, and, after his death, succeeded to
his practice. The marriage proved to be a very
happy one, and for many years Dr. Birrell had gone
in and out among patients who had faith in his skill
as a doctor, and loved him for his gentle and kindly
speech. But that was in the days of Kinkelvie's
greatness, when a hundred-and-twenty looms made
music in the village, and the kilns had supplied the
whole parish with lime. Now there were not a
score of looms a-going, and the limekilns were ruins.
The old race of hand-loom weavers was dying out.
There were roofless dwelling-houses in the Wabsters'
Wynd, whose tumble-down outside stairs led to
nowhere; while what had been beams and traddles
and lays of once busy hand-looms, rotted with the
rafters of roofs that had sheltered them, buried
beneath plastered partitions and the pulp of thatch;
decay, and desolation, and death, which kindly
Nature was happing away in her everlasting green.
It was in the palmy days of Kinkelvie that Dr.
Birrell had lived and thrived, leaving his daughters,
when he died, with a roof over their heads, and

enough for their simple wants. "They lived on the interest," the villagers explained, considering them "passing rich on forty pounds a year." Nowadays there was no doctor in Kinkelvie at all. The nearest practitioner lived at Milnforth, five miles distant, and only visited this village in his rounds. But he was not in much request, nor held in high esteem. For coughs and colds, for sprains and bruises, the villagers had cures of their own, nauseous and efficacious—let Dr. Gregor sneer at them as he might. As for bronchitis, rheumatism, and such maladies incidental to old age, these were part of Nature's law, and "bid to be tholed."

When Urquhart dressed, and drew the blind, he looked out on the back-garden—a long strip of ground, just the breadth of the house, running between two dry-stone dykes to the edge of a park. Red and black-currant bushes ran the whole length of one of the dykes. Against the dyke opposite were a small greenhouse and a hennery. Through some half-dozen apple trees, scattered irregularly through a potato bed, he could see at the head of the garden a green and a summer-house. Beyond the garden, fields stretched away to the loch, lying like a silver fringe along the velvet-green hillside. The rain had ceased, leaving the sky clear and cloudless, bending over fresh green pastures. He thought of the usual Sunday morning in Edinburgh, breaking muggy and gray across dilapidated chimney-cans; the peace and quietness of the day of rest broken with the unending tread of feet on the reverberating pavement, and the rattle of an occasional milk-cart. Here was Nature at her devotions, calm and majestic, kneeling in prayer. A

D

great peace came upon him, and his thoughts wandered away beyond the fields and the loch and the
hills, and his heart was filled with a chastened
gladness.

Presently a voice broke the stillness, timbre and
shaky, but withal of a peculiar sweetness.

> " The Lord 's my shepherd, I 'll not want,
>   He makes me down to lie
>   In pastures green ; He leadeth me
>   The quiet waters by."

He peered through the window as he listened, for
the sound came from the garden ; but he could see
no one.   And the singing ceased.

" *Orlington*," he murmured, " an old favourite of
my father's."

Then the psalm was taken up in the garden
adjoining.

> " My soul He doth restore again,
>   And me to walk doth make,
>   Within the paths of righteousness,
>   Even for His own Name's sake."

This time it was the deep voice of a man, walking,
as Urquhart guessed, with the slow movement of the
music.   He recognised the voice, however, before he
saw Watty Spence climb, and seat himself on the
corner-stone of the dyke between the two gardens.
Then a figure glided from the summer-house, and
sat down on a garden-chair close under where Watty
was perched.

Urquhart watched, wondering.   No word of greeting passed between them.   The lady seated herself
without even looking at Watty, whose face, bent
towards her, was touched with a great tenderness

and pity. But he saw them from a distance, and
this might be only imagination. Was it usual for
them to meet thus, or was this only a chance
meeting? Evidently they had spoken, the one to
the other, in the words of the twenty-third psalm.
And now there they were together, the only figures
in the landscape, and the air so still that he had
heard the rustle of the lady's dress as she crossed
the green.

He drew back from the window with the sense of
intrusion even at this distance. But his eyes were
fixed on the strange couple, Watty still in his every-
day garb, and the lady in gray silk—it seemed to
be—and garden-hat.

Without raising her eyes she opened a book, and
handed it to Watty. "A bible," Urquhart assured
himself, noting Watty's tender handling of it. He
laid it face down over his knee, keeping the place
until he had drawn on his spectacles. Then he lifted
it reverently, and began to read. Urquhart could
hear the sound of the voice borne down through the
garden, as it had been the murmur of a bee outside
the window. And all the time the lady listened with
bowed head, her hands lying on her knees, clasped in
prayer. She received the book from Watty's hands
when he had finished, and, without a word, glided
back to the summer-house. With a red bandanna
handkerchief Watty wiped his spectacles, and sat for
a minute or two looking thoughtfully towards the
loch. Then climbing down from the wall, he walked
slowly away.

After a bit, Urquhart gently lifted the window.
The air came breathing in of the fields, and bringing
the faint aroma of burning peat. The wind rustled

through the ivy, and a brook murmured not far distant. All else was still, the fields reaching to the loch, and the loch touching the silent hills.

When he went downstairs to breakfast, he found the lady whom he had seen in the garden seated at table. She was introduced to him as Mrs. Rae, but beyond wishing good-morning she did not utter a word during the meal. Nor was it a quiet meal, for the Misses Birrell had much to talk about and talked well. Miss Agnes, the younger, was the more talkative and vivacious of the two. Something of dramatic instinct she had, and a lively imagination, that lightened and illustrated all she said. Expression played across her face like the light and shade chased by the wind over a field of barley. Her eyes, at times sparkling with merriment, might change in a flash to express the tenderest pathos. Not her words alone, but her whole body, every action and movement, helped towards her meaning, giving to her conversation a piquancy and charm that no amount of writing could convey. The elder, on the other hand, was quiet and equable, speaking little, but always with a quaint tenderness that suggested the beauty of an autumn evening. Indeed, though Mistress Janet, as she was called, sat at the head of the table and presided over the tea, it was Miss Agnes who said grace and did the honours of the table generally.

But in spite of the fascination of Miss Agnes's talk and Mistress Janet's sweet urbanity of manner, Urquhart could not keep his eyes from Mrs. Rae. What was it in her face that so moved him to pity? Her hair was perfectly white, yet she was not aged. Her face had the expression of one who had come through trial and tribulation, and still suffered in secret. And this expression was not so much in the eyes as in the eyelids, a melancholy resignation written in its every line and in the whole contour of the face. When she did raise her eyes he thought them lifeless and vacant. They were the eyes of one who had lost all interest in life. That she took no part in the conversation was of itself strange, but apparently she did not even listen.

He thought of her when he strolled about the garden, smoking, after breakfast was over. There was something in her face which attracted him, but what the fascination was he could not tell.

After a little while Miss Agnes joined him, and began talking of the garden and the flowers, which were her especial care.

"Most of the gardens here are little else than rose bushes and fuchsias," she told him; "but I have a liking for chrysanthemums and dahlias as well. The dahlias, you see, are almost gone now, but if you had been here a fortnight ago you would have seen them at their best. The one day they were a blaze of colour, and next morning black and withered; one night's frost had nipped them."

"Still you must have been rich in roses too," he observed, noticing the array of bushes.

"Oh, yes," she answered with a smile. "I don't neglect the old favourites although I introduce new ones. We are old-fashioned folk here, and like the old-fashioned flowers. You'll smell mint and southernwood in church to-day. Here are balm and thyme, you see, and there's quite a tree of apelringey—that's what we call southernwood here. It was a bush before I was born, and that's neither

to-day nor yesterday, Mr. Urquhart." She smiled so
playfully when she said this that he could not help
smiling in answer. "But come," she proposed, "you
must see my fuchsias and geraniums in the greenhouse."

Inside the greenhouse, however, she turned and
spoke very gravely, not of the flowers.

"I saw you observing Mrs. Rae," she said. Her
eyes were fixed on him with an appealing tenderness.
"Poor body!" she sighed.

In a flash Urquhart knew what had fascinated
him in the face. It was a face with a history
behind it, a history of sorrow and suffering; of
trial that had broken her spirit until she had suc-
cumbed.

"She is——" Miss Agnes touched her own forehead significantly. "You know?"

"Yes, yes," he answered, catching something of the
old lady's tenderness of speech. "Poor thing!"

"She's a lady born and bred," she continued;
"anybody can see that. But we don't quite know
her story. As far as we can find out, she lost her
husband, her child, and then her reason—all in one
week. For some years she was in a private asylum
before she was brought to stay here—this being a
quiet country place, you know. She used to come
and sit in our garden when she lived with Mrs.
Gordon, and after Mrs. Gordon's death her guardians
asked us to take care of her. We had not the heart
to refuse, poor thing, not that we were in need of the
money—and they keep her like a lady, as she is. No
child could be more gentle; and we felt so much for
her! She has been somebody's body, Mr. Urquhart,
and she is ours now."

" Is she always as quiet as she was this morning,
Miss Agnes ? "

" Oh dear, no ! " she assured him.   " We have long
talks often, but the past is a blank to her.   It is only
on Sunday mornings she is so quiet, after Walter has
read her chapter."

" I saw him this morning," Urquhart said ; " it was
a touching sight."

" She met Walter when he was digging our garden
one day, and made friends with him on the spot.
He seems to recall to her something of her former
life—I expect because he is a gardener ; for when
she mentions her home she always speaks of the
gardener—never of father, or mother, or husband,
only of the gardener—' who was a true friend,' she
says."

" Does Watty read to her every Sunday ? "

" Yes, she saw him at the head of his garden the
first Sunday she was here, and brought a Bible and
put it into his hands.   He is a kind-hearted man,
Walter ; and he seemed to understand at once what
she wanted.   Anyhow, he sat down on the dyke
then, just as you saw him this morning, and read
to her ; and he has not missed a Sabbath morning
since.   If it is wet or cold they sit in the greenhouse
here.   And do you know," she asked in a whisper,
" it is always the same chapter she gives him to
read—the one he read to her first ? "

" That 's Watty at the head of his garden now, I
see."   Urquhart caught sight of him through the
glass.   " He 's ready for church."

" Yes, and it 's time I was ready, too.   That was
the ten-bell ringing as I came up.   If you talk with
Walter, don't mention seeing him this morning.   He

doesn't like people to speak to him about the reading
—or about any kindness he does. But you'll learn
to know Walter yourself, and like him, I'm sure."

He strolled to the top of the garden, and watched
Watty moving about in the garden beyond. He
wore a vest of flowered satin, but had not yet
donned his frock-coat and hat. These were not for
the garden, and his white shirt-sleeves reached to the
cross-pockets of his old-fashioned full-fold trousers.
He was standing silently regarding some dilapidated
beehives when Urquhart addressed him.

" The honey was a failure, the year," he observed,
following his own train of thought before answering
Urquhart's greeting. " Ay, it's a braw mornin' after
the rain. D'ye notice the hill ower the houses clear
agin the blue? It's the first mornin' it's wanted a
nicht-cap this eight days. We'll be wearin' frost-
wise afore the week's out."

" You'll all be weather-prophets here, I suppose?"

"Weel, the feck o' us! But we dinna aye 'gree,
an' that keeps us safe : there aye bid to be some o'
us richt. Rob keeps an e'e on the birds ; I gang by
the busses an' nettercaps maistly, an' the moon when
she shows hersel', as Sir Patrick did afore me, ye'll
mind ; Donal' havers o' rain ower a plug o' baccy,
an' he's sometimes no faur wrang ; but auld Mich'el's
bottle's a safe thing to haud by. Howsomever, the
weather-wise maun a' be early birds. It's when the
day's young ye can judge o' it's natur' best. I saw
ye'd been early asteer yersel' this mornin'."

"Yes, Watty ; I observed you, too, and Mrs. Rae,
from the window."

"Ay? It's a good point to be observant. I
like a man that keeps his e'en open an' his mouth

steekit. The twa aye gang thegether as faur as I 've
seen. . . . Ye 'll be Auld Kirk, I 'm thinkin'. Aweel,
we micht dander down thegether. Your ladies 'll be
awa' a'ready; they 're Free, an' haud twa services,
winter an' summer. But we tak' things cannier i'
the Auld. I' the back en' we begin wi' ane a week,
an' it contents us a' the cauld weather."

"I 'll be very pleased to have your company,
Watty."

"Ye can meet me at the half-hour, than." He was
moving away as he spoke. "They 'll a' be on the
outlook for the new master."

Urquhart stood watching him walking cannily
down the garden-path, resting his eyes now on a
flower-bed, now on the bushes at his side. "And
Watty 's an observant man himself," he thought,
"and a shrewd. How quietly he closed himself
against my curiosity! Yes, I am curious about
Mrs. Rae; and Watty knows more of her than the
Misses Birrell do; I can see that much."

MUIREDGE Farm, according to the tradition of Kinkelvie, had been in the possession of the Muirs from time immemorial. But time moves slowly in country places, and a century outlives the longest memory. The farm could not have been so old as most of its neighbours, for it was all reclaimed land, and at one time must have been part of the bed of the loch. But the farmhouse had been built by a Muir, as the worn lintel-stone of the front door still evidenced, and that was enough to proclaim the antiquity of the family. Those who examined the stone curiously detected a date straggling between the initials, that showed the building to be little more than a hundred years old, and this only the oldest part of it. For there had been additions from time to time, and, indeed, it was these newer parts, in great measure, that gave the house its quaint and antiquated appearance. But the villagers of Kinkelvie were content to see only the initials "A.M." and "G.S."; for there was history to be read therein; something of human interest; of love and marriage, and of the customs of their forefathers. "Andrew Muir," they said, "and Grace Sime his wife"; for tradition had preserved the names, although it had forgotten the date. The same initials were to be seen on the sun-dial standing in the middle of the lawn ; and a sun-dial always gives assurance of age and respectability.

There may have been something also in the conjunction of the names, suggestive of a long pedigree. Muir of Muiredge sounded like the name of a country family ; the one belonged to the other, the farm to the family, and the family to the farm, and they must have grown old, very old, together. Moreover, in the farms adjoining there had been changes within the memory of living inhabitants ; but Muiredge had descended from father to son since the day when A.M. had brought his wife G.S. to the home he had built by the edge of the moss. Old Nance Bruce could tell of Taylors and Haimes in Balbingry before the reign of the Muckersies. She remembered even of Rintouls in Waughmill, although the Misses Souter now held their heads so high there ; but the Muirs had been in Muiredge "a' her ocht."

The farmhouse and steading stood close to the Peat Moss, surrounded with trees. From the front door one had a glimpse of the loch, seen through a sombre line of firs, while the windows at the back looked towards the kirk, standing high by the road, as it wound round the eastern flank of the hill. Originally it had been no more than a four-roomed cottage, with the byre and stable and cartsheds forming a courtyard behind. But rooms had been added from time to time, now on the one side and now on the other, and latterly a great flagged kitchen and dairy behind, carrying it back almost to the door of the byre. A couple of rose bushes, one on either side of the door, and narrow strips of flower beds bordered with boxwood, under the windows, were all it had of garden in front; but the grass of the lawn was soft and close like the pile of velvet, and must have been as old as the grey sun-dial standing at its centre.

On the west side of the house was the rose garden, screened with a flat-topped holly hedge, and cut off from the cottage garden behind it by a high brick wall, trellised with pear trees enjoying a southern exposure. This had been planned and laid out by the last Andrew Muir, who, in the language of the village, "had married a wife wi' a tocher, and led the life of a gentleman."

The marriage had not proved in all respects a happy one. Mrs. Muir had not been brought up to a life of work, and scandalised the wives of the neighbouring farmers by playing the piano when, as they asserted, she should have been bustling about the byre looking after cows and calves. She reigned in the drawing-room, while they ruled in the dairy. The young wife was quick to resent hints about idleness and the vanity of dress, knowing that she was living within her means. She would have been pleased to associate with those wives had they minded only their own homes; but they insisted on looking after hers as well. So it gradually came about that she lived pretty much by herself, rarely having a visitor and rarely visiting. Even her husband came in for his share of neighbourly advice because he dressed to please the wife he loved, and not according to the fashion of his brother farmers. They accounted him "stuck up," and in the pride of poverty consoled themselves with charitable re-

flections on the vanity of riches. But he loved his
wife with all his heart, and, what was more, loved her
ways. It was a pleasure for him to see her moving
about the room with easy grace; and through the
long winter nights he delighted to listen when she sat
playing at the piano. What a wonder it was to hear
the ivory keys answering her touch, and speaking of
things his mind could only dimly comprehend! But
those slim fingers of hers were fit for anything—save
for the rough work of kitchens and byres. She had
brought money to him, and why should she not live
like a lady, doing as she would with her own? So
reasoned her husband, and clung the more to his
wife. That they were happy in their home and in
their love for one another was indeed true, but the
human heart craves more than this, and there was
always a sense of loneliness in their love.

By-and-bye children came, and there was little time
for feeling lonely, but the children grew up apart
from the sons and daughters of the neighbouring
farmers, accounted proud and stuck-up as their
parents were. For the world visits on the children
what it is pleased to consider the sins of the parents.
This is a divine law, and there is great virtue in
enforcing it.

Hardly anything could the mother do that was
pleasing to her neighbours. Her children were not
dressed as they ought to be; she was training up her
boys in idleness; her indulgence would bring her
daughter to beggary. And what a scandal it was
when she brought a governess from Edinburgh to
teach them!

" The very laddies as weel as the lassie," remarked
the good wife of Waughmill, " sit thumpin' awa' at

that pianny. How can onybody expect them to come to guid? But she was brought up episcopalian, poor cratur'! My lassies both kilted their coats i' the dairy afore they were i' their teens, an' look at them now! Both weel married, wi' a good doun-sittin', an' their butter an' eggs sellin' in E'nburgh! An' Dav' gat mair schoolin' in stables nor books, an' now his name's printed i' the very papers an' kent ower a' the country side. Twa' first prizes for stots, an' the silver medal for ploughin'! It's come to a gey pass when a mother pays a stranger to look after her bairns. She should ha'e payed another to tak' the labour an' travail aff her hands as weel!"

Mr. Muir heard, if even his wife did not, what others said, but he took no notice; what his wife did must be right, and it was they who were wrong.

One day, Andrew, a boy about ten years old at the time, came home black-eyed and bleeding, yet bearing himself like a hero. "I was fighting David Hutton," he told his mother, "and he's bigger than me."

"But why should you fight, Andrew?" she asked, almost crying at the sight of his blackened eyes, yet at the same time proud of his spirit. "Why did you fight and come home to me with your face swollen and bleeding?"

"But I gave him worse, mother."

"Oh, Andrew!"

"He pulled the feather out of my glengarry and laughed at my velvet jacket," Andrew sturdily explained.

"You shouldn't have heeded him at all, Andrew. You ought to——"

"I didn't strike him for that," he broke in. "I

didn't strike him till he said we were gentry, and then I fought him; and I beat him, I beat him," he repeated; "and sent him home crying."

When the boys grew beyond the lessons of their governess they were sent to school in Edinburgh; and this also was a new departure in the ways of farmers, and a grievance to those whose sons finished their education at the parish school. Andrew, after two years at school, came home to begin work on the farm, for he was the first-born and would succeed his father, but Robert went straight from school to the University of St. Andrew's. Most probably he would have gone in for the Church, but before he had even got through his Arts course he was suddenly called home to take his place as head of the family. His father and brother driving home from market one stormy Saturday had been thrown from their gig, and Andrew killed on the spot. The father lingered on for about a week, his strong constitution battling against a complication of injuries; but he died without once having regained consciousness.

Then followed a terrible time for the poor widow. The death of her husband and son was a visitation. Neighbours called and sympathised; but their sympathy was not of a soothing tendency. "Pride goeth before a fall," they quoted in their virtue, and that was all the consolation they had to offer. For just such a catastrophe had she all along in her worldly pride been preparing; for just such a righteous retribution had they been devoutly waiting. And now that it had come, who were they that they should deplore the mysterious dispensations of Providence? She was not even allowed to forget that the horse which had carried her husband and

her first-born to an untimely end, was the horse she
had bought for Andrew on his twenty-first birthday.
Surely in this was visible the chastening hand of the
Lord.

Mrs. Muir was never afterwards seen abroad. She
kept to her room watching, when she could, the tall
figure of her second son as he moved about the
fields. But the sorest trial of all was the runaway
marriage of her daughter. Word came from Edinburgh that Elsie and the drawing-master in the
school she was attending had disappeared, whither
no one could tell. Robert set off at once, and
managed to trace their flight to London, and lost
them there. He came home weary and dispirited,
just in time to bid a last good-bye to his mother, yet
unable to give her in her dying moments the comfort
she desired. After her death the hearts of her
neighbours softened, and they spoke no more against
her. The managers and elders of the church even
went the length of accepting the legacy she had left
for the purpose of buying a harmonium for the
church. They had refused the gift—by a majority—
when she was alive; but, now she was dead, it was
magnanimous to observe her dying wish. The harmonium was bought, and Mary Hutton, who had
learned to play the piano with Elsie Muir, when she
came to give her lessons in sewing, was appointed
harmoniumist. That also was in deference to the
wishes of the dead, although it was not generally
known that a sum of money had been left to help
towards her salary.

Robert Muir took scant notice of his neighbours'
belated sympathy. He had seen how his mother
had suffered at their tongues when she was alive,

and their effusive condolences over her grave counted for little now. He was of a quiet disposition, and heard what they had to say much as one might listen to the functional small - talk of garrulous Society. After the funeral ceremony was over he sought what consolation he could in his work on the farm during the day, and in his library at night; making friends of his books and of the teeming life of field and hedgerow rather than of the men he met day by day. His brother-farmers could take their own ways; he kept by his. And in spite of his love for books, the farm prospered under his hands. He came to be recognised as a man of substance, and, moreover, in spite of his reserved ways, one who was willing to help, if his help were required. It was certainly a weakness in a farmer, this book-learning; but there were extenuating circumstances in his case, and his brethren excused him. After all, he was a man to be respected; and the old enmity was allowed to die down.

Eighteen years passed away; he was a widower, with two boys—the younger ten years old—before he again heard aught of his sister. And what he did hear, the country-side could only guess. It was known that he had been called suddenly to Edinburgh, and had remained away for about a week. The day after he left, the *Scotsman* announced "the death of Elsie, relict of the late Arthur Austin, art-teacher, and daughter of the late Andrew Muir, farmer, Muiredge." Then, when he came back again, he had brought with him a young lady, some sixteen or seventeen years old. This was Elsie Austin, who had come with her uncle to Muiredge, and come to stay.

The old farmhouse was soon a brighter place to

E

Robert Muir than it had been for years. The
rooms seemed to change with his niece's presence;
for she brought into them not only the sunshine of a
happy nature, but also all a woman's love for things
beautiful. The whole house began to look neat and
tidy again, as it had done when his wife was alive;
and Elsie was soon a great favourite with the boys,
coming to them as she had been an elder sister and
knew their ways. Nor was it long before she had
made friends with all the villagers. She moved
amongst them with her winning ways, cheering the
aged and taking the hearts of the young at a look.
Yet she did not resemble the Muirs. The Muirs
were a dark race, haughty and silent; she was fair,
full of the play of life, vivacious, and laughter-loving.
The village wives tried to see in her some likeness to
the Elsie they had known, but were baffled, which
was disappointing; for it forced them to attribute
her features as well as her fairness, her sunny nature
as well as her delicate complexion, to her father—a
man whom they had never known. But the chief
thing, after all, was that they loved her for herself,
the men worshipping her openly, and the women
beholding their devotion without jealousy.

For over four years now Elsie Austin had stayed
at Muiredge, and, in spite of having been brought
up in town, had enjoyed her country-life thoroughly.
She had her little pony-phæton, and could drive
about as she pleased; and so had made many
friends—not only among the families of the farmers
round about, but also in the towns of Milnforth and
Inverorr. Moreover, she had come to take the
place of mistress at Muiredge; and that gave her
an abiding interest in the farm and in farm-life. In

the city she had been merely "a Miss Austin"; but
here she was "the Miss," presiding over a household, and holding a recognised position in Society.
Amongst the farm-servants and villagers she could
play the part of the Princess Bountiful, dispensing her
favours evenly and openly; and it was not Andrew
and Robert alone who were her willing slaves.

Being fond of music, she had ever taken an active
interest in the church choir; and after Mary Hutton
accepted a place as housekeeper in Torbean, and
left the village, it was Elsie who took her place at
the harmonium. Nor was it altogether because of
the saving of a few pounds yearly that the church
managers had gladly availed themselves of her
services. She played well in the first place; but,
better than that, she had found favour in the eyes
of the old precentor, who was a cantankerous body.
Never afterwards had Dauvit a word to say against
"the kist o' whistles"; and there was harmony in
the choir now, as well as in the music.

Probably Elsie's coming made more difference to
Mr. Muir than to anybody else. He had taken to
her as she had been his own daughter, and she had
brought back to him that feeling of home in his
house, which he had hardly known since the death of
his wife. Very likely he was more of her slave than
even the boys were; for boys have games and ex-
peditions of their own in which they do not ask
girls to join, but the father's thoughts were all of
his children—and she was one. He may even have
been more indulgent to her than he would have been
to a daughter, but Elsie's nature was not one to be
easily spoiled, least of all by such unselfish love as
Mr. Muir's.

Such then was the household of Muiredge when
Mr. Urquhart came to be schoolmaster in Kinkelvie,
and it was of Mr. Urquhart that the farmer was
thinking when he rose and dressed this Sunday
morning.   He meant his boys to have a good education, as he himself had had ; and he thought he
might ask Mr. Urquhart to give an evening or two
a week to their studies.   Mr. Buchanan, the late
teacher, had done what he could for them, especially
in mathematics, but classics had not been his strong
point, and Mr. Muir had given them a start in Latin
and Greek himself.   Now, however, that a graduate
had been appointed to the parish school, his boys
might have the chance of being educated at home ;
they could be with him until one or both left for the
university.   The salary of the schoolmaster was by
no means a princely one in Kinkelvie, and probably
this Mr. Urquhart would not object to make a few
guineas more a month by private teaching.

So he thought of his boys and of the new teacher.
It did not enter his mind to think of him and Elsie
Austin.

CHAPTER SIXTH

A NEW VOICE IN THE CHOIR

"GOOD-MORNING, Uncle." Elsie Austin came into the large, low-ceilinged dining-room, and bending over her uncle's chair touched his temples with her lips.

"Good-morning, Elsie," he said, rising. "Have you been decking yourself out for conquest? Here have I been waiting quarter of an hour for breakfast, while you've been doing up that hair of yours, no doubt admiring its golden threads, and wondering if this new teacher —— "

She placed a hand over his mouth and held back her head with the dignity of a queen. "Now you have said enough, Uncle. It's just because you know that I positively hate teachers that you speak so; and this Mr. Urquhart will be no better than those loud-voiced boy-men I used to meet so often in Edinburgh. Not a word, now," she warned, with a playful light in her eye. "Here are the boys famishing as usual."

A couple of boys banged into the room as she spoke, and noisily seated themselves at table. Andrew, the elder of the two, was in his sixteenth year, and Robert, although eighteen months younger, might have been taken for his twin brother. They were dressed alike in rough tweed; had the same shaggy head of dark-brown hair, with their hands and faces almost as brown; and both bore themselves with the swing of those who are accustomed to walking across furrowed fields. Strong, healthy lads they looked, and quite equal to the capacious plates of porridge set ready for them on the table. Although they resembled each other so strongly in figure and face, a second glance noted a marked difference, but the difference belonged more to expression than to feature. Andrew had the same eyes as his father, steel-grey and steady, but there was a look in Robert's, soft and dreamy, which he must have inherited from his mother. The village wives often told him that he "looket at them wi' just sic' an e'e as his mother," and hoped he would grow up as kind and gentle as she had been. But Robert did not remember his mother; she had died when he was only a few months old.

A servant now brought in the coffee and a dish of ham and eggs. How delicious it smelt when the farmer lifted the cover—home-cured ham, and eggs taken from the "crib" that very morning! The boys did not take coffee. After their porridge they had a plate of ham and egg, and an extra jug of milk.

"You have a strange prejudice against teachers," Mr. Muir began again, when they were seated at table; "and you quarrel with Mr. Urquhart before you have seen him."

"Quarrel, Uncle?" she asked, smiling. "There is no quarrel; only I don't want to know him. Teachers are all the same. How they used to bore me!"

"But you were a mere girl then, Elsie; and I'm afraid you can't help meeting him, for I mean to ask him to coach the boys in Latin and Greek."

Andrew screwed his face behind his jug of milk, and Robert smiled.

"He has excellent testimonials too," their father pursued.

"Oh Uncle, Uncle," she cried, shaking her head at him, "they all have. A good many teachers used to call at home, I suppose because father had been a teacher, and mother took an interest in them all. And when they wished to be very kind to me they would present me with copies of their testimonials. What funny reading it was, and what proper and irreproachable young men they were, every one! Greek, Latin, Mathematics, English, Geography, History, French, German, Political Economy—all the sciences—Writing, Drawing, Music; oh, what did these young men not know! They knew all the little trifles other people think hardly worth knowing, consequently they esteemed themselves wise above their neighbours, and thanked Providence in their walk and conversation that they were not as other men."

"You are growing sarcastic, Elsie."

"Not at all," she assured him. "It was really good fun in a way. There was one young fellow who used to explain to me every time we met, the difference between interest and discount."

"An interesting subject, surely," her uncle answered unguardedly.

"That's as bad as any one of them," she said. "Let me fill you a fresh cup of coffee. If they had heard such an execrable pun they would have

squirmed in their seats, and made a mental note of it
for their next house of call.   Some used to discourse
on the subtleties of grammar, showing the difference
between subjunctive and potential, and others on the
niceties of algebra.   And there was one little fellow
—he was at the training college when I left Edinburgh—could have given you the derivation of any
word in the language.   Dr. Johnson was his only
author; he had written a dictionary.   Poor Sandy!
I rather liked him too; he was so dreadfully in
earnest."

"Somewhat intellectual gatherings these, Elsie?"

"Oh, but they were more than intellectual, Uncle.
They could sing, and play the piano, and recite, and
dance, and yet with all their accomplishments," she
said, breaking away from banter and speaking
seriously, "they used to bore me dreadfully.   I was
too ignorant for their learned world."

"It would be great fun if Elsie were to fall in love
with Mr. Urquhart after all," Robert remarked to his
brother.

He had been listening to the conversation, and was
already, with all a boy's love of romance, making
a story of startling developments.

"What nonsense you do talk, Rob!" Elsie regarded him from the superiority of her great age and
experience, and talked to him like a mother, smiling
indulgently at his childish folly.   "It's time you
were preparing for church, both of you."

But Andrew was more practical and saw no
romance whatever.

"I know what I'll do if he talks to me about
interest and discount, and all that nonsense," he
observed.

" And what will you do ? " his father asked.

" I 'll ask him the difference between mushrooms and toadstools. Elsie didn't know, and she 'd been at a ladies' college."

" And she didn't know a linty's egg from a blackie's," Robert remembered.

" And you mind what she said when we showed her a mavis's nest ? " Andrew pursued. " Oh, what a funny thing ! Who made it ? "

" But I know better now," Elsie laughed. " You know I do."

" How many eggs does the bat lay ? " Andrew interrogated.

" Away with you boys, away," their father said, rising.

" Five," Elsie cried at a venture after the retreating boys.

" Five, five, oh ! oh ! "

The boys shouted all the way upstairs, and after their bedroom door was shut she heard them still laughing at her ignorance.

Mr. Muir smiled too as he turned away, and Elsie laughed herself. With all her young ladies' college accomplishments, her French, and music, and painting, she was no match for these boys, who, with infinitely less book learning, knew a thousand and one things of which she was totally ignorant. What information she had, she had got from books, a second-hand information at best. But her cousins were full of a knowledge not to be learned from books—secrets which Nature whispers to those only who love her. The hills and the loch, the moss, the fields ; trees and hedges, and streams ; birds and beasts, and creeping things ; spring and summer, and autumn and winter; these had been their teachers, and now they came to books with a full mind. After all, she was no better than the teachers she despised; for her knowledge was the very knowledge she derided. This thought flashed through her brain now, as she stood by the window looking across the moss to the loch, sparkling frostily in the hard sunshine. She had never thought of her accomplishments in that way before, and she blushed, standing alone.

"Bah!" she exclaimed, turning impatiently and walking to the window opposite. "It's their little pedantic ways I despise; and all teachers are the same, lady teachers too. I don't wish to know him, and I won't."

Through the trees she could see the old church, with its stunted belfry standing grey against the hillside, and the bare hedges on the east, where the high-road dipped down to the village of Wells-green. Here and there a narrow foot-path showed like a wisp of brown against the green, as it wound down the hillside and through the Three-Neukit Plantin, bringing from unseen cottages shepherds and their families to the churchyard gates. Here could farmers and ploughmen from outlying homesteads forgather once a week and enjoy a crack before the beginning of the morning service. Some figures were already moving about, black and sombre-looking, amongst the tombstones. It would be time to be going presently, and she went up to her own room.

It was more than half-an-hour's walk from the farm to the church, going round by the Sandy Loan, which led by a winding and easy incline to the high road, opening on it about midway between the church and the east end of the village. But

the farm folk usually went by a private pathway, climbing from the cottage garden straight
up to a side-gate in the churchyard. The boys
had gone on ahead by themselves, and when
Elsie and her uncle entered the churchyard, there
was a group waiting to receive them. Elsie herself
would merely have bowed good-morning and passed
on, leaving Mr. Muir to talk, as was the custom, with
the men. But the two boys stood right in her way,
grinning, and, before she was aware of what was
happening, Watty Spence had very formally introduced her to Mr. Urquhart, the new teacher.

She had been fairly caught, and was annoyed.
She bowed frigidly, uttered some conventional phrase
of welcome—she hardly knew what—and turned
to the church door. But she carried away in a
glance the picture of a striking face, and she felt
a pair of clear, keen eyes following her right into the
church. When she seated herself at the harmonium
she was feeling hot and uncomfortable. This was
not the introduction she had made in imagination, and she had not borne herself with the dignity
and hauteur she had put on when rehearsing the part
with her reflection in the mirror that very morning.
And it did not tend to her composure that she presently became conscious that the two lads were
eyeing her with grinning delight. She would lecture
them when she got home, she resolved. Such levity
was unbecoming the dignity of a cushioned and
curtained family pew. A voluntary was played with
uncertain fingering, and she was glad when it was
over, and the congregation male came trooping in.
There was a sense of relief in the familiar sound
of cheeping Sabbath-day boots, and she began to be

herself again. The usual Sabbath peace had returned,
and in the unchanging routine of praise and prayer
her discomfiture would be wholly forgotten.

But here was Watty Spence ushering Mr. Urquhart
into the choir, setting him down, alas! in the corner
seat of the bass, where, if she lifted her eyes from the
music, she must look him straight in the face. A
chuckle of laughter choked in a handkerchief sent a
flush to the roots of her hair. Oh, those wicked
boys! Above, the minister droned through the
opening psalm, and she heard not a word; the very
music danced before her in mockery. Happily she
knew the tune, and could play it mechanically, and
soon the sound of song arose, drowning the
harmonium, as it was caught up and carried down
the church till it became one voice, and the scattered
worshippers a compact congregation.

But there was a new voice in the singing to-day—
a vibrating voice that she seemed to hear with her
whole body. A deep bass voice has always this
power of making itself felt, as well as heard; it is
as if it played on the nerves like one singing across
the key-board of a piano, and compelling a sympa-
thetic vibration. And Urquhart's voice rolled and
boomed through Elsie in every tone. She felt it
in her arms, in her throat, even in her hair. Then
she thought again of that introduction by the churchyard gate; and she felt angry with Watty Spence,
angrier still with the boys, but angriest of all with
herself. It was to her, all through, a painful service.
Now his voice was ringing through her in the
praise; now his eyes were piercing her through and
through during the sermon, reading her thoughts, she
imagined, and knowing that she had made up her

mind to meet him with the most frigid politeness. She was glad when the benediction was pronounced ; and she played the congregation out, impatient of the last loiterer, so that she might hurry home and regain her composure in her own room.

In the churchyard, while Muiredge stood talking with Urquhart, and Watty Spence was introducing all and sundry to the "new master," he caught sight of Elsie hurrying down the pathway, and wondered what was wrong. She generally had a word or two to exchange with the other women folks, waiting till he was ready to accompany her. Urquhart saw her, too, and his thoughts followed her to the farm. He spoke absently to the friends Watty was haling round to shake hands with him, for the face of Miss Austin haunted him. He had certainly not met her before; yet there was something in her expression when she was introduced which had appealed to him like a memory—a momentary flash of unremembered recognition, and in a moment gone. "Mr. Urquhart, our new master, Miss Austin," Watty had said; and, as he met her eyes, and saw the colour for a second fade from her cheek, the picture of the bible-reading in the garden that morning rose before him, and he heard again Watty's voice droning against the window. Then, as suddenly, her face was suffused with red, and the picture faded from his mind. He saw only a young lady, in a blue-serge frock, gliding towards the church door, with the sunlight playing on her golden-brown hair as she went. But the recognition of a face he had known came back to him again and again, although he had only seen it for a second, and lost it even as it was seen.

" We 'll see you then to-morrow night," Muiredge was saying, " and have a talk about the boys. I should like them to begin at once."

Urquhart accepted the invitation, hardly conscious of making an engagement. He was watching a figure that, from the end of the lane, turned to glance back towards the church before entering the garden.

" I expect Balbingry here may look in, and take a hand at whist; and—you 're a singer, I see—Elsie will give us some music."

" Elsie ? "

Urquhart started, and the name fell from his lips before he was aware of what he was saying. But Muiredge only smiled broadly at his astonishment. Naturally, he was not to know who was meant by Elsie.

" That's Miss Austin that ye 've just been introduced to," Watty explained. " I thought a young chap would ha'e picked up that by a kind o' instinct. Balbingry wouldna ha'e needed a second tellin', I 'se warrant."

But Urquhart was not listening to Watty's explanation, and did not hear Balbingry's chuckle of approval. He was standing arm in arm with Gavin Crombie under the Tron Church, and hearing a young fellow, blear-eyed and thick of speech, hiccoughing her name.

All the way home Watty kept talking of minister and of members; of the family of this one, and the history of that; and Urquhart walked along by his side, quietly inattentive.

CHAPTER
SEVENTH

THE OFFENDING

INITIALS

AFTER dinner, Urquhart went out to have a look
about the village, and turning up the Wabsters'
Wynd, came to the foot of the hill. A cart-road led
round by the Appex to the old kilns. There were
still the ruts left in the sandstone, which wheels had
slowly hollowed going and coming from the limekilns, that were now a ruin. But for years no cart
had wound round this road, here rumbling over the
solid rock, there ploughing deep in sand. The
furrows, however, remained, like the wrinkles of
age, telling of former struggles and of difficulties
overcome; while the kilns to which they led had
fallen in, in masses of mason-work that still in ruin
proclaimed the virtues of the lime that had here
been made.

Urquhart followed the road past the kilns until he
stopped at a wooden seat set against a wall of red
sandstone showing through the thin soil of the hill-
side. This rock was named, and initialed, and dated
from top to bottom. Some names had been cut
deep, as if to defy the effacing finger of Time, yet
now were hardly traceable. Most had been done in
couples, and there was a kind of romance in reading
them. Had T. G. and M. R. still kept together

through life, as their initials had done since 1850?
Or was this now the only memory of a summer-day
walk?   He spelled through the list with a dreamy
feeling, hardly to be called thought, that suited well
with the stillness of the waning afternoon and the
impressive solemnity of the scene.   The village
lay below, the houses huddling together as if they
felt the loneliness of the landscape, and had crept
closer for companionship and warmth; away beyond
a streak of loch and the strip of moorland; here a
very palimpsest of names unknown, and towering
above, the round summit of the hill—sphinx-like,
immovable, eternal.

Who was G. D., Paris, and what had brought him
here?   Where was he now?   Idle thoughts!   Vain
speculations!

He was turning away, when he caught sight of a
name almost at the top of the rock.   Standing on
the seat, he could just touch the letters, which were
partly hidden by an overhanging branch of whin.

Elsie?   That name again!   Was he never going
to get away from it?   Was it going to haunt him
continually now like a memory?   It was clearly and
boldly cut, and the same hand that had traced the
name had also carved under it the initials F. D.

Urquhart let go the branch he had lifted, with an
expression of impatience.   Why he should be
annoyed, he did not ask himself.   With or without
reason, he was angry, and in a mood for quarrelling
with some one; it could hardly be that he was
jealous; and he gloomed at the harmless initials
with a sense of personal injury.   Again he saw the
helpless figure at the Tron, but not now with the pity
and contempt he had felt on Friday night.   All at

once F. D. became to him a living personality, not
merely a passing picture of dissolute youth, to be
dismissed from the mind with an unctuous "Poor
devil!" Here was a man to be reckoned with, a
possible factor in the shaping of his own life. And
meantime, what had happened to bring about such a
change in his feelings?

"H'm!" he sniffed with a pretence of indifference.
"Why should I bother about F. D., or Elsie either?
What's he to Hecuba, or Hecuba to him?"

Then a sudden thought seemed to strike him. He
took out a pocket-knife and began to cut the offending initials deep out of the rock. He smiled at
himself while he did it, as if there had been two
persons present, one taking an artistic pleasure in
doing the work neatly, and the other superciliously
looking on.

"Ye're surely busy?"

He turned with a start. So intent had he been on
the work, that he had not heard the sound of
approaching footsteps, and here was Watty Spence
standing below, regarding him with a look of grim
humour. There was no smile on his lips, but his
eyes were charged with meaning, and Urquhart
stood for a space looking down on him, feeling
supremely foolish. He might have been a schoolboy
caricaturing the master, and caught in the act.

"It's you, Watty?" he stammered, drawing the
blade of his knife across a branch of whin, and
trying to appear calm and unconcerned. "I didn't
hear you coming."

"No!" said Watty.

"It's a delightful evening, isn't it?" He stepped
down, letting his eyes wander round the whole

country-side, as if to give some relevancy to his remark. "A delightful evening, for November."

"An' for stone-cuttin', I wouldna doubt; no frost to hinder ye; though I canna say the day was weel chosen for the wark."

Urquhart laughed uneasily. "It was a sudden whim," he explained. "Sometimes one wishes it were possible to blot those endless initials out at a sweep and leave the rocks naked as Nature made them."

"For a new generation to put its mark on? Na, na! We maun a' scart our names on something; an' there's less harmless ways than on dead rocks. Ye've howkit *his* out, I see; but man, ye leave an ugly gash ablow hers."

Watty looked scrutinisingly into the face of the young man as he spoke, and Urquhart blushed.

"An' ye would be thinkin' your ain name a fitter ane, no doubt? No sooner ha'e ye clappit e'en on a lass than ye're plannin' an' plottin' to leave your mark on her heart. You're a young man yet," he added solemnly, "an' dinna be tryin' on thae tricks."

"No, Watty, you're wrong. I had not the slightest intention of leaving my initials behind me. It was only a sudden fancy to erase his, because——"

He stopped abruptly, with the consciousness of treading on dangerous ground. But he had said too much already. Watty laid a hand on his shoulder, and looked him straight in the eyes.

"Ay?" His teeth closed on the word, as if snapping it off from the thought behind, and the two stood facing each other through a second's awkward silence.

"An' what way his? Were there no others easier

come at, if it was but to amuse yoursel' on a Sabbath day afternoon?"

"Plenty."

Watty, without turning his head, pointed solemnly in the direction of the village, and spoke like one who was not to be trifled with.

"Ye've said ower muckle or ower little, Mr. Urquhart. There's his father's house, a man bowed, an' no wi' the weicht o' years, an' a mother wi' a hud on life frail as the breath she draws. What ken you o' Francis Downie?"

"Nothing, Watty."

"That'll no do, Mr. Urquhart. You say 'nothing,' an' mean 'nothing to his credit.'"

"So be it, Watty, if you will have it so. But, indeed, I know little or nothing."

"An' can that little no be telled? Maybe it's no to your ain credit, either?"

"Look here, Watty," Urquhart burst out with a feeling of irritation, "I don't want you to misunderstand me from the first; yet I am not bound to tell you how or when I saw Francis Downie."

"But you can tell a lie, an' no speak. Had we no better come to an understandin' afore ye speak o' me misunderstandin' ye? If ye've onything against the lad, would it no be better to be a man, an' ha'e it out an' done wi'?"

Urquhart stood whisking away with his handkerchief the sandstone from the seat, impatient of Watty's persistent questioning, yet almost inclined to laugh at his terrible seriousness over such an insignificant matter.

"This is a veritable tempest in a tea-cup, Watty," he said.

"Or in a gill-stoup, Mr. Urquhart?"

"Perhaps you're right; the tea-cup is more to my own taste. I mean that you are making a mountain out of a molehill."

"A molehill brak' the neck o' a king—I needna tell you that—just because it was a molehill, an' no a mountain; an' your onintelligible insinuations mak' mair mischief than the solid truth."

"But I make no insinuations, Watty. I merely say I know little, and little as that is, my mouth is closed. I did not think I should ever hear the name of Francis Downie again, until I met you at the inn last night."

"Met me? Sit down, man, an' speak no mair in riddles."

"I don't mean you," he answered. "I meant the company."

"Ah, I have ye now," Watty said, a little less drily. "Ye mean Rob Buchan—Carrier Rob, as we ca' him here. That wasna the first time ye'd met him?"

"No."

"Weel, then, ye may as well tell me a' ye ken, though Rob meant ye to keep it to yoursel'. I could see he was a kind o' out o' his ordinar', when he spak' to ye first; but I understand now. Howsomever, ye may speak wi' a' freedom; for though I ha'ena the likin' for the lad that Rob has, he's Mich'el's and Marg'et's ae ewe lamb, an' I would do muckle for him for their sakes. Tak' a seat, sir."

They both sat down, and there on the hill-side Urquhart told of meeting Francis Downie under the Tron on Friday night, and of old Rob leading him, half-carrying him down the street, till the two were lost in the darkness.

Watty heard him in silence, and then sat muttering to himself, as if he had altogether forgotten Urquhart's presence. "Poor Mich'el! Ay, ay, poor auld Mich'el! An' yet I've ha'en my ain thoughts about him this while back. Excuse me," he said, suddenly breaking off from his reflections, and laying a hand on the younger man's shoulder; "I can see what way ye wanted to keep it to yoursel', but it's as weel that I should ken. Rob has never said a word to me about his ongauns, though I whiles read it in his face when he cam' frae Edinburgh. I saw there was something amiss weel on for a year syne; but Rob has aye ha'en an awfu' work wi' Frank, an' keepit it a' a secret; a sorry secret it has been to him, I'se warrant."

Watty stopped, and Urquhart, watching his face, thought again of the look in the carrier's eyes when, for a moment breaking through his natural reserve, he had pleaded, with the suspicion of a sob in his throat, talking to the young man of his father and mother. And it was of the father and mother also that Watty was thinking now.

"He didna keep himsel' that straight, I thought," Watty continued, "when he was here i' the summer. I mind he didna come hame frae Cairncleuch, the nicht o' July fair, an' Rob brocht word that he'd fa'n in wi' some fellow-student, an' was bidin' ower the nicht wi' him. But I thoucht it a strange thing for Rob to gang trampin' back again, a matter o' seven mile, an' no getting hame till the sma' hours o' the mornin'. I'm thinkin' the student he fell in wi' was John Barleycorn, no a desirable acqua'ntance for auld or young."

Urquhart felt sorry for Watty, and tried to speak hopefully to him.

"It may not be so bad as you imagine," he said. "I only saw him once, you know, and——"

"Aince is bad enough, Mr. Urquhart, to be in the state you saw him; an' it's no for a young man like you to mak' light o' it. But I ken weel ye dinna believe it was the first time or the second time either."

"I can't say it *wasn't* his first offence."

"Dinna waste words, Mr. Urquhart. There's no use tryin' to beguile me wi' 'maybe's' when I ken the thoughts o' your heart."

Urquhart filled his pipe and began smoking. He did not know what to say. What fate had led him to meet this young fellow at all? He was sorry that he had ever chanced to meet Francis Downie before coming amongst his friends. "It's a sad case," he reflected; "but I hope it may not be so hopeless as you seem to imagine."

"Think o' his father an' mother," Watty broke out. "What a heart-break to them! An' Rob! Ay, Rob has the worst o't, kennin' what's gaun' on an' keepin' it a' to himsel'. The apple o' a father's e'e, an' their only bairn! Man, man, it's awfu'. Sooner or later they're bound to ken, an' it'll be their death. A' the toun was out to wish him weel when he gaed awa'; but what a hame-comin' he's preparin' for!"

It was now almost dark, and a few lights were beginning to show in the village windows. They rose and walked silently homewards.

"Look," said Watty, pointing to a light appearing in a little four-paned window, "there's where he was wont to study; an' Mich'el'll just be takin' a look at his laddie's belongin's. It'll break the auld man's heart when he kens, an' his mother's if she lives to hear o't."

"And the young lady—Elsie—what of her, Watty?"

"Ou," he answered with a touch of constraint, "she'll get ower it, although she'll be wae for the auld folk's sake. It's no as you think," he added in explanation, and somehow or other Urquhart's heart bounded with relief. He was glad for her sake, and his thoughts of Francis Downie were at once gentler and more pitiful than they had been.

"That was *his* doin'," Watty continued, jerking his thumb back towards the initialed rock, "no hers. He hasna kent her that lang an' sees little o' her when he's at hame. I cam' on him at the cuttin' i' the summer past, an' telled him to his face he was a fule. Laddies an' lassies now-a-days fa'in' in love, as they ca' it, just to fa' out o' it again, I canna awa' wi'!"

"I thought it had been a case of growing up together from childhood," Urquhart told him; "and I read quite a tragedy to-day on that rock."

"No, no," Watty assured him, and it was as if he spoke with thankfulness. "She's only been here a year or twa. She comes frae Edinburgh, like yoursel'; but I thoucht the e'en o' a young man would ha'e seen that in her carriage. She hasna the swing o' country roads about her, an' there's something in her very dress different frae the young ladies here about. I ken na what it is, but I thoucht you'd ha'e ta'en it in wi' a look.—But here we are at our doors. No; that was but a silly freak o' his last summer holiday, after a bit ploy he'd been at down at Muiredge. It was a' Bauby Buchan afore that. They've kent ane another since they were bairns an' aye been good friends. Ay, it's Bauby that he should keep by; a winsome lass she is, an' a good wife she'd mak' him. Rob himsel' 's a second father to him a'ready. It 'll be a sair heart to Bauby, poor lass, if he gangs the gate o' his uncle, Sodjer Sandy. But we 'd as weel keep what we ken to oursel's an' hope for the best. It 'll a' be kent soon enough if he gangs on as he's doin'. Ye might look ower after tea if ye can spare the time, an' we 'll ha'e a crack about books. I 've some auld anes ye might like to see.—I 'll look for ye then? There's Mistress Janet at the door; I 'm doubtin' we 've keepit them waitin'."

"Poor Mich'el!" Urquhart heard him muttering as he turned away. "Poor auld Mich'el!"

But his own thoughts were of Elsie Austin.

"So she's not engaged to him," he reflected tranquilly. "I 'm glad of that for her sake. I wonder where I have seen her face before; somewhere, I 'm certain. What a pretty name Elsie is!"

CHAPTER EIGHTH

ATHY IN SCHOOL AND OUT OF IT

IT was dull and chilly when Mr. Urquhart set out for school on Monday morning, and a feeling of depression, like some vague foreboding of evil, came upon him as he picked his way along the muddy street. First impressions of a place do not count for nothing, even with older and less imaginative natures than Robert Urquhart's; and one ever fondly hopes to enter on a new sphere of labour under favourable auspices. The sun should be shining and the air musical with words of welcome when the young come to a strange land, to make in it their home. But this morning the sun was invisible, and the hill was hiding in mist. The voice of the wind was no more than a moan, which the dripping branches, with a few solitary leaves, shivered to hear.

There was only one boy in the playground, and his was hardly a face that one would call propitious. Heavy browed and sullen he looked, and when Mr. Urquhart caught his eyes in passing, they stared at him without a smile, without even a spark of childish curiosity. He stood against the wall of the playground, holding his slate and books under his arm, and, if his face was expressive of anything at all, it was either of dull incurious stupidity or of sullen defiance.

"Ex uno disce omnes." The words came into the teacher's mind of themselves, and he started as if someone had whispered them in his ear. "I hope not; I trust not," he muttered in the tone of one trying to shake himself free from an evil suggestion. But in the school room he found himself unconsciously repeating the words as he noted the maps, peeled and ragged, hanging awry on the white-washed walls. White-washed they had been at one time, but they looked grimy enough now, and the whole place was reeking of damp. The windows were a network of diamond panes, at any time letting in as little light as possible, and on a muggy morning like this, barely enough to disperse the darkness and gloom of night. He looked from the windows to the desks, from the desks back again to the windows. "And this is where I am expected to teach," he reflected. "A cheerless prospect in all conscience! And here is the worst omen of all."

His eyes had rested on the fireplace heaped up with peats. Bits of half-burnt wood hung from the "ribs," and "birns" had smouldered themselves out on the cold-looking hearth. Nothing looks more desolate than a dead fire, especially in a damp room, and in the month of November when the ways are wet; and the young teacher shivered more from a sense of depression than from actual cold.

"This will never do," he muttered, pulling himself up. "I shall grow melancholy before I begin work at this rate."

Going to the door he called to the boy he had seen in the playground, who came over, slowly and unwillingly it was apparent, and looked up in the master's face with his stupidly sullen eyes.

"Can you kindle a fire, my lad?" Urquhart asked. "The school fire has gone out."

"Ay!"

The whole face changed in an instant. The eyes brightened, and there was an expression of eager intelligence on his heavy features. Throwing down his books and slate beside the door, he bounded to an outhouse built against the gable of the school.

"I ken whaur to get everything," he cried.

Urquhart waited till he saw him return with some firewood and an armful of birns, when, turning into school again, he sat down at the master's desk, and was soon busy with log-book and registers.

"She's awa' now."

He looked down and saw the boy with his knees on the fender gazing admiringly into the blazing fire.

"I see you know how to kindle a fire. I hope you can do your lessons as well as you do that."

The boy's face fell at once, and Urquhart saw that he had made a mistake in mentioning lessons.

"Never mind," he said; "I know you'll do your best. I know boys clever with their books, who couldn't kindle a fire at all. I couldn't do it myself."

The boy looked up surprised. "That's quite easy," he said. "I kin'le ours every mornin'."

"Well, I think we must make you stoker for the school. Will you look after the fire all day?"

"Ay!" he answered, quite eagerly.

"That's settled, then. What's your name, my lad?"

"John Cochrane."

He looked the name up in the register.

"I see you're in the first class, but——" He

stopped, yet the boy knew from his eyes what he had meant to say, and his face fell.

"Perhaps you can't help it, John?"

"I'll aye come reg'lar now," he burst out, "as sure as——"

"Ssh, ssh, John! I've no doubt we'll be great friends. I must get all the big boys to help me, and you know if you're irregular I'll need to appoint somebody else stoker."

"I'll no play truant again."

"That's right, John. Now you've got half-an-hour yet before school time, and I hear some of the boys in the play-ground.—Good morning, Miss Mitchell."

The schoolmistress entered just as John hurried out to join his companions.

Miss Mitchell was an ex-pupil teacher, who, for a salary of thirty pounds, presided over the infant department, and taught the girls sewing. By the thoughtfulness of the Misses Birrell, who had invited her to tea on the Sunday evening, Urquhart had been already introduced to her, and they met now not as entire strangers. By the time he had learned from her all that she could tell him about the school and the different classes, it was nine o'clock, and the school children came trooping in.

The day passed off more favourably than Urquhart had anticipated. School children, girls as well as boys, try their best to get the upper hand of a new teacher, and deliberately set themselves to watch for any signs of weakness. They may be slow at lessons; but studying a teacher is work after their heart, and they bring their best enthusiasms to the task. The teacher is their common enemy, and with united forces they make a trial of strength. If victory be theirs in the beginning of the struggle, it will be months before the master recovers lost ground, if he ever recover it; and during that time his life will be as hard as the tyranny of childhood can make it. For boys show no mercy to the vanquished; they worship strength, and serve devotedly him who shows himself their master.

But Urquhart went about his work with eyes and ears open, and he was not slow to notice that he had found a faithful lieutenant in John Cochrane. John knew where everything was kept, and had copybooks, pens, or pencils ready as they were wanted. It was easy to see that the bigger boys took their cue from him, and were on their best behaviour.

Urquhart could hear now one and now another talk to him—*Athy*, they called him—but John answered them with the dignity of an assistant, impressing all with a sense of his responsibility. Altogether, at the close of the day, the new teacher felt that he had made a good beginning, and he looked to the future with assurance. Now that he knew the arrangement of the classes, and had made the acquaintance of his pupils, he might reasonably look forward to doing some good, though it might be unpretentious, work. So far, too, he had been left alone. Not a member of the School Board had called to see how he got on, and he augured much good from that.

At tea he talked about his work with the Misses Birrell, and spoke enthusiastically. The ladies were delighted. Even Mrs. Rae, listening, became interested, and appeared to catch something of his joyous spirit.

"The building is not all that one might desire," he admitted, "and the appliances are not quite such as I have been used to; but after all, the school is the children, and I think we'll get along very well together."

"You'll be very good to them?" Mrs. Rae tentatively asked, and answered for herself, "I know you will." Then she looked at him earnestly and added, "But you'll go away, and leave them again."

"I hope not, Mrs. Rae; at least, not for a long time yet."

But Mrs. Rae shook her head, and would not be persuaded. "You'll go away again after you have taught them to love you," she told him; "they all go away."

The sound of wheels was heard outside, and Miss Agnes rose and went to the door.

"That's the carrier," she announced, and Urquhart hurried out to look after his trunks, which Rob Buchan had just brought from Inverorr.

Rob touched his cap as Urquhart came out, greeting him in his own austere way, in which there was something of awkward dignity, and, without talk, began to lift the trunks from the cart.

"And here's Athy come to help, I've no doubt." Urquhart gaily called, "Come, Athy, and let us see how strong you are."

But instead of coming forward to help—and, indeed, he had followed Rob along the road in the hope of being asked to help—the boy stood still, looked at Urquhart for a moment with sullen defiance, then, without a word, turned and trotted away.

Urquhart watched him scudding along the street, and wondered what in the earth was wrong.

"Strange," he remarked to Rob, when they had got the boxes upstairs. "I thought Athy was just waiting to be asked."

"Maybe no so strange as ye think, Mr. Urquhart," Rob answered drily. "Laddies are as touchy on some points as men.—I would like to ha'e a crack wi' ye, sir, if so be ye have the time."

"I am going down to Muiredge," Urquhart answered, with some hesitation; "it's almost time I was going."

He guessed at once what Rob wished to talk about, and feared the "crack" might be a pretty long one.

But Rob was not to be put off. "That'll answer fine," he told him. "I've a bit parcel here for the Miss, an' I'll ha'e your company down, if ye dinna mind."

"I'll be delighted, Rob. It's getting dark already, and you'll be pilot down the Sandy Loan. It looks a rough-and-tumble road at best."

"I'll see about gettin' Jenny stabled then, an' be wi' ye in a wee."

Rob was back again by the time Urquhart was ready. It was almost dark, and a heavy mist still hung about, dimming the stars. Rob trudged along for a while silent and serious, having something to talk about, but unwilling to begin. Urquhart looked now and again at the face of the old man, and knew what it was that lay so heavily on his mind.

"What was wrong with Athy," he asked, making an attempt to begin conversation.

"John Cochrane, ye mean? I wondered to hear you ca'in him 'Athy,' mysel', you that should be an example to the bairns in a' things."

"I heard the boys calling him 'Athy,'" Urquhart argued, "and I thought he'd be rather pleased to be called by his nickname."

"A kind o' condescendin' on your part, I wouldna' doubt?"

In the mouth of another the words might have been a sneer, but Rob spoke so quietly that Urquhart accepted them only as a rebuke, and was humbled.

"They ca' the laddie 'Athy,'" he continued, "but 'Atheist's the name that sticks to the father, an' that's a heavy reproach to a man hereawa' The laddie has ha'en to fecht his way i' the school; for what bairns hear whispered at the fireside they cry open-mouthed on the cause'ay. Little do they ken what Atheist means, but John gangs to neither kirk nor Sabbath school, an' that's enough."

"Yet he doesn't seem to object to the name from the school boys," the teacher urged.

"No, because he has licket every ane o' them, an' he's open to ha'e it out wi' them ony day they like. But wi' aulder folk he canna fecht, an' he tak's the name off their lips, I've seen afore, as a reproach an' a bye-word."

"I'm sorry I used it," Urquhart mused, "for I thought I'd got to John's right side this morning."

"I was thinkin' that mysel', when he speired alang the road, if the kists belanged to the new master, an' cam' alang to gi'e a hand. But I'm doubtin' ye'll no see John in a hurry again. He's awfu' touchy about the name.—But it wasna about John, poor laddie, that I wanted to speak. Maybe ye'll ken, sir, what was on my mind."

"Yes, Rob; you want to speak about Francis Downie."

" Ay, an' another.   Tak' care o' your feet, sir."

They were on the Sandy Loan by this time, and Urquhart went stumbling along, now jolting down into deep wheel-ruts, now kicking against the grassy ridges the carts had left. He heard the wimple of a burn by the road-side, and was trying to keep clear of it, but his steps were in darkness. All he could see in front of him was a belt of wood which only served to show that the sky above it was not perfectly black, and seemed to recede as they advanced.

" Keep to the middle o' the road, Mr. Urquhart," the old carrier advised, " an' ye 'll get alang safely. Mony a time have I gi'en Frank the same advice. Ay, ye're a' richt now. It 's heavy ower the sand, no doubt, but ye 're sure o' your feet. I ken every stap, an' can pick my way alang the bank.—It was about a Mr. Wyllie I thought ye micht ken."

" Mr. Wyllie !"

" Ay, Frank telled me that nicht, or mornin', rather, that he didna ken ye, only this Mr. Wyllie had pointed ye out to him at some concert or other, as the new teacher that was gaun to Kinkelvie. Now, I would like to ken something about this Mr. Wyllie."

" I know a Mr. Wyllie, Rob, but ——"

" Ye dinna think muckle o' him ? "

" Honestly, I don't."

" Is he a lawyer body ? "

" Something of that kind, though I can hardly say. He 's a man about town more than anything else, and a mystery to everybody."

" Ay, it maun be the same. Frank has never been the lad he was, since he kent him, and that 's weel on

G

for three year syne; an' he's gaun to the devil
a'thegether now."

"Dick Wyllie could hardly lead him any other
road."

"Ay, ay! man, it's a sair heart-break to me, an'
I'm doubtin' if I'll be able to howd it frae the auld
folks muckle langer. But you that kens the toun,
sir, do ye no ken ony way o' gettin' him out o' this
man's guidance?"

"Frank must have money to spend, or Wyllie
would not make him a companion."

"Ower muckle, I'm comin' to think. He has the
parish bursary; he gets money frae his father; he
has gotten it frae me, too, an' I'm awfu' feared he
had some frae Watty the last time he was here.
Forbye a' that he has some laddies teachin' i' the
afternoon, an', I'm thinkin', gets weel paid for it.
I didna ken o' that till the last time I was in
Edinburgh."

"I'm afraid Wyllie will stick by him as long as he
is in funds."

"Could your friend no help me, sir?"

"My friend?"

"Ay. Excuse me askin' so muckle. Ye ken it's
no for my ain sake I do it. But I was ta'en wi' his
face that nicht I saw ye thegether."

"You mean Gavin Crombie."

"I dinna ken his name; but I thoucht he micht do
something to save Frank frae Wyllie, an' frae his ain
sel'."

"I don't think he could be in better hands than in
Gavin Crombie's; and I'll say this much, that
Crombie would do a great deal for you if he could."

"I thoucht he meant what he said when he spoke

to me that nicht; an' I was plannin', if you could gi'e me his address—"

" I shall certainly do so; and I 'll write to Gavin, telling him when to expect you."

" Thank ye, Mr. Urquhart, thank you; an' the blessin' o' his father an' mother be wi' ye. Here we are at the gate, an' our roads part; I gang round by the back.—That 's the Miss singin' the now. I mind o' Frank an' me standin' i' the very same place an' listenin' to her singin', no' that lang after she cam'. He listens to waur voices now. Guid nicht, Mr. Urquhart. I 'll just hand in my parcel, an' awa' back. I ha'ena ha'en my tea yet.—That's Ba'bingry's laugh, I hear. Keep friendly wi' him if ye can, but no' ower thrang. A pleasant nicht to ye; an' thank ye sir, thank ye."

Rob shook hands with him, a thing he rarely did, squeezing Urquhart's like a vice, and trudged away.

CHAPTER NINTH

LUCKY AT CARDS
UNLUCKY IN LOVE

MR. Urquhart was not a whist-player, but he had to take a hand. The parish minister had been asked to meet him; Mr. Muckersie was there to make up a party; and he could not well refuse. But he knew little or nothing about cards, and made bad mistakes. The very fact that he had as partner the minister, who was accounted the best whist-hand in the parish, did not give him confidence. He could never hope to play up to the style of one with such a reputation. Balbingry, who was eager to beat the minister, was ready with encouragement. All that he had to do, he told him, was to remember the cards that were out. But this was what Urquhart could not do, however hard he tried.

"I thought teachers could do anything," Miss Austin remarked, so naïvely, that Balbingry grinned all over, and Urquhart winced.

It was difficult to say whether she was sarcastically asking for information, or expressing an ingenuous opinion.

The game was a very quiet one. Whist is a serious matter in country houses, and the players spoke little. The two lads lay curled up on the sofa, George fighting with the dread Apollyon, and Robert

potting cannibals on the island of Juan Fernandez.
From the piano stool Elsie, apparently trifling with
crewel work, saw every card that was played; and
Urquhart, all along conscious of her eyes on his hand,
felt that he was simply making an exhibition.   It
was bad enough, after hanging over a card for some
time and then playing the wrong one in the end, to
see Balbingry's smug smile, but the creaking piano-
stool told him that other eyes had been watching,
and he knew he was, as Grant would have phrased it,
playing like a fool.   It was a relief to him when she
folded away her sewing and turned round to the
piano.

"That's the signal," Mr. Muir remarked, watching
Elsie adjust the music in front of her.

"Oh, you're sure to finish this game, Uncle, with
four to their one," she answered lightly.

"I've heard a whist saying," Urquhart ventured,
"that four never wins."

"So you do know something about whist, Mr.
Urquhart," Elsie said.   "For, of course, you must
have *five* to win."

"I know that a small trump beats the ace of
another suit, Miss Austin, and that serves my purpose just now."   He trumped an ace of Balbingry's
as he spoke.

The minister pulled himself up on his seat, and his
eyes sparkled.

"We'll make a fight for it yet," he said.

Elsie began playing, and the game proceeded in
silence, till Urquhart lifted the third last trick, where-
at the minister chortled in his joy.   "Played!" he
shouted.   "And now the next two are mine.   Six,
nine, twelve; won in a canter!"

"I don't grudge you the rubber, Mr. Dawson. That last was a beautifully played game. Mr. Urquhart, you 've simply had a walk over."

"Have you lost, after all, Uncle?" The music ceased, and there was disappointment in the voice.

"Beaten off the field, Elsie."

"It's easy playing when ye have the cards," Balbingry grumblingly admitted.

"Easier to make mistakes," Muiredge told him. "Give in, you 're beaten, and by worthy opponents. Come, now, and we 'll have a bit of supper. Elsie."

"You 're quite right, Mr. Muckersie," Urquhart confided to him, walking to the dining-room; "for I didn't know whether I was playing right or wrong. But I had good cards and six of them trumps."

"I hope that means that luck 's to be with you in Kinkelvie," Mr. Muir said, when they were seated at table; "though it 's a common saying here, 'Lucky at cards, unlucky in love.'"

"That 's a hard saying," Urquhart said, laughing. "I should much rather be unlucky at cards in that case."

"But you 've got a companion here under the same bann," the minister told him, nodding at Elsie, who was seated between them at the end of the table, "I never knew one with such a run of luck at whist."

"You say nothing about my fine play, Mr. Dawson," Elsie objected.

"I say that you always win, Elsie."

"Because I like to win."

"Now, are all glasses charged?" Mr. Muir called from the head of the table. "We 've got to drink to Mr. Urquhart's health, and wish him a long stay in Kinkelvie."

"Luck in both counts, Mr. Urquhart, cards and love!" The old minister bowed across to him, and then turned to Miss Austin, "Elsie!"

"I had a mind to look in upon you in school to-day," he continued, "but thought better of it. I judged you'd rather be without intruders until you had got fairly settled. I hope you have made an auspicious beginning."

"I have begun fairly well, I think," Urquhart answered. "I secured a new assistant this morning, a boy, John Cochrane, whom his companions call 'Athy.' But I'm afraid I've lost him already."

Mr. Dawson assumed a very solemn expression, but his thoughts were evidently too deep for words. "Ah," he sighed, profoundly.

But Elsie was interested. She forgot for a moment that Mr. Urquhart was a teacher, and that she was to be no more than frigidly polite to him. "I should call that a splendid beginning," she observed with enthusiasm, "to win over John to your side. It was months before I made anything of him, but now he's——"

"An ardent admirer and a devoted slave," her uncle finished. "Elsie must drag everybody at her carriage wheels."

"Athy swings behind," George corrected; "and it's just to get the pony to hold."

"She hasn't been able to drag him to the Sunday School yet," the minister commented.

"Because I have never tried, Mr. Dawson, and I don't wish to try."

Mr. Dawson shook his head, but his eyes were twinkling. "The little heretic!"

"I have tried to get him to attend the day school,"

Elsie answered, "but I have only got him to go occasionally."

"Then I can hardly hope to succeed where you fail, Miss Austin; although he promised me, this morning, of his own accord, to attend regularly."

"Promised?" Elsie echoed. "Then John will attend."

"But I have offended him since then; offended him against hope of pardon, I'm afraid."

"How so, Mr. Urquhart?" she asked, looking at him curiously. Then all at once her expression changed. The light of interest died out of her eyes; her lip curled with contempt, and she answered for herself. "Ah, I know what John resents. You have called him 'Athy.'"

"That was all, Miss Austin."

"All?" She laughed, and Urquhart felt his cheeks redden. "I admire him for resenting it. It's a sign of grace in him. But you've lost him all the same."

"He's a very sullen-tempered boy," the minister sententiously observed.

"Sullen?" Elsie asked, her eyes flashing again. "It must be a sullen nature, indeed, not to appreciate the condescending familiarity of a master. I am sure you meant it all in kindness, Mr. Urquhart."

Urquhart had nothing to say in reply. He felt that this young lady held him in scorn. Rob Buchan had spoken to him in much the same words, and he had listened humbled; but now he was like one held up to ridicule, and he had not a word to utter in his own vindication. And this after coming here so eager to stand well in the eyes of Miss Austin!

Balbingry sat at his side, silently and complacently

sipping his whisky. Yet Urquhart almost felt that
he heard him purring in self-satisfaction. Even the
boys had become interested in the conversation, and
were conscious of his discomfiture.

"You mind the first time Elsie met him playing
with us she called him 'Athy,' too ; and he ran away
home."

Robert nodded across to George, and the two
nodded sagely down to Elsie. Elsie flushed now.

"But you silly boys told me 'Athy' was his name.
I thought it was short for Arthur. I certainly did
not know it was a nickname."

"And I did not know its meaning, Miss Austin.
But I don't mean to lose John altogether," he said
quietly. "I shall have him back, yet."

There was a silence, and Mr. Muir glanced uneasily
towards his niece.

"Now, Elsie," he called, "I hope they are keeping
you busy there. Mr. Urquhart? Your glass is
empty, I see."

"Thank you. A small piece of tongue, if you
please, Miss Austin?"

Balbingry's eye twinkled. "Cold," he advised.
But Elsie took no notice, nor did Mr. Urquhart.

After supper, Mr. Muir talked with the teacher
apart, and Mr. Urquhart agreed to take the boys
four evenings in the week, giving particular attention
to Latin, Greek, and Mathematics. The work would
not be drudgery, he imagined ; for the boys were
well grounded in Latin already, and had made a
beginning in Greek. Moreover, he was to be well
paid—better than he had been for similar work in
Edinburgh, and the lads looked bright and intelligent. Surely, also, it would be a pleasure, after

school-work, to walk down to the farm, and spend
an hour, or two hours, in this pleasant household.

His eyes wandered to Miss Austin as he thought
of this. Perhaps there might be music and conversation after lessons. Mr. Muir was a reader, and
talked well; and Miss Austin—well, there was a
nameless charm about her—he hardly knew what it
was; did not even ask. How vivacious she looked
just now, holding her own in animated argument
with the old minister, who delighted to tease his
little heretic, as he called her, into smiling rebellion.
But the light of her eyes must have been only for
such an old friend as he was, for they were certainly
coldly incurious when she bowed Mr. Urquhart a
formal good-night.

The farmer accompanied Mr. Dawson by a private
road to the manse, and Balbingry and Mr.
Urquhart walked away together.

"Weel, an' what think ye o' Elsie?" Balbingry
asked, as they picked their way by the Sandy Loan.

The mist had partly cleared away, and the moon,
with a sickly pallor, hung over the loch. Here and
there a star twinkled and disappeared again, while
the cry of a peewit lost in the darkness sounded
plaintive and eerie. Urquhart groped along almost
resentful of the easy swing of his companion, to
whom every step of the road was familiar. He was
not in a key for talk, and would have lost his
temper on the slightest provocation. The seeming
indifference with which the question had been asked
annoyed him, and he wondered whether it was
Balbingry's Scots or his English that was put on.
At the present moment he was inclined to say that
neither was natural. In the company of the minister

and Muiredge he had expressed himself in English—broad in pronunciation, certainly, but correctly; but no sooner were the two of them alone, than he was addressing the teacher in Scots, just as he had spoken when he had been introduced to him on Saturday night by Donald Macvie.

" Miss Austin comports herself with becoming dignity," Urquhart answered, with pedantic evasion.

Balbingry chuckled to himself. " She has no howf o' teachers at a'. Ye would notice that the nicht."

" I can't say I have carried away the impression of such a prejudice in her." Balbingry's talk irritated him, and he spoke on stilts.

" Ay, weel, ye will ; an' soon enough."

Urquhart did not answer; and there was no more said till they came to the inn, where they separated. It was hardly ten o'clock; but Urquhart declined the invitation to step in for a minute. He was tired of Balbingry's company, and wished to be alone.

When he got to his own room, he wrote some letters ; a long one to Crombie, telling of the talk he had had with Rob Buchan, and then launching out into a description of the village, and its simple-minded inhabitants. He drew a picture of the inn as he had seen it on Saturday night, and of his reception ; of the Misses Birrel ; of Watty and Mrs. Rae; the Muirs of Muiredge; even of John Cochrane, and the first day in school. But in all the letter there was not a word of Elsie Austin.

It was nearing midnight when his letters were finished ; and then he picked out a bundle of note-books from his desk, and began scribbling away in pencil, but not for long. His mind was not on the work; and ever between him and the scribbled page came the face of Elsie Austin—sometimes flushing and beautiful, as he had seen it on Sunday morning; oftener flashing at him a smile of scorn; and then he saw her turn from him with a gesture of disdain. He was sensitive enough to feel that she had spoken to him that night merely as she would have spoken to a stranger who happened to be a guest at her uncle's table. He might go and come from Muiredge as the boys' tutor; and Miss Austin had let him understand that he would be received and treated as their tutor—no more.

He laughed to himself, sitting smoking before he got into bed.

"And why should I wish to be more?" he asked. "Mr. Muir is making it well worth my while to act as their tutor, and the dignified Miss Austin is nothing to me."

But in his sleep he dreamed of her all the same.

CHAPTER TENTH

"LITTLE TOM TUCKER HE SANG FOR HIS SUPPER"

IT was Friday night. The week had been a very long one to Mr. Urquhart. Work in school had not proved so pleasant as he had anticipated from his first day's experience. For one thing he had lost John Cochrane, and he had hoped for great things from John's assistance. When he inquired about him, he was told that John was at work on Bowhouse Farm, on the other side of the loch, and that was half-a-day's journey round by the sluices. He was already over school age, and quite at liberty to leave if it pleased him to do so. But the master was annoyed to think he had lost him by a mere accident.

The weather also had had a depressing effect on him, for it had got worse as the week advanced, and, in spite of Watty Spence's prediction on Sunday morning they were farther from frost than ever. Every morning had broken grey with mist, becoming, as the day wore on, a disagreeable drizzle, and finally settling into a night of rain.

The walls of the schoolroom grew grimier day by day, while the exuding maps peeled and scaled, as if the world were meant to cast its slough of colour with the November rains. Every desk and form and

door was in a perpetual cold sweat, and figures in
chalk showed faint on the greasy blackboard.

Even the best of schoolrooms is far from being a
pleasant place in wet weather, and this barometrical
building, sensitive to the slightest damp, was little
better than a dungeon. Built of a porous kind of
stone, it was draughty without being properly venti-
lated, and in weather like this the air became thick
and heavy with the odour of reeking clothes. But
the weather was not altogether to blame for the
master's growing depression. Already in his first
week, in spite of the smaller classes, he was finding,
as keenly as he had ever felt it in Edinburgh, how
little scope there was for originality in teaching, how
little hope of fostering and developing it in the
children. It may be he had expected too much, and
was fretting himself in the face of impossibilities.
He was something of a visionary and a dreamer of
dreams, a man of ideas and ideals; wherefore unfitted
for the work of elementary education according to
rule and rote. Had he accepted his limitations,
accommodating himself to the Code and Her
Majesty's Interpreters thereof, he might have saved
himself a needless amount of worry, and even from
such a small seminary as this, pupils might have
gone forth crammed with the three R.'s, brimful of
dates, bursting with geographical names and smatter-
ings of special subjects, equipped for the battle of life.
Nor was it that the children had been neglected.
They were slow certainly, but they knew what was
required of them in the different standards. Boys in
the Sixth Standard, who had not owned a shilling in
all the twelve years of their lives, and to whom a
sovereign was wealth unbounded, dabbled in Govern-

ment Stock—whatever that meant—with the capitals
of millionaires, and could invoice and receipt bills
running into four figures. Some there were who
could fling down dates and skip through centuries
like boys over stepping-stones, yet they could not
count back to the year of their own birth. Others,
who had never seen the sea, named lochs on the
west coast of Scotland, one for every letter of the
alphabet. Every boy in Standard Six remembered
that Mount Everest was twenty-nine thousand *and
two* feet above the level of the sea ; but not one
could even guess at the height of the hill behind
them. The oldest boy in the school knew the
distance between the earth and the sun, but for the
life of him, he could not tell how many miles it was
to Milnforth.

But what annoyed Urquhart worst of all was the
simultaneous work that went on in the infant-room.
He had thought that this method of schooling
children was a special feature of gigantic schools,
where one teacher might have charge of a class of
one hundred and seventy-odd children, and he had
fondly imagined that in leaving Edinburgh, he had
seen and heard the last of it. Yet here was the self-
same system, in all its virulence, where there was but
a handful of children to teach. All day long he
heard from the smaller room the voices, now of one
class, then of another, growing weary with much
spelling, and raucous with mechanical reading ; and
he knew that the intelligence of the little ones was
being slowly and surely killed, however memory
might be developed. Their childish buoyancy and
brightness, their healthy curiosity, the poetry and
imagination of childhood, all that was beautiful and

natural in them was to be sacrificed to the exigencies of an annual inspection, and the requirements of a criminal code. Little good came of mentioning the matter to Miss Mitchell. That young lady had a mind of her own, and spoke with all the conviction of a narrow experience. The bare possibility of the existence of a better system, she had never considered; she had never doubted the infallibility of her own. Her answer to Mr. Urquhart was in black and white, signed by Her Majesty's Inspector, who had nothing but praise for the excellent appearance of the infant department, and the discipline maintained by the energetic infant mistress. Moreover, she reminded him, she came from Edinburgh as well as himself, and with the highest testimonials.

All he could do was to adapt himself to circumstances, and try to make the best of them. But his heart was not in his work. He had come here with the enthusiasm of youth in hopes of achieving great things, and now he saw the realisation of these hopes receding day by day. He was as much in the grip of the Code here as in Edinburgh, and as completely under the heel of the infant-room.

It was a relief to get home and have a chat with the Misses Birrell, and Mrs. Rae when she was in a talkative mood, even though she always insisted that he would go away and leave them. And at times, Urquhart heard her without a word of protest. There was pleasure, too, in his private teaching. It was a delight to trudge down the Sandy Loan, guided by the parlour window, now full and clear, now trellised through the trees, and catching for a moment, it might be, a graceful figure silhouetted in its light.

It is possible he thought more about Miss Austin than about his pupils, but he did not admit this to himself. He enjoyed his work with the boys, partly because it was such a change from his work in school, and partly because the boys were bright and intelligent, and took a lively interest in Cæsar's Wars and in the hand-to-hand fights around the walls of Troy. They were eager to get at the story, and learned irregular verbs in the process. Declension and conjugation were mastered with little or no conscious effort of memory, just as children learn to talk grammatically in their own tongue, long ere they are bewildered with the mysteries of analysis and parsing.

But the chief charm of the lesson, to Mr. Urquhart, was the sense of being near to Miss Austin. There was a pleasurable consciousness, that could hardly be called thought, of her presence, even though he was alone with the boys. He heard her moving about in the next room, and there was music to him in her footsteps, in the rustle of her dress now and again when she passed the parlour door. How it was that Miss Austin had taken such a hold on his imagination, he did not ask himself. As yet he was like one in a reverie, dreamily conscious of happiness, not wishful of being wakened to actual knowledge.

After all, he had seen very little of Miss Austin. This was his fourth evening at the farm, and he had only spoken with her twice; and there was a touch of hauteur, if not even of coldness, in her bearing towards him. But this, to Mr. Urquhart, was only a phase of that inborn dignity which he saw in all true womanhood. The first perception of a con-

H

descending politeness in her manner would have roused him from his reverie, and he would have known that he loved her. Or it might be, the dawning knowledge of love would open his eyes to her coldness, and rouse him to resent it. What would his awakening be? A word, a look, and life would never be the same to him again!

Miss Austin, too, in spite of her prejudice against teachers, caught herself thinking about this particular teacher now and again, and wondering if he were really no better than those other raw youths she had met so frequently, whose talk of passes and special subjects was only broken, but never brightened, by occasional lapses into compliment ponderously paid. When she did think of him, she felt his voice thrilling through her, as it had done in church, and his serious eyes probing as it were to her heart. There was something mysterious in those deep dark eyes of his, full of the wonder of boyhood, yet at times piercing and intense with the knowledge that only comes of experience. But what did it matter to her whether he were better or worse than his fellows? It was only when she sat sewing, after tea, that she thought of him at all. Naturally, the boys' books lying ready on the table brought him into her mind. That was all. So she had assured herself every evening, and so she assured—and perhaps deceived—herself now.

The rain was drumming on the window, and she could hear the wind in short, irregular sobs, shivering the holly bushes. She looked at the clock ticking so religiously on the mantelpiece, and after folding away her sewing, put a shovel of coals on the fire around a blazing peat.

"He'll be here presently," she thought, "drenched again. That was his step on the gravel outside."

A glance round the room satisfied her that everything was tidy, pen, ink, and books all lying ready on the table. Then she turned to meet him entering with the boys. She would bow to him with becoming dignity and leave them to their work. But to-night Mr. Urquhart stopped at the door, and looked ruefully down at his feet.

"I am almost afraid to enter, Miss Austin," he said, with an apologetic smile.

"Look," cried Robert, "he is mud right up to the knees."

Miss Austin did look, and forgot altogether about being dignified and distant. She was her own natural self, and spoke with the intuition and decision of womanhood.

"Oh, Mr. Urquhart, you cannot sit with wet feet. Please don't be stubborn now—and stupid," she added, with a smile. "Sit down on the hall-chair, and take off those muddy boots."

He recognised that there was no use protesting, and did as he was bid.

"I was almost ashamed to come in," he said. "I did not know I was so muddy till I came in to the light."

"And do you imagine I would have allowed such boots to touch my pretty carpet? I had no idea that the roads would be so bad."

"I am afraid I must blame myself, not the roads, Miss Austin. The truth is, I walked right into the burn, at the side of the Loan. It was very comical," he laughed, "to be going along with my head among the stars, and all at once to find myself knee-deep in water."

She looked at him, and smiled.

"That's a lesson to you, then, not to go with your head among the stars; especially," she added naïvely, "when the stars are invisible. Put on those slippers now, and the boys will take you upstairs. George can get you a pair of his socks."

In a little while the boys were busy at their lessons; but before they were half finished, Mr. Muir entered the room.

"I think we'll give them an hour's holiday to-night," he proposed, "if you agree to it, Mr. Urquhart. The rain is heavier than ever, and I don't think you can feel quite comfortable, after that ducking Elsie told me about. We'll have a chat, if you don't mind, and a little music before supper."

The books were closed, and George and Robert were already curled up in their different corners on the sofa, with authors they preferred even above Cæsar and Homer.

"Watty Spence was here half-an-hour ago," the farmer continued, "and I told him to leave word with the Misses Birrell that you would stay here overnight."

"But," exclaimed Urquhart in surprise, "I could easily——"

"It's all arranged," Mr. Muir informed him; "so you'll just need to make yourself at home. What do you think, Elsie?" he asked, as Miss Austin entered.

"Mr. Urquhart's cloak is soaking," she answered; "his boots are as damp as they possibly can be, and the rain is heavier than ever. Surely these things will compel him to stay, even if we failed to persuade him."

"But I could be home in half-an-hour's time," he argued.

Mr. Muir shook his head, and smiled.

"I 'm afraid not to-night, Mr. Urquhart; and we don't mean to let you try."

"I do not wish to give you trouble," Mr. Urquhart pleaded.

"Perhaps," said Elsie, addressing her uncle, and there was just a suspicion of constraint in her tone, "Mr. Urquhart may be too independent to accept——"

"No, no, Miss Austin!" he burst out; "you misunderstand me—wilfully, I 'm afraid. I am sensible of your kindness, and acknowledge my indebtedness cheerfully. Thank you very much, Mr. Muir; I shall be glad to stay."

"That's settled, then; and now I think we 'll have some music. Perhaps Elsie has some song you know, Mr. Urquhart."

Robert looked up from his corner of the sofa, and made a suggestion.

"I 'll tell you what, Mr. Urquhart," he said; "sing 'Little Tom Tucker, he sang for his supper.' That 'll get it all right, you know," he added, and turned again to his book.

His father and Mr. Urquhart laughed outright at the suggestion made so seriously, while Elsie blushed violently, turning over a pile of music.

"Is Robert really becoming practical?" his father asked.

"No," said Elsie; "Rob is always romantic, and says silly things."

George wheeled himself round to face the company.

"I know who says silly things," he announced. "Who was it said that the bat——?"

"Ssh, ssh, boys!" their father cried. "No tales out of school, you know."

Elsie left the music in Urquhart's hands, and sat down to the piano. "Perhaps you'll find a song there, Mr. Urquhart. I shall try this new piece till you are ready."

The boys chuckled to themselves till they were again absorbed in their stories, while Mr. Urquhart, having selected a song, sat listening to the music. School with all its worries was forgotten. He was in a world of melody and music, and heard, as in a dream, the ivory keys answering the touch of fairy fingers. His head was again amongst the stars, and this time one star was visible.

CHAPTER
ELEVENTH

*WATTY SPENCE
DISCOVERS
AN AUTHOR*

RETURNING from Muiredge on Saturday morning, Urquhart saw why Mr. Muir had insisted on his staying at the farm all night. The burn, which in summer months was little more than a trickle, had, during the night, become quite a torrent, bringing down from the hill-side branches of trees and stones that were almost boulders. The Sandy Loan lost itself in a little loch, where the tops of only the highest bushes were visible, showing like a string of buoys set to mark the run of the road. It would have been impossible for him to have found his way home in the darkness. Now in the broad daylight he had to cut across fields to reach the high road.

Watty Spence met him entering the village.

"It aye comes like that," he began speaking, as if he were answering a question, or continuing an interesting conversation. "I heard it no that lang after ye left, an' I ta'en my ways down to convoy ye hame by the fields, kennin' the Loan would be a loch in an hour's time. But Muiredge had a better plan. Ye would ha'e a pleasant nicht?"

"A very pleasant night, Watty! Isn't Miss Austin a beautiful singer?"

"Weel," Watty answered drily, "she's been so lang considered so hereabout that we've never thoucht o' speirin' the opinion o' a stranger."

"Now, now, Watty," Urquhart said laughingly; "you must not be sarcastic. You simply snap at me every time I mention Miss Austin's name, as if you considered yourself her guardian."

Watty winced.

"No, no, Mr. Urquhart," he said, almost pleadingly; "no that name. She's nothing to me. I mean," he corrected himself, "I'm nothing to her. Ye'll no mention that again, sir."

Urquhart looked at him, and was surprised to see how much in earnest he was.

"I was only speaking in joke," he told him, "and you take me up in all seriousness. But come away, and have a look at my books as you promised. I haven't got them arranged yet."

Watty was quite himself again.

"That'll suit me brawly," he answered. "My time's my ain the day."

Once in the attic room, Watty was in his element. He was one of those men in whom the love for books seems to be inborn and natural. To such, the very fingering of books is a pleasure. They fondle them as they were living things, until they know every one by hand, and could go in the dark and pick out what volume they please. Watty ought to have been a librarian; and here piled up on the floor was the largest library he had ever been privileged to explore. One side of the room had been already fitted up with shelving, and now it would be a labour of love with Watty, if only Mr. Urquhart would allow him, to fill the shelves with the books arranged

and in order.   He looked at the volumes piled
around him and then at the shelves.

"I'm glad ye gang in for open shelves," he remarked.   "It's but a sma' bookcase I hae o' my ain,
but it's open.   I canna bide glass.   Folk'll tell ye it
keeps out the dust, an' no doubt it does; but, man,
what a pleasure there is in dustin' books!"

Urquhart had seated himself at a writing-table set
in the recess made by the attic window, and picked
up some letters.

"Excuse me a minute, Watty," he said.   "There's
one letter here I've been eagerly looking for."

"Gang on wi' your readin', Mr. Urquhart, an'
writin' if ye like.   I'll look after the books, an' I'll
do it that qui't, I'll no disturb ye a bit.   Write awa'
an' leave the books to me."

So the two worked away all day, with only half-
an-hour's interval for lunch, Watty sorting and
arranging the books, and Urquhart correcting proofs
of work he had sent to different magazines at least
two months before.   After the proofs were finished,
he saw how Watty was progressing, and then he
began to copy out some other work he had already
finished in pencil.   He knew Watty did not want
any assistance, and so let him alone.   The afternoon
was waning, and the light began to fail before he
had finished writing.   Beyond the garden he saw the
fields growing gray, and fading in the distance into
the fringe of wood beside Muiredge Farm.   When
it grew darker, he would catch through the trees,
fainter than a star, the glimmer of the parlour
window.

Turning round, he found that Watty also had
finished, and was now sitting admiring his work.

He lit the lamp, and then Watty had to find out
where to set it, so that its light might radiate the
shelves from floor to ceiling, and the books be seen
at their best. Then it was time for a smoke, and the
two rested from the labours of the day.

Watty puffed away meditatively, letting his eyes
wander round the room, and taking stock of everything. But they always came back to the books, as
if there only they found rest. One volume which
he had not put away with the rest he kept lying on
his knee, opening the cover again and again, but
going no further than the fly-leaf and the title page.
Urquhart watched him fingering it, and knew what
the volume was.

"Would you like to read that story?" he asked
him.

"I've read it afore, Mr. Urquhart; an' a powerfu'
story it is ; but if it be yours to lend, I'd like to ha'e
a look at it again."

"Certainly, Watty."

"It's your ain, then? I see a name here that's no
yours."

"Oh, that's nothing, Watty. I picked up the book
second-hand."

"Niel Gordon from E. R. Baxter," he read aloud.
"Ye wouldna ken this Niel Gordon, would ye?"

"Not I, Watty. Judging from the writing, it has
been a present from a lady ; and he has sold it again
—quite a common thing, although I don't like to part
with books myself, especially presents. I picked it
up cheap."

"He had a sair weird to dree," Watty communed,
turning over the pages, "but my heart aye gaed
out to the poor woman, an' the bit nameless lassie.

I 'm thinking the young man was mair coward than hypocrite."

"And how have you got them all arranged?" Urquhart asked. "Could you lay your hand at once on any one you wanted?"

"Easy, that. There's your nouvelles," he said, pointing to a handy shelf, "wi' Sir Walter i' the place o' honour. Some folk here speak o' him as *Watty*, but I aye mak' a point o' correctin' them. 'Watty' is well enough for the like o' me; there's something hamely an' kindly i' the sound; but it'll no do for Sir Walter. It 's ower familiar like. Then there's Thackeray an' George Eliot, twa I 've heard tell o', but never read: an' Dickens. I 've dippet into him, but for my taste he 's either ower boisterous or raxin' himsel' when there's no need for it. Then there's some I saw was stories, but I 've never heard their names afore; they'll be but bairns aside Sir Walter, I 've no doubt; though their print 's a hantle bigger."

"Perhaps they would like their books to be as bulky as Sir Walter's," Urquhart suggested.

"I was just wonderin' if that was their notion. I 'm thinkin' they'll be like the puddock tryin' to blaw itsel' as big as an ox. Or they're maybe writin' for near-sichted readers an' folk like Donald, decent man, that like to spell as they gang."

"But some of them are well worth reading, Watty, I assure you."

"I 've little doubt o' that if they've been worth printin'. They'll be something to fa' back on when ye tire o' the auld ballads, or weary o' Sir Walter. An' I 'm glad to see ye provided wi' both."

Urquhart smiled, but said nothing. He liked

Watty all the better for his honest prejudice. It was as much a part of him as his Scots tongue, and fitted him like his old-fashioned Sunday suit.

"An' speakin' about ballads," he continued, "I was wonderin' what that might be ye were readin' so earnestly." He pointed to a galley proof hung over the back of a chair. "It minded me o' the sheets they were wont to sing an' sell i' the streets in my young days. At first, I thought it micht be a scroll sic-like as they say the auld Greek books were made, but I noticed it was Christian print."

Urquhart handed him the slip, and explained how proofs were corrected.

When it dawned upon Watty that he was actually speaking to an author, he gazed with something of awe on the young man beside him. But he could not speak. The proofs had touched him at a weak point, and all the reverence he had lavished formerly on Sir Walter and the makers of books and ballads, went out to this novice trying his 'prentice hand in the monthly magazines.

To Urquhart the look on his face was perfectly comical, and he laughed outright.

"Don't look at me like that, Watty," he cried; "it's too funny. I'm certain five out of every twelve men I know write stories, or let themselves out in verse. I've tried both now and again for years; yet I'm certain I haven't made ten pounds a year out of writing. That very story in your hand has gone the round of half-a-dozen editors before being accepted by the seventh; and for this bit of poetry accepted at the first shot, I've had a score of pieces rejected. Perhaps I won't see another story or poem of mine in print for months. All the same, I shall go on

trying, and I shall work for success whether I succeed or no."

" It's no a book ye 're writin', then ? "

" No, this is only a story for a magazine."

Watty breathed more freely. So long as it was
only magazine work and not real books, it was possible for him to feel at ease even in the presence of
an author. Yet the fact that his friend was in any
sense an author must be faced with a degree of
reverence and respect. Henceforth he should always
regard Mr. Urquhart with secret admiration.

"But I have written a book," Urquhart continued,
"only it's not published yet, and may never be. I'm
waiting for word from the publishers to whom I sent
it. This story appearing here may be something in
my favour."

Watty parted with the proof reluctantly, and only
after an assurance that he would "get a read of it"
when the magazine appeared. About keeping to
himself what he had just learned, Watty was not
so ready to make any promise. Knowing that the
town possessed an author, it would be hard indeed
if he were to be debarred from proclaiming the fact
abroad, and boasting that he had been the first to
discover it. After much persuasion he went away,
promising that he would try.

When Urquhart descended to tea, Mrs. Rae
motioned him to the chair beside her.

"Now you've had a visitor all day," she said,
"and you must tell us all about it."

"Why, Mrs. Rae," he answered, "my visitor was a
friend of yours, too. It was Walter Spence who
came to help me arrange my books."

"Ah," she sighed, "Walter does not come to see

me, and he was my friend—a good friend. But that
was long ago, wasn't it? I don't remember. And
there was Niel, too. Where is Niel, Mr. Urquhart?
There was Niel and Walter; they were both kind to
me; and Niel lent Walter books, and went away.
You'll go away, too, Mr. Urquhart. You'll go away
like Niel. You'll lend Walter books, and then you'll
go away. They all go away—all but Walter, and he
does not come to see me."

After that she relapsed into silence, and though
Urquhart and the Misses Birrell chatted all the time,
she did not say another word, did not even seem to
hear.

CHAPTER
TWELFTH

ROB BUCHAN'S
NEWS FROM
EDINBURGH

ROB BUCHAN had got Jenny stabled and suppered, and now had time to think of his own tea. Everything was ready for him when he entered the kitchen, where his daughter Barbara, a rather delicate-looking young woman of some twenty years, sat sewing, while she listened for her father's step.

The room was like most of the kitchens in Kinkelvie, where the principal articles of furniture were a box-bed and a great wooden cupboard reaching from the floor to the raftered ceiling. These two articles looked so gigantic in themselves, that one almost forgot to note the diminutive round table, or to count the four chairs, three set against the high bed, and not over-topping it, and a fourth with an earthenware basin set on it, standing between the window sill and an ancient eight-day clock solemnly ticking in the darkest corner. Even the capacious easy-chair might have looked insignificant had it not been drawn up so invitingly to the fire, whose peat flames danced and flickered in reflection about its America-leathered arms. Everything was scrupulously clean. The doors of the cupboard were white with half a century's scrubbing,

and the lamp over the mantelpiece touched with
innumerable high lights the legs and noses of cast
metal horses and riders blackleaded and polished,
hung round it on the ochred wall. The table set for
tea was covered with a linen tablecloth, and that was
a luxury Kinkelvie families indulged in only on
great occasions, such as baptisms, weddings, and
funerals. But Barbara always had everything
looking its best when her father returned from
Edinburgh. He was sure to be tired and hungry;
and a white tablecloth was like a special invitation to
rest and refreshment. And to-night, when Rob
clapped himself down in his easy-chair, he looked
more worn out than usual.

Barbara regarded him earnestly and tenderly.
She saw how tired he was, and she was also aware of
a troubled look in his eyes, a look she had observed
now and again of late, and only when he returned
from Edinburgh. She waited till she had filled out
the tea before she spoke.

"Ha'e ye ha'en a tirin' day, father?"

"Ay, Bauby! The roads are bad. I 'd to get Jenny
sharpened afore venturin' up the Bin Brae, an' I 've
been at her head a' the way. A cup o' tea 'll freshen
me up again. I 'm gettin' ower easy tired, Bauby."

But the cup of tea did not take the troubled look
from his eyes. He was thinking of other things than
tea and toast, and his thoughts were not happy ones.
It seemed to Barbara that he was hardly conscious of
being at home yet, as if his feet had led him by habit
to his own fireside, while his mind remained in
Edinburgh.

"Did ye see Frank this time, father?"

The question was asked quite naturally, yet the

old man started, like one struck by a marvellous coincidence. He pushed his empty cup away, and wheeled the chair round to face the fire.

"Ay," he answered, "but no' for lang. He was lookin' weel, Bauby, an' i' the best o' spirits. Ye'll mind an' tell Marg'et that when ye gang alang the morn."

"Ay, father; I'll mind. I was alang the day an' I'm doubtin' if she'll see the year out. She's no faur frae the hinder end, an' wearyin' for it. The master was up again i' the afternoon to read a bit, an' he brought her a bottle o' some new mixture frae Milnforth. It eased her cough just wonderfu', I thought."

"That was awfu' mindfu' in a young man. D'ye no' think so, Bauby? But Mich'el an' him get on grand thegether. He thinks a byordinar' lot o' Mich'el, an' Mich'el as muckle o' him. It's a pleasure to hear the twa' crackin'."

Barbara had got the dishes cleared away, and now drew in a stool by the fire and busied herself with a bit of knitting. For a time there was no sound but the ticking of the old clock and the clicking of the wires. The old man heard them both, and their sound was music to him, soothing his troubled thoughts. By and bye, however, his ears detected a change. One voice had dropped out of the duet. Turning, he saw Barbara's hands lying idly over the knitting in her lap, while her eyes were lifted to his with a strange wistful look in them.

"What is it, Bauby?" he asked.

"Father," she whispered, and there was a tremor in her voice; "father, did the master ken Frank afore he cam' here?"

I

"Eh? Bauby, Bauby, that's an onexpected question. What way do ye speir that?"

She turned her face towards the fire, so that her
father saw its light lying rosy on her cheek.

"It was a thought," she answered, speaking more
to herself than to her father. She saw some picture
in the flames, and spoke as she saw. "Ye ken how
Marg'et's aye thinkin' o' Frank. Weel, when she
speired at Mr. Urquhart, if he'd ever met Frank,
he answered 'No' readily enough, but he looked
round at me so shame-faced like when he said it
that I kent——" She turned and looked her father
full in the face again, "I kent he didna mean 'no,'
father."

Rob moved uneasily in his chair. "That minds
me I've to see Mr. Urquhart the nicht," he answered
evasively. "It's about a letter I got to a friend o'
his. That's a', Bauby. That's a'," he assured her.

"I'll no be lang," he added at the door. "Ay,
Bauby, ye're just your mother ower again. She was
awfu' quick o' seein' things. It's a gift some women
have. I'll no' be lang, Bauby, but gang to your bed
if ye're tired."

When he closed the door, Barbara sat down
again on the stool, but not to knit. "It's true,"
she repeated again and again. "He kent Frank
in Edinburgh, an' he's ashamed to own it. Frank's
gaun aside again, after promisin' me so solemnly
never to let it within his lips."

And her father was trudging along the street,
muttering to himself, "It's a gift she has frae her
mother afore her, an' it's, maybe, a God's blessin' it's
denied to men."

He passed Watty Spence on the street, but did not

notice him. Watty turned and watched him walking with bowed head. " He has seen Frank again," he told himself, " an' he 's awa' to tell Mr. Urquhart, but he 'll no' find him in."

He waited till he heard Rob's footsteps on the graveled walk to the Misses Birrell's door, and then sauntered back just in time to meet him again at the gate.

" Ay, Rob !" he began, by way of greeting ; "ye 'll no' ha'e found him in. He 's awa' down to the manse. We micht tak' a dander that airt thegether. I was wantin' to see him mysel' !"

" It 's no muckle matter," Rob answered ; " but a turn 'll do no harm !"

" Ye wouldna see Frank last nicht ?" They had passed out of the village by this time, and Watty spoke like one asking a question at random, merely by way of beginning conversation, and answered for himself, " No, of course ye ha'ena muckle time to spare when ye 're in Edinburgh."

" I did happen to see him, Watty ; an' he was lookin' rale brisk an' spirity."

They walked on in silence again, until they reached the Sandy Loan, where Watty stopped, knowing that Mr. Urquhart might come round by the farm. It was a moonlit night, and the stars looked large and clear in the frosty sky. The Sandy Loan would be quite an easy road on such a night. Standing there, they could count the trees and bushes marking its every bend, right to the edge of the moss. The gurgle of the burn was the only sound to break the silence, save from the hillside a mournful bleat of some sheep suddenly finding itself far from the rest of the flock.

"Look," said Watty, pointing in the direction of Muiredge Farm. "Yon's him, I've no doubt."

They saw a twinkle of light rhythmically flaming and fading four or five times.

"Yon'll be him lichtin' his pipe."

"Bauby was tellin' me he was in seein' Marg'et the day again," Rob mused.

"Ay, was he; an' he telled her he'd never met Frank in Edinburgh. But you ken better, Rob."

Rob turned on his friend almost fiercely.

"Watty, Watty, man, what are ye sayin'?"

"I'm sayin' what's true, Rob; though sorry I am to say it. He has been a sair thought to ye this lang time, Rob; but it'll no howd muckle langer. It's out o' no curiosity I speak to ye now, for I ken fine o' his ongauns in Edinburgh, but for the sake o' auld Mich'el an' Marg'et. Eh, man, what'll they say when they ken?"

Rob turned from him with a gesture of pain, but did not speak.

"Ye cam' to speak to Mr. Urquhart about him," Watty continued. "Was there no an aulder friend to turn to, Rob? But ye did it a' for the best, an' I ken what it has cost ye to keep it to yoursel'. How-somever, I may as weel ken the warst o' 't now if I dinna ken the warst o' it already."

"No, Watty, ye dinna ken the warst. Here he comes, an' I may as weel tell ye both what I ken. I maun get it out some way. But howd it frae Marg'et as long as ye can; howd it frae Marg'et and Mich'el."

Urquhart knew as soon as he recognised the two that they were waiting for him, and that they had news to tell. He could tell, too, without seeing his face, how agitated Rob was ; and he guessed at once what he had come to speak about.

"You have seen Francis Downie?" he surmised.

"Ay, Mr. Urquhart; I've seen him again."

"It's not late yet. You could come and have a quiet talk in my room. Watty has told you how much he knows, I suppose?"

"If ye dinna mind, I would rather ha'e it out here, Mr. Urquhart, whaur there's freedom to speak, an' nobody to hear. I would just be stifled atween four wa's the now. Ye're weel happit up, I see, an' I'll no keep ye that lang. We can sit down on the whin-stanes here out o' the wind."

They found seats on some stones such as are often left lying by the side of country roads to be handy for repairing dry-stone dykes. The moonlight fell full on Rob's face where he sat, and Urquhart could see it twitching with emotion now and again while he was speaking.

"I saw your friend, Mr. Urquhart," he commenced ; "an' he was kinder to me than I can tell, though he'll no be able to help Frank. I was in hopes he micht ha'e become acquaint wi' Frank, an' maybe helpit to keep him straight, but he's gaun aff to London soon. Ye'll read'lys ken that?"

"Yes, Rob; I had a letter from Crombie this week telling me his plans."

"That'll be the writer ye were speakin' about?" Watty broke in, interested at once in another story.

"Ay," Rob answered ; "he was writin' when I ca'd, but that didna hinder him frae comin' out wi' me to ca' on Frank. Frank kent I was comin', but he didna bide in to see me. His landlady said she was to apologise for him, because he had an engagement that nicht."

He paused to collect his thoughts, and they could see his lip quivering before he resumed.

"An engagement to stand wi' some dressed-up counter-loupin' gentry tinklin' their bit glesses at a public-house bar! That was Frank's engagement, for it was there I found him.

"The landlady—an' a decent woman she looket— telled us without shame whaur he would likely be, an' I gaed straight for the howf. Mr. Crambie tried his best to persuade me no to gang in; but I'd come to see Frank, an' would listen to no reason. It would ha'e been better if I'd ta'en his advice; but I'm a dour, auld deevil when I tak' it in my head, an' bid to ha'e my ain way. So in I gaed, an' Mr. Crambie wi' me.

"What a place it was! I was fair dazzled at first wi' the brichtness, for there was enough gless about the place to furnish a' Kinkelvie wi' lookin'-glesses, an' it was bleezin' wi' gas.

"Man, Watty, I see the sicht yet. A string o' young men alang the counter, some wi' beer and some wi' whisky; every ane wi' his glass afore him, an' twa brazen-faced hussies, dressed like valentines, chatterin' and smilin' to wheedle young fools out o' their money."

"Scarlet women," Watty commented in an awed whisper. "Scarlet women."

"Weel, Watty, scarlet may be out o' fashion since the days o' scriptur', but the woman hersel's on-changed.

"An' there was Frank, wi' a wheen mair like him, sippin' out o' their delicate crockery, and bandyin' words with barmaids, if maids ye could ca' them."

He paused again, and looking steadily on Watty,

spoke in a whisper. "Ye mind o' Marg'et's brother, Watty; the awfu' licht in his e'en afore he drank himsel' into eternity? Aweel, the same onearthly licht was in Frank's e'en. I'll never forget it—no, never."

He held his hands to his eyes, as if to blind himself to the sight, and a minute passed before he continued the story.

"I was hardly in, when the babel o' voices stoppet, an' every e'e i' the place was on me, Frank's amon' the lave, but no a sign he kent the man he was lookin' on. When I saw that, Watty—when I saw that, I thought my very heart had stoppet alang wi' their din.

"But I didna stand lang lookin' on. 'What does old Hodge want?' a wee putty-faced cr'atur' speired; an' he whips a spectacle-gless out o' his pouch, an' clapping it ower ane o' his e'en, he looks me up an' down frae head to heel, an' wi' that the noise begoud again. Some roared an' laughed, others chappet the floor wi' their sticks, an' the twa ahent the counter tittered to ane another like a pair o' graceless gaucies keekin' at a puppet show. An' a' the time my face was to Frank, waitin' for a look i' the laddie's e'en just to own that he kent me. But Frank just fiddled awa' wi' his glass for a bit, an' syne turned again to his cronies. It was then I kent that Crambie was richt, an' I shouldna ha'e come in. I was doin' harm whaur I thought to do good, an' I kent Frank would never forgi'e me as lang as he lived. An' yet I couldna just turn an' gang out. I couldna leave Frank without a word.

Just then a lang yard-stick o' a body comes up an says to me, 'I think ye're makin' a mistake, Hodge.

This is no a model lodgin'.' Then there was another laugh, an' I could feel my nieves clinchin', an' something burnin' in my arms. 'Young man,' I said, 'I think it's you that's makin' a mistake.' I had laid my hand on his shouther to fling him across the room, when a great pity came upon me, lookin' at the young faces round about me, some o' them that hadna yet kent the rug of a razor. For I saw ilka ane o' them wi fathers an' mothers prayin' for them, like Mich'el an' Marg'et for Frank. So I just shoved him out o' my way an' stappet ower to Frank.

"'Frank,' I says, 'come out o' this; for your father's and mother's sake, come out o' this hell.'

"Man, his face got red a bit, an' I thought he was gaun to speak to me, when ane o' his cronies broke in. 'Introduce us to your friend,' he says, an' Frank couldna stand that. He turned his back on me, an' flung some coppers on the counter. 'A glass o' whisky,' he said, an' his friend cried loud enough for the whole bar to hear, 'Your best kill-the-carter.'"

Rob drew out his handkerchief, and wiped his face. "Man, Watty, would ye believe it? He was orderin' the gless for me. Would ye believe that o' Frank that used to play about here, the blithest lad o' the place? I didna see his meanin' at first, but Mr. Crambie saw it. 'Come awa' out of this, for God's sake,' he whispered to me. 'Don't you see he's insultin' you before the whole bar?'

"But just then a bit waiter body cam' up an' ordered me out. 'You can't be served here,' he says. An' when I looked at him dumbfoundered-like, he puts his hand on my shouther to shove me out. But I couldna stand that. 'Tak' care,' I says; 'tak' care, my man, or I'll break your back. I'll walk out o' here as I cam' in,' an' we made for the door, the whole hell o' prodigals thumpin' wi' their sticks.

"At the door the bit waiter body turns quite joky. 'Good night, Mr. Parson,' he says, offerin' me his hand, though if there's ae thing in his life he's sorry for it's that; for the devil tempted me, an' I grippet it. 'Guid nicht,' I says. Then he ga'e a jump like a trout to a flee, an' syne wriggled about like the same trout when he finds there's a hook in his gill; an' I cam' awa'. But if there's a whole bone left in his fingers it's no fau't o' mine. That was the last I saw o' Frank."

The others sat silent, for they knew not what to say.

"I'm for hame now," Rob said, rising; "it's wearin' late." And the three walked without speaking towards the village.

When Rob had got seated in his chair at home again, a figure came gliding downstairs and knelt at his feet, hiding her face on his knee. And only then did Rob break down completely.

"My bairn, my bairn," he cried, bending over her and fondling her hair with his hand—the same great hand that had crushed the waiter's fingers, touching her as gently as an infant's might. "My bonnie Bauby! An' you an' him like sister an' brother!"

He felt the body quiver with a sob as he spoke.

"But ye'll no tell Marg'et, Bauby. Dinna let on to Marg'et. It's hard enough for you to bear, but mind how hard it would be for Marg'et."

And Barbara's only answer was another sob.

CHAPTER
THIRTEENTH

*THE COCKBURN
CLIQUE AND THE
BUSKIN CLUB*

ON the Friday following the talk at the head of
the Sandy Loan, Mr. Urquhart made a run to
Edinburgh.

When he first came to Kinkelvie he had not
thought to be in town again before the New Year
holidays, but the departure to London of a member
of the Cockburn Clique was a great event, and could
not be allowed to pass uncelebrated. A special
meeting had to be called, and most of the young
men were perfectly well aware that this would be the
last meeting of their Clique. They had only met
once since Urquhart left them ; and now they were
about to lose Crombie, who, more than any other,
had held the little society together. He it was who
founded the Clique, and edited its magazine. In his
own quiet way, he had kept the members to a
definite scheme of study ; while his enthusiasm for
work had prevented them from becoming merely a
band of literary prigs, looking on themselves as the
salt of the earth, and the elect of Edinburgh ; young
men who have been called to regenerate the world of
letters, and to that end seek to spread their light in
electric flashes of mutual admiration.

All the members owed much to Crombie, and all

owned it gladly—none more frankly than Robert Urquhart. Now that their chief was going to London, it was meet that they should come together and wish him God-speed, even as they had done on the occasion of Urquhart's departure for Kinkelvie. Thereafter the seven would be scattered, every one going his own way, and the Cockburn Clique would be a thing of the past.

Urquhart's thoughts, however, as he sped on towards Edinburgh, were not all of the Cockburn Clique. Since Rob's serious talk to Watty and to himself on Saturday night, he had been wondering whether he himself should not try to see Francis Downie, and plead with him to keep to his studies, and to abstain from even the appearance of evil. He was not inclined to take such a gloomy view of the young man's conduct as Rob Buchan; for Rob, though innocent as a child, and charitable in all things, was an austere man, and a stern moralist. He was one who, while weeping over the sinner, and praying for mercy, would have cried aloud against the sin, cursing it with wrathful denunciation.

It could hardly be that Francis Downie was the hopeless reprobate Rob feared. Thoughtless and foolish he might be—that was no uncommon thing in youth. Yet a son of Michael and Margaret Downie could not but have something fine and beautiful in his nature. This outbreak of his, which the old carrier so deeply deplored, was not to be considered confirmed debauchery; only a temporary aberration from the paths of sobriety. His eyes would surely be opened to his folly, and there would be enough of the man in him to save him from the degradation of drunkenness.

So did Urquhart try to persuade himself. After all, Francis Downie was young yet—little more than a boy. All he needed was a friend who should not be afraid to speak to him seriously. And surely one who knew his parents, and the hopes they had of him, might come to him, and talk to him with the tongue of a brother. He could tell him of his mother, and how her whole talk was of her son—her Frank. Perhaps he was not aware that his mother was dying ; for Urquhart, who saw her almost every day, was convinced that she would never leave her bed again. She might linger on for a few weeks, but the end was near ; and she herself knew it.

When the train came crawling into Edinburgh, Grant was on the station waiting him, and bursting with talk, as usual. He asked questions, and did not wait for an answer, or answered them himself.

He might be paying Urquhart a visit soon : he wasn't quite sure yet. There was a talk about closing the school on account of measles: the attendance was very bad. If it had to be closed, he was going to invite himself to Kinkelvie for a week. Could Urquhart put him up? That was delightful. He should like to see the place, and have a talk with the simple folk.

Now he was explaining about Crombie's appointment ; now he had bumped against some interesting word, and was off at a tangent, discoursing of derivation, and letting himself go in a philological rapture. He had begun a poem about the Clique, too, which was a pæan and a panegyric in one ; he thought he had caught some beautifully lyrical lines, as far as he had gone. But he hadn't decided whether to make it an epic, or to fling it off in a series of sonnets. Which would Urquhart suggest ?

Urquhart advised the sonnet; a sonnet was just the kind of thing one might "fling off." And he might have every one in the series ending with an Alexandrine.

That was a capital idea; and it just suited his name, too. He would think it over. The Alexandrine would be an elegiac touch. Something about a wounded snake, wasn't it? But he might find some difficulty with the sonnet rhymes. There was some peculiarity about the sonnet rhyme, wasn't there? And *L'envoi*? But, of course, the poem wasn't finished yet, and he would have time enough to put it all right. He thought he would have it ready for the next number of the magazine.

Urquhart considered that very likely.

But who would be editor, he wondered, now that Crombie was going. Crombie was very lucky in getting this appointment. It was only an assistant-editorship, to be sure; but still the salary was good, and he was on the right road now. It was all a matter of luck. Crombie had always been a lucky beggar. For his part, he did not believe in luck, except bad luck. That was the only kind he had ever known. He had tried the magazines over and over again. It was always the same. *Declined with thanks!* His best work, too! And here was Crombie getting a good appointment right away. The place had been actually offered to him. Pure case of luck!

Urquhart let him go rattling on. There was not the slightest suspicion of ill-nature or spite in his rambling speech. It was only Sandy's way.

"Perhaps hard work may have had as much to do with the appointment as luck," Urquhart considered.

That was a perfectly new view of the case to Sandy. He had always thought Crombie inclined to be lazy.

"Of course, I knew he was a hard student," he admitted. "But what does he do now? He has the whole day to himself. He should try teaching for a week, and he would know what work is."

"And do you really not know," Urquhart asked in surprise, "that Crombie has been contributing to *The Docket* every week for years? When he was in London this last summer he stayed with the editor all the time. Depend upon it, Mr. Newton knew what he was doing when he asked Crombie to join the staff."

Sandy was staggered. "Crombie!" he exclaimed; "for years? And he has never said a word about it. It's not much of a paper, certainly, and perhaps he wouldn't care to boast about it. I must try that way, too. I'll get on to one paper, and stick by it. I've been at an essay on ancient superstitions preserved in words. I must have it finished at once. I wonder what paper I should try. Which would you suggest?"

"How would *Punch* do, Sandy?"

"Punch?" Sandy cried. "Now that's an interesting word;" and the essay was out of his mind at once. "It has reference to the five fingers; you have it in *Punjab*, the country of the five rivers. It's worthy of an essay, itself. I shall think of it. But here we are at Crombie's door. No, I won't go in just now. See you at the hotel. Dinner at eight, I suppose you know? Ta-ta, old boy. I wish we had Crombie's luck. He *is* a lucky beggar."

The dinner that night was a very quiet affair. The

members knew, though they had gathered to do honour to Crombie, that they were attending the last meeting of the Cockburn Clique. They tried their best to talk gaily, but conversation was all of the happy nights that had been ; and when the toast list was reached, they looked exceeding grave, and drank to Crombie's health with great decorum. Thereafter Gilchrist brought out a fiddle and played some Scots airs very mournfully.

Had it not been for Taylor and Grant, the company would have lapsed into silence altogether, blowing out their incommunicable thoughts in clouds of smoke. But Taylor had been studying Christmas numbers and coloured plates, and, out of the fulness of his knowledge, descanted volubly of the nude. As for Grant, he was never at a loss for words, and to-night he rambled in a very maze of miscellaneous information.

Bernard Kaye, usually the quietest of the seven, was responsible for the one sensation of the evening. He had gone through at least half-a-dozen pipes with hardly as many words, when he suddenly startled the company by getting to his feet and proposing a toast.

"Boys," he said, "you've all drunk success to Crombie, and now I ask you to drink to the other member who goes to London with him. Here's his very good health, and better luck to him !"

Grant stared at Urquhart, and Urquhart at Crombie. They were all taken by surprise. Kaye drained his glass and sat down.

"I've taken the plunge," he said.

"It's yourself, then ?" Urquhart asked.

Kaye nodded.

"You might have told us sooner," came from several voices.

"We'd have had a speech ready for the occasion," Urquhart added.

"Hate speeches," Kaye muttered. "Didn't know, myself till to-night. It's a pure spec. As well starve in London as in Edinburgh. Can't make much here. Been trying black and white months back. In London will be on the spot. Take my chance."

"Do you mean to say," Crombie asked in astonishment, "that you have nothing definite to go up to?"

Kaye shook his head with perfect indifference.

"Expect to be hard up for a while. If oof runs out, get something on these, gold hunter and chain, eighteen carat; only cost a shilling; valued at thirty guineas."

"That was the Lawson Lottery," Grant cried. "Mine was a blank. It always is. But you're a lucky beggar."

"London's a lottery," Kaye reflected; "and some prize may come my way. The de'il's good to his ain, they say."

"That's only four of us left," Grant murmured. "It's too bad. I don't believe there'll be another number of the magazine at all. And my poem——"

"Finish the poem," Haldane advised, "and call it *We are Seven*."

There was silence for a time, so sad a silence that Gilchrist produced his fiddle again and tried to cheer the company with some more of his mournful strains, beginning with *He's ower the hills*, and finishing with *Will ye no come back again?* But music failed to rouse them from their melancholy.

When the meeting broke up about eleven o'clock,

Haldane, Crombie, and Urquhart went away together. Crombie had told him, when he talked of calling on Francis Downie, that the most likely place to see him that night would be the Buskin Club; and it was to it they were going now. Haldane was a member, and was privileged to bring in two friends.

"I'm not often inside it," he told them; "only once in a while. When one has got work to do, late hours—or early hours if you like—won't pay."

"The Buskin is a great haunt of Dick Wyllie's," Crombie said; "and it's as likely as not you'll see Mr. Downie there with him to-night. I was told that you were almost sure to meet the two of them there any night in the week."

"It's very rarely I happen to see Wyllie there," Haldane remarked, "unless I stay after eleven. He's one of the late birds. I daresay I have noticed your friend with him. Fair? A slight scar over the right eye? The very same. Cards! He's a member now. Wyllie used to bring him as a friend."

"Do you mean they go there just to play cards?" Urquhart asked.

"Well, not always cards; it's sometimes pool or pyramids. Dick Wyllie is a deadly potter. You should see him on the spot."

Urquhart was becoming quite distressed.

"You don't surely play for money in your club, do you?" he asked.

"*I* don't," Haldane answered with a laugh; "because I've no money to lose, and the only card game I know is whist. As for billiards, I miss as often as I hit. I suppose there must be something on, of course. At least I couldn't imagine fellows playing nap merely for the game's sake."

"I'm afraid you frighten Urquhart," Crombie said
with a laugh. "He was born and brought up in a
village where they still call cards the devil's books;
and he's virtuous by prejudice. However, we'll put
all that right when we get him up to London. I
mean to look about for a corner for him as soon as
I get there. He has been contaminated with the
innocence of country life; but a breath of London
fog will work wonders."

"Why will you always laugh at me in that way?"
Urquhart asked him. "You always talk to me as to
an inexperienced boy. After six years of Edinburgh,
surely I know something of city life."

"Yes; when you stood on your window-sill, I
remember, you could see the other side of the street.
That, too, was life. Then you sat down, quite a
philosophe sous les toits, and wrote of the country,
dreamed of it, lived in it. But here we are at the
Buskin, and it's a far cry to Kinkelvie, my boy!"

When they opened the door of the smoking-room,
Urquhart saw four seated round a card-table in the
farthest corner. They were the only persons present.
The one facing him was Dick Wyllie, who nodded
recognition in a distant kind of way, and stared hard
for a second on Crombie. Then his moustache lifted
with a smile that was almost audibly a sneer, and he
said something in a whisper to Downie, who, in turn,
raised his head and bleared on the three of them.
There was a perceptible effort to focus his eyes—
evidently he saw six—before he finally fixed them
insolently on Crombie. Then he, too, sniggered, and
again bent over the cards.

"Solo whist," Haldane whispered, when they had
got seated.

Urquhart saw that they were playing for money quite openly, and that they paid up in silver. Hardly a word was spoken. Now and again Wyllie made some whispered aside to Downie, and Urquhart would catch a flash of the eye towards Crombie, and see the moustache lift again with a sinister smile. And every time Frank Downie's answer was the same idiotic snigger that Urquhart shivered to hear. How could he ever talk seriously, even if opportunity presented itself, to one whose very smile was so offensive? It would be sacrilege to mention his mother's name in his presence.

He picked up a periodical, and tried to interest himself in its illustrations, but he heard every card played and, now and again, the chink of silver changing hands; while his eyes would wander, in spite of him, to the pale face bending so feverishly over the cards. Could this really be the son of Michael and Margaret Downie?

By and bye another member entered, and walked right over to the card-party. He was a man old enough to be the father of any in the room, but, in spite of his gray hairs, there was an affectation of the devil-may-care youth in his jaunty gait. They all greeted him hilariously, Downie with a mouthful of irreverent expletives.

"Finished in a minute, Captain," Wyllie told him. "Take a hand at nap afterwards?"

The Captain, as Wyllie had called him, stuck a cigar into the corner of his mouth, and, leaning back against the mantelpiece, gathered a skirt of his coat over each arm, and stuck his hands into his trouser pockets.

"What are you drinking?" he asked.

"T.T.," was Wyllie's answer, which seemed to be taken as an excellent joke.

"And our callow and Downie friend? T.T., too? Very good! Excellent, i' faith! Five whiskies, Buttons, and Pitkeathly. Here I say, Buttons! Anybody in the billiard-room?"

"No, sir; all away, sir."

"What do you say?" he asked, turning to the four, and speaking in a confidential whisper. "On?"

"I'm on," Wyllie answered, scraping some loose silver into his hands.

"All on," Downie shouted. "A damsight too much on! Eh, Sammy?"

Sammy, who sat with his back to the three, stretched himself, yawned, and looked at his watch. "I don't mind," he said, indifferently.

"All right, Buttons,"—this from the Captain— "take the liquors into the billiard-room."

Buttons disappeared, and the five followed.

As Downie passed where the three sat, Urquhart rose, and offered him his hand.

"You don't remember me, do you, Mr. Downie?" he asked.

Downie looked at him unsteadily. "No, I don't," he replied, in a thick voice, "and I don't care. Whoever you are, you're in mighty queer com'ny."

He nodded at Crombie.

"You know what I mean? Eh?"

Then he chuckled to himself. "It was a good joke. I didn't expect old Rob would have done it. The only joke he ever made, and a good one. The wai'er's hand's 'nasling yet."

"Come away; come away!" Wyllie told him.

But Urquhart was standing in front of him.

"My name is Urquhart," he said, "from Kinkelvie."

"Oh, you're Mr. Ur'k'rt? I remember your—face now. A teacher, poor devil! And how is the dam-hole? And Elsie? Know Elsie yet? Eh? She's——"

Urquhart flushed to the roots of his hair, and then his face became perfectly pale with passion. His arms were itching, and he clenched his hands to keep him from smiting the mouth that had uttered that name so grossly.

The young fellow, tipsy as he was, saw Urquhart's agitation, and sniggered again.

"Oh, that's the game, is it? You're gone on Elsie? Eh? So was I? Eh? We're pals. Your hand, old man."

Urquhart turned his back on him and sat down; and Wyllie taking hold of Downie's arm led him out of the room.

Crombie regarded Urquhart with compassion.

"I was afraid it would be a failure," he said. I've seen him three times now, and every time like that."

"They're in for a night of it," Haldane said. "I've seen the billiard-room party before now. They'll begin with nap, and end with euchre or poker."

"I'll see him to-morrow," Urquhart resolved. "The fellow's not in his right senses, and I shouldn't have spoken to him at all. I'll call on him at his lodging to-morrow forenoon. He'll be sober then."

But next morning he did not see him at all.

As soon as he had seen Crombie and Kaye off with the London morning train, he walked straight from the station to Francis Downie's address. He wasn't in, and the landlady could not say when he might be likely to return.

"He went out last night with his friend, Mr Wyllie," she said, "and he has not got back yet. They sometimes go down to Queensferry for a night; so I don't expect Mr. Downie will be back till late."

Urquhart went away grievously disappointed. He had promised Rob that he would try to see Frank. What could he say? Better pretend he had not seen him at all. Certainly the Francis Downie he had seen at the Buskin Club was not the Francis Downie Margaret talked about so fondly and so hopefully.

CHAPTER FOURTEENTH

MISS MITCHELL AND MISS MUCKERSIE

IT was a clear, frosty morning. Every footstep rang out on the hard street, and was echoed again from house to house. The hill stood out clear against a cloudless sky, delicate as amethyst, and of crystal clearness. The frost had continued now for more than a week, and the loch was bearing.

Miss Williamina Mitchell descended the stair from the attic-room, tapped at her landlady's door, and entered.

"May I come in, Mrs. Gray?" she asked, and without waiting for an answer, making across to a vacant chair by the side of the fire.

The schoolmistress never varied her mode of entrance; always asking permission, and simpering herself a flattering welcome. It was not to be imagined for a moment that Mrs. Gray would be engaged when she called. That was outside of consideration entirely; but to announce herself apologetically was gracious and ladylike. And in Miss Mitchell's dictionary, the word "lady" ought to have had a page to itself. It was a beautiful word, and so luxuriously expressive; its four letters syllabling a whole world of ideals—drawing-rooms, music, afternoon teas, dinner-services, dances, shopping,

and the latest fashions. There was not another word
in the language that could express more, always excepting, of course, the dream-word *gentleman*, and that
blessed word *etiquette*. Etiquette was Miss Mitchell's
shibboleth, by which she could distinguish the classes
from the masses, position from poverty; dividing
womankind into mistresses and maids, and classify-
ing men as eligibles and ineligibles. There is more
in the sound of words than logic allows. *Etiquette*
with its nine letters, one for every grace, is a word
that ought to come tripping from the tongue, clearly
and airily uttered, just as the word *Society* should
always be spoken in a whisper, reverently, and with
head bowed. To hear Miss Mitchell's pronunciation
of these two words was an education in itself, and
a revelation as well.

"I thought I should just come——," she was
saying, when she gave a little start of surprise,
recognising that Mrs. Gray had a visitor.

"My dear Miss Muckersie," she exclaimed, greeting
the lady effusively. "I did not expect to have the
pleasure of meeting you. How *do* you do?"

Miss Muckersie, sitting straight and stiff almost on
the edge of a spick-and-span sofa, not in keeping
with any other article of furniture in the room, met
the school-mistress's effusiveness with a jerky nod of
recognition, but did not offer to rise or shake hands.
The nod might have passed unobserved had it not
been for two heavy-headed buds, shooting up like
antennæ from the front of the bonnet. These, rather
than the lady herself, bowed as Miss Mitchell
advanced, and it would have been no stretch of fancy
to have imagined them waving her back from the
rigid and inflexible face over which they presided.

But Miss Mitchell was not at all fanciful.   She only saw that the bonnet was somewhat dowdy, and that the nodding buds looked withered before ever they had burst into bloom.

"I always tell Mrs. Gray," she simpered, looking from the forbidding face of the visitor to where Mrs. Gray sat sewing, "that she keeps all the good things to herself."

She retreated backwards as she was speaking to the chair by the fire, where, settling herself so that she could face both women, she drew a scrap of crochet from her pocket and began knitting.

"You know, Miss Muckersie, I believe Mrs. Gray would have allowed you to go, without even having told me that you were in."

She shook her head with playful reproachfulness at the offending Mrs. Gray, while Miss Muckersie's only comment was a most unladylike snort, evidently intended to express approval.

"But I told you when the Misses Soutter called to be fitted on," Mrs. Gray meekly protested, "and you didn't come down to meet them."

Mrs. Gray, when she was only Miss Bruce, had been lady's maid to an old and opinionated lady at Torbean House, and it was to her she was indebted for much of her meekness, and most of her English.

"Indeed you did, Mrs. Gray," the schoolmistress admitted, "but there are visitors and visitors," here she smiled with insinuating sweetness on the inflexible face, "and the Misses Soutter are not Miss Muckersie."

But Miss Muckersie was unimpressionable. "I saw you at the window," she said, "as I came along the street, Miss—eh—Mitchell. Yes, I always do forget that name, common as it is!"

"Ah, but, Miss Muckersie, I was reading; and you have no idea how I become engrossed with French. I have eyes for nothing but my book."

"A dictionary, I suppose?" Miss Muckersie grunted. "No? H'm! Well, you'll have my dress ready this afternoon, Mrs. Gray? Send it down between six and seven."

"But, my dear Miss Muckersie, you are not really going away already?"

The schoolmistress assumed an expression of disappointment.

"We hardly get a sight of you before you are gone, and your visits are like angel visits, you know, few and far between."

"The fewer the better," the visitor snapped out brusquely. "Angel visits are always a visitation here, and it's only the gravedigger that would have them oftener. And, speaking of that," she said, looking to Mrs. Gray, "have you heard how Marg'et Downie is keeping?"

Mrs. Gray shook her head.

"I'm doubtin' she's sinkin' fast," she answered, sympathetically falling back on the speech of her girlhood. "This sudden frost telled heavy on her, an' Mich'el's just waitin' on her nicht an' day. He aye had a fell wark wi' Marg'et, an' he has a sair wark wi' her now."

"Is Francis home?"

"No, but they're expectin' him; next week bein' the Christmas holidays. Rob Buchan aye brings back some encouraging word about the laddie."

"My brother has a different story to tell about

Francis Downie." Miss Muckersie spoke defiantly, like one who advocates an unpopular view. "He's a thoughtless youth."

"By the bye, Miss Muckersie," the schoolmistress interposed, "your brother would not be at Muiredge last night?"

"No, he wasn't." She looked fiercely at the schoolmistress, asking with a look what business it was of hers, whether her brother went to Muiredge or stayed at home.

"Oh, Mr. Urquhart was there last night, and stayed overnight again," Miss Mitchell said with affected indifference. "I saw him returning little more than an hour ago."

Miss Muckersie had risen to go away, but she seated herself on the edge of the sofa again, laying her umbrella over her knees, and crossing her black-gloved hands above it.

"The master?" she queried.

Miss Mitchell had got the conversation she wanted begun. She drew a footstool nearer, and set a dainty slippered foot upon it, carelessly lifting her skirt just sufficiently to let the firelight play about the white-stockinged ankle.

"Are you not cold sitting back there, Miss Muckersie," she asked caressingly, "on such a frosty day as this?"

"No," was the short and ungracious reply. "I keep good thick-soled boots for frosty weather and rough country roads. I leave dolls' shoes for—dolls."

Miss Mitchell simpered like one listening to the most delicate flattery.

"It's quite true, Miss Muckersie, Mr. Urquhart stayed all night at Muiredge again. That's the

second time now, and—you know what people say,
Miss —— "

" No, I don't know what people say, Miss—eh—
Mitchell," she snapped viciously. " And I don't
believe it."

" Oh, Miss Muckersie ! " the schoolmistress exclaimed with dilated eyes, " How can you ? I don't
mean anything wrong. Only, you know when a
young man visits a house regularly, and meets a—
well, fascinating young lady every time, people will
talk."

" People always talk Miss—eh—Mitchell ; and
generally talk nonsense."

" That's true," Mrs. Gray commented with un-
necessary emphasis. " I remember they talked when
I was married ; and there was nothing in it. It
wasn't true."

"And what are people talking about now ? " Miss
Muckersie asked, interested in spite of her ex-
pressions of indifference. " And what do you
mean ? "

" Oh, Miss Muckersie, you are really too innocent,"
the schoolmistress told her, with a giggle.

She changed her foot on the foot-stool, smoothing
her skirt from the knee down, and displaying again
just the least little white ribbon of ankle. " You
know how engaging and—eh—fascinating Miss
Austin can be ? " she queried.

The twin buds nodded and becked over Miss
Muckersie's face. That was as far as she would
commit herself.

" And Mr. Urquhart "—here the young lady
looked at the two elder ladies, her lips parting in a
smile pregnant with meaning—" Mr. Urquhart is a

most impressionable young man—O dear, dear! What am I saying? I didn't mean to say that. But he is, really; I assure you."

"I think he's very nice," Mrs. Gray ventured timidly. "Isn't he? He has been very kind to Marg'et."

Miss Mitchell smiled playfully. "You're just an innocent, simple, loving old dear, Mrs. Gray," she said, smoothing the knitting over her knee, and speaking her thoughts to it rather than addressing herself to her landlady.

"And so this young man is impressionable, is he?" Miss Muckersie snapped out with an ugly gleam in her eye. "And Miss Austin is fascinating, forsooth? Well, Miss—eh—Mitchell, they are a pair of fools, both of them; and so are the people who talk about them."

The schoolmistress affected to be deeply interested in her knitting, turning it round and round on her knee, and examining the pattern minutely. "He just came back this morning," she communed with herself, "in time to meet the friend he was expecting from Edinburgh; some teacher friend of his whose school is closed on account of measles; and now they're both away out again with their skates over their arms. Mr. Urquhart may have arranged a party for skating, you know."

"I hope the loch's safe."

Mrs. Gray looked up from sewing, her face seriously apprehensive of the worst. "You mind how the three sisters were drowned, Miss Muckersie? Three bonny ladies they were. I was at Torbean at the time, and it was Richard that brought me the news."

"Yes," Miss Muckersie reflected, "and the dog too. I remember my father saying there wasn't its match, as a sheep-dog, in the county."

"He told me in school yesterday," Miss Mitchell continued musingly, "that he expected this Mr. Grant—I think that's the name he said—and asked if I would join them at skating. I'm sure he mentioned Miss Austin as one of the party."

Miss Muckersie listened, actually looking interested now, but still she sat as formal and prim as the white tidy pinned symmetrically over the middle of the sofa back behind her.

Of course I refused," the mistress continued. "I knew I was just asked to complete the party. Fancy me skimming along with a complete stranger, just to let Mr. Urquhart have the opportunity of skating with Miss Austin. No, thank you!" She laughed softly to herself, and looked down admiringly at her dainty feet. "Besides," she added, as if it were an afterthought, "I haven't got my skates here."

"No, nor your winter boots either," Miss Muckersie commented, looking disdainfully at the delicate slipper resting luxuriously on the footstool; "and I daresay you'd have preferred Mr. Urquhart yourself, Miss—eh—Mitchell; an impressionable young man, as you say, and eligible, of course!"

"No indeed, Miss Muckersie! Mr. Urquhart is not my style—oh yes, Mrs. Gray, he's very nice out of school; but—well, I see the real Mr. Urquhart, and you have no idea of his conceit. He is positively unbearable. Why, he actually presumed to tell me how to teach, the very first day he was in school!"

"And you older than he is!" Miss Muckersie ejaculated.

"No, I'm not," Miss Mitchell answered hotly. "It was the only sign of temper she had shown, but surely the provocation was great. Her cheek flushed with anger, but in a second she was looking as serene as ever.

"It's very funny, I assure you, Miss Muckersie, to see him teach. You couldn't tell whether it was work or play, and he has no idea of keeping his place with the boys. I don't believe the children could tell you whether they were getting geography and history or just playing a game."

"Disgraceful!" Miss Muckersie grunted. "Does my brother know of this?"

"Oh, I let Mr. Muckersie see the blackboard one afternoon—he dropped in just after school was over. Mr. Urquhart had been giving one of his lessons in —everything—history, geography, reading, and I don't know what more, all jumbled together. The board was like a page out of one of those vulgar illustrated papers."

"Disgraceful!" Miss Muckersie grunted again. "I don't know the vulgar papers you mean. Is that what you were reading this morning? No? And what did my brother say?"

"Oh, he wasn't pleased, I can tell you. He said it was no better than the drawings boys filled their slates with; and, if it taught them anything, it could only be to waste their time. He talked to Mr. Urquhart about it, but you know his high-handed way. He thinks nobody can teach but himself; and he just cleaned the board, and asked your brother to mind his own business."

"What?" Miss Muckersie looked stiffer, straighter, fiercer than ever. "I should have dismissed him on the spot."

"But Mr. Muckersie is a gentleman," Miss Mitchell simpered. "Had it been any other member of the Board! Well!"

The sound of wheels was heard outside, and the schoolmistress screwed herself round in her chair, to peer through the window.

"Well, I declare," she cried. "There's Muiredge and the two boys driving towards Milnforth, and Miss Austin must be left with those two young men alone."

"Disgraceful!" Miss Muckersie ejaculated a third time. "I must tell my brother about this. He oughtn't to allow her to flirt about with any young man that comes in her way. Disgraceful! And Mr. Urquhart a teacher of the young, too! Eleven o'clock, Mrs. Gray? I should have been home by this time, and it's all your fault, Miss—eh—Mitchell, with your hateful gossip. But I'm glad you told me about Miss Austin's ongoings, and that impressionable young man! A pair of fools, both of them! Good morning, Mrs. Gray. Before seven, mind."

The door was slammed, and Miss Mitchell beheld through the window the tall, angular figure striding along the icy street.

"She's not going to see Marg'et," she remarked to Mrs. Gray. "She's away straight home; and I believe she'll tell her brother every word."

She laughed to herself, and drew her knees closer to the fire.

"I wonder what he'll do, Mrs. Gray. Isn't she

a horrid old fright, and positively insulting, too?
But I'll have it out with her some day."

Mrs. Gray sat quietly sewing.   She was too meek
a person for the clever little schoolmistress.

"I—I rather like the master," was all she ventured
to say.

"Fiddlesticks!" the ladylike Miss Mitchell exclaimed.   "He has eyes for nobody but Miss Austin,
a haughty, stuck-up minx!   And I don't believe she
cares a snap of the finger for him.   Oh, dear, dear!
I wonder what Mr. Muckersie *will* say when he
hears that the schoolmaster—his servant—is actually
trying to—— Oh, it's too funny, Mrs. Gray!"

But poor Mrs. Gray was quite bewildered, and
only shook her head.

CHAPTER FIFTEENTH

WEARS YET A PRECIOUS JEWEL IN HIS HEAD

IT was a glorious morning, the frosty air dry and exhilarating, without a breath of wind. Urquhart and Grant tramped along, hearing their footsteps ringing on the road, and echoed across from hedge to hedge. The hill, with winding footpaths and sheep-tracks, and water courses veining its sleek flank, shouldered itself into a sky glittering with frost. Every crack and fissure in its beetling brow was so distinct that the sharp jagged edges of the rock could almost be felt. From the hedges on the other side of the road gray-green fields, dotted with sheep nibbling a scanty herbage or nosing fresh turnips, sloped gently to the single file of firs standing sentinel over the sleeping loch. The burn by the side of the Loan breathed drowsily under its sheeting of ice, while the grasses bending over it were hung with a fretwork of icicles flashing and dazzling in the vibrating sunshine. The two young men drew up now and again with a laugh at the pace they were putting on, but presently they would be swinging along again glowing with health, and breaking into snatches of song out of the very joy of living. Already they felt themselves skimming from end to end of the loch, while the skates on their arms

jingled in anticipation. On such a day it was enough
just to know that one lived. The hedges might
be leafless, but to the discerning eye they were
already holding the promise of spring; while the ear
of a poet could have heard from the brown earth
whispering round their roots the endless song of
summers stretching into an eternity.

Miss Austin was out on the lawn to meet them,
and as they came up the walk Mr. Urquhart thought
he had never seen a lovelier picture, never noticed
her so thrillingly beautiful as now. She was very
simply dressed in a skirt and bodice of soft grey
tweed, a deep white collar fastened at her throat
with a cairngorm brooch. Her head was bare, and
the winter sunshine streaked the waving auburn hair
with threads of gold. Her cheeks had the delicate,
pink flush of a sea-shell, and her eyes sparkled
welcome as they approached. Behind and just
above her rose the sun-dial in a green-and-grey
old age, but as yet its shadow hid only the morning
hours, leaving a long day before it bathed in sunshine.

"Good morning," she said, advancing to meet
them. "Isn't it a perfectly ideal skating day?" And
before Mr. Urquhart had time to introduce his friend
she had given him her hand. "How d'ye do, Mr.
Grant? I wondered, when Mr. Urquhart mentioned
your name last night, if you would really be the Mr.
Grant I used to know."

"Miss—Miss Austin!" Grant stammered, almost
dumb with surprise, while Urquhart looked on in
staring bewilderment.

She smiled from the one to the other. "You
both look astonished," she said, "at a very simple

and ordinary occurrence. I assure you there's no mystery, Mr. Urquhart," she added, with a little laugh at his speechless surprise.

"Come away in," she invited them. "I'll give you five minutes till I am ready. I see you are dying for each other's explanation."

In the parlour the two men looked at each other for a second or two. Urquhart was the first to speak. "This is certainly a surprise," he declared. "What a couple of fools we must have looked !"

"Well, old fellow, *you* did, anyhow."

"No more than yourself, Sandy."

"Why it's years since I met her," Sandy explained. "You know, she lived almost opposite us in Edinburgh, and I used to visit regularly. The house was a rendezvous of teachers, you know ; the mother had such a kind motherly way with her that we all took to her. Those were great times, I can tell you. You remember Jackson and Galbraith, and Wallace and Lowrie, and old Somerville even. Why, we all used to meet there. And now I meet her here again, of all the places in world."

"Miss Austin must have been quite a girl then."

"Well, yes ; though half the fellows were gone on her."

"Shut up, man !"

Sandy whistled. "That's how the land lies?" he whispered with a grin. "It's all right. I wish you luck, old man."

"Enough, Sandy," Urquhart answered brusquely, with a gesture of impatience. "You don't know what you are talking about, and I don't suppose I could make you understand."

"She was always very dignified, I remember,"

Sandy continued. "She didn't seem to enjoy intellectual talk. Of course, she was too young to take part," he generously admitted, "and she may have felt bored."

Urquhart looked at him steadily. "Was it philology, Sandy?"

"Well, sometimes; though, of course, one couldn't get a chance often if the other chaps were there. You know yourself how that lot used to talk."

"Unfortunately I do," he answered, "and how badly. No wonder she appeared dignified and distant. Jackson," he began, ticking off the names on his fingers, "Interest and Percentages and Algebraic Formulæ! Galbraith, English Literature, second stage! What an insane babbler he used to be! All the literature he knew could be bought for ninepence, thirteen as twelve."

"Oh, Galbraith's all right, old boy," Grant objected, "he's in the running for the next head-mastership."

"And Wallace," Urquhart continued, "what was his fad? Second-stage French! I've heard him tell the *Je suis faim* story a score of times. Lowrie could talk about nothing but Passes and Percentages; and as for old Somerville, he was a bore, silent or talkative. And last, but not least, Sandy, there was yourself, sane on every subject except Philology."

"Oh, philology's all right," Sandy assured him; "it's the science of language, and the most poetical of all the sciences. It has thrown a new light on history; it——"

"Yes, yes, Sandy; I know. It lightens up everything except conversation."

"And that reminds me," Grant went on, drawing a

note-book from his pocket, " I got a beautiful new word this morning——"

"What about Mrs. Austin, Sandy, Miss Austin's mother?"

"A perfect beauty, I assure you," the philologist averred, consulting his note-book. "I heard it at that old inn this morning, just beyond Balgowrie. Coming from the station, I looked in——"

Urquhart crossed the room, and placed a hand over the note-book. "Give philology a rest for one day, Sandy. I was asking for Miss Austin's mother. What did she think of those gatherings?"

"Oh, well, you know, she was very kind to us. She couldn't help being kind to anybody. The old boy had been an art-teacher, or something of that sort, at one time, although he was a terrible wreck when I remember him. He fancied himself a great painter, neglected by the Academies; he was certainly a cranky, ill-natured, peevish old humbug."

"Are you speaking of Miss Austin's father?" Urquhart asked, somewhat angrily.

"Well, not exactly. I remember Elsie Austin as quite a girl. She wasn't their child, you know. They adopted her, and were well paid for it, too; had money settled on her, or something of that kind. I forget the whole story," he added, indifferently. "Mother could put you through it all right."

Urquhart gripped him by the collar, and placed a hand over his mouth. "Ssh," he whispered, with menacing eyes, and indicating the open door. They heard footsteps on the stair. "Do you know what you're saying, Sandy?"

Sandy released himself. "Don't get into a funk, old fellow. I'm not saying anything wrong. It's quite true—I know that; and there's no harm in telling you."

"Well, are you ready to go?"

Miss Austin looked in at the door, hatted and gloved, and with a thick fur-boa round her neck. "Why, Mr. Urquhart, have you not recovered from your surprise yet? You are quite pale. Are you ill?"

"I, Miss Austin?" He laughed at the question. "I never felt better in my life. It would be a shame to be ill on a day like this. Shall we go now?"

At the door they came upon Mr. Muir and the boys bringing round the trap. The farmer invited the young men to tea after their skating. "We shall be back from Milnforth about five," he called. "If you are home before then, Mr. Urquhart, I shall pick you up at Donald's."

The three cut across by the moss to the burn side.

"Now," said Elsie, when they had got to something like a path, "we'll walk three abreast; and, Mr. Grant, you must tell me about all our old Edinburgh friends, Mr. Somerville, Mr. Galbraith, and all the rest of them."

"I'm afraid I know little or nothing about them now. I have got out of touch with that lot, and haven't seen any of them for ages."

"And is it still derivation, Mr. Grant?"

Sandy beamed with satisfaction. "Do you still remember about that, Miss Austin? Those were jolly times. By the way, I heard a beautiful word this morning on the way from the station, perfectly new to me; two, indeed, both new."

"New to you, Mr. Grant? That must be worth

hearing. But where could you hear a word on the way from the station? You must tell me that, Mr. Grant."

"Oh, I—I—just happened to hear it, Miss Austin, and it's a perfect beauty. I looked in at the——"

He was cut short by a sharp scream from Miss Austin, whom he saw turn and cling frantically to Mr. Urquhart.

"Oh, Mr. Urquhart," she screamed; "what is it? What is it?"

She was almost beside herself with fright, and clung close to him, as if she would be safe under his care.

Mr. Urquhart's arm was around her with the instinct of protection, and he held her close to him in assurance of safety.

All this had taken place in a second, and now a rustle in the grass at their feet showed the cause of her alarm.

"See, Miss Austin," Urquhart said with great tenderness, and pointing to a gigantic toad hopping away from her skirts, "that was all."

Grant was after it at once like a school boy.

Miss Austin gave a little hysterical laugh, looking down at the animal equally frightened, but still she clung for a breath's space to his shoulder. Then she grew conscious that his arm was round her waist, holding her firm. She raised her eyes slowly, and looked into his. He was gazing steadily upon her, and in his eyes, under the long lashes, there was a peculiar light that she had never seen there before. Or, had it been there all along, and was it only now that it seemed to her to have a meaning? She was quivering yet from her fright, and her eyes were timid under the intensity of his gaze. Her heart was beating against her breast—he must have felt it—and her eyelids fluttered and fell. A blush stole into her cheeks, yet it could hardly be called a blush, it crept so softly across her face from neck to forehead.

"May I—go—Mr. Urquhart?" she asked, and the voice was the voice of a child.

She was firm on her feet again, and Urquhart smiling reassuringly upon her.

"Did you think you could be so frightened by a toad, Miss Austin?"

"It must have been wiled out of its hole by the pleasant sunshine," Grant called from the burn side, where he stood watching the animal making ineffectual attempts to hide away amongst some frost-hardened clods.

"Well, never mind him now," Urquhart advised; "here we are at the White Sands, and, see, Miss Austin, a marvellous convenient tree-trunk provided expressly for you. Allow me."

He lifted the skates from her arm, and she seated herself on the fallen trunk.

"Whoop!" Sandy was off like a shot, skimming in a breath's space, a quarter of a mile away.

Elsie looked down at Mr. Urquhart kneeling at her feet and adjusting her skates. How tenderly his hands touched her foot!

"Mr. Urquhart," she said, almost in a whisper, "I forgot to thank you."

He looked up at her and smiled. "I don't think you hurt the toad," he said. "It must have been the toad Shakespeare mentions, that wears a jewel in his head. I mean to win that jewel."

"Did you know those friends of Mr. Grant," she

asked, when he sat down to put on his own skates,
"Mr. Somerville, Mr. Galbraith, and all the rest of
them?"

"I have met them, Miss Austin."

"What did you think of them?   Now, tell me
true, as the children say."

"They must have bored you fearfully with their
scholastic babble."

"Yes," she answered, with a shiver, "they did ; and
—will you pardon me, Mr. Urquhart?—I thought all
teachers were the same."

"I should be sorry to have you think so, Miss
Austin."

"I said *I thought*, Mr. Urquhart."   She looked at
him with innocent eyes.   "Now," she proposed, "a
race for the island.   Off!"

And she was away across the loch like an arrow,
the clear ice ringing as she went, and hardly keeping
a trace of her course.

CHAPTER SIXTEENTH

A DAY ON THE LOCH

THEY had the whole loch to themselves. Down near the sluices they came upon a solitary individual who had drawn a rink for himself, and was practising curling. But he was the only being on the ice besides themselves. The stones rumbled musically from tee to tee, but the player himself was silent and serious, taking his enjoyment soberly. One who had never witnessed a club match, would, watching him, have imagined curling to be the quietest and most solemn game in the world.

"There's little of the roaring game in that," Sandy remarked as they shot past him, and Miss Austin only laughed for answer. Her heart was so light and happy to-day that she wished to be always laughing. Had she been alone, she would have skated from end to end of the loch, letting her happiness out in a low tremulous gurgle of laughter.

To Urquhart, skating by her side, she looked another being from the Miss Austin he had known for the past few weeks. There was a timid sweetness about her to-day that was new to him. She was transformed in his eyes and transfigured. The hauteur and dignity with which she had formerly met him were gone, but they must have been softened into something finer and tenderer, some-

thing more gently trustful. Up till now he had only
seen Miss Austin in armour; now she had doffed
her mail, and he beheld her in all the beauty and
child-like simplicity of trustful maidenhood. He
glanced at her face now and again at his side. The
cheeks were still delicately flushed, and her lips were
half-parted in a smile of content. Surely also there
was a new light in those eyes, which the long lashes
so shyly curtained. Her face was the face of one
who dreams a happy dream and smiles in sleep.

From the sluices they raced back again to the
island. Sandy had to do most of the talking; the
other two were content to listen. But that did not
annoy Alexander Grant in the slightest. He was a
noted talker, as any member of the Cockburn Clique
could have told; and to-day he excelled himself.
Miss Austin answered his witticisms so readily with
a musical ripple of laughter, and Urquhart his wise
sayings with such a sage and contemplative nod,
that Sandy rattled on as if his best things occurred
to him on skates.

In the middle of the loch there was a slight breeze
blowing, and the three joining hands sped on before
it almost without effort. In a minute or two the
island was far behind them. Away to the north
they saw the village nestling to the hill, the peat
smoke curling upward, and softening its green slope
in a mystery of blue. In front, as they flew along,
the red-tiled houses of Milnforth began to grow
distinct in the distance, where they huddled together
at the far end of the loch, coming nearer and clearer,
until they could count the windows in the houses,
and heard the carts rumbling through its tortuous
street.

They drew up within fifty yards of the shore. They had had a four miles' run, and their faces were glowing with exhilaration. Urquhart gazed earnestly down on Miss Austin's face. Her eyelids still drooped over the eyes, hiding their light, but she felt the earnestness of his gaze, and raised them for a moment to his face. Then they fluttered and drooped again. But Urquhart had seen the light that was in them, soft and dreamy, as if it were sleeping there ; and he fancied he heard the faintest breath of a sigh, as she glided from his side, a sigh of restfulness and peace. His heart leapt to his lips ; he felt the blood coursing through his veins, tingling with a happiness he sought not to question or understand. What change was this in this beautiful being whom he had met so frequently since he came here, yet had not known till to-day ? He had noted the beauty of her eyes before now—hazel and brown, he called them—now he saw not their colour at all for the soul that looked through them speaking to his. He had worshipped her afar off, as one unworthy ; but in a flash she had come into his life, and he knew that he loved her. That was the thought that shot through his brain, almost staggering him with its intensity. His breath came quick and hard ; he felt it in his heart ; he heard it buzzing in his ears. He held his head erect, and closed his lips firmly. This surely was being born again. He had come into the fulness of his manhood, and knew that in the great scheme of creation he had his place and his purpose. He was a part of the great centuries behind him, life lay all before him, and the future was his. In that second the present, the past, and the future were one ; for love is a god, and the gods are immortal.

Miss Austin was a step in front, and he followed. When he got to her side he spoke calmly, like one who can speak with power, but holds himself in rein.

"You have enjoyed the run, Miss Austin?"

"It was glorious," she said.

"What is the programme now, old man?" Sandy, who had been busily curving on the outside edge, now joined them.

"I think we should go into Milnforth for lunch," Urquhart proposed; "and then skate back again in time for tea."

Elsie's eyes sparkled. "Oh yes, do! And we may astonish Uncle and the boys."

She set off first for the bank, the gentlemen pursuing, but just as Grant was passing, he tripped, went dashing wildly forward, turned a somersault, and finally settled down, he could not tell how, on the grassy bank.

"Oh, Mr. Grant!" she cried. "Have you hurt yourself?"

Sandy looked about him, stupidly gathering his senses. "You couldn't do that, old boy," he said.

"I shouldn't care to try," Urquhart answered with a laugh. "Are you sure you are not hurt?"

"I'm as right as the mail myself, but," ruefully holding up an acme, "my skating's done for the day. Here's this catch snapped in two."

"The acrobatic exhibition was hardly worth the cost, Sandy."

"It's all well enough for you to laugh, old man. You two will skate home in no time, while I come limping miles behind."

"You can get a drive back with Uncle and the boys," Elsie suggested; and then she blushed, evidently without reason. "It's seated for four."

They undid their skates and walked up to the hotel for lunch. Mr. Muir had driven past that morning, the landlord told them, but there were some parcels left at the hotel for him, and he was sure to call on the way home. So it was arranged that Sandy should wait at the hotel till Mr. Muir called.

The lunch was a great success. They were all blessed with healthy appetites, and not ashamed to eat with hearty enjoyment. After their forenoon's skating in the bracing air, they were ravenously hungry, and there was little talking for a time. They enjoyed the lunch, because they had enjoyed themselves so thoroughly, and enjoyed themselves all the more in that they enjoyed the lunch.

"Your best plan will be to get off at Kinkelvie," Urquhart advised when he found time to speak, "and I shall meet you there. I have a little bit of writing to finish this afternoon. After it 's done, we can go down to the farm again together."

"Oh, by the bye," Sandy cried, "I read that short story of your's, 'Mysie's Marriage,' in *Langland's Magazine.*"

Urquhart interrupted impatiently. "We 're discussing lunch just now, Sandy, not literature," he told him pedantically. "We 're out for a day's enjoyment, and I don't wish to be dragged into shop talk."

"Lunch, not literature!" Sandy echoed, aping Urquhart's tone. "I beg pardon, old man. The fact is I didn't think I was discussing literature. And literature is shop now-a-days? What next?"

Urquhart laughed. "Shut up, man! Hand up your plate. You 've a good drive before you."

Elsie looked from the one to the other with questioning eyes, but before she could speak, Urquhart had turned the conversation into philology, and Grant was talking like a dictionary.

Sandy went down with them to the loch, and saw the two skating away hand-in-hand. "By Jove," he muttered to himself, "perhaps it's just as well my skate gave way. I don't believe they'll miss me a bit. What a stunner she has turned out. And she has money, too. Urquhart's in luck. He always was a lucky beggar."

They kept close by the shore as they skated back, following the bends of the bays, and coming so close to the land in places, that they could touch the branches of fir in passing. Now sweeping round a corner, they would startle a hare prospecting for a drop of water, and send it scampering off in fright to the open fields. Again, they would raise a flight of sea-gulls to circle round them, sadly silent, then settle again to pick up a scanty meal where some streamlet trickled into the loch. Beyond Balbingry Burn, they caught sight of Mr. Muckersie striding along by the side of the wood, and shouted to him a joyous recognition. But he did not hear or did not heed.

"Let us join both hands," Elsie proposed, "and go flying past him. I'm sure he sees us well enough."

Away they went again, Elsie swinging gracefully, and laughing to herself—or rather it was smiling musically—for very joy; Urquhart silent, because he was too happy for speech. Another bend of the land was passed, and Muckersie was lost to sight. They were within sight of the White Sands now, little more than a mile ahead.

"We'll take it slow, now," Elsie suggested.

" Tired ? "

" No, but we are nearly home now, and I want to ask you a question, Mr. Urquhart. You won't be angry ? " she asked playfully. " Nor think me inquisitive ? Well, it 's just this. Did you write that story, ' Mysie's Marriage ' ? "

" Must I confess, Miss Austin ? "

" Ah, you have confessed already."

" But why do you wish to know, Miss Austin ? I hardly ever mention anything I write."

" Because I have read it."

Urquhart felt his cheeks glow with pleasure. "And enjoyed it, I hope ? " he ventured, bending as if he would read the answer in her face.

" Ah ! " she answered. " Must I confess, Mr. Urquhart ? It 's you who are curious now. But I won't tell you. I 'm afraid I cried over it," she added, naïvely.

" I thought I had given it a very happy ending," he protested.

" Ah, that 's why." She looked up into his face for an instant, and smiled roguishly. " You don't understand," she said, "even though you do write stories about young ladies."

" Wait a minute, please ? " she asked, disengaging her hands. " I 'm afraid my brooch has become unfastened. See, yonder 's Mr. Muckersie in sight again," she added, inconsequently. " Will you pin it for me, Mr. Urquhart ? You haven't any gloves to take off. I wonder how you can go without them."

She lifted her chin a little, and Urquhart began fumbling with trembling fingers, trying to fasten the pin. He felt her breath on his cheek, and he knew that her eyes were smiling at his awkwardness. She

M

let her throat touch his fingers, and felt them trembling.

"He must be going to Muiredge," she remarked, "and he seems to be in a great hurry. Must I really help you, Mr. Urquhart? Can you write stories, and not pin a lady's brooch? Ah, you have managed it at last. Thank you!"

Urquhart raised his head. He was breathing hard; yet Elsie just laughed at him.

"It's harder than writing stories," he declared. "That's the first time I have ever fastened a lady's brooch, Miss Austin."

"Indeed!" She spoke as if she were delighted to hear it. "And yet you presume to write about young ladies! Come on, now; join hands for a run to the White Sands. We'll pass Mr. Muckersie again. Doesn't he look doleful, poor man?"

"I didn't know you wrote stories," she breathed, skimming along. "You didn't think it worth while telling me."

"I'm only trying, Miss Austin; I don't think many people know. I have kept it pretty much to myself."

"Here we are, now," she cried, drawing up at the shore. "What a day it has been! I wish one might be allowed to skate on Sundays. Is that a wicked wish, Mr. Urquhart? Mr. Dawson calls me his little heretic."

She seated herself on the trunk again, and he knelt to unfasten her skates.

"Perhaps you'll give up school," she mused, addressing herself to the back of his head, "and write novels."

"You don't like teachers, Miss Austin?"

He had spoken very quietly; yet an expression of pain came into her face. She did not answer.

"Take my arm," he said, when they were ready to go. There was more of command than entreaty in the tone, as well as in the words; but she laid her hand lightly on his arm all the same, and they walked away in silence.

When they came to the gate she stopped, and began taking off a glove. "Now you are going to meet Mr. Grant," she said. "It's just four o'clock; and mind you must be back by six. You'll all be hungry; and I'll have a delightful tea awaiting you."

"You have made this a most enjoyable day for me, Miss Austin."

"It has been enjoyable—very."

The air was still full of light, and the sky clear, although the crescent-moon was just beginning to glisten like an ivory bow, and a star or two trying to twinkle above them.

She looked up into his face, and her voice trembled a little.

"May I say something serious to you, Mr. Urquhart?"

"Is it very serious?"

"I have often been very rude to you——"

"Miss Austin!"

"Oh, yes!" she insisted. "You know I have. At least, I myself know, and——"

"But," he objected.

"Please don't interrupt me till I am done, Mr. Urquhart. That will be kinder to me. I have been rude; and it was just because I thought so much of myself, and—and I didn't know you."

"And you think you know me now, Miss Austin?"

"I do know you—better. The boys helped me
first. Andrew and Robert like you; and Mrs.
Downie speaks about you every time I visit her
now."

"That's because of her son. I listen to her talk
of Frank, and she thinks a world of that. That's
all."

"Not all! I know more. I was wilfully blind,
and she helped to open my eyes; and oh, I was so
ashamed of myself! There, Mr. Urquhart, I have
told you what has been upon my mind to tell you
for some days now. I had to tell you; and I feel
ever so much better now that I have done it. You
must forgive me, Mr. Urquhart."

She laid her ungloved hand on his arm, and looked
pleadingly up into his face. Her eyes were glistening.

"But, Miss Austin——"

"Mr. Urquhart," she commanded, "say 'I forgive
you.' That would be a kindness to me."

He looked into the serious eyes. "I forgive you,"
he repeated after her; "but for what, I don't know.

"I know," she answered. "You have been very
good to me."

He placed his hand over hers, and held it. "And
now, Miss Austin, may I say something serious?"

Her face was suffused with a serene happiness, and
she spoke calmly. "Not now," she asked him; "it
has been a happy day, and I would dream over it."

He bent and kissed her hand once—twice, and she
did not withdraw it.

"Au revoir!" she said, with a smile.

"Till six!"

CHAPTER   *AT THE EDGE*

SEVENTEENTH   *OF THE WOOD*

URQUHART did not go straight up by the Sandy Loan. A great happiness had come to him, and he wished to be alone for a space to think of it, to accustom himself to it, as it were, so that he might meet his fellow-men calmly, and talk with them on trite and trivial things, without flaunting in their faces the good fortune that had befallen him. Surely he was blessed above others, for never had love come to man before with such sweet awakening. O blessed day, that had brought a joy so exquisite he was half afraid to speak of it, even to himself, lest it might escape him in the very utterance! How could Grant, or Crombie even, or anyone, ever comprehend such rapture? They were groping in the valleys; he was on the heights, and love had crowned him king. Looking down, he pitied them, all knowing not the joy of loving, nor the blissful hope, that was almost certainty, of being loved in return.

Unconsciously, his steps had followed the path down by the moss to the edge of the wood. Here, in the shadow of the silent firs, that seemed to live in unbroken contemplation of mysterious things, could his heart throb out its happiness, whispering its secret to the trees and the grass; to the chaste moon and the listening stars; to the breathing air, that would sing of it round and round the world.

Nature is always the lover's first confidant. Freely and fully may he open his heart to fields, and flowers, and trees, because they listen silently, and their silence is always accepted as sympathy.

But Urquhart did not now find the solitude he sought. He had reached the boundary of the moss, and, with a whoop of boyish glee, he took the burn at a bound, landing at the edge of the wood, and face to face with—Mr. Muckersie.

"Hillo!" he ejaculated, and there was as much of annoyance as of surprise in the sound. He had come here to be alone, and the presence of another was an intrusion.

Mr. Muckersie stood in the shadow of a gaunt Scotch fir, still as a statue, and he stared at the younger man, but did not answer either by word or gesture.

Urquhart drew himself up, and returned the stare resentfully. What right had this man to look at him so? In the waning light, he was aware of an ugly expression on the face; and not only expression, but even the features appeared to have changed from what he knew them to be. The mouth was hard and cruel; the eyes had grown smaller, and glowed with a dull, smouldering light. Even the nose looked drawn; and, from the set of the shoulders, one might have guessed that his hands were locked tightly behind him.

"I was startled, jumping upon you so suddenly," Urquhart explained. "I didn't expect to meet you here."

A slight movement of the moustache might have

passed for a smile, had there been any answering flicker of light in the eyes. But still he neither moved nor spoke.

Urquhart was getting irritated. He did not know what to think. "It's not a corner where one would expect to meet a friend."

"A friend?" He had moved his lips as if to moisten them before he spoke. "That's just what brings me here. It's out o' the way, and," indicating with a lift of the eyes where Muiredge Farm lay, "you have a fine view, and can see without bein' seen."

Urquhart followed the direction of his eyes, looking back across the moss straight to the gate where he had just parted with Miss Austin. He felt the blood rush to his cheek, and there was contempt as well as anger in the look he flung at Mr. Muckersie. Had this man been watching him as a spy?

Mr. Muckersie spoke again, and there was a gleam now, and an evil one, in his eyes.

"I've seen that gate frae this very spot every nicht for years; this is the first nicht I cursed looking."

"Indeed?" Urquhart commented, with an affectation of indifference. "You'd be glad to break the monotony of blessing, no doubt; though you might have waited for weather more suitable. I had thought this would be a day for blessing rather than for cursing."

"That remains to be seen, Mr. Urquhart. Dinna mak' licht o' a serious matter, glib tongued though ye be."

"I have no desire to do so, I assure you; nor do I have the time, even though I understood what you are talking about, which I don't. Good night!"

"No so quick, Mr. Urquhart. I cam' to see you, and when I noticed ye crossin' the moss, I waited 'here to speak wi' ye."

"It's a pity you have chosen such an unfortunate time; for I'm afraid I must forego the pleasure of listening. You see you have consulted only your own convenience in your arrangements."

"I've consulted nobody's convenience, least of a' would I seek to consult yours."

Urquhart shrugged his shoulders and turned to go. "I'm afraid if you will speak, your speech will be a soliloquy. I really must go; I have an engagement."

"No so quick!" the farmer repeated. "I waited to speak to you, and I'm damned but you'll hear."

"Very well, then, fire away, and get it over as soon as possible. I daresay I can give you five minutes."

Muckersie showed his teeth, and his eyes grew smaller still. "I saw the twa o' ye on the loch the day," he said.

"You did? Well, I must say you took a rather peculiar way of showing it."

"I saw mair than you think," he burst out, savagely, "mair than I want to see again."

"I don't care a button what you saw, Mr. Muckersie, or what you didn't see. You don't imagine we went out on the loch to hide ourselves, do you?"

"Dinna be so sharp o' tongue, Mr. Urquhart. It's easy to lord it ower school-bairns; but ye'd as lief keep a calm sough when it's a man ye've to deal wi'. Ye may be a man amon' laddies, but ye're but a laddie amon' men yet."

"But what is all this pother about?" Urquhart cried impatiently. "Explain yourself, and be done with it."

"That'll no tak' me lang, Mr. Urquhart. I've seen enough o' this flirtin' an' philanderin', an' I'll ha'e no mair o' it."

"And is that what you came to tell me?" Urquhart asked, with a sneer.

Muckersie answered with à nod.

"And you've really no more to say?"

"That's a', Mr. Urquhart, an' plenty. Dinna let me ha'e to tell ye again, or I may tak' a different way o' tellin'."

Urquhart glanced at him with scorn. "Well, Mr. Muckersie, you might have saved yourself the trouble. I shall visit Miss Austin without consulting you, and I shall say and do just what I think right. Good night."

The farmer stepped forward, and held him by the arm. "Dinna try me ower faur, my man. I was the means o' bringing you here, an' I could get ye out as easily."

Urquhart laughed aloud. "Excuse me," he said, "but this is too funny. Do you imagine I am dependent on you or your peddling School-Board? If you wish to dismiss me, you'd better hurry up, or you may lose the opportunity. Away with you, man, and not talk like a fool! Who are you, that you should dare to come and talk to me as you have done?"

"And who are you," the farmer hissed almost at his ear, "that you should come between me and Elsie——?"

"Miss, if you please," Urquhart quietly corrected.

"You and your town talk be damned! Miss she may be, and will be, to you; but she's Elsie to me. Do you hear?"

"I'd be deaf if I didn't."

"I've watched her for years," he continued, speaking rapidly, and in his passion becoming dramatic and eloquent—"watched her and worshipped her. Yet never ha'e I whispered a word o' love, or sought by kiss or caress to wauken her into her womanhood. She's but a bairn yet. But you, after an acquaintance o' only as mony weeks, dinna hesitate to walk wi' her arm in arm, as only ane should ha'e the richt; to frake and palaver, to—to kiss her, you hound! Man, when I saw ye on the ice, wi' your hands frakin' about her throat, I could feel mine at yours, an' wi' little o' the frake in them. I saw you again at the gate, with some of your new-fangled love-story capers, bendin' bareheaded an' kissin' her hand. My God! you'd better no try it on again."

"And if I do," Urquhart asked calmly, "what right have you to interfere? You speak as if Miss Austin were your affianced bride."

"An' so she will be. Wha was there here to win her but me, afore you cam'? Is there another here or hereabout she micht marry? No, I tell ye. An' here you come an' stap in atween her an' me. But for your comin' she was mine; ay, an' mine yet, in spite o' you an' your glib tongue. I've thoucht it a' out ower an' ower again, lang ere you cam' here, an' I'm ready an' willin' to marry her."

"Willing, did you say? Really, Mr. Muckersie, you are far too condescending."

"Keep your sneers for yoursel', Mr. Urquhart; I ken what I'm speakin' about, an' it's no every man that would marry Elsie Austin—ay, even wi' her money. Maybe it's a matter o' no consequence wi' your town-bred gentry whether your wife be nameless or no; but country-folk, thank God! ha'e some respect for their good name, an' to marry a bastard——"

What more he would have said was lost. Urquhart jumped back from him speechless with passion; then he rushed at him, and struck at him with all his force. But he hit out blindly, and his knuckles only grazed the other's chin. Slight as it was, it was a blow, and Muckersie needed no second invitation to fight. It had come unexpectedly, however, and it staggered him. They faced each other in deadly silence for a second's space, and even in the darkness Urquhart could see that there was murder in Muckersie's eyes. But while the blow seemed to have made him a very maniac, the dealing of it had a different effect on Urquhart. All his ungovernable fury had been let out in that one blow, and he regretted it almost as soon as it had been given. But the deed was done, and he would stand the consequences. He planted his feet firmly on the ground, and stood calmly waiting. He had roused a madman he could see, and he was determined to defend himself, be the end what it might.

The farmer came rushing at him, his moustache, where it touched the beard, already flecked with foam; but his great arms were flung about without skill, and there was little direction in his blows. It was well for Urquhart that he was able to keep his wits about him, for this great giant of a man could have felled him at a blow, or taken him as a wrestler does and crushed the breath out of his body. Well, also, that he had left his overcoat at home! Neither had stripped or thought of stripping for the fight, and

Muckersie was heavily handicapped in his thick homespun.

All that Urquhart attempted to do was to defend himself, to dodge his adversary's charges, and, if possible, land him a blow on the shoulder as he lunged past. Twice had the farmer missed his man, and brought himself up against the trunk of a tree. His knuckles were hacked and bleeding, and Urquhart could tell from his peculiar breathing that he was half-stunned. If he could only keep cool for a minute longer the victory was his.

But the farmer, gathering strength for a final charge, came forward with head lowered, like a bull at a gate, and Urquhart's feet, in stepping aside, caught an exposed root, and he fell backwards.

Muckersie pulled himself up at the tree, and drew his hand across his forehead. He looked down on Urquhart, lying prone at his feet: he did not offer to rise. Bending over him, he saw that the eyes were closed, and there was not the slightest sound of breathing. Something gleamed in the moonlight at the side of the head, and he touched the blade of a skate. How cold it was! And the grass about it was already warm with blood. He drew back his hand with a shudder, "Is he? My God! But it was his ain fault. And on his ain skates, too! There's fate in that."

He peered round and round in the darkness. There was somebody moving about in the wood. Or was it only fancy? His ears were buzzing, and his head surged with confused noises. But, no! Something was creeping towards him stealthily through the dry grass, man or beast he could not tell. He got to his feet again, and steadied himself against the tree. Even as he did so, he saw a dozen figures rise out of the ground in front of him. With a groan of pain and horror he turned and staggered away. "It was the skates," he muttered.

He was reeling like a drunken man, and figures rose from every bush and whispered a fearful word as he passed. He shuddered at the name they called him, and hurried on. "It was the skates," he shouted at every one of them, "it was the skates ; and there was fate in that ! "

CHAPTER EIGHTEENTH

ALEXANDER GRANT, PHILOLOGIST

ALEXANDER GRANT was enjoying himself. Mr. Muir had set him down at the Inn, and he passed the time, waiting for Urquhart, revelling in talk. In conversation, according to Sandy's judgment, while there might be many listeners, there ought to be but one talker.

Good listeners, however, are rare: so much is expected of them. They have to be appreciative without interruption and critical without protestation. A nod of approval now and again, and a mono-syllabic expression of agreement, are permissible, if not indeed commendable, and at suitable times questions may be put, provided they be pertinent and brief. Sandy himself was a bad listener, although, in justice to him, it must be admitted that he was aware of the fact, and did not seek to hide it.

To-night the ideal audience had been found. Watty Spence had dropped in to introduce himself as a friend of the master's; Rob Buchan was there, quiet as ever, while the landlord sat smoking, ready to listen to anything, and to applaud where he understood. All were eager to hear the voice of a stranger, the more so that he was a man of learning and a friend of Mr. Urquhart's. And Grant was not one to miss such a glorious opportunity. Besides all this, he was at peace with himself and all the world. The forenoon's skating, and the drive from Milnforth in the bracing air, had acted on him like a stimulant, and it was a pleasure now to take his ease in his inn. He seated himself on the only chair in the room, and stretched his legs out towards the peat-fire blazing and buzzing so invitingly.

From the chair he could watch the faces of his three companions, and he gauged their mental capacities at a glance. Here were men who would listen so long as it pleased him to talk; so he discoursed to them of country life. He had many interesting things to tell them about their hill and their loch, about their home life and their unsophisticated ways. And he illustrated all he told them. Every phase of life he chronicled was fossilised in some penny weekly's rejuvenated joke that had once been Scots and humorous, but was now, alas! Scotch and phonetic. Yet the three listening were duller than he had imagined them, and did not catch the point of his stories. Wherefore he talked of humbler things, bringing himself down to the level of their intelligences. He told Watty about gardening, and lectured Rob on stables and sanitation. Donald, he discovered, knew a little about fly-fishing, and he told him a great deal more that was new to him and marvellous. But he always came back to the charm and simplicity of village life. He would have discoursed to them of their village for hours, if he had found them intelligently appreciative. But they were stolidly incurious, and he forbore.

"You know," he wound up, " I should like to come and stay here for a month or so. There are a number of interesting old customs still kept up here, customs that have altogether died out in the town; and the ways and sayings of a quiet, out-of-the-world place like this would make a delightful study. I feel certain I could write a book about the place; and I think I will."

"A book?" the landlord echoed, taking his pipe from his mouth, and staring with astonishment at the speaker. "A book about Kinkelvie! Na, na! We're past that now. The toun's no so thrang as it was wont to be. There was aince a man made a book about the hill an' the loch an' the weavers an' the looms, an' so on : he died a young man."

" Really, Mr. Macvie, I didn't know you had ever had an author amongst you. That's very interesting, very interesting indeed."

" Weel, sir, some folk considers it interestin', but it's dreich, dreich readin' to me."

" Then there's Macgilvray, down by Balbingry," Rob reckoned. " He has made up a book o' poetry, a' lees, they tell me."

" Ay, *he's* livin' yet," Donald conceded ; " but he's a lameter."

" Still living?" Grant cried. "And writing? That's more interesting still, Mr. Macvie."

" Weel, it's no very interestin' to the wife, poor body ; for she has to keep him. Ye see he lies in his bed a' day makin' up his screeds, an' whenever he has as muckle as his head can carry he loups outower an' bangs it down wi' pen and ink. Then he crawls inower again to rest after his labour, so to speak, an' maybe mak up some mair."

"I must have a copy of that book," Grant excitedly declared. "I wonder if I could get a copy of it here. It must be teeming with words, full of them."

"It is that," Watty assured him, speaking with humorous emphasis; "an' little else."

"D'ye mind the awfu' state he was in last hogmonay?" Rob asked with quietly twinkling eyes. "The wife had ga'en out i' the mornin' forgetting the ink-bottle was toom, an' about twal o'clock he loupet frae the blankets just burstin' with verses. But try as he liked he couldna get them out. There was pen an' paper, but no a drap o' ink. Man, he got into an awfu' raptur', an' gettin' haud o' his stult he gaed rampagin' up an' down an' roarin', ye never heard the like. I suppose it's a way wi' poets. They're no accountable for their actions. Weel, would ye believe it? A man that had never been out ower the door for years cam' stultin' a' the way frae Ba'bingry richt up to Robbie Jamieson's shop to buy a bottle o' ink! The whole toun liftet to see him, an' he bid to stand and lay aff to them about how his wife had treated him, him a poet and a lameter. An' warst o' a', when he got the ink, he'd forgotten what he wanted to write. It had clean escaped him like a fluff o' wind. An' it was the finest po'm he'd ever made, he'll tell ye. He taen to his bed ower the head o''t an' never put pen to paper for a month. The doctor gae his trouble a lang-nebbet name; but it's my belief it was po'try that ailed him."

"Ay," Watty drily concurred; "an' a sair ailment it has been for years back; waur than his rheumatism, for that bothers nobody but himsel', but his po'try's the plague o' the parish."

N

"I must really have a copy of his book," Grant decided. "He writes in the vernacular, I suppose?"

"He writes i' the kitchen," Donald answered seriously; "an' he makes it a' up out o' his ain head."

"I mean is the book English or Scots?"

"Ou," Watty sneered, "it's what passes for the Scots tongue in thae degenerate days, but no as Burns or Sir Walter wrote it. It's a' i' the spellin', as if sound, no sense, made it Scots. Every poem's a puzzle—in spellin'; an' folk compliment themsel's when they've warstled to the meanin', though it's no worth the trouble."

"That will make it all the more interesting to me," was Grant's opinion; "for it's words I want. I think the study of words the most beautiful study in the world. Perhaps you have never heard of Philology?"

"No that I'm aware o'," Donald considered, "it'll read'lys no be in my line. But I've heard Watty amon' his flowers, moubandin' some words that sounded like it."

"It's the study, or rather the science of words," Sandy explained, "and there's poetry, tradition, history, everything almost in it."

"A' words!" Donald mused. "Ay!"

"Now for instance, I heard a couple of words this morning that I thought beautifully expressive, and I must trace their history. They are perfectly new to me, and I added them at once to my collection. I am collecting for an exhaustive essay on the subject."

He drew a note-book from his pocket and consulted it. The first word was 'jaw-box.'

The three looked at him in surprise. Perhaps this was one of those smart young fellows from the town, who try to hold up quiet country folks to ridicule. Yet he appeared to be speaking in all seriousness, and looked really interested in what he said.

"You'll no ha'e studied Sir Walter, ha'e ye?" Watty asked. "Or come across a jaw-hole."

"Well, not thoroughly. It's terrible plodding to get at his examples."

"Ploddin'!" Watty simply stared.

"On my way from the station," Grant proceeded, "I looked in at that wayside inn beyond Balgowrie. I like to explore those antiquated places."

"The halfway house?" Donald asked. "The place is little else than a jaw-box itsel'—the jaw-box o' the parish. I'd be geisand afore I gaed in there for a dram. Tammas hasna the name o' good drink."

"*Geisand!*" Grant cried delightedly. "*Geisand!* That's the other word. *Jaw-box* and *Geisand*. The words are quite new to me, and I must find out their history. I cannot tell whether they are French or Anglo-Saxon. You see, I happened to ask for a glass of claret, and Tammas, as you call him, said he was out of it. Just a day or two ago, a couple of bottles had gone sour, and he had emptied them into the jaw-box. I had never heard a sink called a jaw-box before. I do hope it's French."

Donald sat bolt upright in his chair and looked at Grant, his face a perfect picture of consternation.

"Tammas—toom—wine—into—the jaw-box!"

Every word was uttered as if it were a sentence in itself, and had nothing to do with its neighbour. "Na, na! Ye needna come here wi' sic' a story. Tammas Fordel's no the man to pour wine either into jaw-box or condy."

"*Condy?*" Grant caught up. "*Condy?* What's

that ?   That's another new one to me, and it sounds like French."

Rob Buchan looked at him, his eyes twinkling.

"Ye've a nose for queer words, young man.   *Jaw-box* and *Condy !*   Ay, it's a pecu-li-ar taste."

"Condy ?"   Donald answered him.   "What's a condy but a condy, of course !"

"It's the name for a drain hereabout," Watty told him.

Grant got up from his seat, walked about the room, and sat down again.   He was delightfully excited, and Donald looked at him amazed.

"What a find !" he shouted.   "What a find !"

His note-book was in his hand again.

"How do you spell it ?"

"Smell it ?" Donald asked indignantly.

This was getting beyond a joke.   The man was either openly insulting them, or he was stark mad.

Watty looked at him and, smiling grimly, spelled the word for him.

"Now that's another," he shouted ; "pure French, without a doubt.   French *Conduit, Conduit !*   I'm in luck to-day.   There's not the least doubt the Scots have got that word from the French.   It is a beautiful and well-preserved relic of our old friendly relations with France."

"If it's French-Scots words ye want, I could gi'e ye a better ane than that," Watty told him ; "ane ye'll hear i' the toun ony day i' the week.   Here-about we ca' a noisy crowd o' folk a *canallye ;* an' the master told me himsel' that was French."

"What ?" Grant cried, whipping out his note-book again.   "You don't say so ?   French *canaillé !*   Why, I'll have my essay begun at once.   This is most interesting. Let me see. *Geisand, jaw-box, condy,* and *canallye.* They are perfect; most beautiful; really most beautiful!"

"Beautiful?" Donald flung the word back at him. "Ye dinna ca' them beautiful, div ye? *Jaw-box, condy, canallye?* My man, ye 're easy pleased; an' I maun say I dinna admire your taste."

"Oh, but you don't understand," Grant began to explain.

"No, an' I dinna want to."

Rob now spoke, and in his quiet way. "Ye 've gotten a foursome that are faur frae bein' considered bonny, hereabout. Yet, if I was you, I wouldna let on about sic an extraordinar' likin'."

Grant tried to show in what way the words had a fascination for him; but the explanation was thrown away—on Donald, at least. He saw the absurd side of it now, however, and chuckled to himself where he sat, shaking his mane of hair, and slapping his knee. "I 'll ha'e Eesie telled about this," he said to himself again and again. "Eesie 'll see the fun o' this in a blink."

Watty saw that Grant was annoyed, and tried to change the subject.

"Have you ever made a study o' the auld ballads?" he asked.

"The ballads!" Grant echoed, with beaming eyes. "Oh, yes; I 've made my largest collection of interesting and historical words from the ballads. They 're a perfect mine."

"Words?" Watty echoed indignantly. "Words be damned! Man, ye 've gotten words on the brain. A man to read our grand, auld ballads just to gather a pokefu' o' words, is like the couple that poured out the tea, as they'd poured 'tatoes, an' syne suppet the leaves."

Grant turned away in disgust. What was the use of his throwing pearls before swine? Country-folks were a most uninteresting lot, after all. "I wonder what's keeping Urquhart?" he asked. "It's past six o'clock already, and we were to be at the farm by six."

"He'll be waitin' ye down there," was Watty's opinion. "His skatin' was ower twa hours syne, at ony rate."

"No," said Grant. "We arranged to meet here, and Urquhart always keeps an appointment."

"He does that," Watty agreed. "But here's Muiredge himsel' to tak' ye down."

The door had opened, and Mr. Muir stood looking round about him. His face was troubled, they could easily see.

"We have been waiting you, Mr. Grant," he said. "Has Mr. Urquhart not finished his writing yet?"

Grant's heart almost stopped beating. "He hasn't returned yet, Mr. Muir. Is Miss Austin home?"

"They were home from the loch by four o'clock, and Mr. Urquhart left then to meet you here."

They were all on their feet now, and stood looking into each other's faces, all afraid to speak the fear that had gripped their hearts.

"Donald," said Rob quietly, "ye have a couple o' lanterns; bring them."

"If he has tried to skate ower the moss hole!" Watty cried in anguish. "It never bears, it never bears."

Grant caught him by the arm. "But you don't think he——"

"On wi' your hat, young man," Rob told him. "This is no time for words. Come awa' now. Donald, you can come, too; it's no ower thrang for Eesie the nicht."

Rob appeared to be the only man amongst them who kept his head. Watty was trembling from head to foot, and Mr. Muir looked actually ill.

"A gill o' the best brandy i' your pouch," was Rob's last injunction, and they set out, a silent company.

CHAPTER NINETEENTH

ATHY'S NEW NAME

THERE was a sound like the roar of a train coming nearer and nearer, until he heard the regular thud of the piston-rod, and could feel the heat of the furnace scorching his face. His forehead was burning, and as the noise died away he opened his eyes. Something was beating in his head like a hammer, and there was a buzzing sound, as of rushing waters, in his ears. Looking up, he saw through a veil a thousand points of light twinkling down on him, for all the world like stars. Surely it must be he was dreaming. Yet when he raised his arm to rub his eyes and see whether he was awake, he felt that he was cold and stiff. Reaching up, he touched a hand laid lightly on his forehead.

"Who's there?" he asked. "Where am I?"

"Ye've cuttet your head on your skates, an' I've tied your hanky round it. It was bleedin' awfu.'"

"And who are you?"

"John Cochrane."

Urquhart closed his eyes again, and lay still for a second. Something had happened, but he could not tell what. Try as he liked, he could not recall anything. Thought was chaotic. All he knew was that he was lying outside, and that John Cochrane was beside him.

"Did I fall, John ?"

"Ay," John answered readily, and it was as if he spoke with jubilation. "Ye fell ower a branch. He didna knock ye down."

"He, John ? Ah, I remember now ; Mr. Muckersie ! "

The whole events of the day came rushing back upon his mind, roaring and confused at first, like water that has been dammed up and now carries everything before it. Gradually the tumult of thought subsided, and his mind grew calm. He saw everything clearly and in order, from the time of his setting out in the morning till the end of the fight, when he fell backwards. After that all was blank. What a miserable end to a day of such joyousness and promise !

"It was a grand fecht," John declared. "He was winded afore ye fell. I wish ye hadna fa'n."

Urquhart groaned. He had fallen, indeed. What would Miss Austin say ? What could she think ? And yet with the very thought of her came a thrill of savage delight in having dealt that first blow. With the same provocation he knew he would do it again, ay, and fight again, though he might be pommeled out of recognition.

He dragged himself round, and leaned up on his elbow. His whole body was aching, and his legs were cramped with cold. "You must help me up, John. Is it late ? They 'll be wondering what 's wrong. Let us hurry home."

But when he was assisted to his feet he found that he could hardly walk, far less hurry.

John came to his side, and asked him to lean on his shoulder. So they began moving slowly along

the edge of the wood. The foot-bridge was quarter
of a mile further down the burn, and by it they must
cross. Urquhart had leaped across the burn little
more than an hour ago, but now he could hardly lift
the one foot beyond the other. The stars twinkled
coldly above as they crept along ; he heard the wind
sighing sadly through the firs. Even the moon, where
it hung over the loch, regarded him reproachfully.

"Is it late ? " he asked again.

" It 'll be past six now."

The master's heart sank within him, and his face
twitched with anguish. The physical pain was
nothing to this. "The first tryst !" he muttered,
altogether forgetful of John's presence. "The first
tryst, and broken ! "

"Ba'bingry's awa' hame waur nor you," John
confided, thinking to comfort him. "Ye dodged
him bonny yon time he gaed bang against the tree."
He chuckled with joy at the recollection. "But ye
should ha'e licket him. Ye ta'en it ower easy, I 'm
thinkin'."

John talked like a critic, as he was well entitled to
do. He had fought his way through every class
in the school, and could speak from a long and
varied experience.

"Ye could ha'e gotten into him easy. He doesna
ken how to guard."

"Did you see it all, John ? "

"Ay, I was ahent the bus' a' the time. I would
ha'e knocket him down mysel' for ca'in' her yon.
That's what he ca'd his hagman last year, an' Jock
ta'en it out o' him. He stretched him wi' a hay-fork."

Urquhart heard him rattling on, hardly heeding.
His head was throbbing wildly, and his whole body

was racked with pain. They had not reached the bridge yet, and he felt that he had been walking for hours.

"I foucht every laddie i' the school," John informed him, and he spoke like a hero, "just for cryin' 'Athy' to me, an' yon was waur."

"I think I should have done it myself, John."

John gave a gulp of pride. "Mind your feet now," he warned. "We're just at the brig, an' it's slippy. Ye'll never ca' me 'Athy' now," he added, with a tremor of joy in his voice.

Urquhart stopped and looked down at him. "No, John, I did not know what the word meant, or I should never have used it at all. When Rob Buchan told me the meaning of the word I was exceedingly sorry I had used it."

"'Abody cried it at me—aince," John answered, "but no mony now."

"I think I'll need to find another name for you," Urquhart proceeded. "What do you think of the 'Good Samaritan'? Yes, I think I shall call you the 'Good Samaritan' after this."

It is doubtful whether John had ever heard of the Good Samaritan, but he knew that the master was speaking in his praise, and he understood the word "good" at least. He felt himself more of a man, and asked Urquhart to lean heavier on his shoulder. "I carried a sack o' 'tatoes frae the pit to the byre this forenoon," he assured him.

"Look," he cried, when they had crossed the bridge, at the same time pointing in the direction of Muiredge Farm, "look, yonder's men out wi' lanterns, twa o' them. D'ye see them?"

He stuck his fingers into his mouth and whistled,

a piercing sound that shot through the darkness, away over the moor, startling a few shrilly-protesting peewits and finally sighing itself out in the wood halfway up the hill-side.

For a second the lights were still. ·Then they saw them held aloft and swung from side to side. A voice came to them out of the darkness.

"That's Rob Buchan," John confided to himself. "They'll be out lookin' for ye, thinkin', maybe, ye had fa'n into the moss hole."

Urquhart hung his head and set his teeth together, cursing himself for a fool. Already in fancy he saw every gossip of the village telling, with excited eyes and staccato ejaculations, the story of the fight, and how the master was brought home. It would be the talk of the parish, and his shame would be in the mouths of the very school children.

He staggered along hearing John whistling regularly at his side, and the answers of different voices ever coming nearer.

"Three, four, five o' them!" John counted as they approached, "Donald, an' Watty Spence, an' Rob, an' Muiredge, and a stranger. I dinna ken wha he is."

Urquhart almost fell into Rob's arms, and Grant came dancing round him, sobbing with excitement.

"My head's badly cut," Urquhart explained, taking the first word, "and I must have lost a deal of blood."

"Thank God, it's no waur, sir," Rob answered devoutly. "It was the moss hole that I was feared for."

"But how did you do it?" Grant cried wildly. "How did it happen? After such a glorious day, too! Where was it? You know——"

Rob gripped the young man's shoulder and swung him out of the way. "The man's red-wud," he muttered; "clean red-wud. Tak' a drap o' this, Mr. Urquhart."

"Red-wud," Grant repeated to himself; "red-wud. That's another new one. What's *red-wud?*" he asked, turning to Watty.

"That's the richt word i' the richt place," Watty answered shortly. "It means 'Hurry up.' You an' John there'll hurry up to the house as hard as ye can an' tell them to be ready. We'll be at your heels."

"Yes," Muiredge added. "And tell Elsie to have the couch ready."

"That has done me a world of good, Rob. I feel ever so much better already." Urquhart was speaking almost cheerfully. "I fancy I'm stiff and sore with nothing but cold. I had fainted when John found me."

"Come on," John shouted to Grant, setting off at a trot, and Sandy had to follow.

"Red-wud," he kept saying to himself, puffing along at John's side, fearful lest the word should escape him before he could fix it in his note-book. "That's the fifth new word to-day. This is a rare place for words. *Jaw-box, geisand, condy, canallye, red-wud!* Five new words in one day isn't bad, is it? I wish I could get another just to make out the half-dozen."

"Samaritan," John suggested. "That's what the master ca'd me. Red-wud just means ye're daft. Ssh, man! Tak' it slow, now. Yon's her comin' hersel' to the gate."

CHAPTER TWENTIETH

AND THE SUN-DIAL WAS— MUCKERSIE

MISS AUSTIN had been moving about, unable to settle to anything, ever since Mr. Muir and the boys had returned from Milnforth. She had gone to the door when she heard the sound of wheels, half expecting to meet Mr. Urquhart and Mr. Grant as well; for it was half-past five then, and Mr. Urquhart might have had his writing finished and have joined the party at Donald's. But he had not even reached home when Mr. Muir drove through the village, nor had they passed him as they came down by the Sandy Loan. She could not understand it at all, and felt sure that something had happened. He had gone across by the moss, she had seen, when he left her. What if he had slipped and fallen somewhere? He had sprained his ankle, perhaps, and was unable to walk home. And now? It was too dreadful to think about, and she tried to drive the notion from her mind. Mr. Muir just laughed at her fears, and assured her that Mr. Urquhart would be perfectly safe; he was old enough and big enough to look after himself. But when six o'clock struck, and neither he nor Mr. Grant made an appearance, the farmer himself began to be uneasy. It would not take him long to walk back to the village, and he set off to see what kept them.

Elsie tried to busy herself with some sewing while waiting his return, but her fingers were too nervous for such delicate work, and her mind was filled with the wildest imaginings. What about Mr. Muckersie? She remembered, with a start, that she had seen him evidently making for the farm; yet he had not been here. Where else could he have been going? Perhaps Mr. Urquhart had met him on the moss. And then? She shuddered as she thought of this. No, no! That was too terrible to contemplate.

Again and again she went to the door, and listened for the sound of voices or approaching footsteps. But all was still; so still that she heard from the trees the frosty crickle of twigs, and, now and again, a low rumbling moan from the fettered loch.

There was a sense of impending catastrophe in the very air. The stars seemed all to be yearning over her when she stood at the open door, and there was an infinite pity in their gaze. She tried to throw the feeling off, and to laugh away her fears. The excitement of the day was still upon her, she told herself, and making her alive to the faintest sound. She was nervous; that was all. But something—instinct or some spiritual sense—was stronger than reason; and as the minutes passed, suspense became almost unbearable.

Mr. Muir had surely had time to go to the inn and return again; and yet there was no sign of him, no sound of voices, no beat of footsteps on the frosty ground. In this still air she could have heard them half-a-mile away; while Grant's high-pitched voice would have carried from the head of the Sandy Loan.

Suddenly the silence was broken. A piercing whistle clove through the darkness, flashing across her face in a shriek of agony; and then the silence closed round again, deeper than ever. But only for a second. The whistle was answered by voices, and, peering through the interlacing boughs, she saw glimmers of light waving over the middle of the moss.

She knew what that meant, and, for a moment, it was as if the fingers of death had clutched her heart. The noise of the boys clattering downstairs must have kept her from fainting.

"What's all the noise on the moss, Elsie?" they asked in a breath.

She did not answer, did not hear. Her eyes were fixed on the moving dots of light, and her thoughts were out on the moss.

"That was John Cochrane that whistled," Andrew affirmed. "He's the best whistler in the world."

In proof of which assertion, Andrew stuck his fingers into his mouth, and made a weak imitation.

A second whistle was heard, coming as in answer to Andrew's, which must have sounded faint no further off than the sun-dial.

"There," he cried exultantly; "he heard it, you see, and answered."

They heard the whistle again and again, at regular intervals, and the answering voices, and Andrew tried his best every time.

"It's Indians," Robert imagined. "They have surrounded him, and his comrades hear him across the prairie—or wolves."

The whistling had ceased now, and the lights were hidden.

"Perhaps he's tomahawked by this time," Robert continued.

"Ssh, boys!" said Elsie; "go in now." And she spoke so seriously that they were awed. "I shall walk down to the gate. I hear somebody coming now."

She was at the gate when Mr. Grant and John Cochrane came up.

"Don't be alarmed, Miss Austin," were Sandy's first words. "Mr. Urquhart has met with a slight accident, but he will be here presently. Mr. Muir says you might have the couch ready."

"He's no awfu' bad," John informed her, for he thought she looked frightened; "he's walkin himsel'. He walket half-way ower the moss wi' me."

Elsie turned to the house at once, and Sandy and John followed. Outwardly now, she was perfectly calm. There was work to be done, and she alone to do it. It was a relief to have something to do— anything, so long as she need not stand waiting helplessly, and wondering what could be wrong.

She led the way into Mr. Muir's sitting-room, and told them to wheel the couch round towards the fire.

"He fell and cuttet his head on his skates," John told her; "but I tied his hanky round it, an' it's a' richt again. It was bleedin' awfu'."

In a very little time everything was ready. John and the boys had brought a supply of coals, and a gigantic fire was roaring in the grate. The servant-girl saw that there was plenty of hot water, and had water-bottles ready; while Elsie herself brought blankets, and piled them on the couch. The room looked quite like a hospital ward when they had finished; and now they were awaiting the patient.

O

Andrew and Robert would be just in the way if
they remained, Elsie considered, and she asked them
to go upstairs again to their stories; while Grant,
now that he had a moment to himself, seized the
opportunity to consult his note-book.

"I have got quite a budget of words to-day," he
remarked; "most interesting words, and all new to
me. This is a splendid place for words. I had no
idea Urquhart had come into such a marvellous
place. You know," he declared quite confidentially,
"he used to bore me about the country. I thought
it was all nonsense; but, really, it is interesting and
attractive. I don't believe he was very far wrong,
after all, in coming here—if only he would take up
philology."

He looked at the book again, and made a note.

"But I wonder if that is right.   What is the proper
spelling of it—I mean the provincial spelling?"

He looked up from his book, and questioned
Elsie, who was standing with her arm resting on
the mantelpiece. Her face was very pale, even in
the ruddy firelight playing on it; but Sandy did not
notice.

"Red-wud," he explained.   "That old carrier fellow
said I was 'red-wud.' It's a peculiar word, isn't it?"

"That old carrier fellow?" Elsie asked, dreamily.
"Is Rob Buchan with them on the moss?"

It was evident from the tone that she had not
heard the question at all. Her ears had caught only
the words that had any interest for her at that
moment.

"An' the master ca'd me the 'Good Samaritan,'"
John broke in.

"Good Samaritan?" Elsie echoed, with more of

interest than before. "I think you deserve the name, John."

"But about 'red-wud,' Miss Austin?"

"I think you deserve it, too, Mr. Grant. John," she added, turning to him, "you might see if they are near yet."

John made for the door at once, and Sandy became again very interested in his note-book. He did not know the meaning of 'red-wud,' certainly; but Miss Austin had spoken so quietly, and yet so pointedly, that, without understanding why, he felt snubbed. Elsie left him to his meditations, and followed John.

When she got to the lawn she saw John, with his back to her, dodging about a corner of the sun-dial. He had not heard her approach; and she stood watching his manœuvres listlessly at first, then with a wild interest, when it flashed upon her what he was rehearsing.

"There!" he said, "tak' that!—an' that!" He launched out first with his right hand, then with his left, slashing at an imaginary foe lurking in the shadow of the sun-dial.

He was back again in position at once, his feet planted firmly, and his arms ready for action. His head lay on his shoulders as though he had no neck at all, and he taunted his antagonist to come on and get the same again.

"That ta'en the wind out o' ye, my man."

All the time he was speaking his head was dodging imaginary blows, and his arms were dealing death-strokes right and left.

"How d'ye like that, now—an' that? There! there! You would ca' her a name like yon! Have ye forgotten how Jock Jarvie stretched ye wi' a hay-fork for what ye ca'd him? Eh, my man, ye'll no seek that a second time."

Looking at him as he danced and capered, dodged, and dealt blows, Elsie could hardly help smiling, although every blow he delivered she felt like a stab.

But John was at it again, watching and sarcastically criticising every move of the enemy.

"Have you no ha'en enough yet? Oh, I see your game. Ye're gaun to run at me like a bull, are ye? Come on, then; I'm ready whenever ye like. Sheuch! Sheuch!"

Elsie turned away sick at heart, and crept back to the room. She understood it all now. She knew how Mr. Urquhart had met with his accident, and it was all her fault.

Even to Grant the change in her face when she entered the room again was apparent.

"Miss Austin!" he cried in alarm.

But she waved him back. "Let me alone," she moaned. "Go! There they are now. I hear them. I am all right. I will be all right."

She held her head up like a queen, and walked with a firm step to the door.

"Elsie—Miss Austin!" a weak voice whispered; and she laid her hand on his arm, taking him from their charge, and leading him in.

"Come," she said; "you shall rest here. See what a nice, comfortable couch I have ready for you."

"Thank you very much, Rob," she said, turning to them after Mr. Urquhart was within the room; "and Watty, and you, too, Donald."

They watched her, wondering. They had not

known that she was a woman till now. Her face was graver than they had ever seen it before; her whole bearing was more womanly and dignified. More striking than the excessive pallor of her cheeks was the expression of serenity which looked forth from her eyes and lay on her brow, speaking of an inward happiness and peace they could not comprehend.

And how was it that she should receive this young man from their hands, taking him into her keeping as one that had a perfect right?

Not only Rob and Watty, but Sandy even, must have been impressed, for he was silent, and helped Urquhart to take his boots off, without asking him a single question. John Cochrane hung in the background till he saw that he was no longer required, and then slipped away unseen.

Watty looked about him for a minute, like one trying to collect his scattered senses. Then he stole out of the room with a comical display of unobtrusiveness, walking on tip-toe, and dragging Donald with him.

"We're no fit to be inside there," he whispered in the lobby. "What a nasty smell thae lanterns set out!"

Rob lifted his cap reverently, and followed. This room was sacred in his eyes; he felt that he was treading on holy ground.

CHAPTER TWENTY-FIRST

THE OLD, OLD STORY

THE ten o'clock bell was ringing when Urquhart awoke next morning. His head was beating painfully where it had been cut, and he was tired and shaken. Otherwise he felt quite well. The stiffness and soreness had gone from his legs and arms already, and he could move them easily and without pain. As he lay watching the frosty sunlight lying in clear-cut lines across the carpeted floor, the events of yesterday came back to him, sharp and distinct, up to the fight. After that all was confused, like something that had happened to him in dream.

He had a hazy recollection of being led home, and of stretching himself out on the couch. Mr. Muir had helped him out of his coat, and Grant had taken off his boots. He remembered also lying half awake, half asleep, while the wound in his head had been bathed and bandaged. How gently and tenderly it had been done! He knew whose hand that was. Then he had been wrapped round and round in blankets, and had had hot water-bottles to his feet. Last of all, some one had brought him a tumbler of something delightfully warm, and he had drained it drowsily—falling asleep, it must have been, as he was drinking.

Yet surely there was something else. Or had he only dreamed it? Had not some one come just as he was falling asleep, and kissed his forehead? But no! That must have been only a dream. Yet, well, how pleasant to think it might be true!

It was not till he rose and walked to the window that he knew how weak he was. He felt little or no pain, however. All he wanted was to rest, and he sat down on the couch again, leaning back amongst the soft blankets. How luxurious it was just to recline like this, doing nothing, not even thinking! He must have fallen asleep again, for Mr. Muir was in the room when he opened his eyes.

" How is the invalid?" he asked cheerily. "Ready for breakfast, I hope."

Urquhart stood up, to show that he was all right. "I feel quite well," he answered, "only most unaccountably weak."

Mr. Muir smiled. "If you knew how much blood you had lost you wouldn't say 'unaccountably.' Get into this dressing-gown, and we'll go into the dining-room. The sight of your own coat would frighten you."

Urquhart felt the walk to the easy-chair wheeled close to the dining-room fire, quite long enough, and he was glad to sink amongst its cushions.

Mr. Muir placed a little table at his side. "See, here is something to tempt you to eat. Elsie has been experimenting in tit-bits all the morning."

Miss Austin herself now brought in tea, and sat down at the other side of the table. "We shall have *our* breakfast now," she said; "I couldn't get mine with Uncle and the boys."

"So busy with tasty dishes!" Mr. Muir commented.

Urquhart watched her while she filled the cups.

There was a delicate pink flush on her cheek as if twin rosebuds had left their reflection in the transparent skin, to remain there always. Her eyes were soft and liquid, brimming with untold dreams; and when she spoke, it was with a tremulous tenderness of tone that one imagines in the sound of a brooklet gurgling amongst grasses, or hears at times in the undertone of a sigh.

They hardly talked at all. It was a happiness just to be near each other. What need of words when each knew the other's thoughts? There was a happy secret known only to themselves, yet neither had whispered it, had hardly even given it a name.

When breakfast was finished and the table lifted away, Mr. Muir and the boys came in again before setting out for church.

"You're looking brighter and stronger already," Mr. Muir told him. "We'll be seeing you quite yourself again when we come back from church. Elsie will stay to look after you."

He laid his hand on her head and smiled on her. "I didn't know till last night she could be such a capital nurse."

"Who'll take her place at the harmonium?" Urquhart asked.

"Miss Mitchell will be delighted to perform. Nothing would please her better than to occupy Elsie's place altogether."

After they were gone Elsie went to the piano, and played and sang a few hymns very softly, until she knew by his regular breathing that Mr. Urquhart was asleep. Then she brought a footstool and sat down beside him, leaning her head where his hand

rested on the arm of the chair. The flames danced
and flickered, and she heard in their crooning the
song that was flooding her heart with music.

So it was, sitting so near to him, that Urquhart
saw her when he awoke. He laid his hand gently
on her hair, bending her head back till he could see
her eyes. She looked up into his face fearlessly,
proudly.

"Elsie," he whispered ; "Elsie !"

The flush deepened on her cheek, but she did not
speak. Only, by the slightest movement, did she
seem to draw nearer to him.

He leaned down and kissed her lips.

Her eyes were glowing, and she still kept them
fixed on his.

"Elsie," he whispered, "do you know what that
kiss means? Does it tell you my secret? Does it
say what I wished to tell you yesterday?"

Her answer was a sob — only in a sob could
the joy of her heart find expression. She reached
up and caught both of his hands in hers, laying her
face on them. Her breath came quick and warm,
and he felt her lips pressed to his fingers.

"Elsie," he whispered again ; "Elsie !"

"Say it," she breathed ; "say it to me. Let me
hear you say it."

"Say that I love you, Elsie? My heart would
say nothing else. I love you ; I love you ; I love
you. I have loved you ever since I saw you that
first Sabbath morning. I loved you when I did not
know it. And now my heart is so full that I can
hardly even tell you. But, Elsie, my love for you
is not everything. I wish to be loved as well."

"Have I not told you?" she asked, still holding

his hands to her face. She kissed his fingers again. "Is that not telling you, Mr. Urquhart?"

"Mr. Urquhart, Elsie!"

She laughed softly to herself. "Let me say it all by myself. Robert, Robert, Robert."

"I love you," he prompted.

She was silent for a second. "No," she said. "That is for you to say to me. I can only do it in my own way."

She lifted her face, still keeping hold of his hands, and, drawing him towards her, offered her lips.

He kissed her again and again.

"That's how I say it, Robert."

"Now," she said, leaning her head once more against the arm of the chair, "we shall be very quiet. Let me sit like this. I have something to say to you. Ssh! Don't speak yet."

For a few minutes they sat thus. His hand was laid on her head again, and his fingers trifled with her tresses. She did not change her position when she began to talk to him, but spoke self-communingly, watching pictures in the fire.

"It is all my fault that you were hurt," she said. "I did very wrong, I know; but I was so happy on the ice yesterday, and so proud. I knew I was loved. It was just because Mr. Muckersie was looking that I asked you to fasten my brooch. I wanted him to see, and—and it was wrong of me. I shouldn't have done it."

She felt his hand trying to press her head back, so that he might see her face, but she would not allow him.

"Please, Robert, not till I am done. No, don't interrupt me. Listen. I made him angry, and he waited to meet you, and you quarreled, and fought. It was all my fault. You fought about me. Oh, dear, I wonder if you will ever forgive me."

"Forgive you, Elsie? It is I who need your forgiveness. If you knew how ashamed I am of the whole miserable business, you would pity me and forgive *me*."

"But you are not ashamed of fighting for me, Robert?"

"No, Elsie. But I shouldn't have heeded him. He lied, like a coward, and I struck him in passion. I ought to have treated him and his calumny with the contempt both deserved. I simply degraded myself by touching him at all."

Without turning her head, she reached over and fondled his hand. "I am glad you struck him for me. I am not a flirt," she burst out vehemently. "He had no right to speak about me at all. I never have given him any encouragement to—to——. You know I haven't, Robert."

Urquhart's heart bounded with relief. She did not know the name Muckersie had called her, and his lips would never mention it, never.

"Tell me all about it," she said. "Did you beat him?"

"I don't believe he hit me once," he said musingly. "He was so blind with rage that he could no more fight than fly. I know he was dazed and bleeding before I tripped and fell; and skates don't make a comfortable pillow, Elsie."

"I'm glad you won."

"I don't think there was any winning for either side," he said, with a laugh. "You might put it we were both beaten."

"Isn't it strange I should love a teacher, after all?" she asked dreamily. "I used to detest them; and I don't do things by halves. When I dislike people, I dislike them seriously; and when I love them——"

"Yes, Elsie. You love them——"

"With my whole heart," she finished.

"But you had met rather an unfortunate lot," he told her; "certainly not to be taken as types of the teacher—in Edinburgh, or anywhere else. And you have grown out of such an absurd prejudice now."

"I don't know," she answered playfully. "You wouldn't have me fall in love with them all, would you?"

"Some of my best friends are teachers," he said; "and they are as fine fellows as you could wish to meet."

"But I don't want to meet fine fellows," she argued; "not now. I have got one teacher, and I don't want any more. Perhaps I shall be a very rebellious pupil—sometimes."

"And perhaps I may not be a teacher long, Elsie. I have had a long letter from a friend in London, which requires serious consideration; and this fight may help me come to a decision."

"Will you be a writer?"

"Perhaps. I have done some little in journalism, and I may go in for it now altogether."

"Will you go away to London?" she asked ruefully.

"I may, Elsie; but I shall come back again. You know that."

"Yes," she answered; but there was little of joyousness in the tone now.

"Don't speak any more about it yet," she pleaded; "You shall tell me again. Oh, why should you teach me to love you, only to go away and leave me?"

"Elsie, Elsie," he protested, "you mustn't put it in that way. How could I help loving you?"

"No; I shall not say that again, Robert, or you'll be vexed with me." She rose, and smiled down on him. "Now I shall leave you all by yourself. The church will be out presently, and Mr. Grant will be coming down to talk about words." She leaned over the chair, and touched his forehead with her lips. "There, I'm glad we had such a long talk before *he* came. Good-bye! I know you are wearying for a sleep again. Lazy boy!"

But he had not the chance of sleeping again. Elsie was hardly out of the room, when the servant announced the Misses Birrell and Mrs. Rae. The ladies came in, in a great state of excitement, and could hardly speak at first for joy at seeing the master so well. Grant's story had almost frightened them out of their wits; and they had come with faltering steps, expecting to hear that he was dangerously ill, perhaps unconscious, and unable to see them. Now here he was talking to them quite cheerily—paler than usual, no doubt, and weak, but still able to be up, and to receive visitors. They seated themselves around him, nodding and smiling upon him and upon one another; asking questions, and, when he attempted to answer, warning him not to speak.

Urquhart determined to confess everything to them at once, blaming himself entirely, and admitting no extenuating circumstance whatever. But when he told them he had been fighting, they refused to be shocked. He must be quiet, Mistress Janet told him, and not excite himself.

It wasn't his fault, Miss Agnes knew. He must have been compelled to fight in self-defence; while Mrs. Rae thought he must be very brave.

Urquhart had imagined that they would be horrified at the very name of fighting; and here they were smiling on him with unmistakable approval. It was quite a revelation to him that they took it so lightly.

Miss Austin entered the room as they were rising to go.

"Excuse me not coming in sooner," she apologised. "I thought you would like to see Mr. Urquhart alone. Don't you think I have made a very good nurse, Mistress Janet?"

The Misses Birrell regarded her bending over the chair, her young face beaming with happiness; and they observed how Mr. Urquhart looked up at her with an answering smile. What a lovely picture it was! Old maids though they were, they felt their own hearts—young in spite of their years—glowing in sympathy; for they knew instinctively that these two were lovers, and had already told each other the tale of their love. Miss Agnes touched her eyes with her handkerchief. She felt a little gulp at the throat, and a far-away memory came back to her of her own youth, and of one whom the gods had loved.

Mrs. Rae watched them earnestly and came over to Elsie's side. There was a strange look in her eyes as of one bewildered with dim, impalpable recollections.

"Elsie," she said, "Elsie! I remember your face; but it is all so blurred. Kiss me, Elsie."

Elsie regarded the poor lady with something of fear and something of pity, and, laying her hands on her shoulders, she leaned forward and kissed her. There was something in the face—she could not tell what—that attracted her strangely, yet she touched the lips with fear and trembling.

Mrs. Rae took Elsie's face in her hands and gazed on it scrutinisingly.

"I know, Elsie," she said, "you love him. Does he love you, Elsie?"

"Yes, Mrs. Rae"—quite in a whisper—"and I am so happy."

Leaving Elsie, she came and touched Mr. Urquhart's forehead with her lips. "Be kind to her," she said. "Yes, I know you will. But you'll go away now. Ah, I told you so. You'll both go away and leave me."

"See!" she cried, turning suddenly on Elsie, "here is my present for you."

She took from her neck a gold chain, drawing with it a locket which must have lain next her heart, and fastened it round Elsie's neck.

Elsie had evidently lost the power of speech. She thought she ought not to accept the gift, but Mrs. Rae fascinated her, and not a word either of thanks or refusal would come to her lips. Before she had recovered herself the visitors had gone.

Kneeling by the side of the chair, she took hold of her lover's hand, and looked up into his face. "What is wrong with me, Robert?" she asked. "What is wrong? There is something about her— I cannot tell—oh, I do feel so strange."

Urquhart stroked her hair and soothed her, till her nervousness was gone.

"You are too sensitive," he said; "and the gift was unexpected."

"That's not all, Robert. Oh, she looked at me so; and see, the locket is exactly the same as one I have which belonged to my mother; on the one side the monogram E. R. B., and on the other N. G."

She opened it and looked inside. "This one has a photograph, however, and mine is empty. I wonder if this is Mrs. Rae herself when she was young. I think it must be; it is very like her. Look, Robert."

"I think it is like my Elsie, strangely like," he said, "only not half so beautiful."

She closed the locket with a snap. She was quite herself again. "Now you are speaking flattery," she said, " and you mustn't, or else I shall —— "

"Shall what, Elsie?"

She rose and kissed him. "Here are the boys coming from church. Uncle will be here in a minute. Have you a long story to tell him, Robert? There!"

With a ripple of laughter she left him alone.

CHAPTER   *THE VOICE OF*
TWENTY-SECOND   *THE PARISH*

IT was not often that Kinkelvie had a fight to talk
about, and now that one had taken place, and
at its very door, so to speak, the village was stirred to
its depths. In the churchyard on the Sabbath
morning some vague rumour of it had drawn the
scattered knots of farmers, ploughmen, and shepherds,
into one compact crowd that the last toll of the
church bell could hardly bring into church. But no
one could speak with knowledge on the subject.
One had heard this, and another had heard that; it
was all hearsay together, and exaggeration. Balbingry's name was freely mentioned, however; so
was the master's; and when neither appeared at
church everybody knew at once that the fight had
been a very serious affair indeed. And why was
Miss Austin absent? Some of the members looked
very wise when they saw Miss Mitchell presiding at
the harmonium, and they complimented themselves
on their knowingness with a nod and a smile, or with
a deprecating shake of the head, according as they
regarded the fight from a romantic or a religious
standpoint.

When service was over they trooped out eager
to buttonhole Muiredge, but they were disappointed

For he was one of the first to leave, and was half
way home before the kirk had "skailed." That was
unusual with him, therefore suspicious; and the
tongue of gossip began wagging as vigorously and
as unsatisfactorily as ever.

After all their talk, they had to go home perplexed
and wondering. They had only heard enough to
make them wish to hear mc.e, and their curiosity
increased the longer it remained unsatisfied. Every
night that week brought its contingent to the village,
shepherds from the hills, and ploughmen from
outlying farms, all eager to hear, and all piously
hoping for sensational developments.

In the village it was the talk of the loom-shops.
and women discussed it at their pirn-wheels. For
this was no ordinary fight, like that between the herd
and the hagman from Saughton three years ago.
That had been merely a feeing-fair quarrel between
two men whom everybody knew to be rough tykes
at best; but a stand-up fight between a schoolmaster,
who was expected to be in all things an example to
others, and a farmer, who was a member of the
School Board, was a vastly different matter.

Miss Mitchell, of course, as behoved one in
her position, and as became a lady of refined and
delicate sensibility, was shocked, and took care to let
everybody know it. It was such a fearful thing for a
teacher to do. What an example to the boys! She
shouldn't wonder though the parents refused to
allow their children to attend school so long as he
remained schoolmaster. Example before precept,
you know! Then she would shake her head and
say the same thing over and over again.

She got little sympathy from her landlady, whom

she preached at every night after tea. Poor Mrs.
Gray felt that she was in a sense responsible for the
fight, and blamed the little schoolmistress for her
insinuating talk to Miss Muckersie on the Saturday
morning.

"I should have warned you not to talk to Miss
Muckersie as you did," she told her. "I knew she
would go and tell her brother every word you said;
and the Muckersies have always been a very bitter
family."

The schoolmistress only laughed.

"What if she did, Mrs. Gray? She was only
telling him the truth, which he was bound to learn
sooner or later. I think Mr. Muckersie was quite
right to interfere; and if Mr. Urquhart would fight,
it was his own fault, and he deserved all he got.
I have always considered him vulgar, and this only
proves it."

Mrs. Gray shook her head. She couldn't argue the
matter with such a clever talker as Miss Mitchell;
but though she was silenced she was not convinced.
It was a pity for the master, and she was sorry for
him. Mr. Muckersie must have provoked him or
he would not have fought, never! She was certain
of that.

"Ah, Mrs. Gray," the schoolmistress pityingly
observed, "you do not know Mr. Urquhart. Why,
the school is a different place already under his
friend Mr. Grant. He is so clever, and a perfect
gentleman!"

"And how is he able to take Mr. Urquhart's
place?" Mrs. Gray asked. "I thought you told me
he was a teacher in Edinburgh."

"Yes, but his school is closed for a week or two on

account of measles, and he came here to have a
holiday. A nice holiday!" she sniffed; "to have to
take up Mr. Urquhart's work for him! I should
have allowed him to find a substitute, or give up the
place altogether, as he ought to do if he had any
self-respect. I wonder he's not ashamed of himself.
As far as I hear, he's mooning about Muiredge
Farm, and perfectly well."

"Well, Mr. Muckersie's not."

Mrs. Gray evidently found consolation in this
reflection and spoke emphatically.

"More shame to Mr. Urquhart then! I'm afraid
I can't convince you, Mrs. Gray." She sighed profoundly. "I am sorry for you. You are bound to
see him in his true colours yet; and it is such a disappointment to find one we have respected to be
altogether unworthy. Truth will out, Mrs. Gray;
though sometimes it is hard to bear. I know."

When Miss Mitchell called on the Misses Birrell
to ventilate her feelings about fighting in general,
and to hint at the heinousness of Mr. Urquhart's
offending, in particular, she was dismayed to find
them as unsympathetic as her simple-minded landlady. She had always considered the Misses Birrell
models of propriety, and it was a sad disillusion to
find them so callous in respect of a matter of such
gravity.

They had just finished tea when she entered, and
she drew out her invariable scrap of crochet, and
set herself for a comfortable chat. But the Misses
Birrell were not so meek and mild as Mrs. Gray, and
she had to talk warily. They were not persons
whom she might hope to dominate by sheer emphasis
of opinion.

"Isn't it terrible, Mistress Janet?" she asked, speaking with an affected emotion.

Mistress Janet looked at her and smiled.

"Not so very terrible, Miss Mitchell."

"Oh, I'm so glad you take it so lightly!" she said, with a sigh of relief. "You know," she explained, "I thought——" And then she stopped to examine her crochet.

"Yes, Miss Mitchell?"

"I thought," she ventured, as if she were now speaking in the strictest confidence; "I thought you would be so shocked."

"Oh, dear, no!" Miss Agnes treated the matter quite airily.

And Mistress Janet smiled with great serenity. "Not in the least!" she corroborated.

Miss Mitchell knitted a while in silence before replying. She must strike out on a new tack, she saw.

"You know I took it quite to heart; really, Mistress Janet, I thought it so serious."

"But he is quite well," Miss Agnes told her calmly. "He'll be back in school in a day or two."

The conversation was not turning as the school-mistress wished; the Misses Birrell were somewhat obtuse. She smoothed the crochet on her knee and talked to herself this time.

"I think fighting is such a terrible thing." She gave a little shudder. "Don't you think so, Mistress Janet? And so—so vulgar, Miss Agnes!"

"Indeed!" This was Miss Agnes's favourite word when she was annoyed. "Then it's a very vulgar world we live in, Miss Mitchell; and this is the most vulgar country in it."

Mrs. Rae looked up from the sofa where she had been listening.

"I think it was very noble of him," she averred. He fought for Elsie."

"Ah!" sighed the little schoolmistress; "poor Miss Austin! Fancy her name in everybody's mouth now; and people will be sure to couple her name with his too."

"And an excellent couple, I should think," was Mistress Janet's opinion.

Miss Mitchell sighed.

"Oh, I shouldn't like to think anybody had fought about me."

Miss Agnes was getting angry by this time.

"Is there any likelihood of that, Miss Mitchell?"

"I should hope not; I should sincerely hope not."

"And I should think not!" Miss Agnes smiled on her visitor quite benignly. "So there's no use citing improbabilities, is there, Miss Mitchell?"

After that little more was said. The schoolmistress discovered that it was getting late, and she remembered she had some work waiting her at home.

"Mr. Urquhart hasn't fallen in love with *her*," Miss Agnes remarked after their visitor had gone, "and a good thing too!"

In her insinuating way, Miss Mitchell tried to prejudice others in the village against Mr. Urquhart, but with little success. The Muckersies, of Balbingry, had never been favourites with the villagers, nor even with their own servants, and there were few to put in a kind word for the farmer now. He had been defeated in a stand-up fight, in which, most probably, he had been the aggressor. That he had got the worst of it there could be no doubt now, for he had not been seen since Saturday afternoon, and the doctor from Milnforth had been at the farm twice since then. Mr. Urquhart had been victorious. There could be no mistake about that, and it was reasonable they should look upon him as a hero, after he had beaten a man of Muckersie's weight and build.

Every night in the week when the men met at the Inn, and argued the matter out professionally, they arrived at the same conclusion, and the verdict was not in Balbingry's favour. Nor were the women inclined to be too severe, even on a teacher, for fighting, when they considered the cause of the quarrel. For, of course, Balbingry and the master were rivals, and had fought about Miss Austin. That raised the fight to the level of romance.

It was Saturday night, however, before the fight was fully and finally thrashed out. Then the back-room of the Inn had a gathering worthy of the subject. There were ploughmen from Balbingry, from Muiredge and Saughton; from Waughmill, and one representative even from the Bowhouse. Jabez Orrock, the smith from Balgowrie, looked in; two herds from Glenpow; and last, but not least, the policeman for the parish.

There was other interesting news to be talked about; for everyone entered the room holding a little handbill, which Old Mousie the beadle was delivering into the hands of all who passed his door. This bill announced an evening service on the Sunday following, when the Rev. Mr. Gordon, from Carse-cowden, would preach a Christmas sermon. Now, a Christmas sermon was a novelty, almost an innova-tion, in Kinkelvie; and evening services were un-

common enough to excite curiosity when they did
come. But a fight was more uncommon still, and,
for unsophisticated folks, had more of human interest
than a sermon in prospective. The visitors, as they
dropped in, gave a glance at the handbill, and folded
it away in their waistcoat pockets. Their wives,
perhaps, would be interested in this; they were met
to consider a weightier matter.

Ian McLeod, the police constable—and not merely
for the village, but for a whole parish—was a person
of authority in a meeting like this, and he took the
chair at the head of the table. Yet, while fully
cognisant of the honour that was due to him, Ian
was a cautious man. Wherefore, he doffed the
constable-cap and unbuttoned his tunic, to let it be
understood that anything he might say was to be
accepted from him in an unofficial capacity. The
others filled the benches alongside the table, or
swung their legs from the high window-sill. Donald
himself sat nearest the door, for easy access to the
bar as occasion required.

"Ye'll no be gaun to mak' a case o' it, will ye?"
Donald asked, to open conversation, after having
seen that all glasses were charged.

Ian regarded his glass meditatively, and sampled
its contents. This was not a question to be answered
off-hand, and he must talk discreetly.

"Well, you see," he began, speaking with a decided
Highland accent, that his long stay in the village
had not in the slightest toned down. "You see, it is
just this. What is the precise charge? I know
something about law"—which he pronounced 'lah'
—"having been twenty-five year, come the sevent'
day of Aprile, Her Majesty's police constable."

"Is it a' that, Ian?" the smith asked. "Ay, an' a young man yet."

"And twenty-wan years of that time," Ian continued, "have I peen in this parish; and there's not another police constable in the county can say so much, or half so much."

"You're richt there," Donald answered. "The first I saw o' ye was at the doctor's funeral, an' that's twenty-wan year past last term. It was a grand funeral, yon. We ha'ena seen the like o' it i' the parish since syne."

"And so," the policeman concluded, "I should know something about law—more especial the law as pertaining to this parish."

He looked round the company, to see if there might be anyone who would say him nay; but the company nodded, to a man, and moistened its lips.

"Then that prings me to the point of my argument, lads."

Ian leaned forward, and, grasping his glass with his left hand, he stretched out his right as far as he could reach, so that, resting his elbow on the table, he could work the forearm through forty-five degrees of emphasis.

"What is the charge?" he asked. "What are we to call it?"

"I would ca' it a fecht," Saughton's herd considered; "neither mair nor less; an' a braw ane, if a' stories be true."

"Ah, but that is just where my knowledge of the law comes in! The law does not recognise fights at all; it will not commit for fights; for a fight is no charge. What can we call it, then, to pring it within the law? Preach of the Peace? The fight was in a lonely spot, in a retired place, where they disturbed nobody but their two selves. So it is, I do not think you can call it Preach of the Peace. What remains, then?"

"But do ye mean to say," Jock Jarvie, a burly, six-foot specimen, asked, "that if I was to gang to 'e hill-tap, an' fecht Tam here, the law couldna lay a hand on me?"

Tam Lowden took his pipe from his teeth, and spat contemptuously. "To 'e hill-tap to fecht? I wouldna gang ae fit. So what comes o' your argument now, Jock?"

"They gaed to the Muiredge Wood to fecht it out," struck in Jabez Orrock, who was a known poacher. "Could ye no mak' it a case o' trespassin' in pursuit o' game? The game doesna need to be specified."

Ian thought the smith was not treating the question seriously, and he did not answer. He hoped to argue out that case some day with Jabez, elsewhere. He was biding his time.

"There is only one other charge," he announced, "and that is Assault and Pattery. If you, Jock, thrashed Tam, then it is within Tam's power to have you summoned for Assault and Pattery. Or if Tam thrashed you——"

"Thrashed me?" Jock exclaimed. "Tak' a look at the twa o' us, man, an' no blether nonsense."

"I am taking a case just for the sake of argument," Ian began to explain.

"But we're past arguin' by this time," Jock interrupted; "an' fechtin' it out wi' closed nieves at 'e hill tap. I'll allow Tam'll lick me in arguin', for he's a glib-tongued deevil; but no in a stand up fecht. No, no!"

"Still, if Tam did by chance thrash you," Ian persisted, "then it is within your power to take him up for Assault and Pattery."

"De'il the fear o' me, Ian. I would just tak' it out o' his skin."

The door opened, and Watty Spence joined the company. Room was found for him next the policeman. If he did not know as much about law as Ian, he, at least, knew more about this particular fight, and so was accorded a place of honour.

"I was just saying," the policeman explained, "that your friend Mr. Urquhart, which is a beautiful Highland name, might summon Balbingry for Assault and Pattery."

"Is it no mair likely to be the other way about?" Watty asked. "Here's the master been back i' the school twa days, an' lookin' as well as ever. But Ba'bingry's no able to be out ower the door yet. Will it no be Ba'bingry that'll summon the master for assault and battery?"

Jock Jarvie laughed aloud.

"Na, na," he cried; "he's ower proud. He has gotten a thrashin' an' he'll say nothing about it. He has never fashed me since the day I stretched him wi' a hay-fork."

"Then," the policeman concluded, with judicial gravity, "if it be so that Balbingry will not move, nor your friend neither, the one to summon the other, there can be no case. It is not Preach of the Peace, and it is not Assault and Pattery neither. No case, Donald! I haven't had one since July Fair fifteen year."

"The next question is," Jabez Orrock announced, "if the law canna lay a hand on them, 'What is the School Board gaun to do?' They canna let the matter pass. It's the clash o' the countryside by this time, an' they're bound to tak' notice o' it. They'll gi'e him his leave as sure as guns is iron."

"An' what about Ba'bingry himsel' in that case?" Donald asked. "He's as bad; an' he's a member o' the Board. If the master has to shift, they should shift him as weel."

Jock Jarvie scratched his head. "Ay, Donald, ye have them there. That'll be a kittle question for them to settle. Ay man, I never ta'en thought o' that."

"It's a complicated case," the policeman admitted.

"They'll gi'e them both another chance," Saughton's herd surmised.

"To fecht again?" Jock exclaimed. "Ba'bingry'll no tak' it. It's aince beaten aye cowed wi' him."

"Fechtin' wi' a common, ordinary man is bad enough," Tam Lowden argued, "but fechtin' wi' a Board, or a Committee, is ten times waur; an' they'll gi'e him his leave on the spot. If he'd come off second best they micht ha'e looket ower it, but it maun be a sair downcome to them to get the warst o' it."

"Ye're speakin' about things ye ken nothing about," Watty informed them. "The matter's settled a'ready; an' the Board'll no ha'e the chance o' dismissin' him. Mr. Urquhart has gi'en up his place, himsel', an' he'll be out o' this in a month's time."

This bit of news fell on the company like a thunder-clap. Nobody ventured to speak for a time.

They knew Watty had been with the master that afternoon ; and what he said must be true.

"Aweel, it's a damned shame," some one muttered, and the remark was accepted without protest.

"He's leavin' the teachin'-way a'thegether," Watty continued ; "an' ye dinna ken what ye've lost. Here was a man that was an honour to the toun, a writer o' stories an' poetry, an' we canna keep him amon' us three months."

"Writes stories?" Donald ejaculated. "Man, man! An' he looket a douce, decent chap too. I thocht it was the other ane, Mr. Grant, that followed that line. Ye mind how he havered here last Saturday."

"No to be compared!" Watty grunted.

"Ay, ay!" Jock Jarvie moralised. "That explains the fecht now. Thae writin' chaps, they tell me, are a bad lot. I've heard about some awfu' ongauns they ha'e in London."

"An' what would ye ha'e done yoursel', Jock?" came a voice from the window. It was the ploughman from the Bowhouse who spoke. "I had the story frae John Cochrane, that saw the fecht frae beginning to end. An' d'ye ken what Ba'bingry ca'd her afore the master ga'e him atween the e'en?"

"I wouldna wonder but what it was the same name as he ca'd mysel'," Jock complacently observed.

"It just was, Jock. An' can ye wonder at the master takin' the Miss's part?"

"He ca'd me an ugly name, no doubt," Jock reflected with the utmost composure, "but I ca'd him ower."

Watty Spence had risen to his feet, and the eyes

of all were now on him. His face was livid, and his eyes were blazing. "What did ye say?" he cried. "Did Ba'bingry ca' the Miss a——a——. Wha *telled* him? Wha telled *him*?" He shook his trembling fist at the company, and sank again into his chair. "I'm makin' a fool o' mysel'," he apologised.

"Ye are that," Jock told him, "to tak' ony o' Ba'bingry's ill names in earnest. It's a failin' wi' the family. Downbye, they have only twa kinds o' folk i' the world, an' they're either Ba'bingries or Bastards. It's just their way; an' the auld runt o' a sister is as ill-tongued as himsel'."

Watty accepted the explanation with a sigh of relief. "That'll be it," he agreed. "I spoke without thinkin'."

"I've heard him say mysel'," Donald corroborated, "that the sister—that's Miss Elsie's mother—was never married to the pictur'-man ava'; an' that was the way she never looket near Muiredge again."

"Weel," was Watty's answer—emphasised with a blow on the table that made the glasses ring—"he telled a damned lie; an ye can fling that in his teeth the next time ye see him. Now, I'll say Guid nicht, chaps; I'll need to be stappin'. I was expectin' to see Rob in the nicht, Donald."

"He was hame frae Edinburgh afore seven," Donald answered; "an' he spak about lookin' in."

"We'll be seein' ye at the kirk the morn's nicht, Watty," Jabez Orrock called to him as he was going out. "Ye'll ha'e seen the bill?"

Watty took the bill handed to him. "No, I haena seen the announcement, though I heard some word o' a Christmas service. Some big gun, no doubt?"

He read the bill, and stood staring at it for almost a minute.

"Can ye no mak' it out, you that's sic an awfu' reader?" Jabez asked.

Watty moistened his lips, but he spoke quite huskily when he answered. "Mr. Gordon, o' Carse-cowden! Ay!"

"We'll be seein' ye there, then?"

"Ay, Jabez, it's likelys I'll be there. God willin', I'll be there."

CHAPTER TWENTY-THIRD

MARG'ET

WHEN Rob Buchan returned from Edinburgh on Saturday afternoon he had told Donald that he might look in that evening, and gladly would he have come for an hour or two, not to talk, not even to listen, but merely that he might sit silent amongst a company of talkers. For Rob had a terrible task to perform, and he would have been thankful for an hour's respite. Yet he did not dream of shirking it, or seeking any means of escape from doing it. He regarded it as a solemn duty imposed upon him, and it would try him sorely. He might be the better of a night's rest, he reasoned; and on the Sunday morning he would nerve himself to its performance. In the back room of the Inn, surrounded by talkers who would let him sit undisturbed in their midst, the hours would not drag so slowly, he thought; and bedtime would come to him more quickly there than if he sat wearily waiting for it at his own fireside.

But when he reached home he found that his task was not to be postponed. It must be done now or never.

Barbara had his tea ready for him as usual, and everything looked as bright and inviting as ever; but she explained that she could not wait, and that he must take his tea alone. She had just hurried along from Marg'et's bedside, to have everything ready for his return.

"The doctor was here this afternoon," she said; "an' she's no expected to see ower the nicht. She's no so shaken wi' the cough now, for the breath comes easier the nearer she draws to the end; but she's wearyin' to see you, an' hear news o' Frank."

Rob drew his sleeve across his eyes, and groaned aloud. What a terrible ordeal he had to go through!

Barbara laid her hands on his shoulder. "Is he no comin' the nicht?" she asked. "Is he no comin', after you tellin' him she was on her deathbed?"

"I haena seen him at a'," the old man confessed wearily. "Bauby, Bauby, dinna speir ony mair. It wasna for want o' seekin' for him."

"Has he left the town? Father! father! what has happened him?"

"Nothing has happened him that he hasna brought on himsel'. He's safe an' sound, as far as I ken—in body, at least."

She kneeled by the side of his chair, and clasped his knees.

"Father!"

"Bauby, my bairn, dinna tak' on like that. I canna tell ye mair. Ye'll learn a' soon enough. Oh, Bauby, dinna speir. Gang awa' alang, like a good bairn. I'll just drink a cup o' tea, an' follow ye."

She rose, threw a shawl over her head, and went out.

Left alone, Rob lifted down the family-bible, and laid it on the table; but he did not open it. Perhaps his mind was too agitated for reading; or it may be that while he sat with his head bowed on its covers

Q

he was pouring out his heart in silent prayer. Any-how, it did him good ; and if his eyes were still troubled when he raised his head again, his face was more composed, and he looked like one fortified against evil. He had set himself resolutely to do his duty, however hard it might be, and there would be no backsliding now.

Having filled out a cup of tea—strong, and, by this time, half cold, he took it at a draught.

"Now," he said to himself, "I maun see the master about this, an' we'll gang alang thegether."

Urquhart, who had just returned from seeing Grant off to Edinburgh again, was busily writing when Rob was shown into the room, and the look in the old man's face went to his heart. He rose and pointed him to a chair which Rob, without a word, lifted to the table, and sat down.

The room had been silent enough before he entered ; but now to Urquhart it seemed that the silence had deepened, until he could hear the sound of his own breathing. The ticking of his watch on the mantelpiece became almost painful ; and he heard the eerie sound of shivering twigs outside the window. He noticed that the fire was burning low, and he rose and broke it up into a cheerful blaze ; and yet the room felt strangely still.

"Marg'et's sinkin' fast," Rob observed, in a passionless voice ; "it's no likely she'll see ower the nicht. I thought you might gang alang wi' me, and see her afore she slips awa'. She thinks a by-ordinar' lot o' you," he added, as if to show reason for his request.

"You were to see Frank, to-day," Urquhart observed. "Is he coming by Inverorr to-night ?"

"He 'll no be here this nicht, Mr. Urquhart; if ever he be here again."

Urquhart looked at him, and his voice fell to a whisper. "What do you mean, Rob?"

For answer, Rob drew out some letters from his pocket, and laid them on the table.

"What am I to understand from these, Rob?"

"Frank has left his lodgin'," the old man explained. "I didna see him; an' that's a' he left ahent him; an' this——"

He put down a pass-book beside the letters.

"But these are all letters addressed to Frank himself, Rob."

"Ay, an' we 'll open them atween us."

"Open them?" Urquhart echoed, in surprise.

"Ay," Rob answered, in a monosyllable.

"But, Rob, this is a very strange thing to do; a—a criminal thing. Are you aware of what you are proposing?"

"I 'm aware o' what this is," Rob answered, touching the pass-book. "It 's the bill for his lodgin', an' it stands at seven pound odds. Can ye no mak' a guess at the others?"

"Bills?" Urquhart murmured faintly.

"Weel, we can look an' see."

"But what of Frank himself?" Urquhart asked, with something of fear in his voice.

Rob put down the letter he had been about to open, and looked steadily on the younger man.

"Francis Downie," he said, in a tone of hopeless resignation, "has 'listed."

Urquhart leaned back in his chair, sick at heart.

"'Listed!" Rob repeated.

"What an end! What an end!" Urquhart burst out.

"If it be the end! God grant it may be but the beginnin' o' a new life."

"It will break his father's heart, Rob."

"It may be a God's blessin' it 's ower late to break his mother's."

"And could you not see him at all?"

"No. The regiment he 's 'listed in is lyin' at the Castle; but Frank himsel' is packed aff to some station i' the North."

"Did he not leave any word?"

"Only a scrap to say he 'd disgraced himsel' an' a'body belangin' him, an' wanted to be forgotten. God grant that that be but a sign o' grace. His regiment 's ordered foreign soon—India or Africa, I forget; an' the young anes—the recruits—are bein' prepared for the journey. Let us see what we have here now, Mr. Urquhart."

They opened the letters one by one. They were all bills.

The first Urquhart opened was from Richard Wyllie. "He wants seven pounds," he read out to Rob. "He cannot claim it legally, he says; but it is a debt of honour."

"A debt of honour!" Rob growled. "Into the fire wi' it! Into the fire wi' it, this minute! A debt o' dishonour an' shame that it 'files the fingers to touch!"

Urquhart took the others and summed them up. "Seventeen pound, three, and fivepence," he said. "I don't believe Michael has that sum in his possession."

"We 'll no ask him for a penny," Rob answered, gathering the bills together; "but they 'll be paid to the uttermost farden my next journey."

"I shall certainly give a little, Rob; but I can't give much. You know the life I'm going to launch out on in London is a very precarious one, and the little I have saved I shall need to take with me."

"I ken ye would gi'e willingly, sir, if I needed it; but we'll manage. Watty an' me'll manage this atween us — no that I need even Watty's, but he would tak' it ill if he was to be left out."

"But I can give a little," Urquhart protested.

"No," Rob told him decidedly. "It wasna to ask ye for onything that I brought them here; but I couldna face the responsibility o' openin' them mysel'. Now, sir, we have other wark afore us, an' a sair job it'll be. We have to break this news to Marg'et afore she gangs."

Urquhart started from his chair. "Rob, Rob, you're not going to do that?"

"It has to be done," Rob answered quietly; "an' wha else is there to do it?"

"I can't, Rob, I can't; spare me inflicting pain on that noble woman."

"Mr. Urquhart," Rob addressed him solemnly, "I'm no gaun i' my ain strength, or I would cry out against it mysel'. I've seen this afore me a' day, an' my heart has been cryin' out, 'Spare me, spare me.' But Marg'et's waitin' for it, an' that's a' she's waitin' for now. Will ye no gang wi' me an' help me?"

Urquhart put on his overcoat and hat without a word. "Come," he said, screwing down the light; "I'll go with you."

When they entered the room they saw Marg'et sitting up in bed propped round with pillows, for only in such a position could she breathe at all.

Michael sat at the bedside, his hand resting fondly
on that of his wife; but his eyes were vacant, as if
he heard and saw nothing.   Only by a caressing
movement of the hand now and again did he show
he was conscious of what was passing round him, or,
at least, of what was passing away from him, out of
his life.

Barbara, who had opened the door when she heard
their footsteps outside, set chairs for them close by
the bedside; but they preferred to stand.

Rob took off his cap, and looked earnestly at the
wasted figure on the bed.   What a change from the
Marg'et he had known for so many, many years!
She was changed indeed, but beautiful still; yet the
radiance of her face was not of this world, and her
eyes glowed with a spiritual light.   But there was
the same scrupulous cleanliness and neatness about
her now, on the brink of the grave, that had made
her a name among neighbours through all the years
of her life.   The linen was spotlessly white, and the
convolvulus frills of the cap she wore looked as if
they had come that minute from the Italian iron.
Michael appeared not to have noticed their entrance.

"My Frank, Rob!" the dying woman whispered.
"My Frank! Is he comin' afore I gang?"

Urquhart could see Rob's lips twitching, and the
veins standing out like cords on his temples; but
when he spoke, it was in the same steady, passionless voice.   To Urquhart it sounded like the voice
of Fate.

"Frank'll no be here, Marg'et.   He canna win to
see ye.   He has putten his hand to the plough, an'
there's no lookin' back; no, neither for father nor
mother."

Old Michael looked up, catching at the words, and spoke like one answering mechanically to his cue. "No man having put his hand to the plough, and looking back, is fit for the kingdom of heaven."

Then he let his head drop on his breast again, and took no notice.

" But, my Frank!" came the voice from the bed. "Am I no to see him an' bless him afore I gang? I 'm gaun on my lang journey, Rob ; my lang journey."

" He canna come, Marg'et. Had it been the Lord's will, I would ha'e brought him to your bedside; but it wasna to be. Frank 's preparin' for a lang journey as weel. It may be to the heathen cities o' India, or the plains o' far-awa' Africa, whaur the name o' God 's unkent."

" India ? Africa ? "

Marg'et's eyes looked larger and brighter than ever in the pallid sunken cheeks.

"Bauby, Bauby," she cried, "bring me the book ye were wont to read thegether as bairns. The third on the tap shelf, Bauby. India? Africa? To heathen lands, Rob ? "

" Heathen lands, Marg'et."

Barbara brought the book and laid it down beside the wasted hand. It was the lives of Moffat and Livingstone. Urquhart turned away with a sob. This was terrible.

" My Frank, Rob!" she said again, fondling the book. " He hath chosen him to be a soldier."

" A soldier!" Rob echoed brokenly.

" My heart yearned to see my laddie, Rob ; but he canna come, an' it would be wrang o' me to complain. Rather should I cry out in thankfulness o' spirit, 'Lord, now lettest Thou Thy servant depart in

peace.' For what saith our Lord himsel', Rob?
'There is no man who hath left house, or parents,
or —— ' "

She lay back among the pillows and closed her
eyes.

"Father," Barbara whispered, frightened at his
stricken face. "Father, leave her now. She's sair
needin' rest. Tak' him hame, Mr. Urquhart. Tak'
him hame."

Rob stepped to the bedside, and bending over,
kissed Marg'et's wasted hand. Then he patted
Michael on the head, as he would have patted a
bairn. "Mich'el, Mich'el, Mich'ellie! Poor auld
Mich'el!" he muttered.

Urquhart could stand no more. He stuck his
handkerchief in his mouth and stole downstairs.

"The good Lord forgi'e me! God forgi'e me!"
Rob repeated again and again, when he was in the
open air. "God forgi'e me for deceivin' her, Mr.
Urquhart; for I didna try to deceive her, an' she's
gaun awa' so proud o' her son an' so pleased. God
forgi'e me."

But Urquhart could say nothing at all.

"After a'," he went on, "it may be the Lord's
doin'. He may ha'e so putten the words in my
mouth just to ease the wa-gaun o' a faithfu' servant.
For I didna gang i' my ain strength, as I telled ye;
but I lippened to Him to put in my mouth what I
was to say."

When they reached Rob's door, Urquhart bade
him good-night, and set out for a long walk. The
scene had been too much for him, and he was too
excited to sit quietly at home that night. And so it
was that the saddest sight of all he missed. For

just as twelve o'clock was striking, Rob's door
opened, and Michael entered, bareheaded; his
sparse grey locks looking as if some wild wind had
been blowing about them.

Rob, who sat dozing in his chair waiting for
Barbara, started up in fear.

"Mich'el, Mich'el," he cried, taking the old man by
the shoulders, "calm yoursel', calm yoursel', Mich'el!"

"She's awa'," said Michael quietly; "an' she gaed
wi' his name on her lips an' his book in her hand."

"Poor Mich'el! Poor auld Mich'el!"

"But, Rob, what was that about India and
Africa?"

"God forgi'e me, Mich'el! God forgi'e me. I
didna mean that."

"Ay, Rob; the Lord has forgi'en ye a'ready, an' I
forgi'e ye; for Marg'et passed peacefu'."

"Mich'el, Mich'el, it's awfu'."

"A soldier, I heard ye say," Michael continued
calmly. "It's in the blood, Rob. He's gaun the
gate o' his uncle afore him; an' what an end was his!
Ay, Rob, ye deceived her, but ye didna deceive me.
I saw it i' your face when ye cam' in. I saw it
plainer i' the face o' the master, though he never
spak' a word."

He stopped and lifted a pathetic face to Rob's—
pathetic in its unnatural calmness.

"Frank has 'listed, Rob?" he whispered.

"Ay!"

"Marg'et's gone an' Frank's 'listed. An' I'm o' no
mair use i' the world. Guid nicht, Rob."

He turned and tottered again to the door.

Rob sank into his chair and, strong man as he was,
sobbed aloud.

CHAPTER
TWENTY-FOURTH

MRS. RAE
REMEMBERS
A RHYME

URQUHART sat in his room on the Sunday afternoon, doing little but smoking and thinking. He had tried to read after dinner, but had to close the book. Now his thoughts were of his own affairs; now they were of Michael Downie, as he had seen him the night before, sitting like one in a trance, and fondling his dying wife's hand. He saw the picture of Rob standing in the agony of his stern sense of duty, talking to Marg'et of her son, yet merciful in spite of himself. But the picture that came and blotted out all the others was the face of Elsie Austin. When he looked on her face there was no room in his mind for any other picture.

He drew the easy chair up close to the fire, and gave himself over to reverie, dreaming of the past and planning for the future.

If he turned his head towards the window he could see, over the village and across fields, the dark patch of wood which hid the homestead of Muiredge, and in thought he lived over again the blissful Sunday forenoon when he had told her of his love, and he had heard her syllable his name.

He had just parted with her, having gone round by the farm from the church, and she had walked

with him as far as the old saugh tree, where the
Sandy Loan bent in towards the moss.   Yet his
thoughts, as he sat gazing into the fire, were not so
happy as the thoughts of an accepted lover ought to
be.

He had made up his mind to leave Kinkelvie.
His resignation was already sent in, and there was
no going back on it now.   How long he would be
away after he left the village he did not know; a
year, perhaps more ; and all that time he would be
afar from the woman he loved.

He also saw clearly enough how Elsie, even
though she approved of his going away, and
entered so heartily into his plans, dreaded the
thought of separation.   He had talked with her of
what he expected to do in London ; of his chances
of succeeding ; and she, listening, saw the future far
brighter than he painted it ; for she was in love with
him, and believed in him.

But if he happened to mention casually the date
of his departure, she looked at him so wistfully that
he could not bear to say more.

" Don't," she would say ; " don't say more.   It will
come too soon, and I shall be desolate.   It is strange,"
she had told him that very day.   " Had you never
come here at all, I should have been perfectly light-
hearted and gay.   Now I am changed, happier, with
a happiness that is new and wonderful to me; but I
don't know what I shall do when you go away.   I
shall miss you awfully, Robert.   Let us be happy as
long as you are here, and forget about your going
away altogether."

It was not without earnest and anxious consideration that Robert Urquhart had decided to throw up

his situation as teacher, and to embark on the somewhat precarious craft of journalism.   He was not
one of those raw youths who imagine that all they
have got to do is take a ticket for London, and
thereafter their fortune is assured.   The first article
they write will be accepted, and, once they have
appeared in all the glory of print, editors will be
outbidding one another for the favour of their con-
tributions.

He knew young men who had gone to London
and come back again poorer and wiser men; he
knew of others who had gone and had not come
back.   Whether they were there still, or whither
they had drifted, who could tell?   Robert Urquhart
knew well enough that the streets of London are not
paved with gold; but he also knew that he had a
certain capacity for hard work; and he put his trust
in that.

Then of late he had been becoming more and
more dissatisfied with the work of teaching in an
elementary school.   There was something radically
wrong with the whole system, he had come to think,
and the Code was a monumental failure.   Neither
teacher nor pupil had a chance under it.   It crushed
the life out of the one; it dwarfed and stunted the
whole nature of the other.   The old parochial system,
which he was old enough to remember, had not concerned itself so much with reading, writing, and
arithmetic, perhaps, but it turned out men and
women.   The whole aim of the present system was
to turn out machines—calculating machines, geographical machines, reading machines, but machines in
very truth, and generally defective.

He had never at any time been in love with the

Code; it was too hard and fast; there was too much
of system and science about it; but it was only of
late that he had come to regard it as a great educa-
tional blunder. His eyes had been opened wider to
the defects of the system since he came to Kinkelvie;
for in Edinburgh he had traced all its evils to the
gigantic schools; now he was discovering that these
evils were inherent in the nature and constitution of
the Code. He was tired of teaching under a cast-
iron system that was daily becoming more and more
distasteful to him.

But what could he turn to if he gave up teaching?
There was only one thing he could think of, and that
was journalism. To this he had been, in a sense,
serving an apprenticeship for years, devoting all his
leisure to writing both for the daily Press and for the
more pretentious monthly magazines.

Then, certain things had happened, which, considered singly, might not have had much weight with
him, but taken together, had determined his decision.
First of all, Crombie had gone to London, and Kaye
with him. Crombie, certainly, had gone to a situation
where he had a fixed salary, but in a long letter to
Urquhart he had urged him to throw up teaching
altogether and come to London too, even though he
came merely as a free lance. He could guarantee
him a little work every week on *The Docket*. " I am
nominally assistant editor," he said ; " but practically
editor." It might be a very small beginning, but in
time he could work up a connection with other
papers. All that was needed was a start; and that,
Crombie could assure him.

On the heels of Crombie's letter had come an intimation that his novel was accepted, and, if he agreed

to the terms offered, would be published in the Spring. The terms, as far as Urquhart was able to judge, were very fair, and if the book had anything like a sale, he was bound to make some money by it.

Last of all, there had been the fight. That, more than anything else, had led him to send in his resignation to the School Board and turn his back on teaching. He knew well enough that after a fight which had been the talk of the parish, he could never have the same standing as formerly in the eyes of the douce folk of Kinkelvie. The school children themselves would not now regard him with the respect a schoolmaster ought to command.

Moreover, he preferred resignation to dismissal; and it was as likely as not, if he did not resign, that the School Board would dismiss him. If they did dismiss him—and they would be quite justified in doing so—he knew that he could have no appeal against them.

These were the considerations that had led him to sever his connection with the School Board of Kinkelvinwood, and with elementary teaching altogether. He had sent in his resignation on Saturday, addressing it to Mr. Muckersie, who was Clerk to the Board, as well as being a member of it. Then he had written to Crombie, telling him what he had done, and when he expected to be in London. Not a word did he mention of the fight; for he could not have spoken of that without bringing in the name of Elsie Austin. He would tell Crombie about his engagement when he got to London ; he could not write of it yet.

He went over the whole circumstances in his mind again and again, looking facts in the face. No, he

did not regret what he had done. In fact, he had a
sense of freedom now that was altogether new to
him. He was his own master, and the making of
his life was in his own hands. What although he
did not make much money to begin with? He did
not expect to. But he could work at his hardest, and
he did not despair of success in the end.

The only hard thing was that he must leave Elsie,
and he knew also how hardly she would feel it.

He got up and walked to the window, but the
shadows of night had already fallen athwart the
fields, and Muiredge Farm was blotted out. Yet not
quite. He could see the twinkle of light that was
the parlour window. "May God watch over her, and
bless her," he said aloud. "Some day I shall come
back and claim her as mine own. Some day! some
day!"

"All in the dark, Mr. Urquhart?" came the pleasant
voice of Mistress Janet at the door. "We are wondering if you have forgotten about tea altogether this
afternoon."

"I must have forgotten about time, at least," he
answered her; "for I was not aware it was nearly
tea-time. And the darkness might have told me."

"You like the gloaming, Mr. Urquhart?" she asked
tenderly. "To me the gloaming is full of poetry,
and it is then that I like to sit and converse with all
my absent friends, and friends of long ago."

"Then I suppose you'll be seeing me in your
gloaming pictures soon, Mistress Janet, and counting
me amongst your absent friends."

"Yes," she sighed, "you are going away just when
we know you. But then we are assured you will
come back again, Mr. Urquhart, and that is a con-

soling thought; and Miss Elsie will come to see us
often when you are away."

Urquhart laid his hand on the old lady's shoulder.
"You are very good, Mistress Janet," he said. "I
think I must claim you and Miss Agnes as my aunts.
It must be pleasant to have relations. I have none
in the world now, excepting a cousin in Australia.
Do you know that I always think of you and Miss
Agnes as two poems."

"Dear, dear!" she answered him playfully, "very
prosy poems, I assure you. It's you and Elsie who
are the poem just now to us; and you have no idea
how sweet a poem it is to two old maids, Mr.
Urquhart. But what of Mrs. Rae?" she asked.
"Can you not think of her as a poem too?"

"A puzzle poem, Mistress Janet, or sometimes an
elegy."

"Poor dear!" she sighed. "Well, we'll better be
going down now, and not keep tea waiting, or else
we'll be late for the evening service."

At tea the talk was again of his going away. Mrs.
Rae was much troubled about it.

"Isn't it just what I told you, Mr. Urquhart?"
she asked mournfully. "I said you would go away.
They always go away. Just when we have learned
to love them they go away and leave us, and they
never come back again."

"But I am coming back, Mrs. Rae."

He spoke hopefully to her, but she refused to be
comforted.

"He must come back, you know," Miss Agnes
assured her. "He must come back for Elsie, and
that will be a great day. We must all look our very
best then."

"Is he going to leave Elsie?" she wailed. "Oh, poor, poor Elsie!"

They looked at her in astonishment. It was rarely that she was so genuinely moved. She was trembling with agitation, and in her eyes was a look of anguish.

"But he's coming back to Elsie," Mistress Janet told her again.

But it was to no purpose.

"Poor, poor Elsie!" she wailed. "Why do they all go away from Elsie? Why should he go away when Elsie loves him so much?"

"But I shall leave Elsie in good keeping, Mrs. Rae," Urquhart said, trying to soothe her. "You shall go and see her, and she shall come and see you. You'll both be good friends; and you must comfort her when I am away."

Mrs. Rae looked at him anxiously. "Is that true, Mr. Urquhart? Shall I comfort Elsie till you come again? Yes, yes, I shall be kind to her, for I know. Ah!"

She leaned across the table and spoke in a low, solemn voice. "I was Elsie once, and he went away. That was long, long ago; oh, so long ago. But I can't remember. It's all locked up here." She touched her forehead with her finger. "All locked up, Mr. Urquhart."

"Now, Mrs. Rae," Miss Agnes called, "you are not eating at all; you are talking too much. Let me fill your cup again. We'll need to be preparing for service soon."

"I was thinking to-day," Urquhart remarked, "that I might leave most of my books with you when I go, taking with me only what I actually

R

need. They can remain here till I come back
again."

"I am sure we shall be pleased to keep them,"
was the reply; "and we shall take great care of
them, Mr. Urquhart."

"I suppose we shall be at liberty to read them?"
Miss Agnes smilingly asked. "Or must we leave
them religiously on the shelves?"

"I think I may allow you to read them," he
answered with mock gravity, "provided you only
read one at a time."

"I promise not to read more than one at a time,"
she said; "and I shall always return it with the
corners of the leaves not turned down. I daresay
you don't know the rhyme old folks used to write on
the fly-leaf of a book. This was in the days when
books were fewer than now.

"'This book belongs to Mr. So-and-so.

"'If thou art borrowed by a friend,
    Right welcome shall he be,
To read, to study, not to lend,
    But to return to me.'"

"Oh, I know, Miss Agnes, I know," Mrs. Rae
cried, interrupting her. "I know it.

"'Not that imparted knowledge doth
    Diminish learning's store;
But books, I find, if often lent,
    Return to me no more.'"

"Yes, Mrs. Rae," Miss Agnes said, applauding
her. "And do you remember the moral?"

"Let me see," she answered. "This was it.
'Read carefully; pause frequently; return duly,
with the corners of the leaves not turned down.'

That's it," she cried gaily. "I remember it; I remember it. Oh, Mr. Urquhart, it is so pleasant to
remember something. And that was long, long ago.
It was Niel who gave it to Walter. Niel wrote it in
a book he gave to Walter.

"'This book belongs to Walter Spence.'" And she
went over the rhyme again.

"But where is Niel, Mr. Urquhart? Where is he?
Ah, he went away. He went away from Elsie and—
and—I forget."

"Come now," said Mistress Janet, "we must get
ready for service. Mr. Urquhart, we'll leave you
here to have your smoke. Are you going to the
service to-night?"

"Yes, Mistress Janet; I shall go with you."

"Is Elsie to be there?" Miss Agnes asked
roguishly.

Urquhart laughed. "Do you think that is the
only attraction that could drag me to an evening
service, Miss Agnes? Yes, both she and Mr. Muir
are coming up to it."

The ladies went upstairs, and Urquhart sat down
to enjoy a pipe till they should be ready.

CHAPTER TWENTY-FIFTH

A SENSATIONAL SERVICE

THE ladies were hardly upstairs, before the door opened very gently, and Walter Spence entered the room.

He looked exceedingly serious; and as he crept in on tip-toe, he held up a warning hand to Urquhart, enjoining silence. He was dressed ready for church; and, taking off his Sunday hat, he set it carefully down on the table before he spoke.

"I cam' in to ha'e a talk wi' ye yoursel', Mr. Urquhart," he said, in a low, earnest voice.

"But sit down, Watty; sit down."

"No, sir, thank ye. It'll no tak' me a minute. I was at the door, wonderin' how I could see ye without disturbin' them, when I heard the three o' them gang upstairs."

Urquhart looked at him in surprise. This was not like Watty at all. And now, when he observed the face closely, he saw how pale it was, and that it wore an expression of uneasiness and pain. The eyebrows were drawn together; the lips, when he was not speaking, tightened over the set teeth.

"When I heard them gang upstairs," he continued, "I saw that was my only chance, an' I stappet in."

"Yes, Watty?"

"Are they thinkin' o' gaun to the evenin' service?"
he asked.

"Yes, Watty; they are upstairs, getting ready just
now, and we are all going together."

Watty took a step forward, and placing a hand
on the back of the chair, whispered hoarsely, "Dinna
gang, Mr. Urquhart. For God's sake, dinna let
them gang."

Urquhart regarded him keenly. He saw that the
man was in earnest, whatever it might be he had on
his mind. But this was a strange request to make;
and he could not understand why it should be made
at all.

"But why, Watty, should they not go; or how
can I keep them at home, if they wish to go?"

"Dinna ask me, sir," Watty pleaded, almost tearfully; "but for God's sake do what I tell ye, an'
keep them at hame."

"But I can't, Watty. I don't know what to say
to them. I can't tell them, when they come downstairs, that they must stay at home because I
command them. They'd think me mad."

A spasm of pain crossed Watty's face.

"I dinna ken what to say to ye," he acknowledged;
"but dinna let them gang. I've been feared for
this for years, an' it has come at last. But surely,
Mr. Urquhart, ye can get some excuse for keepin'
them at hame."

"I don't understand you, Watty. What harm can
there be in going to church? And their hearts are
set on it, too. This Mr. Gordon is accounted an
able preacher, and they are eager to hear him."

"That's it," Watty whispered; "that's just it.
He'll be ower muckle for them."

"You mean," and Urquhart smiled, in spite of
Watty's seriousness, "that he is a sensational
preacher, and that his sermon will excite the Misses
Birrell ? "

"Ay, that's it."

"Well, Watty, I must confess I think your fears
groundless. The Misses Birrell, I am certain, will
listen as calmly as you or I. I really think you
are talking nonsense, Watty."

"Oh, man, man," Watty burst out, "can I no
convince ye? Will Mrs. Rae be able to stand his
preachin', think ye? She's a nervous cr'atur', ye
ken yoursel', an' it would tak' michty little to shake
her to pieces."

"Well, Watty, to tell you frankly, I don't think
a sermon, however sensational, could do that; and
I should be quite willing to risk it."

"Keep her at hame," Watty pleaded again; "tak'
my word for it, an' keep her at hame."

"But, Watty, if you have any other reason, known
only to yourself, why don't you say so straight out?
And I should try to help you; but really I can't
imagine what you mean."

"Oh," Watty sighed, "I canna persuade ye; an'
here they come. I thoucht ye might ha'e done this
for me. Is Elsie—I mean Miss Austin—gaun?" he
asked abruptly.

"She is."

The ladies entered the room, and Watty picked
up his hat to go.

"Are we all going together, Watty?" Mistress
Janet asked him.

"Ay, Mistress Janet; Mr. Urquhart an' me will
gang down wi' ye."

"I didn't hear you come in, Walter," Miss Agnes told him; "but we're glad to see you all the same. It'll be pleasant to go along together."

"Do you know," Mrs. Rae asked, "that after our chapter this morning, Walter asked me not to go to church to-night? And here he is going himself. I told you I would go, Walter."

"Yes, Mrs. Rae; an' I thought I'd just come ower an' gang wi' ye."

"Now," she cried, "that's nice; and you are really going with us? It is very good of you, Walter. But you were always good, long, long ago, before they all went away. And Mr. Urquhart is going away too, now, and leaving Elsie—poor, poor Elsie!"

It was still hard frost when they got outside, but there was a slight wind blowing now in short, irregular puffs, and the stars were seen but dimly through a film of cloud. From the hillside they heard the bleating of sheep, evidently gathered into a flock, and not far from the hedges. Over the noise of their bleating came the plaintive cries of peewits, expostulating, wailing, screaming, like restless spirits wantoning with darkness. As soon as they had passed out of the village, Urquhart buttoned the collar of his coat up about his throat. The wind moaned so mournfully across the fields, that the very sound of it was chilly. He was depressed, too, as with the sense of impending storm; and Watty's peculiar behaviour that night had touched him with a vague foreboding of evil.

Now and again he gave a glance at Watty, trudging along at his side, painfully silent. What was wrong with him? He walked with head bent; and though Urquhart could not see the face under the old-fashioned, broad - brimmed hat, he was certain that it was still as grave and troubled as he had observed it when Watty had come in to talk with him. Allowing the ladies to go on in front, he fell behind, and tried to draw him into conversation, but to no purpose. Watty answered his questions briefly, and often irrelevantly. His mind was occupied with other things, and he hardly heard what was said.

"What has gone wrong with the sheep to-night?" Urquhart asked. "I don't think I have ever heard such a mournful bleating before. And this shivery feeling in the air? Is there going to be a change?"

"A change?" Watty echoed. "Ay, there 'll be a change the nicht, but no onexpected; though we 're maybe no prepared for it when it does come."

"You 've been waiting for it, then?"

"Ay, waitin' for it for years. It was bound to come sooner or later, him bidin' so near; an' now it 's come at last."

Urquhart gave him up. He couldn't understand him at all to-night, and this air of mystery and melancholy about him was laying hold of himself as well. The very church bell, when it began to ring to-night, seemed to have changed its tone, and tolled most funereally.

Something soft and cold sighed against his cheek, and clung to it.

"Why," he exclaimed, "it 's snowing!" He turned his face to the sky. There was not a star to be seen now. "We seem to be in for a regular snow-storm."

"Snowstorm?" Watty echoed. "Ay, I smelt it i' the air this mornin'. It 's to be a nicht o' storm, Mr. Urquhart. Here we are now at the kirk door, an' it'll read'lys be a thin congregation—that's ae blessin'."

The congregation was indeed thin, as Watty had hoped, and the church felt cold. Some half-dozen lamps, hung round the walls, hardly served to disperse the gloom. A heavy, damp smell of oil met them as they entered, and it pervaded the whole building. One of the lamps, which had not been properly trimmed, kept fizzling away, as if it were trying to warm itself; but it could not raise heat enough to dry its clammy globe.

Had the worshippers come together, and filled the front pews, they might have looked a goodly congregation; for although it was not a night for shepherds and their families from the hills, or for ploughmen from the surrounding farms, there were representatives from almost every family in the village. But they sat in scattered knots and units, with yawning blanks between, and this only served to make the church more chill and cheerless. They sat in a dim, religious light, indeed; and the odour of incense in their nostrils was of paraffin oil.

Mr. Muir and Miss Austin were already seated in the very first pew when they entered. Urquhart would have sat down beside them had Watty allowed him, but he was forced right to the front, and then pushed into the pew behind the Misses Birrell and Mrs. Rae. He shivered as he sat down. How cold and comfortless everything was! He hoped Mr. Gordon would really be the powerful preacher Watty said he was; for it would require a man of great earnestness indeed to rouse one from this lethargy of gloom.

But when the preacher mounted to the pulpit and

began the service, Urquhart had little opportunity either of joining heartily in the praise or of listening humbly in prayer. During the reading of the opening psalm, his attention was caught by the strange behaviour of Mrs. Rae. She was sitting right in front of him, and, though he could not see her face, he was aware that she had become terribly excited, and that the voice of the minister was affecting her strangely. She moved about in her seat, opened her Bible and closed it again and again, looked hard and earnestly towards the pulpit for a second or two, then hid her face in her hands, only to fling them wildly away again, and again fix her eyes on the preacher.

Watty had also noticed her agitation, and when Urquhart looked at him he shuddered at sight of his face. Whether it were murderous hate, or merely mental anguish, or something of both, he could not tell, but the expression frightened him. This was not the Walter Spence he knew. The face was so changed that he hardly recognised him; and all through the service, in praise or in prayer, he sat in the same immovable attitude, like one stricken, his chin on his breast, and from under his contracted eyebrows, his eyes fixed on the minister in a steady, malignant stare.

Not a word could Urquhart remember of what that minister said. He filled the church with his stentorian voice, reciting psalms, or thundering out the Word as if the Bible were a book of denunciation; he cried aloud in bitterness of tongue, or wrestled in an agony of prayer; but it was all lost on Mr. Urquhart. He could not take his eyes from Mrs. Rae becoming more and more agitated every minute.

Or, if they did leave her, it was just to fling a glance at Watty sitting motionless at his side, and then turn to her again.

He saw that the Misses Birrell were doing all they could to quiet and soothe her; but they were at their wits' end, and knew not what to try. Occasionally a hardly audible moan escaped her, and she pressed her hands to her forehead, and sat still for a time, but not for long.

It was not, however, till the sermon was reached that the poor woman gave way altogether. The minister had hardly given out his text when she jumped from her seat, and stood stretching her hands out towards him entreatingly. She was sobbing with excitement, and for a time could not utter a word; then her voice rang through the church, agonised, imploring, "Niel, Niel, Niel! Come back to me, Niel!"

The silence of death for a second!

She sank to her seat exhausted, and her face fell forward on the open bible.

The sound of breathing was heard again in church. The minister still stood with one hand outstretched, the other resting on the bible, as he had been standing when Mrs. Rae interrupted the service. Watty had not yet moved, Urquhart saw; but sat there—his face as hard as ever, the same stony stare in his eyes.

The minister's hand fell, and his eyes were turned to Urquhart. "Some one might take the poor woman home," he said, "and we shall proceed with the service of God."

Watty was on his feet at once, and the Misses Birrell, too. "We'll gang hame, Mistress Janet," he said ; "we'll tak' her hame. Mr. Urquhart, if ye dinna mind——"

Mrs. Rae allowed herself to be led away quietly and meekly. At the door, however, she stopped, and held out her hands to Miss Austin. "Elsie," she pleaded, "Elsie, my child, come with me."

Elsie rose at once and came to her, looking at her with terror-stricken eyes. Watty, having been brought to a halt while this was taking place, turned round and shook a fist at the minister. He was beside himself with passion, and it was a time before he got his voice. Then he shouted in terrible tones, "And Nathan said unto David, '*Thou art the man!*'"

They marched out into the blackness of darkness. It was snowing heavily, and every feature of the landscape was blotted out. Already the snow was half-an-inch deep on the ground, and they walked with noiseless footsteps. They were hardly out of the church, when Mrs. Rae stumbled, and would have fallen, had not Elsie been at her side, and caught her. Her bible went flying from her hand, but she did not seem to miss it. Urquhart picked it up, and came to her side.

"Take my arm, Mrs. Rae," he said. "Now we'll manage nicely."

She clutched his arm convulsively, and clung to it. "Niel, Niel," she sobbed, "you have come back again."

Watty Spence came to the other side, but she would not part with Elsie. "No, no," she cried, when Watty offered to take Miss Austin's place ; "I have got Elsie and Niel, and I mustn't let them go again."

They had to struggle on in the blinding storm as best they could. Urquhart led the way, and tried

to keep to the middle of the road; but he marched
right into the hedges at least half-a-dozen times
before a watery glimmer of light told them they
had reached the end of the village. Watty and
Muiredge, struggling along behind with the Misses
Birrell, fared no better. They could only turn their
faces in the direction in which they knew the village
lay, and push forward, knowing that the hedges would
keep them from wandering astray.

Mrs. Rae was utterly exhausted by the time they
got home; but she refused to let Elsie go. They
might have done with her what they would; but no
persuasion would let her part with Elsie.

"No, no; stay with me," she pleaded; and Elsie
had to accompany her to her room.

And it was just as well that Miss Austin was with
her; for the Misses Birrell could do nothing. The
poor ladies had lost their heads completely, and were
almost as helpless as Mrs. Rae herself.

Urquhart went straight into his study, taking Mr.
Muir with him. There they sat silent for a time,
looking to each other now and again, but not knowing what to say. They heard the ladies moving
about in the room below, and their thoughts were
of Mrs. Rae and Elsie.

The scene in church had impressed itself so
forcibly on their minds that they were already regarding it as a thing apart from themselves, something which they could look back on and study
without bias or prejudice. But look at it as they
liked, it was all a mystery to them and a tragedy.

Mrs. Rae's life, before she had come to Kinkelvie,
was curtained off from them; it was a blank to
herself. Had they had a glimpse to-night of what

lay behind that curtain, and beheld for a moment
the terrible tragedy that Urquhart had so often
imagined must have crushed her spirit and left her
the poor, helpless being they knew?

"Well," Mr. Muir asked, after a long pause, "can
you make anything of it at all?"

Urquhart rose, and began pacing from end to end
of the room. "I don't know what to think, Mr.
Muir. It has quite unsettled me. Who is this
Mr. Gordon, do you know?"

"He's a minister from Carsecowden, and he's
staying a day or two with Mr. Blyth. That's how
he comes to be preaching here. But his name is
Niel, Mr. Urquhart, or Nathaniel in full. Surely,
Mrs. Rae must have known him at one time."

"That does not concern me so much, Mr. Muir."
Urquhart came and leaned on the mantelpiece as he
spoke. "How does Elsie come to be mixed up in
this business?" he asked slowly and deliberately,
looking Mr. Muir straight in the face.

"What do you mean, Mr. Urquhart? Elsie?"

"Mr. Muir, excuse me speaking plainly to you. I
did not mean to mention this at all, but I must get
to the bottom of this mystery now. And surely you
will recognise that I have some right in asking you
about Miss Austin? Certainly, it is not out of
idle curiosity that I speak. Miss Austin is not
really your niece, Mr. Muir?"

"Mr. Urquhart!" The farmer's eyes were blazing,
but beholding Urquhart's anxious face he became
calm on the instant. "Excuse me," he said, "you
have a perfect right to know. Elsie was an adopted
child."

"And whose child, Mr. Muir?"

"That I don't know. My sister brought her up from infancy; that is all I can tell you. You do not blame me, Mr. Urquhart, for not mentioning this to Elsie herself? My sister was all the mother she ever had. I could not tell the girl—that—that she had no right to the name she was called by, if she had the right to—to any name. Surely, you don't blame me for that, Mr. Urquhart?"

"No, Mr. Muir; I should be the last in the world to blame you for your kindness to Elsie. Do you know her mother's name at all, Mr. Muir?"

"Elsie's full name is Elsie Baxter Austin. Baxter was her mother's name. That tells you a sad story, Mr. Urquhart. But surely you won't give her up for that. You are not thinking of that, Mr. Urquhart?"

"Never! Elsie is mine. No, never!"

Mr. Muir leaned forward, and gave him his hand. They clasped hands in silence. There was no need of words. They recognised each other as men, and a grip of the hand said all they wanted to say.

Urquhart went and sat down at the table. "Do you know why I struck Mr. Muckersie?" he asked. "I gave the first blow in that fight, and it was because he called her a name —— "

"Muckersie!" Mr. Muir ejaculated. "The miserable wretch! And yet he doesn't know. It's only his dirty mind. The Balbingries were ever the same. Every woman has her price, they think. They have always insinuated that my sister was not married to Mr. Austin, but they are wrong. You know my sister's was a runaway marriage?"

Urquhart nodded.

"They went to London, but they didn't stay long there. They came back to Edinburgh, and all my sister's money was lifted as soon as she came of age. That's all I knew about her till I got word of her death. I suppose the marriage didn't prove a happy one, and she was too proud to let me know anything about it."

Urquhart, who sat fingering the leaves of the bible he had brought in with him, suddenly started from his seat.

"What is it?" Mr. Muir cried. "What's wrong?"

Urquhart brought the bible, and put it into his hands. "That is Mrs. Rae's bible," he said. "Read her name—*Elsie R. Baxter from Niel Gordon.*"

Mr. Muir sat holding the bible with trembling hands. "I cannot read it," he said. "But it cannot be, Mr. Urquhart. It is surely a mistake."

Nearly all that Mrs. Rae had ever said to Urquhart came rushing back into his mind now. Everything went to confirm the story he read on the fly-leaf of this bible. Then there was the locket she had given to Elsie, with its double monogram. He had remarked at the time how like the little photo it contained was to Elsie. He saw it all now.

He sat down at the table again and laid his head on his hands. The whole world seemed to be whirling from beneath his feet. Then he rose and put on his coat. "There is only one man who knows this story," he said calmly, "and I must see him. I must see Watty Spence; and I'll get it out of him though I have to wring it word by word."

"Watty Spence, Mr. Urquhart! Are you mad? Watty Spence!"

"Yes, Mr. Muir, Watty Spence!"

CHAPTER   *THE MEETING IN*
TWENTY-SIXTH   *THE VESTRY*

WATTY SPENCE had returned with the Misses
Birrell from church, but he had stopped at
their garden gate. As soon as he heard the door
shut behind them and knew that all were inside,
Mr. Muir and Miss Austin as well as Mr. Urquhart,
he turned and went back the road he had come. It
was snowing heavier than ever, and darkness rose in
front of him like a wall. But Watty heeded neither
darkness nor storm. He pulled his hat down almost
to his eyes and strode along with head bent, as if he
were boring a way for himself through the palpable
blackness. He kept to the middle of the road, and
there was no swerving now either to right or left.
Had he deliberately tried to pick his way, he would
have walked with uncertain steps, zigzagging from
hedge to hedge. But his mind was already at the
end of his journey, and by a kind of instinct or
unconscious memory, his feet kept to the road
straight and true as they would have done in the
broad light of day.

He wore no overcoat, and the thin black frock-
coat hung loose from the shoulders; for that is the
way frock-coats must be worn in country places,
summer and winter. It is a Sabbath-day fashion

S

which has become a religious convention, sanctioned and approved by the tradition of the elders. His bible was still held in his left hand; in his right the great bulging umbrella which completed the outfit for kirk or funeral. But it never entered his mind to put it up. It was tied tightly in the middle and carried under his arm. Umbrellas were only for rain, and not even then unless it were coming down in earnest.

Chains of snowflakes came twining and twisting, swirling under his chin and clutching at his throat. But Watty did not mind them a bit. They crusted over his black silk scarf till it was white as his spotless shirt; but he did not feel their cold. There was a fire in his breast and in his brain to-night: let the snows come, chill as the hand of death, if they would, the blood would be warm in his veins, his fingers be tingling at fever heat.

He must have been as far as the head of the Sandy Loan, when he ran right into another person coming towards the village. They had both been walking quickly and they staggered back, the one from the other, with the force of the collision. And even then, peering through the blinding drift, each was conscious only of a shapeless shadow intensifying the darkness immediately before his eyes.

Watty adjusted his hat, which had suffered in the encounter. "I dinna ken wha ye be," he said; "but ye'll excuse me on a nicht like this. It's no the kirk comin' out a'ready, is it?"

"Is that you, Walter?"

Watty recognised the voice of the minister, Mr. Blyth.

"No, the church is not out yet," he said. "I

followed shortly after you had left, because I could not wait till service was over. It's nothing serious, is it, Walter?"

"Weel, sir, they're housed a' richt enough now. I just left them at their door an' cam' stappin' awa' down to the kirk again. But the ladies themsel' will be blithe to see you. They're sair putten about. I'm doubtin' if ye'll see Mrs. Rae. She's in a terrible state."

"Yes, Walter, I must go and see them. I have never seen Mrs. Rae so excited before. That was an extraordinary scene in church. I saw Mr. Gordon was exceedingly agitated when he got begun to his sermon."

"Ay, sir, it was a tryin' scene."

"But you don't mean to go back to church yet, Walter? Service will be over almost as soon as you are there."

"I'll tak' my chance, sir; guid-nicht." And Watty again bent his head to the storm. "That's the best thing that could ha'e happened," he kept assuring himself, as he trudged along; "the best thing that could ha'e happened. I'll see him himsel' now."

When he reached the church he heard the voice of the congregation in the closing paraphrase, sounding as plaintive and mournful as the soughing of the wind outside.

> "Come then to me, all ye who groan
> With guilt and fears opprest;
> Resign to me the willing heart,
> And I will give you rest."

He stood listening for a minute, and then made his way round to the vestry at the back of the building. Cautiously opening the door, he put in his head to see that the room was empty before he crept in on tiptoe, and stationed himself in the corner, thrown into shadow by the opened door.

The room was bare enough to have been mistaken for a hermit's cell. There were two chairs—one of them dilapidated and rickety, and a plain deal table standing in the middle of the floor. On the table were set a carafe of water, a cracked tumbler, and a smoky little lamp shedding a light so meagre that it failed to reach further than the edge of the table on which it stood. In the corner, opposite to where Watty stood, was a diminutive fireplace where a few cinders tried to keep themselves warm and sputtered reproachfully now and again against occasional snow-flakes that had strayed down the chimney by mistake, to perish ignominiously. Over the mantelpiece was the only respectable article of furniture in the room —a dainty mirror—and it must have felt sadly out of place. Originally meant for some lady's dressing-room where beaming eyes would have looked into it night and morning, seeing a wealth of uncoiled tresses sweeping round a shapely shoulder, here it hung from Monday to Saturday, reflecting nothing but cold, bare walls, and a colourless window that hid the green ivy-leaves tapping to be allowed to see inside. Twice on the Sunday it saw nervous fingers adjusting stiff white bands under a shaven chin. That was all, except it might be an occasional glimpse of the old beadle's gray-whiskered, lantern jaws.

But it is questionable whether Watty took notice of anything in the room at all. He had laid his umbrella on the floor, setting his hat beside it, and placing his bible on the top. Then he stood still as

a statue, waiting.   The paraphrase died away in a
kind of wail, and he gave a sigh of relief.

"Now," he murmured, squaring his shoulders, and
staring straight in front of him, "now.

He did not change his position when Mr. Gordon
entered ; did not by the slightest sound or movement
betray his presence.   The minister, with a nervous,
irritable jerk of the arm, flung the door close behind
him, and, walking straight to the mantelpiece, laid his
head on his hands, and groaned.   He had not stayed
to take off the pulpit gown, and Watty looked at the
black-robed figure, but not in pity.   There was only
the table's length between them, and he could see
from the contraction of the shoulders that the man
was in agony.   But his heart must have been har-
dened against him ; for he only drew his eyebrows
closer and tightened his lips over his teeth, making
his face sterner than ever and harshly forbidding.

For about half a minute the minister stood like
one agonizing in prayer, then he raised his head
wearily and began muttering to his reflection in the
mirror.

"After all those years !   O God, what I have suffered !   And Nathan said unto David, '*Thou art the
man !*'   Thou art the man ; yes, thou, Niel Gordon !
And Walter Spence too ?   I didn't know the face
again, but that voice !   Walter S——.   God help me !
Walter ! Walter ! spare me.   I have sinned, and suffered.   Walter !"

While he was speaking he had flung his head back
from the glass in a very paroxysm of fear ; and now
he stood staring into it with terror-stricken eyes, his
hands pressed to his temples, and his fingers like
claws buried in his hair.

From where he stood Watty could see even in the
dim light the reflection of an ashen face, with the
dilated eyes staring fearfully on him. Still, he did
not move.

The minister's agitation was but momentary. He
saw that the face in the glass was no spiritual apparition, no illusion conjured up by an uneasy conscience
for his torment, but the reflection of a bodily presence
in the room beside him. His hands fell to his side,
and he turned and faced Watty with an expression
not quite of fear, nor yet altogether of shameless
effrontery.

They regarded each other in silence. What the
minister saw was a face hard as marble, and a figure
as white. For Watty was crusted over with snow, which
the chill air of the cheerless room had been unable to
thaw, and he had not taken the trouble to shake it
off before he entered. No wonder the sudden
apparition of such a figure—and especially with
the face of Walter Spence—had scared him with a
sense of the supernatural.

Mr. Gordon saw that he was expected to speak
first.

"What do you want, Walter?"

Watty moistened his lips, but it was the lips only
that moved when he spoke.

"Do ye need to speir that. You, Niel Gordon?"

"What can I do, Walter?" he cried in a kind of
whining irritation. "It's all past and gone now;
dead—and buried—for years. Ssh!"

He stepped over and opened the door.

"All right," he said to the beadle; "just you lock
up the church door now and go. I'll take the vestry
key with me to the manse."

"Ye'll mind and put out the licht, Mr. Gordon? An' tak' care o' yoursel' gaun down. Keep a grip o' the palin' till ye're at the door. It's a sair nicht."

"Yes, thank you; I'll remember. Good-night."

"Guid nicht, sir."

And they heard old Mousie's steps shuffling and echoing in the empty church. Mr. Gordon came and stood again with his back to the fire.

"What can I do, Walter?" he asked. "You have found me after all these years."

"Found ye, Mr. Gordon? Found ye, did ye say? I could ha'e laid hands on ye if I had liket ony day for the last twenty year. But a' I was concerned about was keepin' her out o' your way. Ye dinna think, surely, that onybody wi' the spirit o' a man in him would seek to find out *you*."

"You are too hard, Walter. Have I not suffered?"

"Suffered, Mr. Gordon? Dinna let that word cross your lips onless it be said o' her. What ha'e you suffered? Ye suffered yoursel' to become a paid servant o' God. Ye've suffered a trustin' congregation to believe ye a saintly man sent to minister to the pure in heart, an' to keep the feet o' your flock to the paths o' virtue. Ye've suffered yoursel' to be made o', an' flattered by the purse-proud o' your congregation, that have marriageable daughters wha worship the godly Mr. Gordon. That's how you've suffered, Niel Gordon. I ken you, an' I ken Carse-cowden. But what o' her ye brought to a bed o' shame? Cursed by her father, an' disowned by her ain flesh an' blood; no a friend on the face o' God's earth, savin' only mysel'; an' little it was that I could do! Her life ruined; her mind darkened; an' growin' up apart frae the bairn that was born her!"

The minister writhed in pain, and held out his hands as if warding off blows.

"Don't, Walter, don't," he groaned. "Every word is stabbing me. You don't know what I have suffered all those years. Life has been a daily torment; for I have lived with a sin eating into my soul and the curse of a ruined life upon my head. You don't know; you can't comprehend. I knew nothing about—it, while I was in Germany. I had no letters."

"Ye kent nothing about it? Man, man, dinna shuffle wi' words. Ye kent o' the sin, but ye had shut your e'en to its consequence. That was a'."

"And when I came home," the minister continued, "what could I do? She had left home."

"But you had my letter, an' kent whaur to find her if ye'd been willin'. Had ye come at that time her reason had been spared her: for though a' had scorned her, she had faith in you. But you—you had a pen an' ink an' the sophistry of a prize-medalist. Man, as lang as I live I'll never forget the nicht I had to read her your letter. She had a seam in her hand, a bairnie's bit frock. Man, if I had ha'en my hands at your throat that nicht, you wouldna ha'e been livin' this day; an' I would ha'e strung for it willin'. But ye're no worth it."

"Walter, Walter, have you no mercy? The evil had been done. There were my father and mother, whose hopes were centred in me. I had to choose. Had I gone to her then I had been ruined; my prospects blasted."

"Prospects!" Watty hurled the word at him. "Maun women aye be sacrificed to men's prospects? An' I suppose it was better that she should be ruined than you; that her life should be wrecked, so that

you micht become a minister o' the gospel. Have
ye no conscience ava? Div ye never think when
ye're mountin' the pu'pit that every step is ower a
woman's body?"

"Walter, Walter, spare me. Have I not told you
I suffer? My ambition was attained, and I have
lived in hell ever since."

"Man, if ye'd ha'en the spunk o' a louse at that
time ye'd ha'e come to her, kirk or no kirk. I would
ha'e seen a' the pu'pits in Scotland bleezin' in hell-
fire afore I'd ha'e played the part o' a coward an' a
murderer."

The wind gave a weird and unearthly sough outside, and a branch of ivy pattered on the window.
Mr. Gordon shivered with fear, and sank down on
the chair, clasping his hands and letting his head fall
above them on the table.

Watty looked at him pitilessly as ever. This was
a display of weakness, in his eyes. He considered
him a coward even yet, and despised him.

"This is what ye'll ca' your sufferin', no doubt?"
he said; "a bit fit now an' then o' whingin' an'
whinin' self pity, wi' twa three words o' prayer that's
little better than blasphemin'; an' it's a' ower. Ye
rise wi' a conceit in your sufferin', as ye ca' it, that ye
think is the consolation o' God. Eh, man! The
prayer o' the Pharisee was mair worthy than sic' a
yirn and yelp as yours—you that would beslaver the
gates o' Heaven for a soul that's no worth savin'.
'Lord, Lord, I've suffered,' ye dare to cry to Him!
Shame on ye, ye poor insignificant cratur'."

The minister only answered with a groan, and
Watty continued, unheeding—

"Think on what ye've made her suffer. Forget

about yoursel', if that's possible, for aince i' your life, an' try to imagine what life has been for her. If life has been a wreck and a ruin to her, it was your doin'; an' ye had it in your power, if ye'd been a man, to make life to her as sweet as a love-sang an' as bonny as a summer day."

"Walter, Walter, it was impossible. You don't know the terrible ordeal I had to pass through; you forget what torture it was to me. Was it less painful that I inflicted it; that I had brought it on myself?"

"There ye are again. It's aye yoursel' ye think about, an' pity. Ay', an' the suffering doesna end wi' her. Ye ken that, or ought to ken. That's the warst o' it a'. Think on the sufferin' waitin' the bit lassie—though she'll bear it bravely when she comes to ken; for she doesna tak' after her father. I dinna need to tell you that the sins o' the fathers are visited on the children. That's a favourite owercome o' yours i' the pulpit when ye're in a holy raptur' an' drivin' sin hame to the hearts o' your innocent flock. An' wha should ken better than you? Poor simple-minded folk hangin' on your words, an' tryin' to accustom their shou'thers to your sinfu' experience! Did ye never pause i' the middle o' your sermon sometimes an' think ye were quotin' Scriptur' to your ain damnation?"

"Stop, Walter, stop. You will drive me mad."

"I could say nothing harder than you say in your sermons, hurlin' hell at the heads o' your hearers. I ken about your preachin' in Carsecowden; an' if I had ane o' your sermons i' my hands the now, I could draw blood wi' a whip o' your ain makin'. But what's the use?"

"Yes, what would be the use? For it's all past, and the penalty has been already paid."

"Already paid, Mr. Gordon? If I thought that, Mr. Gordon, I would leave ye, as I'd leave a headless adder on the moss. But what o' the lassie, if the mother's sufferin' be by?"

"A girl, Walter? A girl?"

"Eh, man, do ye no even ken that? Did ye close your very e'en and ears when ye closed your heart? Were ye beggared even o' natural curiosity if ye had no higher feelin'?"

"Walter! Walter!" the minister groaned. "You don't know. Do you imagine that I have never thought of them? Is it nothing to me that I have never even seen my own child?"

Watty looked at him, and made a gesture of contempt and loathing.

"How can ye tell ye've never seen her, Mr. Gordon? Ye've never tried to see her, an' wouldna ken her, though she were to sit under ye an' listen to ye ilka Sabbath mornin' prayin' for the blessin' o' God on your bible-class. Ay, ay, man; an' ye think ye havena seen her?"

The minister raised his head, and what a haggard face it was that Watty saw now. But the look of pain and horror in the eyes did not touch him with the slightest sensation of pity.

"Last year ye drove through Kinkelvie," he recalled to him with quiet scorn. "I saw ye mysel'. But ye didna ken, Niel Gordon, that the young lady that had gien ye a lift frae the station was your ain flesh an' blood."

The minister sprang to his feet, and held a hand over his eyes.

"O God!" he cried; "O God! And that face
has haunted me ever since. It was the face of her
mother—once."

"Ay, aince, Mr. Gordon; and if she hasna sic a
happy face now, wha's to blame?"

"I have thought of that drive many a time since.
She was a girl any father might have been proud of;
most accomplished, I thought, and refined."

"Accomplished an' refined? She's a' that; though
it's no you she has to thank for bein' either the ane
or the other."

Mr. Gordon let his chin fall on his breast, and he
reeled against the mantelpiece.

"Water," he whispered; "give me a drink of
water."

Watty filled the glass and handed it to him.

"Thank you—I am ill, Walter—leave me. You
are—very—hard on me."

"No, sir. I canna leave ye here on sic a nicht as
this. I'll see ye as far as the palin', an' ye'll be able
to find the way hame yoursel'. It would be the
death o' you to stay here."

The minister looked at him curiously.

"Perhaps that would be the best—for everyone,"
he said.

"No," Watty answered decidedly. "Ye'll excuse
me sayin' it, Mr. Gordon; but ye're no ready for
that yet. Now, if ye're a' richt we'll gang."

"But what do you want me to do, Walter?
Why did you come here if it was only to torment
me?"

"I want ye to get out o' Kinkelvie, Mr. Gordon;
that's a'. Ye can leave the morn's mornin'; an' I
wouldna like to see your face on earth again. It

brings back memories o' a time I would rather forget."

"But, Walter, before I go, could I not see ——?"

"No, that's out o' the question. Ye've managed for ower a score o' years, an' ye'll be able to thole awa' till the end."

"My daughter, Walter?"

Watty laughed harshly. "You've no daughter, Mr. Gordon. What would Carsecowden say to that? Na, na; gang back to your flock, an' be the godly man ye've been. It wouldna do to begin immorality at your time o' life."

The minister turned to the mantelpiece, and again laid his head on his hands.

"Walter," he muttered wearily, "you are without mercy. My daughter? And she will be nameless."

"Weel, sir, it's ower late to think o' that now; an' it may be a hard thing to say an' harder to hear, better to be nameless than takin' her name frae you. God grant she may get an honest man's name afore lang."

Mr. Gordon turned and faced him.

"Is that the case?" he asked anxiously. "Is there any hope of that? I suppose she *must* be a woman now?"

"Weel, there may be hopes o' it; but hope's no certainty. If she doesna, ye'll read'lys ken at whase door to lay the blame. Come awa', now. There's somebody at the door. It'll be Mr. Blyth on his way hame again."

The door opened, and Mr. Blyth looked in upon them. The light was too dim for him to observe them closely, and he did not notice how haggard and pale Mr. Gordon was.

"Not home yet," he asked cheerily. "You are taking a long stay, Walter."

"I cam' to tell him they were a' right," Watty answered; "kennin he would be putten about wi' what happened under his e'en."

"That was very thoughtful of you, Walter; very thoughtful indeed. Well, are you ready? Dear me, Mr. Gordon, you haven't got the cloak off yet!"

"It's a comfortable thing, a cloak," Watty reflected, "an' it fits him fine."

It was still snowing when they came out. Watty crossed with them to the paling-side, and bade them good-night there. They got hold of the top spar, and he watched them disappear in the direction of the manse.

"Twa ministers," he communed with himself, after they were lost to sight; "an' what a difference! Niel Gordon wi' the wreck an' ruin o' a life on his head, an' Mr. Blyth as innocent an' pure as a bairn! But for a' that, it's Niel that's the great gun; a rousin' preacher an' powerfu' in prayer. There's no mony can haud a can'le to the godly Mr. Gordon o' Carsecowden. An' here's Mr. Blyth in his corner o' the vineyard—a corner, it's well named—wi' but a handfu' o' worshippers, an' onkent outside o' Kinkelvie. It's queer."

But Watty was a simple-minded man.

CHAPTER TWENTY-SEVENTH

MISTRESS JANET met Mr. Muir and Mr. Urquhart when they came downstairs, and told them that Elsie had made up her mind to stay all night with Mrs. Rae. They had got the poor lady to bed now, but she was too excited to sleep, and she would not allow Elsie out of her sight.

"I can't make it out at all," she confided to them. "She has never had a turn like this before that we remember, certainly not since she came to stay with us. She is usually so quiet and bidable, but the service to-night has been too much for her. Mr. Blyth himself is a very quiet preacher, and we had no idea she would be so affected by a stranger. It has upset us very much, Mr. Muir, and you'll allow Elsie to stay, won't you? I don't know what she would do if Elsie were to leave her just now."

"I suppose I must," Mr. Muir answered, somewhat reluctantly it must be admitted. "Elsie herself will know best. But I trust Mrs. Rae will be all right after a good night's rest."

"Thank you very much, Mr. Muir. You don't know what a relief it will be to Agnes and myself to have Elsie with us. Mrs. Rae is perfectly quiet so long as Elsie is beside her, and does whatever she tells her; but she takes no notice of us at all, does not even seem to know us. It is very strange."

The gentlemen bade her good-night, and went out. At the gate they met Mr. Blyth, and only recognised him when he spoke to them. He had merely come to inquire about Mrs. Rae; she was all right now, he hoped.

Mrs. Rae was very much quieter, they told him, but the Misses Birrell themselves were terribly upset, and would be pleased to see him. It was very thoughtful of him to come along on such a night, and the ladies would certainly appreciate his kindness.

"I met Watty Spence on his way back to church again," he said; "so I concluded that there was nothing very serious to be apprehended, though I hardly knew what to think in church to-night. Anything like that appears worse than it really is, when it happens in church."

"You met Watty Spence?" Urquhart asked him. "I was just on my way to see him. I shall probably meet him coming home. Well, good-night, Mr. Blyth. Your visit will certainly be a great comfort to the Misses Birrell; they are almost as ill as Mrs. Rae herself."

What could have taken Watty back to church again? It was certainly not to hear the sermon; Urquhart was sure of that. He must have gone back to see the minister, he reasoned. What else was there to make him trudge away along the road again, on such a night as this?

"I may as well walk a bit with you, Mr. Muir," he suggested, after they had left Mr. Blyth. "Perhaps we may meet Watty returning, if we are able to see anybody at all to-night."

They took the middle of the road, and bent their heads to the storm. The last house in the village had hardly been left behind them before they heard the voices of the congregation returning in a body. Urquhart drew Mr. Muir in close to the hedge, and allowed them to pass. They could not make out a single figure in the crowd, but they heard them talking as they came, shouting to one another through the darkness, and raising their voices because they did not see the faces of those whom they addressed.

But it was not the sermon they discussed. Urquhart could hear Jabez Orrock's voice high above the others, and he was speaking of Mrs. Rae and the scene in church.

"Watty's not with them," he observed, after the voices had gone away again into the darkness. "I can tell that from their talk. He must have stayed to see Mr. Gordon. That's what has taken him back again. Depend upon it, Mr. Muir, Watty knows more of this mystery than anybody else."

They stumbled to the middle of the road and pushed forward once more, but by the time they got to the church the door was already locked, and there was no light in the windows.

"What's to be done now?" Mr. Muir asked. "He must have passed us on the road. One might easily miss a regiment in this blackness. I suppose you'll be going straight back again. I shall keep right on to the kirk, now that I have got so far, and go down by the footpath; it will be easier than the Loan in this storm. I shall look up in the morning and see how they are keeping. Good-night."

They shook hands, giving each other a grip that

T

said more than either could have expressed in words,
and parted.

When Urquhart got back to the village he was
again disappointed, for Watty had not reached home.
However, he had made up his mind that he must see
him, and he kept walking about, up and down the
street, but never going far from the door, until he
should make his appearance. The villagers were all
indoors, and there was no one to see him and to
wonder what he did abroad on such a night.

From lighted windows he heard now and again a
psalm raised, and the voices of father, mother, and
children joining in praise. Outside, only the impene-
trable darkness and the wailing of the storm! He
waited till the singing had ceased and the windows
round about had begun to darken, and still Watty
had not returned. The lights from the Misses Birrell's
window were the last to go out, and even after they
had darkened he heard, as he passed the gate, a voice
from the window above, and paused to listen. It
was Elsie singing *Rock of Ages*, and he heard every
word. She was singing to Mrs. Rae, he knew; for
that was her favourite hymn.

There was something so pathetic and pleading in
the voice coming to him, calling to him he felt, that
he could not drag himself away even when he heard
from the other side of the street the tap-tapping of
snow-laden boots against the jamb of the door. That
was Watty returned, he knew, but he waited till the
hymn was finished and he heard again the sobbing
of the wind in the solitary street.

He was almost sobbing himself as he turned away.
There is something almost spiritual in the sound of
singing coming out of the darkness and quivering

through the silence of night; and now, when Elsie ceased, and he felt on his face again the clammy breath of the storm, he shivered with a sense of loneliness and desolation. It was as if Elsie herself were lost to him—had sung in that hymn a wailing farewell, and passed out of his life for ever.

Try as he might, he could not shake himself from the fear that something had come between himself and her he loved, and now she was lost to him. And to one who loves, the only curse of God or man is the curse of separation.

Watty had just got the lamp lit, and was seated by the side of the fire when Urquhart entered.

"Sit down, Mr. Urquhart," he said quietly, nodding him to a chair opposite. "I was expectin' to see ye the nicht. Hang your top-coat on the back o' the door."

"You expected me, you say," Urquhart began as soon as he had sat down; "and I take it you know what I wish to speak about?"

"Maybe I div, an' maybe I divna, Mr. Urquhart. But ye'll admit now I was richt. Mrs. Rae shouldna ha'e been there the nicht. She ought to ha'e been keepit at hame, as I telled ye."

"That may be, Watty. But how was I to know that she had known this Mr. Gordon in her youth? You alone knew that, and you kept it to yourself."

Watty looked at him searchingly.

"Ye evidently think ye ken a' about it now," he said, with something of constraint in his tone. "Where may you ha'e gotten your information at a moment's notice, so to speak?"

"Look here, Watty," Urquhart answered impatiently; "I know more than you think, but I want to know more, and that is why I come to you. You must tell me what you know."

"Must, Mr. Urquhart? That's no a word I'm accustomed to hear, an' to tell ye the truth I dinna like the sound o' it frae a young man's lips."

"Watty, Watty," he burst out, "don't let us be at sixes and sevens. This is as serious a matter to me as it is to you. Where did I get my information? It has come to me in many ways. It has been coming to me all the time I have been in Kinkelvie. There is one of the sources of my information lying almost at your hand. Whose are the names on that book I lent you?" he asked, pointing to the volume lying where Watty could just reach it on the table.

Watty started, and looked up with anxious eyes.

"The very same names are on Mrs. Rae's Bible," Urquhart continued. "What am I to learn from that?"

"What am I to learn frae what ye tell me?" Watty asked in his turn, "onless it be that ye've been pryin' whaur ye've no richt to pry? Or what need ha'e you to learn onything at a', for that matter? What are the names to you?"

"Much, Watty. You know what Elsie Austin is to me now, and it is for her sake that I come to you to-night."

"For her sake?" Watty echoed wearily. "Man, man, would it no be better for her sake if you learned nothing at a'—if a' this was dead an' buried an' forgotten? What way will ye seek to rake up what I've happit awa' for years? If the story concerns only Mrs. Rae, what is that to you?"

"This is merely trifling with me, Watty. It concerns more than Mrs. Rae, and you know it

does. You are simply trying to put me off, but it
won't do. You went to church to-night to see
Mr. Gordon?"

"I did," Watty answered curtly. "That was my
concern, an' nobody else's."

Urquhart leaned forward, fixing his eyes steadily
on Watty's face, and spoke in a whisper.

"No, you are wrong," he said; "for it concerns
others. It concerns Elsie, and it concerns me. You
went—to see—Elsie's father?"

Watty fell back in his chair. If Urquhart had
struck him a blow, it would have hurt him far less.

"I knew it, Watty; I knew it." He drew himself
up again, and talked self-confidently. "Perhaps
you'll know now how this matter affects me."

Watty, who had not been able to utter a word for
a second, now rose to his feet and turned on the
younger man. His eyes were blazing, and he hurled
at him a torrent of words, eloquent with indignation.

"An' that's your meanin', Mr. Urquhart?" he
asked. "I see what you're drivin' at now, an' I ken
the thoughts o' your mind. They do ye little credit,
an' ye're no the man I ta'en ye to be. You would
come an' worm a story out o' me, a story against the
name o' her ye've pledged yoursel' to heart an' soul;
an' now that ye think ye ken what ye want, ye would
break wi' her for what was no fau't o' hers. An' ye
think I'm the man to help ye in your cowardly
intent? Little div ye ken me, Mr. Urquhart, an' as
little did I ken you."

"Yes," Urquhart answered very quietly, "you do
indeed know me very little if you think so meanly of
me. I shall never give her up. What has this twenty
year old story got to do with our engagement?"

Watty regarded him a little less sternly. "Nothing," he answered. "It has got nothing to do wi' it, Mr. Urquhart, an' so what need ye question or ken about it at a'?"

"But you don't seem to understand, Watty. What will Elsie say to me when she knows? She will think she ought to give me up. I know she will; I know Elsie's spirit, and I am certain of it. And, God help her, I think she knows already."

Watty sank into his chair again.

"Do ye think she kens?" he asked wearily. "Do ye think she kens? Surely no! Surely ye're wrang, Mr. Urquhart."

"I am almost certain she has already made a guess at the truth," he said. "I saw it in her face to-night in church. There is a mystery about Mrs. Rae, she knows that, and Elsie will find a clue in that present she got from her only last Sunday."

He told Watty of the two lockets and their monograms; of Elsie's own one which had belonged to her mother, and of the other that Mrs. Rae had given her.

"It was the last present he ga'e her," Watty murmured; "the last present; an' I mind o' her gettin' the neighbour made to it in Edinburgh. That was afore the bairn was born; an' it was to be hers. She had some queer fancies afore the time."

"What is the whole story?" Urquhart asked.

"Excuse me for a bit," Watty pleaded. "I'm a' shaken the day, for I've kent what was comin' ever since I read his name on the bill. I saw it a' happenin' afore we ever cam' near the kirk; an' it was a tryin' time I had wi' him i' the session-house.

I'll fill my pipe, if ye've no objections, an' tell ye the while I'm smokin'. Ay, it's hard on you, too, Mr. Urquhart. I didna see it in that licht; but ye've a richt to ken a' now."

And it was a sad story that Walter Spence had to tell. It was pretty much the story of his own life from the time that he had left his father's house in Kinkelvie, and gone out to fight for himself in the world. After serving at different places, he had settled down as gardener and coachman to a Mr. Baxter who occupied a large house near the village of Milndour. The very first summer he was there he had become acquainted with Mr. Gordon, a divinity student at the time, who was on holiday and had taken a lodging in the village. "We got on fine," Watty said ; "for I was a great reader, an' he used to lend me books, an' him an' Miss Elsie got on as well—ower well for her, poor lassie ; for the sufferin' an' shame fell only on her. Niel Gordon wasna the man to bear either the ane or the other.

"She was an only bairn, an' motherless as well," he continued ; "an' there was nobody to warn her against sic-like as Niel Gordon. It's aye the innocent an' pure that suffer in that way, Mr. Urquhart. When a lassie's choke fu' o' the knowledge o' good an' evil, as ye might say, she's aye on her guard, an' she's virtuous just because the thoughts o' her heart are no clean. But the heart that is as clear an' pure as crystal is as easily broken. But he's a scoundrel that breaks it.

"Niel Gordon didna gang muckle near the house, for Mr. Baxter was a proud an' pompous kind o' body, an' looket for something better for his daughter than a minister. But they used to forgather i' the gardens, an' I thought a lot o' mysel' at the time, makin' the world bright, as I thought, for a couple o' innocent hearts. My head was burstin' wi' poetry an' romance. Mighty little poetry there was i' the summer followin', after he left her, an' a' the romance was turned to tragedy. He gaed awa' travellin' on the Continent, kennin' little, an' carin' less, what he'd left ahent him.

"Eh man, man!" he burst out, "think o' her actually comin' to me—for her father was a man o' little sympathy—an' a' but tellin' me what was wrang. Poor lassie! I gaed hame an' grat for her that nicht, though little good e'er cam' o' greetin'.

"The next thing was that she ran awa' frae hame, an' the father let on she'd gone to bide wi' her auntie in Edinburgh; but he learned what was wrang, an' cursed her as no daughter o' his. He blamed me for lettin' them meet i' the gardens; ay, an' I blamed mysel', for my better nature had never trusted Niel Gordon, only he'd played on my weakness for books, an' I'd been content for that bribe to wink at wickedness. I saw my duty then was to try to mak' some amends for what I might ha'e prevented, had I no been so blinded wi' my ain conceit.

"I left Milndour and gaed to Edinburgh, where I was fortunate enough to get work in a nursery, an' then I set mysel' to seek her out. She wasna wi' her auntie. Na; she had turned her to the door when Mr. Baxter wrote sayin' he disowned her; for the auld hypocrite had a son, an' well she could guess wha might fa' heir to the money that should ha'e been Miss Elsie's.

"I trampet the streets every nicht, an' I had been to every hotel i' the town afore I met her just by chance, an' she was so changed that she kent me afore I kent her."

He paused and refilled his pipe.

"But what's the use o' gaun ower a' that again?" he resumed. "The first thing was to see about decent lodgin's for her, an' I advertised i' the *Scotsman.* Ane that answered my advertisement was a Mrs. Austin, an' it was because I wondered if she would be the Elsie Muir I used to ken that I tried her first. She didna ken me, but I kent her, worn and weary though she looket, an' I ta'en the rooms. I was sure she would be well cared for there, an' I had a kind o' thought that the twa o' them bein' Elsie, they would get on wi' ane another. It was when she gaed there that she ca'd hersel' by her middle name, an' she has been Mrs. Rae ever since.

"My next business was to see her lawyer, for she had some twa hunder or thereby a year in her ain richt, frae her mother; an' it was a blessin' she was so weel provided, or it is hard to say what would ha'e happened her. They gi'e lawyers an ill-name, Mr. Urquhart, but that ane was kindness itsel' to me, an' he has been like a brother to Mrs. Rae ever since. Ye'll never hear me say a word against lawyers."

"But what of Mr. Gordon?" Urquhart asked. "Did you not try to see him when he returned?"

"What can you say about him, Mr. Urquhart, but that he was a scoundrel, a damnable scoundrel. He cam' back frae his wanderin's, but he wouldna meet me, an' the letter he wrote to me was——. Eh, man, Mr. Urquhart, ye little ken the power the devil has ower a man that's fashed wi' ambition. Mind that when ye gang to London, an' keep him at arm's length frae ye. Whenever ye begin to mak' a

paction atween yoursel' an' your conscience, you 're
in his clutches, an' he doesna need to bother himsel'
about ye ony mair.   He kens he 's sure o' ye, for he
has putten your feet on the road, an' ye'll follow your
nose to hell.

"It was that letter that killed her; for the Elsie
Baxter I kent has been dead and buried since then.
Mrs. Rae 's only her tombstone.

"She had meetin's wi' her lawyer twa or three
times, an' a' her affairs were left in order, for she
was like ane makin' a will an' preparin' for death.
But I kent little about that; a' I ken was that she
never saw the bairn that was born her, an' that she
was i' the Throstlebrae Asylum afore the Elsie you
ken was a month auld.

"It was then that I gaed an' saw the lawyer again,
an' through him managed to get a place as gardener
at the Asylum.   Little good I could do her, but
I kent it was my duty to be near her an' watch
ower her ; an' the wonderfu' thing is she aye kent
me.   Ay," he mused, with a kind of pride, "she
minded nobody but me."

"And Elsie—the child—remained with Mrs. Austin,
I suppose ? "

"Ay, she 'd no bairns o' her ain, and the feck o'
the money, I found, had been settled on the bairn
afore ever she saw the licht o' day.   Mrs. Austin
hersel' was a jewel o' a woman, though the man,
I thought, was a kind o' cantankerous cr'atur'.   But
it was little I saw o' him.   I expect he did little
to keep the pot boilin', an' Elsie was a godsend
to the poor wife in mair ways than ane.——That 's
Elsie Austin's story, Mr. Urquhart, an' her mother's,
an' a sad, sad story it is."

"And when did Mrs. Rae come here, Walter?"

"Weel, that's wearin' on for eight year syne. Ye see, when my father died, I thought I might come an' just troke awa' as he'd done afore me, wi' the bit market-garden ahent, there, forby doin' the delvin' an' sic like i' the gardens o' them that's no able to do that wark for themsel'. A' the manses here are weel provided wi' garden, an' I've my ain work wi' the three o' them.

"I saw the lawyer again, an' suggested to him that she might be as well livin' wi' some woman that would look after her, in a quiet country place; an' it was him that got her settled here. She lived at first wi' Mrs. Gordon, but on her death he got the Misses Birrell to look after her—an' ye ken the rest yoursel', Mr. Urquhart. She couldna ha'e been in better hands."

They sat and smoked for a while without talking, and the thoughts of both were of Elsie, Watty pondering over the hard and cruel fate of the Elsie he had known, once so light-hearted and happy; Urquhart wondering uneasily what of joy or of suffering life had in store for the Elsie he knew.

Twelve o'clock struck before Urquhart rose to go.

"Tell me, Watty," he said at the door, "Is she like what her mother was at her age?"

"Terrible like; terrible like. I hadna seen her frae she was a bairn till she cam' here, an' it was an awfu' start to me. I sit an' look at her i' the kirk whiles, an' it's her mother I see. I've often wondered about her an' Mrs. Rae livin' so near, mother an' daughter, an' strangers the ane to the other."

"I don't know how it will be, Watty. I'm certain Elsie knows by this time, and—but I'm not going to lose her now. I won't."

"Keep her, Mr. Urquhart, an' tak' care o' her for her ain sake an' for her mother's sake as weel. Think on her life. An' that scoundrel, God pity him, preachin' the gospel o' love!"

"I shall be spending my holiday this week in town, Watty. Perhaps it would be a kindness to her not to speak of this till I come back, though I shall find it hard to wait. But she will be calmer by that time."

"Ay," Watty answered, musingly, "I believe ye 're richt, Mr. Urquhart. That 'll be the best thing ye can do. Guid nicht, an' may the blessin' o' God rest on both you an' her."

CHAPTER TWENTY-EIGHTH

URQUHART left for Edinburgh on Monday morning, where he stayed till the end of the week, and a long weary week it was to him. It had been arranged, before the events of Sunday had come to upset all their plans, that Elsie herself should drive him to Inverorr. But that was out of the question now; and, besides, the roads were so heavy after the snow-storm that driving was impossible. His easiest way was to go to Powmarsh, a wayside station on the single line between Milnforth and Ladyburn. That would mean half-a-day's journey to Edinburgh, no doubt; but Powmarsh was little more than two miles from Kinkelvie, whereas Inverorr was, at least, three times that distance. And, in the state of the roads, even a two miles' walk would be fatiguing.

Rob Buchan met him at the end of the village, and proposed to walk "a bittie" with him. When he got beyond Balgowrie he could take him by a footpath through the Double Plantin', and that would bring him on to the station.

The clouds had snowed themselves out during the night, and now the whole landscape—hill, and loch, and fields—was a stretch of soft undulating white, glittering and sparkling in the sunshine, till the eyes

were dazzled and blinked painfully, looking round
in vain for a restful spot. It was with almost a cry
of relief that Urquhart staggered into the fragrant
gloom of the Plantin'. Coming into its welcome
shade, he had much the same sensation as one
would have crawling out of the dank and vaporous
darkness of a mine to breathe freely in the healthy
light of day.

Rob insisted on carrying his bag for him, but he
trudged on in front, silent as the firs through which
they passed. It was not till they had reached the
station, and rested in the wretched shanty of a
waiting-room, that there was any conversation at
all.

"Mich'el was expectin' ye'd wait till the funeral
on Tuesday," he said; "he'll be sair disappointed."

Urquhart excused himself as best he could. "I
would have stayed," he told him, "if it had been at
all possible. But circumstances almost compel me
to leave, just now. I have thought over everything
very seriously, and have persuaded myself that it
would be best for me to be away for the week. You
know about Mrs. Rae, I suppose?"

"Ay, I was hearin' about the scene on Sabbath
nicht. How is she this mornin'? I had clean forgotten to speir about her. She'll ha'e gotten ower it
by this time?"

"No, Rob, she's worse; so bad, in fact, that I
could not even see Miss Austin this morning to bid
her good-bye. She won't let Elsie out of her sight;
and I'd merely to get her good-bye from Mistress
Janet's lips."

"Ay, ay, man; I thought ye were lookin' a kind o'
worrited-like," Rob answered, in all sympathy. "It's

a sair thing to thole—I was wi' Watty this mornin',
Mr. Urquhart, an' he telled me a' the story."

"You know about Mrs. Rae and this Mr. Gordon,"
he asked, "and Elsie ? "

He added her name as if he were forcing himself
to do so.

" Ay, the whole story ; an' a heart-break o' a story
it is. Eh, the scoundrel ! the scoundrel ! Ay, man,"
he mused, after a bit, "we a' have our troubles. I
used to consider mysel' sair putten till it, when I kent
what was gaun on an' had to howd it frae Mich'el
an' Marg'et. But think o' Watty for a score o' years !
Eh ? What can ye say about him ? The burden o'
affliction has been heavy on him ; but he has borne
it without a grum'le. But this scene has been an
awfu' blow till him ; an' he 's no himsel' this mornin',
or maybe he wouldna na'e telled me."

" He has taken it as a duty imposed on him to be
near Mrs. Rae, and to watch over her," Urquhart
communed. "It may have been a quixotic idea of
duty, but he has stuck to it like a man."

"Ay, a man ! It 's ae thing for a chap to grow a
beard to his chin an' wale a wife to be the mother o'
his bairns, but it 's another thing to be a man. I 've
kent mony a ane grown to the years an' the stature o'
men that were as gauche an' bairnly as the blubberin'
brats that ca'd them father."

Urquhart hardly heard what he was saying; his
head was too full of his own troubles. With him it
was, Elsie, Elsie, Elsie; nothing but Elsie. A foreboding of evil had been with him ever since his talk
with Watty Spence before they set out for church ;
and all that had happened after, had come, as it were,
to confirm and intensify this foreboding until it had

such a hold on him he could not, try as he would, shake himself free from it.

"You'll be back on Saturday?" Rob asked. "I hear her comin' now. She's barely the hour late, an' that's nothing at this time o' year."

"Yes, Rob; Saturday afternoon, and I wish it was here."

But before Saturday came, Kinkelvie had had another sensation to dissect and discuss; and it was a desolate village to Mr. Urquhart when he returned.

Miss Mitchell, who had been away since the previous Friday, arrived in Kinkelvie before him, and, without delay, set herself to analyse the strange things that had happened in her absence. She prided herself on her power of analysis; it was a gift she had; and she was wont to talk of complex sentences, co-ordinate, subordinate, and co-relative clauses, with an easy familiarity that showed she was on intimate terms with these profundities. The simple wives of Kinkelvie heard her mouthing her sesquipedalia, and thought it almost profanity that she should utter them so lightly. The men heard her in silence, not venturing to speak till she was out of ear-shot, when they shocked the faith of their wives with a monosyllabic reflection that was at once sarcastic, profane, and sceptical.

Once on a time when Miss Mitchell was a pupil teacher in Edinburgh she had had sole charge of a section of a class, and Her Majesty's Inspector in his report had made special mention of the excellent appearance her pupils had made in analysis. And the sentence had not been an easy one either. She remembered it, and quoted it yet. It was a sentence no mortal man had used, one would be

safe to say, from the days of Adam, and such
as it would be impossible to hear outside the walls
of a school room or college. "Into the very middle of
the stream plunged the hunter's very brave dog." That
was the sentence they had got, and the little pundits
of nine and ten had fixed the subject at a glance,
and brought down the predicate without a second's
stalking. Then they grappled remorsefully with the
parsing, and after a brilliant skirmish with the two
"verys," came off with flying colours. Since then
Miss Mitchell had worshipped analysis. She was
sure she had an analytical mind.

But, like those marvellous detectives who shame-
lessly elaborate their slimy experiences, and boast
of what they are pleased to call their analytical
faculties, the little schoolmistress tried to square
facts with her suspicions. Everything that had
happened pointed to Mr. Urquhart. He was at the
bottom of all the mischief.

"Depend upon it," she told Mrs. Gray, after
learning the facts of the case, "there is some under-
hand work here, and you will see it has been the
hand of *one*. I don't mention any name, but why
was he at church with the Misses Birrell that night?
It is the only time he has been to church with
them. And the very first time he is within its walls
this scene takes place. It's very suspicious, Mrs.
Gray."

Mrs. Gray shook her head. "I can't tell what you
mean, Miss Mitchell; the worst happened after
he had left. So how can you blame him? He went
away from here on Monday morning."

"When did they take her away?" Miss Mitchell
asked.

"On Wednesday, poor soul! It was a sad sight, Miss Mitchell, I can tell you."

"Was she very wild? Did she scream and——. You know I've heard, Mrs. Gray, that people, when they are mad, often say awful words. Did she say anything wicked—or naughty, you know?"

"She was very quiet, Miss Mitchell. She was quiet so long as Miss Elsie was beside her, but if she went from her side for a minute she was—terrible. Dear, dear! Don't ask any more, Miss Mitchell. It's very, very sad."

"It's very, very suspicious," Miss Mitchell considered. "Why should she cling so to Miss Austin? And there was a lawyer too, you say, from Edinburgh."

"Yes, and a doctor. The doctor and Miss Elsie went with her, and Walter Spence. But she didn't know anybody but Miss Elsie, not even Mistress Janet and Miss Agnes."

"I suppose there's no use asking them anything," Miss Mitchell sneered. "I was awfully disappointed in them. I used to think them gentle and dainty, you know — quite ladies. But you should have heard their sentiments about fighting? And they've such a high opinion of Mr. Urquhart. Of course, it wouldn't suit them to say a word against him so long as he pays for his rooms. You wouldn't say a word against me, Mrs. Gray," she simpered, imagining in her self-complacence that she was talking nicely to her landlady. "Would you now?"

Mrs. Gray blushed. Whether it was that something nasty in the implied compliment jarred on her, or merely that she could not answer Miss Mitchell's question at once truthfully and politely, she herself perhaps could not tell. But Miss Mitchell was too well pleased with herself to notice her landlady's agitation, and her stammering reply was accepted in all graciousness.

"I suppose Miss Austin is back again?" was the next question.

"Yes; but she has gone away since. She is staying for a week or two, I heard, with the Muirs of Balbie. They are some far-off relations of Muiredge; the two daughters stayed a fortnight here last winter, you remember. She was needing a change certainly, for she was quite knocked up; she hadn't been in bed from Sunday to Wednesday. The sea air will do her good."

"I wonder!" the little schoolmistress mused. "Perhaps Mr. Urquhart is there too. I met a friend of his at a party last night, and he said he hadn't seen Mr. Urquhart since Wednesday. That just exactly fits in with your story, Mrs. Gray. Miss Austin would go away on Thursday?"

Mrs. Gray looked at her in wonder. This young lady was far too clever for her. She couldn't say the simplest thing but Miss Mitchell saw a new meaning and a new story in it.

"Yes," she admitted; "she left on Thursday morning."

Miss Mitchell lifted down the lamp and lit it.

"Depend upon it, Mrs. Gray, that's where Mr. Urquhart is; and it's not proper. Miss Austin may be a very fine lady, and accomplished—she does know a little about music; but if she has gone there to meet Mr. Urquhart, she's no better than she ought to be.—What is that jingling, Mrs. Gray?"

Mrs. Gray listened.

"It must be Mr. Muir in his sleigh," she said;
"yes; that's the tinkle of the bells."

"A sleigh?" Miss Mitchell echoed. "Oh, how
nice! Fancy, a lovely frosty night; and all wrapped
in furs; and the stars; and flying along. How
delightful!"

They had both moved to the door as she was
speaking, and now the sleigh glided past them, and
drew up at the Misses Birrell's door.

"Mr. Urquhart!" the schoolmistress gasped.
"Fancy, Mr. Muir going to the station to drive him.
And I'd to come up in that rickety old thing of
Robert Buchan's. Surly old man he is, too. And
then to lift me right out, wraps and all, as if I had
been a baby! I thought he was going to swallow
me altogether when I screamed. 'Ay', ay', mem!'
she tried to imitate Rob's broad pronunciation.
'They'd loss by you that selled ye by the weight.'
How vulgar!"

"I should have taken that as a compliment," was
Mrs. Gray's opinion.

"Perhaps it would sound pretty in English, but
not in his coarse speech. Look, there's Walter
Spence with them, and here's Mr. Muir coming back
again. Isn't it lovely, Mrs. Gray? Doesn't it make
you think of furs, nice sealskin jackets, and bear-
boas?"

She bowed to Mr. Muir, who waved to them as he
glided past, and they heard the jingle of the bells
after he was lost to sight.

After tea, Miss Mitchell called on the Misses
Birrell. The news she had heard was sensational
enough in all truth, but it was too meagre, and she
could not rest till she had heard more; till she had

learned everything to the minutest detail. But the
Misses Birrell received her coldly, and quietly refused
to gratify her curiosity. When she inquired about
Mrs. Rae, they told her it was too painful a subject
for them to talk about. She would excuse them,
they hoped. They could not speak even to each
other about what had happened. It had been a sad,
sad week to them.

One thing, however, the schoolmistress did learn,
and that was that Mr. Urquhart was terribly cut up
when he knew that Mrs. Rae had had to be taken off
to an asylum. Mr. Muir had gone to meet him at
Inverorr, and had been the first to tell him. He
hadn't known about Elsie either, for he had written
to her from Edinburgh, addressing the letter to
Muiredge. " It had been a fearful blow to him,"
Mistress Janet said, and he had gone straight to his
room as soon as he arrived. They heard him moving
about even now.

The next three weeks passed slowly and wearily
for Mr. Urquhart. He worked as hard as he could
in school, and with the two pupils at night, but still
the days dragged. He sat up half the night trying
to read or write, but it was almost impossible for him
to fix his mind on any work. Occasionally Watty
and Rob dropped in to see him, and sat and smoked
with him. For both knew what it was that was
troubling him ; but they had not much to say. It
was enough to come and enjoy a pipe with him for
an hour or so, and shake hands with him when they
rose to go, giving him a grip that made him wince
with the pain.

He wrote several times to Elsie, but received no
answer, and now the fear that she had merely gone

to Balbie to escape him became almost a certainty. She had learned everything, Mr. Muir told him, and had taken it calmly, like one stunned. She knew that Mrs. Rae was her mother, and that she herself was nameless. And now, so both Mr. Muir and Mr. Urquhart feared, she had determined to break off her engagement, because of the reproach that clung to her. She was branded in the eyes of the world, and unfit to be the wife of an honest man.

"She told me nothing about this," Mr. Muir admitted wearily, "only I could read it in her eyes, and it was terrible, Mr. Urquhart. She has been as a daughter to me, and it cut me to the heart to see her silent suffering. I could do nothing ; that was the worst of it. And when this invitation came from Balbie, I thought at the time that the change would do her good. But when I asked her how long she would stay, she just came and kissed my cheek, that was all. It was like a stab, Mr. Urquhart, for I knew what she meant."

"I don't know what to do, Mr. Muir. It would be unwise to go to Balbie. She has gone there to fight this out alone, and I can only wait till she comes back. I must see her before I go."

"It is a question you must settle for yourselves," Mr. Muir considered, "you and Elsie. I can't help you, and you know I would if I could. You wouldn't have me write and order her home."

Urquhart, as the days passed and it came near to the day of his departure, went about half dazed. He was suffering from sleeplessness, and had become nervous as well as melancholy. He did not know what to do, and it was Watty in the end who helped him out of his difficulty.

It was the Friday night before he left Kinkelvie. He had taught his last day in school, and come home with a little present which the school-children had given him that afternoon. Now he was making ready to go on the Saturday. All the books he wished to take with him were already packed when Rob and Watty entered. Watty was bursting with a brilliant idea; Urquhart could see that at once. Before ever they had got their pipes lit he began.

"Does she ken when ye leave for London?" he asked.

"Yes, I told her I should start from Edinburgh on Monday night."

"A telegram!" Watty cried, delightedly. "Telegraph to your friend, him that's the writer, an' say ye'll no be there till the end o' the week."

"Well, Watty, I have thought of that, but it's no use. She will not leave Balbie until she hears that I have gone from Kinkelvie for good, and she writes to Robert almost every day. She has made up her mind, and no doubt she considers it her duty."

"But gang to Edinburgh the morn, as ye were plannin'," Watty whispered. "Say good-bye to Muiredge an' a' body. Rob an' me will no tell; an' come back again next week. It's Elsie I'm thinkin' on," he added, as a special argument. "It's her mother an' her that I've ha'en to look after, an' now Mrs. Rae has been ta'en frae me, in a sense. She didna ken me this time. That was the sairest of a'. But still I've Elsie left, an' I'd like to see her married."

"Ay," Rob concurred, "married to you, Mr. Urquhart, for both your sakes."

Urquhart rose and shook both men by the hand.

" I 'll adopt your plan, Watty.   I must see her before
I go."

And that was how Robert Urquhart came back to
Kinkelvie again, after having bidden a long farewell
to all his friends on the Saturday night.

When he arrived at Inverorr he drove straight to
Muiredge.   Mr. Muir was astonished to see him, but
when the plot was explained he entered into it heart
and soul.

" Elsie arrives this afternoon," he said, " and you
must be here to meet us on our return."

But Urquhart had another proposal to make.   " I
shall drive to the station myself and meet her," he
suggested ; " that is, if you have no objections.   The
roads are safe enough now, and I daresay you could
trust me with the trap."

So it was arranged, and he was at the station in
plenty of time.   The train was late, and when it did
arrive he stood at the horse's head till a porter came
shouldering her luggage, and Elsie behind him.

She started when she saw who had come to meet
her, and, pale as she was, her cheek became paler
still.

Urquhart looked at her, and for a moment could
not speak, so great was the change he saw in her
face.   It was beautiful still, but with a spiritual
beauty, and he read in a glance the terrible tale of
suffering she had come through.

Then he stepped to her side and took her hand.
She was trembling visibly, and regarded him with
wistful, reproachful eyes.

" Elsie,' he said, " I have come to meet you."

" Robert "—the name was no more than a whisper
—" Mr. Urquhart, why did you come ? "

"Now," he said, with an attempt at gaiety, "you must get in. Allow me." He helped her in, happed her about with the rugs, and then sat down beside her. "That's too long a story to tell here, Elsie. But we'll make it all right at home."

She leaned back and closed her eyes.

"Come now," he said, speaking still with an attempt at cheerfulness, "this is your favourite, Mysie. Will you drive, or are you willing to risk the reins in my hands?"

"You, Robert," she answered, without opening her eyes; "I am tired. Oh, why, did you come; why did you come after I had fought it all out?"

He did not answer, only pulled the haps more closely round her shoulders, and tucked the rug in at her side, and they drove to Muiredge almost without another word of conversation.

When they reached home she sat down in the dining-room before going upstairs. Urquhart left the boys to look after the horse and trap, and came in with her. She went up and kissed Mr. Muir, who took her face between his hands and looked into the eyes. "And how is my little daughter?" he asked with a smile. "I'm afraid the sea air has taken the roses out of her cheeks."

"I'm quite well, only tired," she said, "very tired ; and I have a slight headache. I think I shall go up to bed. "Good-night," she said, turning to Mr. Urquhart, and offering him her hand ; "you will excuse me to-night; I am tired."

"No, Elsie," he answered ; "you are not going yet, nor in that way."

Mr. Muir left them, closing the door as he went out.

"I am going away to-morrow, Elsie," Urquhart continued, "and I wish to have a talk with you before I go."

"I am tired, Robert; so tired."

He took off her hat and her boa, laying them on the table, and then began unfastening her gloves. She let him take them off, too, without a word.

"Now," he said, "you shall sit down in this chair where I sat one happy forenoon, and we shall talk as seriously as we talked then, and I trust as happily. There! You are quite comfortable?"

She laid her face on her hands, and sobbed as if her heart were breaking.

He stood near her, and laid his hand lightly on her head until the sobbing ceased and she grew calm.

Then he went and leaned on the mantelpiece where he could see her face.

"I'm going to-morrow, Elsie," he said again, "and I wish only to say good-bye before I go, and to arrange about writing to each other while we are so far distant, until I come again and claim you as my wife."

"Robert, Robert," she pleaded, "you hurt me more than I can tell. I have been fighting it out these three weeks, and now, when I have fought to the bitter end, you come and make me begin the fight again. It is cruel. It is not manly."

"No, Elsie! There is to be no fight again. Whenever you say you have ceased to love me, I shall leave you alone, and you will never see my face again; but till then I shall not give you up, nor will you give me up."

"You don't know what I have suffered, Robert.

Do you think it has cost me nothing that you talk
so lightly, after it is all past ?"

"I am not talking lightly, Elsie; and it is not past.
It is because I see what you have suffered that I
insist. Would you have your life to be a continual
repetition of the three weeks that you have gone
through ?"

She shuddered, holding her hands to her eyes.

"I am not going to be dismissed like this, Elsie.
You think I am cruel ? I shall be cruel for an hour,
if it must be so, that I may not be cruel to you for
life. Have you not seen enough of sacrificed lives
that you would sacrifice yours and mine ?"

"Oh, not yours, Robert," she moaned, "not yours.
It was to save yours from being sacrificed. Why
will you torture me to tell you what I am ? You
know. You knew when you fought Mr. Muckersie.
Oh, I saw it all so clearly on Monday morning. I
thought he had called me a flirt, but that name—
that horrible, horrible name ! Oh, Robert, spare
me ! Go !"

"I shall spare you, Elsie. I shall spare you a life
of misery ; but I won't go yet."

"Won't ?" She looked up at him, but the light in
her eyes was not of anger.

"I won't, Elsie. And I won't let you sacrifice
either your life or mine. For whether you see it or
not, you are deliberately sacrificing mine."

"Oh, Robert, Robert ! Deliberately ? After all I
have suffered."

"But your sufferings must end, Elsie, and there is
only one way of ending them. Our engagement is
not to be broken off. Do you know how sacred and
binding an engagement is ?"

"Do I know, Robert? Yes; I should have been true to you till death. I shall be true to you till death as it is, for no other shall kiss my lips as you have kissed them."

"Because you love me, Elsie?"

"You know I do; although it is cruel of you to force me to say so now. But is there nothing else than love in the world? There is God's law, as well as love."

"God's law is the law of love, isn't it, Elsie?"

"Oh, Robert, leave me! You torture me. It cannot be. Have you not read, 'Visiting the sins of the fathers upon the children'?"

"That is from the second commandment, Elsie. The only commandment you should lay on me, and make me write on my heart, is the first, 'Thou shalt have no other goddesses before me.' And I won't."

"You are irreverent, Robert, and flippant; and you pain me."

"Because you compel me, Elsie. But I shall compel you."

He bent over and raised her from the chair. The power of resistance was gone from her. He clasped her to him, and she laid her head on his breast and burst into tears.

When she ceased, he bent and kissed her again and again.

"You shall never give me up, Elsie."

She flung her arms around his neck and clung to him. "Don't leave me, Robert, don't leave me. Oh, I love you, I love you because you are stronger than I am. All the agony of these weeks is gone, isn't it? Tell me it's past, Robert, Robert."

He stroked her hair, and she leaned her head again

on his breast. "I was so tired," she sighed. "I
made up a prayer last week to say every night.
'God bless Robert; make him forget me, and send
him some one better, who will love him as much as I
do.' But when I came to say it, I could only say
'God bless Robert.' The rest was too hard. My
heart wouldn't say it; my lips wouldn't say it, and
I rebelled so. Robert," in a whisper, "I shall have
your name some day, and then I won't be—
nameless?"

"Weesht, Elsie, weesht! Mr. Muir will be returning presently, and I must be going. I shall not
see you for a long time, more than a year, but we
shall write every week."

"Yes, Robert; I shall be happy now, though you
are away, because I am not going to lose you, and I
know you love me, and you have all my love. Is it
wrong, Robert? I cannot love Mrs. Rae—my
mother. I only pity her. But I am vexing you;
I won't speak any more about that. Kiss me now.
Here's Uncle."

Mr. Muir was a happy man that night when he gave
both his blessing, but perhaps the happiest men
on earth were Watty Spence and Rob Buchan when
Urquhart met them at the Inn, where he had trysted
to meet them. There was no need of words. He
marched in upon them and gave them his hands.

Watty jumped from his seat. "Three glasses o'
your very best, Donal'," he shouted; "the very best
ye ha'e i' the house."

"Mak' it four, Donal'," Rob corrected; "an'
brandy."

CHAPTER   *GRANT'S VISIT*
TWENTY-NINTH   *TO LONDON*

A LMOST two years have passed since Robert
Urquhart left Kinkelvie.

It is a broiling August day, and the air of London
is sultry and still. Two young fellows are seated
in a room, the windows of which look into one of
those streets branching off Russell Square. Gavin
Crombie has drawn the lounge up to the opened
window, and sits sipping a cup of cold tea, his
favourite beverage. The other, occupying two chairs,
and smoking the identical briar he had filled and
emptied so often at meetings of the Cockburn Clique,
is Bernard Kaye.

It is a comparatively quiet street. They hear from
the Square the roll of 'buses and the rhythmical
patter of hooves, softened almost into music; and
rising and falling now and again, like a voice above
its accompaniment, the tinkle of passing hansoms.

Kaye's hat and stick are laid on the table, so it is
evident he is only making a call, but one can see at a
glance that Crombie belongs to the room, and the
room to him. He has thrown off his coat, and his
feet, lifted on to the lounge, are in seedy-looking
slippers—bauchles they would have been called in
Kinkelvie.

Crombie sipped dreamily at his tea, turning his head to the window every now and again, and listening when he heard the tinkle of a hansom in the street. Kaye finished his pipe and reached for the carafe, but on second thoughts set it down again.

"Nothing better to drink, old man?" he asked. "This water is beastly stuff."

"You know the press yourself. See what you can find."

Kaye crossed the room and returned with a bottle of lager. "Ah," he sighed with satisfaction; "only decent drink I've had this week."

"Broke?"

"Not a bit," he answered, throwing open his jacket and displaying the gold chain. "Redeemed yesterday; in funds, you see. Been saving for the week with Grant. Wouldn't do to let Sandy know of my small economies; he'd carry it straight back to the old folks. Must show him about, too; his first visit to London."

"Have you been out to see the house Urquhart has taken?"

"Yes; out last week. Quite idyllic! When is it coming off now?"

"He goes down to Scotland end of next month, and I expect he'll bring her back with him. The chief and he are chums, and I expect the wives will be great friends, too. Live quite near."

"They should be here by this time." Kaye looked at his watch. "King's Cross, Urquhart said?"

"And here they are," Crombie cried, rising and peering over the window, as the sound reached them of a hansom pulling up below.

A minute afterwards Grant and Urquhart entered. Sandy looked the same as ever, and came in beaming and talking, asking questions and forgetting what he had asked.

"And how are you, old man? Looking fresh. And you, Kaye? In the Academy yet? Suffocating, isn't it? No air at all here. Some chemical preparation, I suppose, made in Germany."

"Don't you know, Sandy," Crombie asked very seriously, "that London air is just filtered fog. They catch the fogs at the East End now-a-days, and pass them through a sieve; it's said to be very healthy."

"You don't happen to know the derivation of *fog*, do you?" Sandy asked. "*Fog* in Scots is moss. I wonder if they are from the same root."

"The same root!" Kaye chuckled, "the same root! That's a good joke, Sandy. Didn't think you could joke at all."

"Chemists and botanists are not quite agreed on that point yet," Crombie informed him, still speaking in all seriousness; "but an hour's walk in a London fog will leave you in little doubt as to its derivation."

"Humbug!" Sandy shoved his bag and a pile of papers into a corner, and, throwing himself down on the lounge which Crombie had just vacated, proceeded to make himself at home.

"Now," he announced, "I'll just stretch myself for a bit, and then we'll go out; I'm eager to explore the place. Suppose we give a look in at Greenwich Hospital—I should like to see that—and the Zoological Gardens. Do you know I hate to hear people speak about the 'Zoo.'"

"Very good," Crombie agreed. "Couldn't we do Kew Gardens, also, and Epping Forest on the way?"

"By all means," Sandy answered. "I must see everything, you know; and I've often read of Kew. Anything special on at the music halls to-night?"

Kaye gurgled with laughter, and Urquhart, standing in his favourite position, his arm on the mantelpiece, smiled down on Sandy rattling away supremely unconscious of his woeful ignorance.

Looking at him as he stood there, one would have seen his face more changed in these two years than the faces of any of the others. His hair was thinner at the temples, and the lines under his eyes had deepened. The mouth, however, was even firmer, although the eyes looked milder, than formerly. It was the face of one who had had his own trials and troubles, and now could sympathise with others in affliction.

Certainly he had had a pretty rough time of it since he came to London, and so had Kaye; but they had struggled along with an air of jaunty indifference, now down on their luck and borrowing where they could, now in funds and lending lavishly. For, in London, young fellows know how hard the battle of life is, and this knowledge makes them ever ready to help one another when they can; and if fortune does happen to smile on one of them, the opportunity of helping a luckless brother is rarely wanting.

Urquhart could have told many stories both of borrowing and lending; of pawning and redeeming. One story he never forgot of a young fellow from Yorkshire, whom he had met now and again, dodging about like himself from office to office, trying to raise money on some personal paragraph or occasional article. "Rum" was the name this youth got to be

x

known by, not from any predilection for a special liquor, but because "Rum" was his favourite ejaculation. He used it in his speech oftener than he used any other word in the language, and there were some who did not know him by any other name.

It was about the end of Urquhart's first six months in London, and he was in sore straits. Everything he could pawn had been pawned, and he hadn't a copper in his possession. True, there were various sums of money due to him for work done; but so long as there is a companion to tide him over a week, the struggling journalist or artist does not apply to the editor for money that must, in the ordinary course of things, be his. He is reduced to the lowest ebb when it comes to that.

In his need at the time, Urquhart thought of Kaye and went to call, only to find that he also was down on his luck; and it was while the two sat talking that Rum came in upon them. He hadn't a farthing either, but he had an idea.

"Tell you what!" he cried. "I'm going round to the office of the *Christian Hoax*"—a name he always gave a certain paper necessity compelled him to write for—"Editor's about as 'cute as they make 'em. Rum, eh? Commercial Christianity is his line, eh? Rum, I tell you. Took this article to him yesterday on what's-his-name's sermon last Sunday. Forget the bloke's name. Rum, eh? What d'you think he told me? Just shows what the *Christian Hoax* is. Said there wasn't enough of *Jesus Christ* in my article. Rum, you bet. Got it back to sprinkle the name in freely. Rum thing to do! Beastly rum! But got to do it. Going back with it now. Cash down, I expect."

Rum came back in about half an hour.

"Eighteen bob!" he cried, delightedly. "And we share equally."

But Urquhart knew he had not had time to go to the office and back, and he noticed now that he had neither watch nor chain.

Crombie had always been inclined to laugh at Rum as a man who was not to be taken seriously; but he had ever spoken of him with respect after Urquhart had told him this story.

But all these days of hungers and bursts were over for Urquhart now, although he was in touch with them still, for there were young fellows round about him, struggling as he had struggled, and requiring now and again that helping hand that had never failed him in his sorest need. He had got into a fairly good post by this time, but his success had not come to kill in him that spirit of *camaraderie* which binds the struggling cliques of professional youths in London, and makes beautiful, lives that had otherwise seemed sordid and mean.

He looked at Sandy stretched at his ease on the lounge, and thought of his teaching days. Had it been well for him that he had left school? He couldn't tell. He had had a hard fight since then; whereas had he stuck to teaching he would have been earning a fixed salary all the time, and facing each morrow without a pecuniary care. But though the fight had been hard, he looked back on it now without a regret—nay, indeed, with a certain amount of pride. Perhaps, again, if he had remained a teacher, he might have gone under, as poor Gilchrist had done; for, just a month ago, he had received intimation of Gilchrist's death. He had been nervous and excitable, just as Urquhart himself was; and who knows but that the strain and worry, the wearisome drudgery of elementary teaching, might have carried him to a similar end?

Sandy turned towards Urquhart. It almost seemed as if he had been reading his thoughts.

"I suppose you heard about poor Gilchrist?" he asked. "One of the members of the Board said that he had been simply killed by the Code. Pretty strong thing to say, wasn't it? It just shows that the members know how exacting the blamed thing is, and would help us if they could. But they can't. And I can tell you teaching's not a bed of roses. You're well off, you fellows. You don't know what work is. It's all play with you, and occasional cheques."

"Very occasional!" Kaye murmured.

"Don't you grumble, Sandy," Urquhart told him. "I used to think it bad enough; but I've come through worse since then. Besides, you don't know London schools, or you would thank your stars night and morning that you were in Edinburgh. It's a killing business here; and the tragedy is that the poor fellows will live on long after they have been killed. Why, the Board actually keeps a staff of detectives—euphemistically called Inspectors—who prowl about to pounce on teachers who may not be teaching according to their time-table. I thought that kind of thing had been satirised to the death."

"That wouldn't hurt me," Sandy complacently observed. "I always stick to my time-table."

"I never did," Urquhart confessed, "and didn't attempt to."

"But bother school!" Sandy cried. "I'm here for a holiday, and what are you fellows going to do? The first thing I want is a wash. Then we go out. When is the Tower open?"

"Wouldn't you like to see the British Museum?" Crombie asked. "It's quite near. That's why Urquhart and I live in this quarter of the town."

"The British Museum!" Sandy exclaimed. "The very place! Let us go at once. I suppose you are allowed to study there; and you can get any book you like. Why, you fellows are lucky beggars. I've been planning out a book of late, but it'll need a lot of reading. 'The origin and meaning of place-names.' And this would be the very spot for it. It's a splendid subject. Fancy how many examples you can have from the Bible alone, all with their meaning and the story of their origin ready to hand. Then think of the North American Indian place-names, and their meanings; and China, and India, and the Highlands, and——but the subject is endless. And the world's just waiting for that book too."

"Issue it in monthly parts," Kaye suggested, "and let me have the commission for illustration."

"No," Sandy said; "I shall launch it in one volume, and you will see it will create a sensation. But there's no chance of undertaking one's *magnum opus* in Edinburgh. Now if I were in London, I should read every book bearing on the subject in the British Museum."

"That's penal servitude for life," was Crombie's opinion.

"Oh, but I should manage!" Sandy confidently asserted. "Why take Scotland alone. Look at those names I got when I was collecting my Scots-French words—*Burdiehouse, Thankerton, St. Ford,* which the natives pronounce *Sangfor.*"

Kaye lit his pipe.

"Go on, Sandy," he said. "This is like old times. Haven't heard a word about—what do you call it again—Piology—or something like that—since I left Edinburgh. Fire away. The Cockburn Clique rises like the phœnix from its ashes. Fish out some lager, Urquhart, and let us enjoy ourselves."

"Now, that's an interesting story," Sandy shouted; "and hundreds talk about the phœnix who don't know what they are talking about."

"I don't," Kaye admitted; "but I don't know what you are talking about, either. So it's all right. Go ahead."

"Then there's Champfleurie ——."

"Used to sketch in that quarter," Kaye interrupted; "near Linlithgow. Fire away, Sandy; it goes down beautifully with this lager. Isn't it like old times, Crombie? You haven't an odd number of the magazine about you, have you, Sandy?"

"Then think of the Keltic place-names," Sandy continued. "Why, half the towns in Scotland are Keltic. Now you, Urquhart, lived in Kinkelvie, and I don't believe you ever tried to find out why the natives called it Kinkelvie, and not Kinkelvinwood. And, by-the-bye, that reminds me! Where's that *Scotsman* I brought up with me? There's an old friend of yours dead there. You remember that old lady who lived with the Misses Birrell? Something wrong in the upper storey?"

"Mrs. Rae!" Urquhart ejaculated.

"That's the name. She's gone. See it there."

Urquhart took the paper and read the announcement—

"At Kinkelvinwood on the 19th inst., suddenly, Mrs. Rae—Elsie R. Baxter—in her forty-eighth year."

He read it out to Crombie, who knew the whole story of his stay in Kinkelvie. They had often talked of it; and Crombie knew how hard he had been working to have everything ready for his marriage, which he was now eagerly looking forward to.

"I think I ought to go to Scotland right off, if I can get away," he said.

"You were intending to go down next month at the latest," Crombie mused. "It's only a case of running off a month sooner than you expected. Yes, old man, I think you should go at once. She'll expect you, I'm certain of that."

"What am I to do then?"

"Go and pack up. I'll wire to the chief—he's in town, isn't he? We'll get a reply in plenty time."

"Wire?" Sandy echoed. "I wonder at you, Crombie, you that used to be such a stickler for style and pure English. Wire is a bastard word, worse than vulgar, even. But why telegraph at all if he's in town? Let us go and see your chief, and explain matters. That seems to me the best way."

Crombie smiled. "We're a lazy lot," he said, "and spendthrift as well. We'd rather spend a sixpence on a telegram, than a shilling on trains. What'll I say for you? 'Called to Scotland; likely be away week.' That'll do, I think. Now you go and turn out your trunk. I'll go round to the office with this."

In about half-an-hour a reply came back. "Take a month, my boy, you need a holiday."

"And my holiday, too?" Sandy bemoaned, "I come to London to see you, and you run off the very first night."

"Can't be helped, Sandy. I leave you in good hands. Kaye is going to take this week with you, and you 'll have Crombie every night after six."

So Robert Urquhart left King's Cross that night for Edinburgh.

CHAPTER THIRTIETH
BACK TO KINKELVIE

URQUHART had not been in Scotland since he first came south, but he had been kept well posted in all the news of Kinkelvie. Occasionally he had a letter from Watty Spence, and, of course, he had corresponded regularly with Elsie. Only yesterday, it seemed to him—yet it must have been at least six months ago—had she written telling him of Mrs. Rae's return to the Misses Birrell. For it was almost always Mrs. Rae she called her in her letters, rarely mother. He had also had a letter from Watty at the same time, a strange, pathetic kind of letter, meant to be bubbling over with the good news of her return ; yet to Urquhart, reading it, every line was touched with an infinite pity for the change that had come over her. She did not know him now. Watty told this again and again with pathetic iteration. He had gone to the head of the garden on the Sunday morning, but she had not, as in the old days, come to him with her bible. All that was forgotten, too, and she remembered neither his face nor his name. Still she was free again, and in that fact Watty found what consolation he could.

Now she was dead. Urquhart could not say he

was sorry. He had been sorry for her since he had first seen her, and perhaps death had been to her now a blessed release. Or was it not rather that she had died many, many years ago, and left only a soulless body to serve out its allotted years on earth?

It was Saturday evening when he arrived at Kinkelvie, but he had telegraphed from Edinburgh to the Misses Birrell, and Watty and Rob were waiting for him at the end of the village when he came.

"Ye've just missed the funeral," were Watty's first words; "but we're glad to see you."

Rob gripped his hand, and scrutinised his face.

"Welcome to Kinkelvie for the second time," he said. "Ye're aulder than when ye cam' first, an' the lines o' labour are deeper i' your face; but that's no disgrace. It's the good ground that tak's the deepest furrows."

Urquhart alighted from the machine, and walked along the street with them. Here was Donald, too, at his door, waiting to bid him welcome, and his sonsy wife smiling at his side. There was little or no change in any of the men from what he had first known them. For all that he could tell, they were wearing the identical suits of clothes he had seen them in, the first night he arrived at Kinkelvie.

And there was as little change in the Misses Birrell. Mistress Janet was still as quiet and sweet as of old, while Miss Agnes bustled about when he came in, with the same beaming restlessness that he had liked in her when he had made his home with them.

What a delight it was to be with them again, and to feel that he was once more in a home! His life in London was already little else than a dream.

Here was his room, too, just as he had left it, his
books lining the walls; the old-fashioned paper-knife
and his favourite pen lying on the writing-table, as if
he had left them there an hour ago.   On the mantelpiece was lying an old briar pipe that he had brought
with him here from Edinburgh.

He sat down by the window, and waited till the
gloaming died into darkness, and then he caught
the twinkle of light through the trees that had been
his beacon in other days.

"God bless her," he murmured again. "Now I have
come back to claim her for mine own, and the 'some
day' I have longed for is here at last."

It was too late to go to Muiredge that night, and
when he came downstairs he found that Watty and
Rob had been invited to have supper with him; and
a happy party the five of them made.   There was no
loud laughter or boisterousness; for Mrs. Rae had
been carried from the house that very day, and it was
meet that they should be quiet and decorous.   But
there was no pretence of inconsolable grief because
of her death.   She had found rest at last, Mistress
Janet said, and they ought rather to be thankful, for
she had wearied for it sorely, and sought it with tears.

"We shall miss her, Mr. Urquhart," Miss Agnes
said; "but it was best for her.   It came sudden at
the last, but it came quietly, and she bade us all
good-bye.   She sent for Elsie and Walter, and we
were all with her when she passed away."

"Ay," Watty told him proudly; "she kent me i'
the end.   She minded me, an' ca'd me by my ain
name—Walter, Walter.   But she never mentioned
him."

Of course, they had to give him the latest news

and tell him about all his friends. Old Michael was still living, but failing sorely, and hardly fit for work now.

"He'll be awfu' proud to see ye," Rob said. "I telled him ye'd come. Of course, ye ken he bides wi' me now, an' Bauby has the twa o' us to look after. He tak's a turn at the loom every day, but very little ser's him. It pleases him, howsomever, an' passes the time."

"I heard that Frank had been home for a week or two," Urquhart said. "How is he looking now?"

"Lookin' weel, Mr. Urquhart," Rob answered with gladness in his voice, "lookin' weel. He's ta'en up what you left aff, for he's a schoolmaster i' the regiment."

"That's splendid news, Rob."

"Ay, man, it was a pictur' to see auld Mich'el gang about leanin' on his arm, so proud-like. The army has made a man o' Frank, and Mich'el has been another bein' since he was here."

"And of course you would hear of Mr. Muckersie's marriage?" Mistress Janet asked.

Urquhart looked surprised. "No," he said; "that's news to me, certainly."

"What?" cried Miss Agnes. "I must ask Miss Elsie what she means. How could she forget such an interesting bit of information as that?"

"She hasn't once mentioned Mr. Muckersie's name," he answered. "And yet, perhaps, it is my own fault. I believe I ought to have known. In a letter she told me that Miss Mitchell had got married, and she left me to guess to whom. I guessed Mr. Andrews, my successor. But I suppose I was wrong."

Watty grinned. "No, she didna manage that; though we'll no' blame her; it wasna her fau't. But she's settled now; ay, an' so is Ba'bingry."

"They were just kirket a week past on Sabbath," Rob said, continuing the story; "an' it was a sicht to see. She was braw, I'se warrant ye, an' carried hersel' like a queen, toddling along by his side, her hand no higher than his pouch."

"High enough for her," was Watty's opinion; "for she'll seek no higher. An' it'll need to be a weel filled pouch to please her. She has made the sister sing sma' a'ready. Helen thought she could snap her fingers in ony woman's face, but the little school-mistress was ane ower muckle for her; an' she's glad now, they tell me, to keep to the kitchen an' the byre, an' she tak's the wife's orders as meek as a lamb."

"Didn't they quarrel the very first day?" Miss Agnes asked.

"Ay, Miss Agnes; there was a war o' words for ae forenoon, but that settled it. Helen left the parlour cowed, an' now she speaks to the servant lasses about 'the mistress.'"

"And what of John Cochrane, Watty? I heard he had left the district."

"Ay, he's in an engineer's shop in Haliston. It was Muiredge that got him there. I'm hearin' that he's pickin' it up wonderfu'."

So they chatted the hours away till it was time for Rob and Watty to be going, and Urquhart went up to bed. How still everything was to him here! Memory carried him back to the first night he had spent in Kinkelvie, and now he felt the awful silence even more than he had felt it then. It was too

impressive for sleep, but at last he closed his eyes,
and slumbered peacefully, dreaming of London and
paragraphs and reviews, and waking to all the beauty
of an August Sabbath morning in Kinkelvie.

He walked down to Muiredge immediately after
breakfast. Just outside the village he overtook old
Michael, out to breathe the air of the fields before
preparing for church.

"Well, Michael," he said, "how are you? I am
awfully glad to see you again."

"Mr. Urquhart," Michael exclaimed, blinking up
into his face, for Michael was sorely bowed, and had
to look up. "The Lord has been good to me, for I
didna think to live to look on your face again."

"Nonsense, Michael; you must live to see me
come again and again."

"The wish is no so kind as it's kindly meant,
Mr. Urquhart. I'm comin' nearer to her every day,
an' I ken He'll no keep me muckle langer frae
Marg'et. Out o' His boundless mercy He spared me
to see my son—my son that was dead an' is alive
again; an' my gray hairs are no to be brought in
sorrow to the grave."

"It's a delight to me to be back again," Urquhart
mused, "and to look again on the hill and the loch."

"Ay, He fills the world wi' beauty an' the earth
wi' gladness, if we would only see an' hear. You'll
be gaun down to Muiredge? She'll be blithe to see
ye. I aye speir for ye when she comes up, an' she
tells me a' about ye. Ay, an' Watty reads a bit frae
your book at nichts to Rob an' me, an' syne we sit
an' crack about ye i' the great Babylon. But haste
ye, haste ye now, an' no let my totterin' steps keep
ye frae her side. May the Threefold encompass ye

both, Mr. Urquhart, an' bless her to ye as Marg'et was blessed to me."

They were as far as the Sandy Loan by this time, and Michael turned back again.

To Urquhart, who had only known Kinkelvie in winter, the Loan was more beautiful than he had ever seen it; while the moss, with its infinite shades of purple and blue, stretched before him a sea of exquisite colour. But the beauty of the landscape was felt rather than seen, for his thoughts were at the farm, and again it was Elsie, Elsie, Elsie; nothing but Elsie. But now it was with a great happiness flooding his heart.

And there she was as he had seen her once before, standing by the sun-dial, waiting him.

He put his arms around her, and folded her to his heart. "Elsie! At last!"

She sighed, nestling to him as one that was weary and now found rest. He felt her breathing like one in sleep, and looking on her face saw that the eyes were closed.

"Elsie!" he whispered, and kissed her.

She opened her eyes. "It was a prayer of thanksgiving, Robert. Come, we shall go in now. I knew you would come, before even I got your telegram. I have wearied to see you. Let me look at your face."

She laid her hands on his shoulders, and gazed into his eyes. "Yes, it is as I thought; you have been working hard. And I doing nothing, Robert. But I shall be with you soon now, and help you. Won't I?"

"Yes, Elsie; that's what I came for. We have waited long enough."

Mr. Muir was in the dining-room, and the two boys came thundering downstairs when they heard Mr. Urquhart's voice. They were both grown almost as tall as their father, but Andrew's hand was the hand of a farmer; Robert, it was evident, was still a student.

They all sat down, and then there was another happy party, questioning and talking, until it was time to go to church.

After the forenoon service, there was the usual gathering in the churchyard, and Urquhart had to renew acquaintance with all his old friends, every one of whom had some profound and original remark to make of London. On one point, however, they were all agreed, that "After a' it wasna Kinkelvie; na, he would be glad to get back to breathe the caller air."

Mrs. Muckersie bowed to him as she passed clinging to her husband's arm, but Muckersie himself looked the other way.

Urquhart felt almost inclined to laugh at the condescending smile she bestowed on him, and the imperious toss the head gave afterwards, as she should say, "I have observed the letter of the law of politeness, and now you may keep your distance."

"There's a mark on his brow he wouldna like ye to see," Watty whispered. "It's whitish for ordinar', but it gets awfu' red when ye mention a fecht."

When the people began to disperse, Watty took him round to the back of the church, and stood beside a newly-turfed grave.

"This is whaur she's laid," he said. "I passed up the lane there yesterday afternoon, no that lang afore

you cam', an' I saw a black figure wi' hingin' face,
standin' at the head o' her grave. He'd come to do
penance, I wouldna doubt, an' readlys gaed back,
thinkin' a fell lot o' himsel'. I let him alane, Mr.
Urquhart, an' didna seek to disturb him. I had
said my say to him that Sabbath nicht, an' left him
to the mercy o' his Maker."

"Is he still in Carsecowden, Watty?"

"Ay; Mr. Gordon, o' Carsecowden, is become a
name—a name for holy livin' an' humility in prayer.
He gae a series o' lectures, the winter past, on the
penitential psalms, waxin' most eloquent, an' risin' to
his greatest powers o' persuasion in the fifty-first,
when he cried nichtly to crowded kirks that he was
the chief o' sinners. Man, it ta'en grand; an' he's
gotten fifty pound added to his stipend. They
should hae made it fifty-one, for he would hae seen
in that the hand o' the Lord. Ay, he's a godly
man, Mr. Gordon, an' humble-minded witha'. He
doesna boast about his godliness either, but rather
glories in his humility; ay, wallows in it, shoutin'
on a' the congregation to look an' see. That's Niel
Gordon, an' he's been the same since he selled his
soul to the devil."

In the afternoon Elsie had to return to church, but
Mr. Urquhart and Mr. Muir remained at home and
chatted of many things, chiefly of marrying and
giving in marriage. Mr. Urquhart would have the
marriage as early as possible now. What was the
use of waiting longer? He had a house taken in
London, and for the past month he had been setting
it in order for her coming. After all, he had only
come north a month or so earlier than he had
expected to come; and now that all things were

Y

ready, he could see no reason for delay. It would be folly to delay it, merely because of Mrs. Rae's death.

Mr. Muir, of course, was not in so great a hurry.

"I know you are right," he admitted; "and I wish to see Elsie happily married, yet you will be taking the sunshine from Muiredge when you take her away. But I am not going to stand in your way. Elsie and you will settle that for yourselves, and fix the date; my part is to give her to you with my blessing."

After tea Elsie and Urquhart walked across the moss and down to the White Sands; and, seated on the fallen trunk, where he had once put on her skates for her, it seemed but yesterday, they fixed the date of their marriage. The burn trickled into the loch almost at their feet, and the waves rippled and sang to them where they sat. The song was of that happy day when the loch was a stretch of ice, and the frosty air rang with the music of skating, and the laughter of young hearts awaking to all the ecstasy of love.

The memory of that day was with the lovers now, and because of the beauty of the past and all the happiness it had brought them, they could face the future with faith, and look forward with an assured hope of even happier days to be.

By and bye there came to them on the breathing air the sound of singing. They listened to it in silence, for their hearts were too full for speech; but thoughts unuttered went out to meet the blending voices from the moss, and were carried away up, up over the trees into the infinite blue vault of heaven and the very gates of eternity.

"Let us go and join them," Elsie suggested. "It

is Watty's choir. Every Sabbath evening in summer," she explained, while they walked back towards the moss, "if the weather allows it, Watty and Rob and a few more take a walk to the moss and go through a few of the old tunes. It is very beautiful, I think, and I like to be with them when I can get."

They heard different psalms raised now and again, and sung through several verses until they reached the company seated on the dry grass near the great Silver Saugh. Elsie went and sat down beside Michael and Barbara.

"This'll be new to ye, Mr. Urquhart," Watty said. "It's a service only for summer weather, an' it's about the only chance we ha'e nowadays o' hearin' the tunes o' our fathers. We'll ha'e time for *Eastgate* afore ye gang."

He took the tuning-fork between his teeth and gave the key.

"Miss Elsie," he said, "you'll help Bauby wi' the air, an' Jenny here'll gi'e ye an alto. It'll be a gey strong bass, Mr. Urquhart, wi' Rob an' you an' me, but we'll no' drown Adam's tenor. Now."

He gave the keynote again, and beat time while they were singing—

> "Behold how good a thing it is,
> And how becoming well,
> Together such as brethren are
> In unity to dwell."

Old Michael sat and listened with wide-open eyes, that saw something fairer even than the beauty of moss and wood around him.

"That's grand," he said simply, when they had finished. "Now for *Glencairn*, Watty, for the finish."

And the voices rose again, floating over the moss,

and creeping up the hillside in the words of the
twenty-third psalm :

> "The Lord's my shepherd, I'll not want ;
> He makes me down to lie
> In pastures green. He leadeth me
> The quiet waters by."

Urquhart remembered how he had listened to the
same words sung to *Orlington*, his first Sabbath
morning in Kinkelvie.

But their shadows were growing long and faint on
the grass, and it was time to be going.

Urquhart walked back over the moss, and parted
with Elsie at the garden gate.

"Do you remember," he asked, "when we stood
here once before?"

She looked at him with earnest eyes. "Can I
forget that day, Robert? Or that night either?"

He kissed her hand again, as he had kissed it then.

"A fortnight now, Elsie; only a fortnight more.
Then I shall take you away. Look round on moss,
and hill, and loch, and the home here, more beautiful
than all. Will it not pain you to bid farewell to
them?"

"Yes; but I shall have you, Robert. And we
shall come back here every summer."

"Perhaps we may come back and live here altogether, Elsie; some day. Who knows?"

"That will be something to look forward to."

He kissed her good-night. "I shall see you
to-morrow morning, and every morning, now; for
we are not to be parted again. Good-night."

He watched her till she reached the sun-dial,
where she turned and waved her hand to him
again   Then he walked away.

The sun had set and the hill was growing gray. A few stars had begun to twinkle faintly in the luminous west, against which were outlined the roofs and gables of Kinkelvie nestling to the knees of the hill. The faintest chirp of a bat now and again, and in the distance the low, unbroken wimple of the burn, falling and winding round by the roots of the Silver Saugh, were the only sounds to break the stillness of the scene. This was Nature, serene, and silent, and beautiful; the fields and the loch composing themselves for sleep, and the everlasting stars sentinel in the sky.

At the head of the Sandy Loan he turned and looked back towards the farm, to see again through the trees the twinkle of light that had guided his steps to the gate of her dwelling, and to the beauty and holiness of love.

And he stood till the deepest darkness of the night had come, and the sky was studded with stars. There were some that blinked down on him tenderly and lovingly, and others that gazed on him with calm and steadfast eyes; but the light of all he took for the light of blessing—blessing him because of his love for her, and, above all, blessing her who was his.

And on this earth the stars have always been, and always will be, accepted of the sons of men as emblems of love, and the types of constancy and truth.

www.ingramcontent.com/pod-product-compliance
Lightning Source LLC
Chambersburg PA
CBHW022209010726
47493CB00002B/476